A SHORT ROPE FOR A TALL MAN

W9-BMZ-083

A SHORT ROPE FOR A TALL MAN

A CARSON STONE WESTERN

NATE MORGAN

PINNACLE BOOKS
KENSINGTON PUBLISHING CORP.

www.kensingtonbooks.com

PINNACLE BOOKS are published by

Kensington Publishing Corp.
119 West 40th Street
New York, NY 10018

First Printing: May 2023
ISBN-13: 978-0-7860-4943-1
ISBN-13: 978-0-7860-4944-8 (eBook)

10 9 8 7 6 5 4 3 2 1

Printed in the United States of America

PROLOGUE

Caleb Burns was a bad man who'd done bad things. Backshot men. Rustled cattle. Highway robbery. He was lying back in bed, smoking a cigarette in his room at the boardinghouse when somebody slipped a note under the door.

He rolled out of bed with a groan, the springs creaking, and snatched up the note, unfolded it, squinting at the words. He could read good enough, and the note was written in neat, even letters. The message was a simple warning. A bounty hunter in Wheeler's Saloon down the street had been asking for him.

The note wasn't signed.

Caleb muttered a string of curses, unimaginative but earnest.

He wasn't surprised the note was unsigned, the hallmark of a man both cautious and enterprising. If this went bad, the man could simply remain anonymous. If it came out right for Caleb, the man could present himself with an open palm for a gratuity. Everybody wanted money. Nobody wanted to stick his neck out.

He smoked the rest of the cigarette and considered his options. He'd only just arrived last night in the rain, had been riding hard across Oklahoma and had finally crossed the

Texas line and seen the lights of the town drawing him on. His plan was to rest up a bit with Kansas and Oklahoma now behind him. He was trying to decide between staying on the southern route to Mexico or taking a big right turn toward California, and he wanted to take a few days to decide with the help of a whisky bottle and maybe some soft gal working the saloon.

He supposed he could sneak out the back, saddle his horse, and go, but the notion of getting back on the trail so soon rankled and decided him the other way.

Caleb mashed out his cigarette butt in the ashtray, pulled on his boots, and grabbed his gun belt, buckling on the Schofield revolver. It hung low on his right hip.

The street in front of the boardinghouse was muddy from last night's rain, but the sky was blue. Caleb squinted up at it. It was going to be another hot one. People were out and about, nobody paying him any mind, which was just what Caleb wanted.

They don't know me here. The bounty hunter will be from out of town, too, if he's been tracking me. Just a dispute between two strangers. I'll need to handle this just right.

He walked down the street to Wheeler's Saloon, taking his time. At midmorning, he doubted many people would be in there. Good. Better for concocting his story.

Caleb paused at the saloon doors, looking inside before entering. The barkeep was a bald, florid-faced man with a mustache almost as big as his face. He wiped the bar with a rag three feet from the only customer, a lanky man, hat pushed back on his head, dusty from the road, a two-gun rig belted around his waist.

The only other person was a saloon gal, hunched at a table across the room, pushing an empty shot glass around with a slender finger like it was the saddest thing in the world. Red hair. Skin white as fresh linen. Caleb might have to get to know her if he worked it out right with the bounty hunter.

He looked around, and when he saw nobody watching him, drew the Schofield and pushed through the saloon doors. He kept the revolver low, down against his leg. He wasn't looking for a fair fight, but shooting the wrong man in the back wouldn't do him any good.

The barkeep offered a friendly nod, but then his gaze dropped to the gun in Caleb's hand. The barkeep slowly sank down behind the bar.

The man with the two-gun rig was reaching for his whisky bottle when he saw what the barkeep was doing and froze. Then he turned fast and saw Caleb. The man had a hard look about him, blue stubble and lines in his face. He saw the Schofield and went for his own guns.

He got them barely halfway out of his holsters when Caleb lifted the revolver and fired.

The room shook with the crack of the gunshot, blood blooming red and wet on the man's chest. He stumbled back against the bar, dropping both his guns. He slid along the bar for a few feet, then fell to the floor with a thud. Caleb approached, his revolver up and cocked in case the man moved.

He didn't.

Caleb went to the bar and saw the barkeep peeking over the top.

"Don't worry," Caleb said. "It's over."

The barkeep didn't move.

Caleb uncocked the Schofield and set it on the bar next to the dead man's whisky bottle. "I s'pose the sheriff will be along. You're my witness. He drew on me."

The barkeep's eyes went to the pistol again.

Caleb reached into a pocket and flipped the coin onto the bar. The ten-dollar Gold Eagle spun and clinked against the bottle before coming to a rest.

The barkeep stood and made it disappear into an apron pocket with surprising alacrity. "Yessir, drew on you totally unprovoked. You had no choice but to defend yourself."

The red-haired gal was next to him in a flash, setting her empty shot glass on the bar. The clink of coins had brought her right quick.

"Shot that fella dead, didn't you?" One lip curled as she smiled. "I like bad men. You a bad man?"

Caleb drank straight from the bottle, then filled her shot glass. "Bad when I need to be, but I can be nice, too."

She grinned, then tossed back the whisky and set the glass on the bar. He took the hint and filled it, then drank from the bottle again, his whole body vibrating from the encounter. He wouldn't go so far as to say he enjoyed killing, but there was a dark excitement to it. *He's dead and I'm alive, and it could have been the other way around.*

He took her by the arm and pulled her close. "Maybe you and me could head upstairs. We could take the rest of this bottle and—"

There was a sharp *pop*, and Caleb felt something in his chest. Something else dripped down inside his shirt, warm and sticky. He looked down and saw the widening red stain on his shirt. He also saw the little derringer gleaming silver in the gal's white hand, gray smoke oozing from the top barrel.

With her other hand, she took the shot glass again and threw back the whisky. She was still smiling, that one lip curled.

Caleb's last thought in the world was, *You've got to be kidding me.*

She watched Caleb Burns fall over dead on top of the man he'd killed, and *of course* that was the exact moment the marshal pushed into the saloon, six-shooter in hand, a deputy next to him pointing a scattergun right at her. She held the derringer, which still smoked like she'd just shot a man.

Which she had, obviously.

"Just keep still, young lady." The marshal had gray in his beard and above his ears, and there was something in his eyes that said he'd seen plenty in his time, up to and including a saloon whore with a little popgun in her hand. "I never seen you before, have I?"

"I'm not from around here, Marshal," she said. "Maybe lower those guns and I can explain."

"Maybe you explain, and then I'll consider lowering this shooter," the marshal told her.

"I'm putting this down nice and slow, okay?" She set the derringer on the bar. "Now I'm going to show you something. Nothing sudden."

He gestured at her with the six-shooter. "Go on, then."

She reached down to the hem of her skirt and pulled it up past her thigh. There was a folded wad of papers stuck in the top of her stocking. She took it out, let the skirt drop, and held out the papers to the marshal.

He nodded to his deputy. "Get it."

The deputy lowered the scattergun, stepped forward to take the papers, then stepped back to stand near the marshal.

"Read 'em," the marshal said.

The deputy unfolded the papers. "One on top's a handbill. Caleb Burns. Wanted dead or alive. Two hundred fifty dollars." He showed the handbill to the marshal.

The marshal looked from the handbill to the dead man and back again. "Not a bad likeness, especially that pushed-in nose."

"Other papers look like legal stuff," the deputy said. "Belongs to Katherine Payne."

"That's me. Kat for short," said the redhead. "I hunt bounties. All legal and proper."

"You're Lady Pain?" A look of appreciation crossed the marshal's face. "I've heard of you."

"I'm not fond of that nickname."

"You were tracking this Burns fella?"

"Actually, no," Kat said. "I'm passing through, but we're staying at the same boardinghouse and I recognized him from the handbill. He gave a different name to the proprietor, but his initials were on his saddlebags."

"What about that one?" The marshal pointed his gun at the dead man under Caleb's corpse. "He your partner?"

Kat shook her head. "Never seen him. Just bad luck being in the wrong place at the wrong time."

"Bad luck, huh?" The marshal holstered his six-shooter. "Follow me, then. We'll wire for your money. Might take a few days."

"Works for me," Kat said. "Can you have it wired to my bank in Fort Smith? I'm headed that way."

The marshal shrugged. "Probably could."

She followed the marshal then packed up her things at the boardinghouse. She changed out of the saloon girl outfit and packed it into her saddlebags. The costume had worked before and probably would again in the future. A pair of man's brown pants and a blue shirt with the sleeves rolled up would be better for riding. Too hot for the vest or the jacket.

She shrugged into the shoulder holster for the .32 rimfire. Kat was no quick-draw artist and preferred the rig to a regular gun belt. Subterfuge was Kat's weapon of choice. Nobody expected a woman bounty hunter.

Her horse was a fast little chestnut. She rode past Wheeler's, saw the marshal leaning on a hitching post.

He flicked her a two-fingered salute. "Feel free to come on back for a visit whenever you're not shootin' folks."

Kat offered him a quirky smile and a wink and then rode out of town.

* * *

Colby Tate sat astride his painted mare in the alley between the dry goods store and the tanner's. He'd watched her come out of Wheeler's and follow the marshal to the jailhouse, and then watched her again after she'd changed clothes and rode out of town. That was her, all right, Lady Pain in all her red-haired glory. He'd met her once in a Topeka saloon a year ago, but she'd been so drunk, he doubted she'd remember.

It had been one of those chance gatherings of bounty hunters. Get a few together and they'd always swap lies about the baddest men they'd ever brought in dead or alive. Tate had listened more than he'd talked. He wasn't one for boasting. He did what he did for the money, not for fame or a thrill. He'd surprised even himself to learn how fast he was with pistols. He hands fell automatically to the twin, nickel-plated Peacemakers on his hips. He fingered the hilts, an idle habit. He'd thought about joining the Pinkertons, but he'd always preferred to be his own boss and setting his own hours. Bounty hunting seemed a good fit.

An hour earlier and Tate would have had him. He'd caught wind of Caleb Burns coming through Oklahoma and had trailed him here. Lady Pain had gotten in ahead of him. It was as simple as that.

Tate sighed and pulled a handbill from his inside jacket pocket. From the other pocket he pulled out a pair of wire-rimmed spectacles with small, round lenses and put them on. He unfolded the handbill and squinted at it. Some would consider the man handsome, Tate supposed, although it was sometimes hard to tell with these illustrations. His right ear-lobe had been shot off, and a scar behind his left ear ran to the collarbone—although the scar was part of the written description and didn't show in the illustration. A man match-ing that description had been seen in Fort Gibson. That had been two weeks ago, and the information wasn't as solid as what'd he'd had on Burns, but it was something to go on. Better than nothing.

Tate nodded to himself. He'd made his decision. "Looks like you're next, Carson Stone."

He turned the painted horse north and headed for the Oklahoma Territory.

CHAPTER 1

Carson Stone stripped off his shirt and chopped wood, a sheen of sweat coating him within minutes. It would get hotter before it would cool off. His shoulders and neck were sore by the time he finished splitting the logs.

He paused when he saw Jenny coming toward him from the main house. She was only eight, butter-yellow hair in pigtails, a front tooth missing. She carried the water bucket with both hands, some of it sloshing out. He stood patiently and let her come at her own pace. He looked around. It was wide-open country and seemed especially empty with the Taylor brothers and the ranch hands off on the cattle drive. He'd worked on a ranch before, and the sudden quiet after months of hard work and mooing cattle always struck him as odd.

Jenny arrived and set the bucket on the stump. "Hot work, Mr. Stone?"

"Hot enough," he said. "And I told you it was okay to call me Carson."

She handed him the ladle. "Ma says not to call adults by their first name."

"Well, listen to your ma, then."

Carson Stone dipped the ladle into the bucket, then brought it to his lips. It went down his throat cool and clean.

He dipped it again and drank more. "You need the rest of this."

"No, sir."

Carson dumped the rest of the bucket over his head, then handed it back to Jenny empty. "Thanks for that."

"You're welcome." She turned and skipped back to the house.

Carson slopped the pigs, fed the chickens, and repaired a stretch of fence on one of the pens. He leaned against a fence post, wishing he had the rest of that bucket of water.

"I don't pay you enough to work this hard," said a voice behind him.

Carson turned to see William Taylor grinning at him.

He smiled at the old man. "Ten dollars a month, meals, and a roof over my head. That's what we agreed on."

"I thought you'd talk me up," William said.

William was the uncle of the two men who ran the ranch. In his midsixties, he'd had enough of the trail and now stayed behind when the others went on the drive. He'd fallen off a barn and broken his arm, which was in a sling. Carson had happened along at just the right time and now took care of the routine chores that usually would have fallen to William.

It was a good, temporary setup, a quiet place and out of the way, although Carson would be moving on at the end of the month.

There were things he had to do.

"The money's not as important as a quiet place to think for a while," Carson said.

"I reckon a man needs that every now and then," William said. "I won't pry into your business, but I'm a good listener if you ever find yourself in the mood."

"It's a dull story, so you're not missing anything. But I appreciate it."

"In the meantime, maybe you'd like to ride into town,"

William suggested. "You could run an errand for me, then get yourself a beer at the saloon or whatever you want. You haven't left the ranch in two weeks. Too much peace and quiet can ruin a man."

That made Carson chuckle. "I'll take that offer. I don't want to risk ruin."

He put on his shirt, and the sweat stuck it to him. He saddled his horse, a big, black gelding he called Jet, strapped on his Colt Peacemaker, and snugged his hat down low on his head. He hadn't worn the Peacemaker since coming to the Taylor Ranch, and it felt both good and strange on his hip at the same time.

It was eight miles into Fort Gibson. The narrow trail along Beggar's Creek took him to the road that went past the fort. The army had been gone for a while, but then the Tenth Cavalry had returned to take over proprietorship of the place a few years ago, just a small garrison that sent out patrols in the area. Most of the Indian trouble had been up toward the Dakotas since Little Bighorn, but Carson supposed folks felt better having the bluecoats around just in case.

The fort wasn't much more than a blockhouse and a palisade and another low building for a barracks. It had the look of a place that was built by someone making it up as he went along, but Carson was hardly an expert on such things. A man in the only watchtower gave him a wave as he rode past, and Carson touched the brim of his hat in return.

The town itself wasn't much farther, and it might even have been a stretch to call it a town at all. A few houses, a very small hotel, a general store, a barbershop that doubled as a dentist's office in case somebody needed a tooth pulled, a stable with a blacksmith's shop attached, and a ramshackle saloon.

Carson dismounted in front of the general store and looped Jet's reins over the hitching post. The store also served as the stagecoach stop and the post office, and Carson had a packet of letters to drop off. William wrote to his brother, two sisters, and a couple of cousins twice a year to keep everyone up-to-date on family business and whatnot. Carson suspected William handed the simple errand off to him just to give Carson a chance to slip into town and get a break from the ranch.

Carson paused before entering the general store and looked around. A few people out on the street. Different faces. William was right. Carson needed this. After he dropped off the letters, he'd head to the saloon for a beer, and maybe strike up a conversation with somebody and get the news of the world.

He entered the store and paid for postage with money William had given him. He took a quick glance around, wondering if there was anything he needed for himself. He couldn't think of a thing, and anyway, he was eager for that beer.

Carson walked out of the general store just in time to see a woman drop a huge armload of packages into the mud. He moved in to help without giving it a second thought, going to one knee in the mud and gathering packages.

"Thank you kindly, sir," she said. "I suppose I should have made two trips, but I thought I could juggle them."

"Happy to help, ma'am."

"I hate to put you out," she said, "but could you help me carry these to the hotel?"

She was easy on the eyes and that was a fact, dressed smartly in a green skirt and a matching jacket, an ivory blouse, and a heap of gorgeous red hair pulled back and tied with a green ribbon. She had the kind of vivid beauty visible a long way off that just got better up close.

Lady, I'll carry your packages to Omaha if you ask me.

But what he said out loud was, "Happy to help, ma'am," which he realized he'd said already. *That's it, Carson. Impress her with your razor wit.*

He followed her across the street to the hotel.

In the lobby, she looked over her shoulder back at him and smiled, teeth about as white and perfect as God could make them. "My room's up the stairs at the end of the hall. Thanks again. I do appreciate it."

Carson's mother might have had a low opinion of a young lady inviting a strange man up to her room, but Carson didn't much care. All he was doing was carrying packages.

He followed her upstairs and down the hall to the room at the end. She went in and gestured for Carson to follow.

"Set those on the chest of drawers , would you please?" she said.

It was a surprisingly well-furnished room for such a small hotel in a Podunk town. Double bed. Vanity. Wardrobe. Washbasin on a separate stand.

Carson crossed the room and set the armload of packages down on the vanity. When he heard the door click shut behind him, his eyes flicked up to the mirror. He saw the woman's reflection. She'd already set her packages on a luggage rack near the door, and her hand was coming out of her jacket. Carson caught a glint of metal.

He spun on pure reflex just as her arm extended straight to level the little gun at him. He backhanded it, the derringer flying across the room, then clattering on the floor. She took a quick step back, hiking up her skirts to reach for a small revolver strapped to her upper thigh.

But Carson's Peacemaker had already cleared the holster, and he pointed it right at her heart. "Don't."

She froze, one hand hovering over the grip. Her eyes locked on his, and they stood that way a moment.

"Well, looks like you're in charge." The woman's lips curled into a sly smile. "You gonna shoot, or are we gonna stand here all day?"

"It's just that I hate to shoot anyone with such nice legs," Carson said.

Her smile widened, almost like she couldn't help herself, but then the top lip twisted nearly into a snarl, giving that smile a dangerous edge.

"But first, I wouldn't mind hearing why you suckered me up to your hotel room just to put a bullet in my back," Carson said.

"There's paper on you," she said. "Carson Stone, wanted dead or alive. And the state of Texas doesn't much care if the bullet goes in the front or the back."

Carson's eyebrow rose into a question. "You're a bounty hunter? A *woman* bounty hunter?"

"Katherine Payne, legally registered out of Beaumont, Texas, to exercise certain legitimate functions of the court." She said the words with a sort of cool confidence, as if they might protect her from whatever Carson would do next.

The first thing Carson thought was that he'd stayed in one place too long. He'd gotten comfortable on the Taylor Ranch, felt safe. And now the bounty hunters had caught up with him—or this one had, anyway—and one was more than enough.

"Can I put my skirt down?" she asked. "I feel sort of awkward like this."

"Take that pistol out first and toss it on the bed," Carson told her. "Slow. Thumb and forefinger on the grip."

She did as told, easing the revolver from its holster. She tossed it on the bed, then let her skirt drop.

"Now go stand in the corner." He gestured with the Peacemaker.

She scooted into the corner.

He eased around the bed, keeping his gun on her, and took the revolver, sticking it in his belt. Then he bent and picked up the derringer. His eye roamed the room quickly, but there were no other weapons in sight.

"I'll leave your guns at the desk downstairs," Carson said.

"You wait in here five minutes. I'd prefer to be on my way without any further trouble, but if you stick your head out of this room before five minutes are up, I'm just going to blaze away. Understand?"

"Five minutes," she said. "I hear you."

"Just so we're sure, I didn't do it," Carson told her.

She sighed like she'd heard that one before. "The State of Texas don't care."

"Well, you tell the State of Texas for me to just sit tight, because I'm in the process of clearing up this whole misunderstanding."

Carson backed out of the room, shut the door, and headed down the stairs fast. He dropped the guns with the clerk at the front desk with a story about cleaning the guns for the nice lady upstairs and she'd be along directly to pick them up. He headed outside, climbed on his horse, and headed out of town at a gallop.

Back at the ranch, William Taylor offered Carson a confused look as he filled his saddlebags with all his worldly possessions and prepared to head north.

"I know I said I'd stay on until the end of the month, Mr. Taylor, but something's come up," Carson explained. "Some business I should have taken care of a long time ago."

William shook his head. "I sure do hate to see you go, but I understand there's some things that just won't keep."

"Thanks for understanding," Carson said. "Truth is, I liked it here. I wish circumstances could be different."

"Me too." William handed Carson a Gold Eagle. "I think the deal was for ten dollars."

"The deal was for a month. I can't take your money, Mr. Taylor."

"You earned it, and you'll need it. Go on."

Carson took the coin. "You're good people, Mr. Taylor. Say goodbye to the girls for me."

"I will, Carson. Good luck."

Carson mounted Jet and took one last look at the ranch.

So much for peace and quiet.

He headed out at a trot, wondering if he'd ever get back this way.

CHAPTER 2

Carson knew he was headed for a place in the Ozarks north of Fort Smith, but he didn't know much more than that, which might explain why he hadn't been in very much of a hurry until the bounty hunter showed up. He knew what he needed to do, just not quite where it would happen.

All Carson could say for sure was that there was a price on his head for a crime he didn't commit. It was past time he did something about it.

Katherine Payne had the air of a determined woman about her, but she didn't seem much like a tracker. Carson took a shallow creek north a few miles, hoping to throw her off just in case. When the creek bent westward, he left the water and kept going north, a bit out of his way, but he wanted to discourage pursuit. He'd eventually have to nudge north anyway.

He spent the night on a level patch of ground with enough trees and bushes to conceal his small cookfire, beans and bacon and coffee. He stretched out on his bedroll. Sleep was slow in coming. His narrow bed back at the Taylor Ranch wasn't what anyone would call luxurious, but it had already spoiled him for sleeping on the ground. He supposed he'd get used to it again quick enough.

Up again with the gray light of predawn. Carson settled for

coffee, skipping breakfast, and soon he was in the saddle again, heading east. By dusk, he was riding into a small town called Clemmensburg. It looked a little bigger than Fort Gibson, but not by much. He hitched Jet out front of the local hotel and went inside.

The man behind the front desk wore little, round spectacles, hair neatly combed and slick, sideburns that looked like they were trying to make a name for themselves but otherwise clean-shaven. He welcomed Carson with an open, friendly face. "Welcome to the Barrymore Hotel. I'm Carl Barrymore. Need a room tonight, sir?"

"Depends on the price, I guess," Carson said. "I need a place for my horse, too. Is there a stable in town?"

"There surely is," Barrymore said. "But we've got a barn out back with plenty of room and hay, and if that'll do for your horse, we'll throw it in for the price of a room."

"Okay, then. I don't need anything fancy."

"Not fancy would be number five," Barrymore said. "A single bed and a window facing the side alley. It's our most reasonably priced accommodation."

"That'll do." Carson chastised himself inwardly. He should be saving his money and getting used to sleeping on the trail again, but he just flat out didn't want to. He signed the register and took the key.

He put Jet in the barn and gave him a rubdown, then took his saddle, saddlebags, bedroll, and Winchester up to his room. It was small, and the bed was even narrower than the one he'd had at the Taylor Ranch, but it wasn't the ground and that was all that mattered. He opened the window to let in some air. The alley wasn't much of a view, but Carson didn't care. He already knew what Oklahoma looked like.

He was dead tired. It would have been easy to kick off his boots and flop into bed, but fate had swindled him out of a beer in Fort Gibson. A minute later, he found himself walking down the town's main street toward the saloon. He could hear the music, loud talk, and laughter before he got there.

Carson pushed his way through the swinging doors, and a grin split his face as he took in the saloon, about two thirds full, smoky, a piano player attacking an upright with more enthusiasm than skill, a couple of card games going, and some pretty women working the room and flirting with the customers.

Carson Stone absolutely loved a good saloon, and it had been too long.

He went to the bar and resisted asking for a bottle of whisky. Too many miles to travel in the morning. The barkeep brought him a beer instead, and Carson paid for it.

He looked at it a moment before drinking. *This has been a long time coming.* He sipped and was in Heaven. He made the beer vanish in four big gulps and ordered another. He planned to nurse this one and simply sit back and enjoy the atmosphere of the saloon. He found a small table against the same wall as the piano and sank into the chair.

He sipped his beer and watched the people. The men playing cards seemed content, both winners and losers alike. The working girls looked just as happy as the cowboys they pulled along by the hand for a good time. Even the barkeep seemed to be in a good mood.

This was all he'd wanted, Carson realized. To do a good day's work, then relax around good-natured people, not bothering nobody, and nobody bothering him. He'd had a chance for a simple life like that and had blown it, not knowing a good thing when it was right in front of him.

I aim to fix that. But not tonight. Tonight I'm going to sip on this beer, and then if I'm still in a good mood, maybe just one more. Too long since I was just happy.

He'd been comfortable at the Taylor Ranch, but he only just now understood that wasn't the same as being happy.

He'd been hiding, avoiding what he needed to do. He'd made a mistake and hadn't wanted to face up to—

Stop it. Not tonight. Be happy.

He sipped his beer and watched the other happy folks in the saloon.

"That bastard can't play piano worth a damn," said the man at the next table in a too-loud voice.

Carson sighed. *There's always one.*

Nobody in the saloon paid the man any mind. The piano player redoubled his assault on the upright.

"Hell, I could play better'n that with my ass," the man said, even louder this time.

Carson turned his head to get a better look at him.

He was big, more bulky than muscled, with a huge beard maybe meant to compensate for the thinning strands on top. Red cheeks. His coat hung on the back of his chair with his hat, and his shirtsleeves were rolled up over thick, hairy forearms. Eyes glassy with whisky. He shared a bottle with a man who guffawed at his outbursts, short and soft-looking, blond hair on his lip trying way too hard to make a mustache out of itself.

Carson had to admit the piano player wasn't the best.

Still, there was no call to heckle the man.

"You stink!"

The man was shouting now, and spoiling Carson's mood. He wanted to tell the man to shut his fat mouth. *Don't do it. Just finish your beer and head back to your room. No point in courting trouble.*

But Carson opened his mouth. He couldn't help it.

"Why don't you just keep shut, you big tub of lard?"

The words startled him, mostly because they hadn't come out of his opened mouth. Carson had been about to say something similar, but one of the saloon gals beat him to it. She stood up from a table near the middle of the room, hands on her hips, the cowboys with her looking half amused and half concerned. She was a tiny woman, not even five feet tall. Carson allowed her another inch or two because of all the glossy black hair piled up on her head.

"Nobody talking to you, bitch," slurred the burly drunk.

The place had gone quiet. Even the piano player stopped and turned around to watch.

Carson sipped his beer and sighed. It had been a pleasant evening there for a few minutes.

The saloon gal stalked over to the drunk, high heels clacking rapid-fire on the wooden floor. The drunk stood up to meet her, and it was almost comical, her glaring up at the bigger man who had at least a foot on her in height.

"You been running your damn mouth all night and nobody's impressed, Hank Baily," she scolded. "Go home and sleep it off."

Hank grabbed her by the arm, face going red and angry.

She tried to pull away. "Let go, you dumb ox."

"Maybe we should all just settle down," the barkeep said nervously.

"You stay out of it. I'm a paying customer."

Baily twisted the woman's arm, and she squeaked.

Carson stood and moved toward the drunk, who was focused on the woman and didn't see him approach, but his blond pal saw and started to push away from the table.

Carson pointed at him. "Sit the hell back down."

The man sat.

Carson grabbed the pinkie finger of the hand holding the woman. He cranked it back. One of the fighting tricks his father had shown him.

Baily howled in pain and let go of the saloon gal. He stepped back, jerking his hand away, hate flying from his eyes like daggers at Carson. "You son of a bitch."

He went for his gun.

Which Carson had expected.

Instead of backing away, Carson stepped in close. Baily's

draw was drunken and sloppy. Carson put his hand over Baily's, preventing the draw, and with his other hand slammed the beer mug into the side of Baily's head right behind the ear. Glass shattered and beer splashed.

Baily stumbled back, eyes crossing and legs turning to water. He fought a moment to right himself but lost the fight and went down. He let out a long groan and closed his eyes. Carson stood over him a moment, but Baily didn't move.

"Somebody ought to fetch the sheriff," Carson said.

A deputy entered the saloon in no particular hurry two minutes later and looked down at the snoring drunk. "Hank again. That figures. You the one that hit him?"

"Yessir. He was stepping over the line with the lady."

The saloon gal and the piano player and a half dozen other folks confirmed that Baily had gone for his gun.

"Better drag him over to the jail and let him sleep it off. Help me carry him," the deputy told Carson.

"Me?"

"You're the one that hit him."

Carson couldn't argue with that, and between the two of them, they took Baily to the jailhouse and put him in a cell. The deputy hadn't asked Carson's name, and Carson hadn't offered. Men on the run don't advertise who they are. Carson walked back to the hotel, his mood shot to hell now. He went up to his room, opened the door, and froze when he heard a gun cock.

The man on the bed looked at him over a pair of round spectacles. He held a leather-bound book in one hand. The nickel-plated six-shooter in his other hand was pointed right at Carson's chest.

"My name's Colby Tate," the man said. "If I might have a moment of your time, I believe a brief conversation might be to our mutual benefit."

CHAPTER 3

"Make yourself at home," Carson said.

Tate chuckled good-naturedly, almost like a man who didn't have a pistol pointed at Carson's heart. "Sorry. I didn't know how long you'd be, and I've been riding all day."

He sat on the bed, legs stretched out in front of him, the oil lamp on the nightstand burning low, and his hat hanging from one of the bedposts.

"Anyway, a chance to do a little reading." Tate closed the book and held it up. "You're familiar with Chaucer?"

"'Fraid not."

Tate set the book aside. "Never mind. An indulgence from my school days."

Carson looked the man over. Tate wore shoes instead of boots, creased trousers, and a matching jacket. A red plaid waistcoat. A gold watch chain hung from one pocket. A thin, black tie. Shirt starched and pressed. He looked like he talked. "You're educated." Not a question. The man wasn't any older than Carson, maybe even a year younger.

"Harvard. Class of '75."

"You're a long way from Boston, Mr. Tate."

"Yes. I remember that every time I get an urge for a bowl of clam chowder. And it's Cambridge, actually, if one felt inclined to split hairs."

"You said a conversation to our mutual benefit," Carson reminded him.

"That's right."

"If we could get on with that, I'd be much obliged. Benefit me how?"

"Well, if we're conversing, I'm not shooting," Tate said. "So I suppose not being shot is the most immediate benefit."

"Talk all you want, then."

"Thanks, I will. I'm a bounty hunter; did I mention that?"

Carson sighed a muttered, "Another damn bounty hunter."

"Pardon?"

"Nothing," Carson said. "Go on with what you're saying."

"There's a bounty on you, so it's understandable that I'd want to collect that . . . considering my line of work."

"But . . ."

"'But' indeed," Tate said. "I can collect two hundred dollars for you dead or alive, *but* I like to think big, and I think you can help me."

"How big?"

"You were with Big Bob McGraw on that business in El Paso?" Tate asked.

Carson frowned when he heard the name. Big Bob McGraw. A mean, dangerous sidewinder and the beginning of all Carson's troubles. "Whatever you've heard, it wasn't like that."

"Let me guess. You're innocent. You were framed."

"You want to know what happened."

"That's right."

"Okay," Carson said. "I never told anybody before. Might as well tell you."

Three years ago . . .

A twenty-one-year-old Carson Stone sat on his horse in an alley, holding the reins of four other horses. He was more nervous than he'd ever been in his life, mouth so dry he couldn't even spit. He kept looking up and down the alley, hoping nobody would come. So far, he'd been lucky.

He rubbed his sweaty palms one at a time on his vest.

Stupid, stupid, stupid. How did I end up here?

Because of his father, he thought, even as another part of him knew that wasn't fair. His father had built the farm from nothing, and they all worked hard, and one night over dinner, he'd said the words he'd said to Carson a hundred times before.

One day this farm will be yours.

Saying that shouldn't have started an argument, but it had. Was Carson's whole life decided for him? Was he going to take over the farm after Pa died, marry a girl he met at church, then leave the farm to his own son? He wanted to see the world, he wanted to . . . well, he didn't completely know what he wanted. Not to be a farmer, that was for sure.

He'd taken off on his own, no plan and even less sense, and had somehow ended up with McGraw and the others talking about holding up a bank. He'd been good and liquored up at the time, so McGraw's talk made sense. Why should rich men have everything they wanted and regular folk like McGraw and Carson have to scratch out a living, breaking their backs with work? Who had most of the money in the bank anyway? Rich folks, that's who.

He'd sobered up by morning and realized he'd swallowed a lot of bunk, but it was too late. He was in an alley, holding the horses for a clean getaway, while the others—

Voices drew his attention to the other end of the alley.

A matronly woman was coming toward him, a young girl with her, maybe nine years old. They bickered playfully, the mom teasing her daughter.

Carson looked the other way. McGraw and the rest would be coming out any minute now. He looked back at the woman and her daughter. *Come on, lady, walk faster. You don't want to be here.*

Carson heard the gunshots and knew they were coming, butterflies kicking the inside of his guts like they wanted out.

The woman stopped abruptly ten feet from Carson. "What was that?"

Carson opened his mouth to tell the lady she'd best move along, but it was too late.

McGraw and the rest of the gang came storming around the corner, shooting at something behind them, bullets flying every which way, gouging holes in the brick walls of the next building. There were screams and shouts, and Carson thought he might wet himself.

The woman saw McGraw with his bandana pulled up over his face and shrieked.

McGraw spun on her with his six-shooter, sticking the barrel right in the woman's face, her eyes going wide. He was a big and intimidating man, not that he needed to be with a six-gun leveled at her. McGraw cocked it with a thumb, and all the blood drained from her face. Carson knew he was going to do it, that he'd squeeze the trigger and blast that poor lady's head off right in front of her child.

But then he didn't.

"Get the hell out of here," McGraw yelled at her.

The terrified woman fled the alley, dragging the girl with her.

McGraw and the others hopped on their horses.

"Out of the other way!" he shouted. "Ride!"

In the next instant, Carson was riding among them, a neighing, galloping calamity of horses and shouting men and gunfire.

They erupted from the alley onto a wider street, and the gunfire redoubled. Carson felt something tug at his shirt-sleeve. He'd been that close to taking a bullet. It was mostly noise and smoke and the crack of pistol shots. As far as Carson could tell, nobody had been killed, and then they thundered out of town in a cloud of dust, leaving Waco behind them.

They rode for hours, until well past sundown, following a stream for a while, then doubling back, ending up in the barn of an abandoned farmhouse McGraw had scouted ahead of time. They figured they'd thrown off the posse—if there was one—and now it was time to lay low.

Whisky bottles were passed around, slaps on the back and loud talk as they all celebrated a successful heist.

Except for Carson.

When everyone finally settled down to sleep, Carson lay awake. He kept seeing that woman and her daughter. How close had they been to death? Some innocent person would get killed sooner or later if Carson strayed down the outlaw path.

He snuck out while everyone else was dead asleep and rode away.

A week later, he'd found his roundabout way back home only to face bitter disappointment. The farm was abandoned, his father buried under a tree at the corner of the property. Word among the folks in town was that he'd had a heart attack and Carson's mother had gone back to New Orleans.

In the next year, Carson burned through his share of the bank robbery money, drinking whisky, playing cards, and even dallying with the occasional saloon gal. Nothing seemed to numb the feeling of wrongness that gnawed at him constantly. Carson Stone didn't know who he was or what he was supposed to be doing with himself.

He pondered that exact situation while haunting the corner table of an El Paso saloon, trying to find answers at the bottom of a beer mug.

Annie passed his table, some random cowboy leading her by the hand. She winked at Carson, her slight smile a promise. Dark hair in tight curls dangling down over bare shoulders. She was near to overflowing out of her low-cut blouse. Of all the girls who worked the saloon, Annie was the only one who'd really caught his eye, and he'd been lonely, and one thing led to another. They'd hit it off right away and found themselves in each other's arms when she'd finished working.

He felt a kiss on the cheek and looked up to see her, that gleaming smile making his insides melt like butter.

"Where's the cowboy?" he asked.

Her smile fell. "Waiting upstairs."

"Well. Get to it, I guess."

Annie leaned down, whispering right into his ear. "You know I can't help it. It's just work. I'll see you later. Don't bring any money. You won't need it."

He squeezed her hand without looking at her, and then she was gone.

Carson's mother would have been disappointed to know he'd taken up with a woman like that, but he tried not to think about it, refused to think about a lot of things, like what Annie was doing with that cowboy, what tomorrow would bring, or the mistakes that lurked in his past. There was only the moment he was living in now, and a fresh mug of beer to numb him to the rest of the world.

He sat that way for another hour, not really wanting to be there but having nowhere else to go.

Carson looked up and saw Big Bob McGraw and his gang enter the saloon.

Shit.

McGraw spotted him instantly and threw back his head, roaring laughter. "Well, if it isn't our lost sheep, Carson Stone. How we do love reunions, don't we, boys?"

They crowded around his table, and Carson offered them a weak smile, although he felt like he might be sick. McGraw was built like a grizzly bear, chin like an anvil covered with black stubble. The world shook when the man walked.

The rest of his gang were all hard men—killers—but they

couldn't compare to McGraw. The man was pure mean, seemed to delight in the feel of meanness running through his veins. If there was one thing McGraw especially despised, it was weakness, so Carson pushed down his fear and attempted a cool demeanor.

"What brings you fellas to El Paso?" Carson asked. "Looking to make a withdrawal from the local bank?"

"Funny you should mention that," McGraw said. "But first things first. Where in the hell did you go after Waco? I don't take kindly to folks sneaking out on me. Makes me think you don't like me. Was it something I said, or do you just not like my face?"

Carson's insides were water, but he met McGraw eye to eye, rock steady. "I like your face fine, Big Bob. It's downright pretty. But the fact is, you and the boys are better off without me. One thing I learned from Waco is I'm not cut out to be no outlaw. I'd just be deadweight to you."

McGraw ran the back of his hand down his jaw. "Prettier if I shave, but I do appreciate the compliment. Just don't go sweet on me." He brayed laughter again, and then, just as quick, his face hardened into a scowl. "Still, it was bad manners. And you know how important manners are to a man like me."

"I know it," Carson said. "And I knew it would be rude to tell the law about your hideouts. Or the names of all the men in your gang. Some they know and some they don't, going by the wanted posters. Cash money reward for Big Bob McGraw, but I kept my mouth shut. Them's the manners that count, if you ask me."

They stared at each other for a long moment, nobody saying a word.

Then McGraw laughed again and pulled up a chair. The tension seemed to go out of the rest of his men.

"You got sand, Carson, and I like that," McGraw said. "Because I'm such a gracious and forgiving fellow, I'm going to give you a chance to make it up to me. I lost a couple men on our last job. You can step in and help carry some of the weight. I'm a champion of second chances almost as much as I am of good manners."

They both paused their conversation when Annie approached the table. She smiled big at Carson, but then her eyes shifted to McGraw and the smile faltered. She started to turn away, but McGraw latched onto her wrist.

"Annie! How's my best gal?" McGraw pulled her into his lap. "Been saving yourself for me?" He brayed laughter again.

Carson had to stop his hand from going for his Peacemaker. He'd be dead in an eyeblink if he tried it.

"I was beginning to think my best customer had forgotten all about me." Annie's smile was so strained, it looked like it might break her face in two. Her worried eyes went to Carson briefly, but she immediately turned her attention back to McGraw, putting a hand on the back of the big man's neck. "You'll need to make time for me when you're passing through next." She started to get up from his lap.

McGraw yanked her back down again. "Oh, I'll be making time for you directly, pretty lady, never you worry about that. I just need to finish some business with my boy Carson first. He and I are going in on a business venture, aren't we, Carson?"

Carson took a deep breath. "I told you, Bob, I'd be no good to you."

"And I told *you* that I believe in second chances, and you *will* be taking advantage of this generous opportunity," McGraw said firmly. "I can be real loud about it if you force me to get persuasive."

Annie wasn't even pretending to smile now, her face pinched with fear. McGraw either didn't notice or didn't care.

Carson mulled his next words carefully. Big Bob McGraw was not the sort to take no for an answer. He could go along with McGraw's second chance, bide his time, and then slip away, but then, if he ever crossed paths with McGraw again, that would be it. If he went with the outlaw now, there'd be no getting out of it. He needed to tell McGraw no, and he needed to tell him right here and now.

Preferably in a way that wouldn't get Carson shot.

"With respect," Carson said. "It's not for me."

The tension that had leaked away just moments ago flooded back double. Everyone went tight and quiet, like a pack of wolves readying themselves to pounce. Carson felt like his bowels would let go any second, but he held McGraw's gaze without flinching.

"Me being magnanimous is sort of like a comet. Only comes around every great once in a while," McGraw said, voice low and menacing. "When it finally does happen, it's a bad idea to ignore it."

Four men erupted into the saloon, guns drawn, a marshal's star gleaming on the black vest of the one in front.

"Bob McGraw, you and your men are under arrest," the marshal said, voice booming throughout the saloon. "Touch those guns and we'll cut you down."

Big Bob McGraw knew better than to go for his gun.

Jake Stuart didn't.

Everyone called him Little Stu. He was short and barbwire skinny, and the only other person in McGraw's gang even younger that Carson. Stu was a hotheaded young buck with a chip on his shoulder and a drastically overinflated sense of how quick he was with a six-gun.

And he was pretty fast, truth be told. Stu managed to clear leather before the marshal turned on him, fanning his revolver, the saloon shaking with the thunder of pistol fire. Red splotches made a trail up Little Stu's front from his belt buckle to his throat. He took three halting steps back, falling over his own chair. He went down hard and never got up again.

McGraw was already flipping the table over, Annie tossed from his lap with a panicked squeal. All hell broke loose.

Carson had thrown himself to the floor and was belly crawling out of the way.

Screams. Shouts. Bullets blazing every which way. One of the saloon whores tripped over him with a yelp, then crawled away under a table.

Carson made it around the bar, then dashed for the back door.

He glanced back once, just in time to see McGraw rise from his hiding spot behind the table and blaze away with his six-shooter. One of the shots caught the marshal in the left eye. It popped blood, the bullet exiting the other side in an explosion of bone and blood and hair.

Carson felt something hot sting the bottom of his ear.

He ignored it and ran. He found Jet and rode as hard as he could until the horse almost quit beneath him. He rested the horse, sleeping in the dark without a campfire, and that was when he discovered most of his right earlobe had been shot off.

He awoke the next day and kept running.

CHAPTER 4

"I never even drew my pistol," Carson told Tate. "A month later, I saw my face on a wanted poster. I thought about finding the nearest law and explaining what had happened, but it was just my word, and with a dead marshal, I figured that was a good way to find myself at the end of a rope pretty fast."

"That explains the earlobe," Tate said. "What about the scar down your neck? Let me guess. Knife fight with an Apache or some such misadventure?"

A reluctant grin. "Nothing so legendary. Farming accident. But maybe I'll start telling people it was an Apache. Now, how about you lower that pistol? You're making me nervous."

Tate hesitated, then lowered his gun. "I believe your story, Mr. Stone. I'm a very good judge of character."

"Not that I don't appreciate it, but we've only known each other a grand total of ten minutes," Carson said. "What makes you so trusting?"

"I've been after you a few days," explained Tate. "Along the way, I had the opportunity to exchange pleasantries with the nice people at the Taylor Ranch. A seasoned old fellow named William has you pegged as a good man with troubles, and a pretty little girl named Jenny seemed especially distraught you'd taken your leave without saying goodbye.

Something tells me if you were a genuine cad, these simple, good folks would have seen through you in a minute."

"Okay, then. You're a good judge of character and I'm a stand-up guy," Carson said. "Now what?"

"I think I have a proposition for you, but let's talk in my room next door," Tate said. "I've seen closets bigger than this room."

"You're in the next room?"

Tate gestured to the open window. "How do you think I got in here? It was an easy climb."

Carson laughed. "Lead on, then."

He followed Tate to his room. It was bigger, for sure. A double bed and a table with a couple of chairs. A sideboard with water glasses and a pitcher. Tate set the glasses on the table and told Carson to sit.

Carson sat.

Tate went to his saddlebags and came back with a bottle of whisky and a thin, leather-bound book. The whisky bottle was half empty, and the book was tied up with twine. He sat at the table across from Carson and filled both glasses. Then he pulled the twine loose on the book.

Carson took the glass and sipped. He'd expected something cheap, but the hooch was good. "Thanks for this."

"Don't mention it."

"Harvard bounty hunter, huh? What do people think of that?"

"I haven't solicited opinions on the subject."

"Just wondering how a fella like you got into such a line of work."

Tate adjusted his glasses and let his eyes drop back to the book. He squinted at the pages. "That's a long story, and there isn't enough whisky."

Carson shrugged and sipped.

"Seems we're both headed to Fort Smith," Tate said. "I

received word McGraw was there. That your reason for going there, too?"

"More or less."

"Which is it?" Tate asked. "More or less?"

"I'm after McGraw," Carson said. "But he's not in Fort Smith. He might have passed through and been seen there, but he's got a place north in the Ozarks. I aim to find him there."

"Do tell. I'm learning things already. So, you track him to the Ozarks. Then what?"

"Bring him back alive," Carson said.

"Dead's less trouble."

"That how you do things?"

"The law takes a better view of my sort if we bring them in alive," Tate explained. "But if I have to shoot, I'll shoot. How important is it to you that McGraw comes back in one piece?"

"I'm not religious about it," Carson said. "But it's my first choice. I want him to tell what happened, to let the law know I had nothing to do with shooting that marshal."

"And you think Big Bob McGraw will clear your name out of the goodness of his heart?"

Carson downed the rest of the whisky. "Maybe. I want to try. Don't misunderstand me. I'm not looking to get killed. If I have to bring back a corpse, that works, too. There's a woman who'll testify on my behalf, but she's afraid of retaliation. If McGraw's dead or behind bars, then that solves that problem."

"But first you have to find him."

Carson nodded. "First I have to find him."

"And he's probably got his men with him."

"That's a distinct possibility."

Tate sat back, took off his glasses, and used his tie to wipe the lenses. "It's just as I thought, then."

"What's just as you thought?"

"You, my friend, need help." Tate snatched up his glass and tossed back the whisky all in one go.

"You're that help, I take it."

"You take it correctly." Tate donned his glasses again and found the section of the book he wanted and ran a finger down the page. "These are the men you rode with in McGraw's gang. Tell me if I get something wrong. Irish Dan Hannigan. There's three hundred dollars on his head. Jimmy Bachman. That's another three hundred."

"Memphis."

"Jimmy Bachman's in Memphis?"

"No, I mean everyone calls him Memphis. He's from there and came West after the war," Carson explained.

Tate wrote down the information in the book. "Gentleman Dick Fleetwood. Why do they call him that? Another champion of good manners?"

"Clotheshorse," Carson said. "Spends all his money on fancy duds—silk waistcoats and pearl buttons and such. You dress smart, but he dresses flashy. Never seen a man use so much mustache wax. You'll usually find him in a bowler hat."

Tate wrote it down.

"Fancy clothes ain't the most important thing to know about Gentleman Dick Fleetwood."

"Oh?"

"He's fast," Carson said. "Fastest I've ever seen."

"Faster than you?" Tate asked.

"Yes."

"I don't generally like to boast, but I'm rather fast with a Colt myself," Tate said.

Carson couldn't stop himself grinning. "A lot of men thought that, then went up against Fleetwood."

"I'm not a lot of men."

"If you're just a little bit fast, you're faster than most," Carson said. "Most men wear a gun because that's just the world we live in. But the majority of folks mind their own business and might live their whole lives and never draw on anybody. A little bit fast is all it takes. That's me, I'd say. A little bit fast, but nobody's idea of a legend. People talk about Gentleman Dick Fleetwood. He's on his way to making a legend out of himself."

"Maybe that's why he's worth four hundred, then." Tate wrote in the book.

"Maybe so."

"Gordon McGraw," Tate read from the book. "Bob's brother. Five hundred dollars."

"With him, you get more of the same as from Bob," Carson said. "Just as mean but quieter about it."

"I suppose we're fortunate to only have one of his brothers to deal with."

Carson raised an eyebrow. "Bob has another brother?"

"Two," Tate said. "Jeremy is two years older than Bob and is serving a stretch in Huntsville for rustling. The oldest brother is nearly sixty, named Elvin. He never much associated with the others, which might explain why he's the only honest one in the bunch . . . on paper, anyway. Works for the Leavenworth, Lawrence and Galveston Railroad Company. That's four brothers all told, but only two of any concern to us."

Carson grinned. "Two's plenty."

"And that leaves the big prize, Big Bob himself," Tate said. "One thousand dollars."

"A lot of money when you add it up."

"A lot more than the two hundred I'd get for you," Tate explained.

"I feel that proposition coming."

"You show me to Bob's hideout in the Ozarks, shout out when you recognize somebody, and I'll forget about the bounty on you," Tate said. "I'm still relatively new to the region, and a guide isn't a terrible idea. You know McGraw and his men.

You point the way, and I'll pull the trigger. You don't have to get your hands dirty if you don't feel like it."

"But I want McGraw alive."

"And I want the thousand dollars."

"This is about more than money to me," Carson said.

"We'll try to take him alive, but if we can't, then we can't," Tate said. "No amount of money matters if I'm too dead to spend it."

"Agreed." Carson stuck out his hand.

Tate shook it.

Tate refilled his whisky glass, then looked at Carson. "Night cap?"

"Not me." Carson stood and headed for the door. "I expect we'll be up before the sun if we want to get to Fort Smith in a timely fashion."

Tate took a pocket watch from his waistcoat. It was bigger than average and gleamed gold. "I suppose a few hours' sleep would be best."

"Nice watch."

Tate turned it over and showed Carson the back. "Harvard crest. Reminder of a former life."

CHAPTER 5

Colby Tate was not at his best in the morning.

As Carson had promised, they were up before dawn. Tate cursed the darkness and cursed the lack of coffee and cursed his saddle, which, according to him, was too cruel to be compatible with his sense of civility.

He cursed—inventively, often quoting Shakespeare—until all the surliness had drained from him, and soon they were riding out of town in the direction of Arkansas. Carson's attempts at conversation met with uninterested grunts. He gave up after a while, and they rode in silence.

When they finally stopped to rest the horses, Carson built a small fire and made coffee. Reasonably soon after drinking a cup, Tate resembled something more or less human again.

"I guess we'll do coffee first thing next time," Carson suggested.

"Apologies." Tate cradled the cup as if it were a rare medication for a fatal illness. "I thrive on routine, so yes, please, coffee first thing would probably benefit all involved."

Carson hid a grin. Tate might have been educated and fast with a gun, but Carson guessed the man wasn't built for the open road. Tate was in for a rude awakening. Carson had just been lamenting the loss of his bed back at the Taylor Ranch, but he felt he'd get used to sleeping on the ground again long before Tate.

They each had another cup of coffee, and soon the horses were saddled again and they were back on the road.

They camped that night with a shallow creek on one side and a clump of trees on the other. Bacon and beans cooked over a campfire and more coffee.

"We'll need to decide our route before we get started in the morning," Carson said. "Down to Fort Smith or straight toward the Ozarks."

"Why bother with Fort Smith?" Tate asked. "You said McGraw wasn't there."

"His hideout's not there, but if he passed through, somebody might know something," Carson said. "And we could pick up some supplies."

"Rebuttal. Asking too many questions about the man might just tip him off somebody's on his trail," Tate said. "Let's go straight to his hideout. There are other places for supplies, surely."

"You're the boss. I'll see to the horses."

Carson strapped a feed bag on Jet and another on Tate's horse. They'd been watered earlier. He wasn't expecting trouble with the animals, but he hobbled both anyway. By the time he returned from checking the horses, Tate had stretched out with his head on his saddle and a thin Indian blanket pulled up to his chin.

"Remember, coffee in the morning before we set out would likely make me a more tolerable traveling companion," Tate told him. "Just if anyone's interested in that sort of information."

"Duly noted."

"I assure you, I'm not usually so fussy," Tate said. "Nor am I a stranger to the outdoors. My family has a place in the Blue Ridge Mountains. Although it has twelve rooms and a smaller cottage for the servants. Now that I say it out loud, I don't think I'm quite making my point."

"Some people like rough living." Carson shrugged. "I won't quite say I like it, but I'm used to it, and that's good enough."

"I suppose if I'm out here long enough, I'll get used to it, too."

"Or you can always go back to Boston."

"No, thank you," Tate said. "The situation back home is not currently . . . to my satisfaction."

"Sounds like a story."

"Stories go better with a comfortable chair and good brandy," Tate said. "Another time."

And a minute later, Carson curled up, using his own saddle for a pillow, and was fast asleep before he'd even had time to count the first sheep.

His eyes opened about an hour before dawn just like usual. Maybe it was all those years of farming that got him into the habit. He resurrected the coals from the cookfire, and Tate sat up, rubbing his eyes, just as Carson poured him a cup of coffee.

Tate took the cup gratefully. "I dreamed I smelled coffee."

"No dream. Reality."

"Something of a harsh reality if the knots in my back are any indication."

"Don't worry," Carson told him. "A day in the saddle will fix that."

"Oh? Riding is good for the back?"

"No, but when your rear gets sore, you'll forget all about everything else."

"Something to look forward to."

Carson saddled the horses while Tate pulled himself together, and they were soon on their way. They camped again that night, the routine much the same, and then halfway through the third day, they spotted the trading post. A wooden bridge took them across a wide creek where a squat log building sat next to a crossroads, a good spot for a trading post, Carson thought. The sign on the door in rough, hand-painted letters read *Meriwether's Supplies & Sundries*. Carson and Tate tied their horses to the hitching post and entered.

Dim inside. A single lantern struggled to illuminate the interior. A stooped man with a black beard emerged from the back room and seemed surprised to see customers.

"Hello there," he said. "Stage came through yesterday, so I thought it might be awhile before I saw anyone else. Apologies for the poor lighting. Hold on a moment." He scurried around the inside of the trading post, throwing open shutters. Sunlight poured in. "That's better. Now, what can I do you for?"

"First, can you happen to tell us if this is Arkansas?" Carson asked.

"Came over the bridge, did you?"

"That's right."

"Well, that's Lee Creek, and as soon as you step foot on this side of it, you're in Arkansas."

"Thanks. Good to know I've been going in the right direction," Carson said. "Are you Meriwether?"

"Meriwether went back East in '71. I bought the place off him. Everyone just calls me Parson."

"Oh, you're a parson?"

"No."

Ah.

"Well, we're keen to give you some business, Parson."

"Sounds good. Tell me what you need, and we'll fix you up."

Flour, sugar, coffee, bacon, beans, and jerky. Simply fare to keep a belly filled. Oats for the horses. There were some good-looking green apples and also some pecans, so Carson added those to the list.

Tate browsed the store while Carson gave his order to

Parson. "How much for the whisky?" he called from the other side of the tall shelf that divided the room.

"How many bottles are there?" Parson called back.

"Three."

"I can sell you one," Parson said, "but I'm making a delivery day after tomorrow, and I need those other two bottles. I don't usually make deliveries, but the fella has a bum leg, and he pays me extra."

Tate came from around the shelf and set a single bottle on the counter next to the flour and coffee. "I can make do with one."

"Thank you kindly, sir," Parson said. "If I forget the coffee or butter, he'll let it pass, but forget the whisky and I'll never here the end of it. Typical Irishman, if you'll forgive my saying such a thing. No offense to anyone's ancestry in particular."

Tate and Carson exchanged glances.

"The gentleman's name wouldn't be Dan Hannigan by any chance?" Tate asked.

"Gives his name as Dan Smith," Parson said. "But sounds a lot more like a Hannigan to hear him talk."

"Big jug ears, lots of forehead, teeth like a horse," Carson said. "Dimple right at the end of his chin?"

"That's him, sure enough," Parson said. "A man can give any name he likes as far as I'm concerned. None of my business, but you described him."

"That's one of the men we're looking for," Tate said. "Where can we find him?"

Parson licked his lips, eyes bouncing between Carson and Tate. "Might be a man don't want to be found. I don't want this coming back on me."

Tate slipped a hand into the pocket of his waistcoat and came out with a coin. Carson caught the glint of gold.

The bounty hunter set the coin on the counter. "Twenty-dollar double eagle. That's over and above a fair price for the supplies. If it's the man we think it is, he won't be bothering you. If it's a different man, then no harm done."

Parson picked up the coin and rubbed a thumb over the smooth surface. "I guess this is one of those no-questions-asked situations."

Tate shrugged. "You can ask."

"Never mind. I don't want to know. Okay, here's how to find the man's place, but if something does go wrong, you didn't hear it from me." Parson made the coin vanish into a pocket. "I suppose I can throw lunch into the bargain while we're at it. There's cabbage and rabbit stew."

Tate wrinkled his nose, but Carson said, "I'll take a bowl of that. Thank you kindly."

"Head out the back door," Parson said. "Tables on the back porch. I'll bring out two bowls with corn bread."

Carson opened the back door, stepped out onto the wooden deck of the covered back porch, and looked straight down the twin barrels of a 12-gauge shotgun. Then the *click-click* of a hammer being thumbed back.

Katherine Payne grinned up at him from her seat at the table and kept the shotgun trained on Carson's face. "I'm starting to wonder if you've gone sweet on me, Carson Stone, following a lady all the way to Arkansas."

CHAPTER 6

Carson didn't move a muscle, but his eyes slid to the open doorway back into Meriwether's. Colby Tate was nowhere to be seen.

Of course. Right when I could use a little help.

He looked back at the woman pointing the scattergun at him. She sat with her back to one of the trading post's open windows. There was an empty bowl and a spoon on the table next to her. "A pleasant surprise to find you here, Lady Pain."

Her grin twisted into a snarl. "I don't care for that nickname. Where did you hear it?"

The *click-click* of a Peacemaker's hammer being thumbed back was slightly different from the sound of a cocking shotgun, but Katherine Payne must have been familiar with it because she froze instantly, only her eyes slowly widening.

Colby Tate appeared at the open window behind the red-haired bounty hunter. "I'm afraid that's my doing. Apologies. I didn't know the moniker displeased you."

"It does," she said, voice steady and seemingly unperturbed. "Mind telling me who's got a six-shooter pointed at the back of my head? It's starting to itch a bit."

"Colby Tate. A fellow bounty hunter. We met once about a year ago, when I first came West."

"Doesn't ring a bell."

"You were pretty drunk."

Carson cleared his throat. "As the only one here not currently pointing a gun at anyone, I'd like to suggest we all just take it down a notch. Maybe we can set the hardware aside and talk things over like civilized folks."

"I told you once already," Lady Pain said. "There's paper on you, Carson Stone. I'd be within my legal rights to blast you straight to hell with this 12-gauge."

"As he's currently in my custody, I wouldn't take it well if you did that," Tate said. "And I'd be within *my* legal rights to take action."

"I don't see any chains on him," she said. "And he's wearing a gun. You and I define 'custody' a bit differently, Mr. . . . who the hell are you again?"

"Tate. Colby Tate. I do admit we're taking something of a lax approach to custody in Mr. Stone's case."

"Lax indeed. If I decided to pull this trigger, I'd dispute before a judge that I didn't consider him to be in custody at all."

"If you decide to pull that trigger, you'll never dispute anything before anyone ever again." A hard edge had crept into Tate's voice.

"I hate to interrupt such slick banter," Carson said, "but that shotgun's probably getting heavy, and if your finger slips, I'll be the one paying the price. Why don't we all agree for the moment that I'm in a general sort of custody and not about to run off. I'll even hand over my six-shooter until we get all this straightened out."

Carson waited a long, tense moment while everyone considered.

"I have a bottle of whisky," Tate said. "Which might facilitate our reaching some amenable agreement."

"Well, why didn't you say that in the first place?" Katherine Payne eased the hammer back into position and set the shotgun on the table. "I'm going to turn around now and have a look at you, Tate. Don't shoot."

"Never fear," he said. "I've already holstered my weapon."

She turned and squinted at the other bounty hunter.

"Is my face any more familiar than my name?" Tate asked.

The woman shook her head. "Nope."

Carson took his gun from the holster and set it on the table in front of her. "You can hang on to that for now if it makes you feel better."

She glanced at the Peacemaker but made no move to take it.

Tate left his position at the window and came around through the back door, followed closely by Parson, who brought the stew and the corn bread.

"I see you met our other visitor," Parson said. "Hopefully, everyone's getting acquainted."

"Getting along like a house on fire," Tate said. "Could I trouble you for the bottle I purchased earlier and three glasses?"

"Gonna make a party out of it, eh?" Parson said. "Back in a jiffy."

Parson left, and Katherine Payne turned to Tate. "Let's make it official, then. I'll show you mine, if you show me yours."

"Happy to oblige." Tate pulled his legal papers from his coat pocket. "I believe you'll find my credentials in order."

They traded papers and both read. A minute later, they both agreed they were bona fide legal bounty hunters.

Carson took one of the bowls and began to spoon stew into his mouth. It was hot and bland, but Carson had suddenly found himself famished. Maybe that was the effect of having a shotgun pointed at him and surviving. Even the lousy stew tasted good.

He wasn't keen to be caught between these two bounty hunters, and he especially didn't want them fighting over him. Twice now, the woman had been prepared—even a little eager—to shoot him.

Just keep shut for now. Let them two talk it out.

But he wished suddenly he'd kept his gun.

Parson arrived with the whisky and three clean glasses.

Tate filled the glasses and held up his for a toast. "What shall we drink to? Not shooting one another, I suppose."

"I'll drink to that," Carson said.

They drank, and Tate refilled the glasses.

Carson let his sit. It was too early in the day to fall face-down into the mud, so he reminded himself to sip slowly.

The woman tossed back her second shot and held out her glass for a third.

"I apologize about that Lady Pain business." Tate refilled her glass. "I didn't say it to goad you."

"Friends call me Kat." She tossed back the shot.

"Kat. I like it. And I do hope we can be friends."

"Keep pouring the whisky. That should do it."

Tate refilled her glass again.

This time she sipped, curious eyes going back to Carson. "I'm not sure we've settled the matter of Mr. Stone's dubious custody. But I'm willing to table the matter. For now."

Carson smiled at her and reached for a piece of corn bread. "Thank you for that."

"But it doesn't mean I'm not curious," Kat said. "I'll take a wild guess and say you two have come to some sort of arrangement."

"We have," Tate said.

"I'd like to hear about it." Kat sipped whisky.

Tate looked apologetic. "Well . . . it's, uh . . . something of a private matter, actually."

"Tell her," Carson said.

"And why should I do that?"

"You found me, and she found me," Carson said. "That ain't coincidence. It's because you're both after the same men. McGraw and his gang. And if that's the case, it's more than likely we'll all be tripping over one another as we move forward unless we come to some kind of agreement now. Tell me what I've got wrong." He sipped whisky, eyes going back and forth between them.

"You're not wrong," Kat said. "I'm after McGraw."

"That's McGraw and his boys, and any new men he's added to the gang since," Carson said. "That's a lot for you all by your lonesome."

She glared at both men. "A lot for two, even."

"A lot for three," Carson said. "But three's better than two. Or one."

"But three's not better when it comes to splitting the money," Kat pointed out.

"I don't care about the money," Carson told her.

Kat raised an eyebrow, suspicious.

"I just want McGraw," Carson said. "Alive, if possible."

"Carson is innocent," Tate said. "He just wants to clear his name."

She grinned, and again it had that sneering quality. "You haven't been very far West for long, have you, Mr. Tate?"

"I guess not."

"All these fellas are innocent. Every single one. Just ask them."

Tate frowned. "I take your point."

"Don't worry, he's an excellent judge of character," Carson said dryly. "Just ask him."

Kat laughed and finished her whisky.

"The point is that Carson might have left me in the dust last night while I was sleeping or the night before, but he didn't," Tate insisted. "He means what he says. He's in this for McGraw."

Kat rubbed a finger around the inside of her shot glass, then put it in her mouth, sucking the whisky remains. Her eyes worked back and forth between the two men, dozens of thoughts obviously dancing in there. *She might not say it, but she agrees with me*, Carson thought. *Taking on Big Bob and his boys all by herself won't work, but she's greedy. She wants that money all to herself, but she's smart enough to know it's a bad play.*

So, greedy or smart. Which would win?

"Okay, then. Three guns, but split two ways," Kat said. "We do our best to bring in McGraw alive, but if it's either me or McGraw that takes a bullet, I vote for McGraw. Sorry."

"I expressed a similar sentiment," Tate said.

"How do you propose we kick off this new partnership?" Kat asked.

"We know where Dan Hannigan is," Carson said. "Or we think we do. Not too far from here."

"Then what are we waiting for?" Kat stood and grabbed her shotgun. "Let's bag us an Irishman."

CHAPTER 7

Parson's directions had been simple enough.

The eastern road bent a little way south to run along Lee Creek for a while, a tall pine forest growing up around them. They wouldn't properly be in the Ozarks for some time, but already the ground was hillier. About a dozen miles out from Meriwether's, they reached Parson's first landmark, where Lee Creek abruptly angled south again, and a much smaller creek crossed the road, known to locals as Little Lee.

There wasn't enough to Little Lee to merit a bridge and was really only a problem at the height of spring thaw. The horses splashed across with no trouble.

"We're about to lose the sun," Carson said. "We were never going to make Hannigan's tonight anyway. Maybe we should have stayed back at Meriwether's."

"If there'd been a hotel, I promise you we'd be there right now," Kat said. "But if we have to camp out anyway, we might as well eat up some miles. This way we can take our time tomorrow, ease up to Hannigan's place nice and slow and give it a good look before we try anything."

"Fair enough, but it might not even be him."

"It's him," Kat said. "There might be more than one jug-eared Irishman roaming western Arkansas, or there might not be. But I have a good feeling."

"I'm inclined to agree," Tate said. "I mean, Kat's good feeling isn't especially scientific, but statistically, how many Irishmen could there be in the area? Boston was lousy with them. Out here? Not so many."

"Let me talk before either of you two start squeezing off lead at him," Carson said. "He was always the most affable of the bunch. I might get something out of him about the others. Or . . ."

"Or what?"

"Or he might see me and just start shooting."

They found a level patch of high ground along the Little Lee and made camp. By the time Carson returned from watering the horses, Tate had the cookfire going.

"That's not a bad fire." Carson tried to keep the surprise out of his voice but failed. "We'll make an outdoorsman out of you yet."

"I prefer hotels," Tate said. "But I've built my share of campfires. I'm no army scout, but I get by."

"I never doubted you for a minute."

"I'm with the professor, here," Kat said. "We can't get back to soft beds soon enough to suit me."

"I'll even take my turn cooking," Tate offered. "Pan biscuits and bacon work?"

"Works fine."

"I'll get to it."

They ate and washed up, and then Kat broke out the whisky. She drank a slug straight from the bottle, then handed it over to Carson, who hesitated only a second, then took it. He drank and passed it to Tate.

"A swallow can't hurt, but let's go easy," Carson said. "We've got an Irishman to run down tomorrow."

Kat took an extravagantly small sip. "I'll go slow, Daddy. I promise."

"How does a woman get into the bounty hunting business?" Carson asked.

"Too tired for stories," she said. "Too *sore*. No matter how much time I spend in the saddle, I can't get used to it. And I *hate* sleeping on the ground." Kat held up the bottle. "This helps." She took another slug.

"It's the devil's own work, trying to pry anything out of either of you two," Carson said. "Fine, keep your secrets."

"It's not that I have secrets," Tate said. "It's just you'd be disappointed. I'm not very interesting."

"I'm downright fascinating," Kat said. "But I don't feel like it."

"Anyway, hearing about Dan Hannigan might be more useful right now," Tate suggested. Is he fast like Gentleman Dick?"

"Nobody is."

"Fast as you?"

Carson considered. "Now that I think about it, I can't remember ever seeing Dan draw on anyone. His weapon was more the gift of gab. He'd talk you into thinking you were pals and then hit you in the back of the head. You can't ride with a man like McGraw and not be able to shoot, but I never heard nobody talk like Dan was some lightning-quick legend."

"You think any of the rest are with him?" Kat asked.

"Couldn't say, but Parson talked like it was just Dan."

Kat thought about that. "If they've all gone their separate ways, that could be both good and bad. Bad we have to hunt them each one at a time. That could take a while. But good we don't have to take them on all at once."

"Regretting our deal?" Tate asked. "Maybe you don't need us to pick them off one by one."

"McGraw will have men with him," Kat said. "Maybe not the same men, but he won't be alone."

"We'll find out tomorrow if Hannigan's talkative," Carson said. "Let's get some sleep."

Kat put the cork back in the whisky and shoved the bottle

into her saddlebag. "Remember that cute little derringer I pulled on you, Carson, when you helped carry my packages?"

"How could I forget?"

"Well, I sleep cozied up with it right here at the ready," Kat said. "So take heed, gentlemen." She turned away from them, her head on the saddle for a pillow.

Tate rolled his eyes. To Carson, he said, "Wake me when it's time to go."

"You'll smell the coffee," Carson assured him.

The night passed uneventfully, and Carson's eyes popped open predawn as usual. He moved around quietly, letting the others sleep, going down to the creek to water and feed the horses. He took his time getting the fire going again, then put on a pot of strong coffee. The sun was humping up pink-orange on the horizon, flooding the pine forest with new light when Tate yawned and stretched.

"You let me sleep."

Carson handed him a cup of coffee. "If Parson's directions are good, we can take our time and still get there with more than enough daylight. I got sugar at Meriwether's if you want it for the coffee."

Tate held the cup in two hands, warming himself. "Black's fine."

"That's how I take it, too."

Kate awoke with a groan and did take sugar for her coffee.

Within an hour, they were traveling again, and soon came to Parson's next landmark. Where the road angled into a valley, another trail branched off north up a hill with an easy slope. The turnoff was marked by an old, rusty bucket hanging from a tall, wooden post. Parson had told them the bucket had been there for as long as he could remember, and who put it there and why was a mystery to him, but locals called the winding path up the hill Bucket Trail.

The three of them steered their horses up the hill, following what was little more than a game trail widened by routine use. A half hour later, they passed an abandoned cabin with the roof fallen in, another of Parson's landmarks. Rock walls rose gradually on either side of them, the path broadening as they now headed up a narrow ravine. They rode single file, the trickle of a stream flowing downhill next to them.

They were getting close and approached each bend in the trail slowly to peek around the corner first.

Carson reined in Jet. "We should walk from here."

They dismounted and tied the horses to a scrawny pine.

They followed the ravine, and a hundred yards later, they saw it. The space ahead opened up significantly. The ravine ended in a large, rocky cul-de-sac, the stone walls a dozen feet high all around. A small waterfall dribbled down the far wall forming a small pool that leaked into the stream. It flowed between a number of boulders that had tumbled down the hill once upon a time. On one side, there was a small pen for animals, but at the moment, it contained only a single mule that had seen better days.

On the other side of the stream, across from the pen, sat a neat log cabin with a flat roof. A small, covered porch. It looked to be in good repair, and smoke rose from the chimney. A door in front with a shuttered window to the left of it.

They watched for a few minutes from the mouth of the ravine, backs pressed to the rock walls, trying to keep out of sight. Nobody came or went from the cabin, nor to the outhouse about a hundred feet away from it.

"You think he's in there?" Kat asked.

"Somebody is." Carson pointed at the chimney smoke.

"Alone?"

"No way to be sure," Carson said. "But I don't see any horses."

He thought about the Winchester he'd left in the saddle sheath back on Jet but figured it was best to leave it. If it was anyone but Dan Hannigan in the cabin, he'd hunker down with the rifle and wait for the person to head for the outhouse.

Might still be the smart play, but we could sit here all damn day. I always got along well enough with Dan. I bet I could talk to him, but not if I walked out there with my Winchester cocked and ready.

"I'm going to try for a closer look," Carson said. "You two wait here."

"Does it look like I'm volunteering to cross open ground?" Kat asked.

Carson rolled his eyes. "That's the sense of teamwork I was hoping for."

"I'll go with you," Tate said.

"Don't," Carson said. "I appreciate it, but one person walking up on him's likely to get a better reaction than three."

Tate gave him a friendly slap on the back. "Good luck."

Carson ventured into the cul-de-sac, thinking he'd take all the luck he could get.

He walked slowly toward the cabin, keeping his hand away from his Colt, being careful but trying not to *look* like he was being careful. Should he call out or walk up and knock? Dan—or whoever was inside—probably didn't get a lot of visitors, and there was no point startling somebody who maybe had an itchy trigger finger.

Carson was just about to call out to the cabin when he saw the shutters open three inches and a rifle barrel emerge from the crack. The gun belched fire, and the shot echoed along the ravine.

Carson's hat flew off behind him.

He ran for the nearest boulder along the creek and threw himself behind it.

"I didn't have to miss," came a voice from the cabin. "Knocking your hat off was just my way of saying bugger off to trespassers."

Irish Dan's brogue was unmistakable.

"Is that how you welcome folks coming to offer a friendly hello, Hannigan?" Carson shouted from behind the boulder.

A long pause. "Nobody here by that name. I'm called Smith. Go on and get back down the ravine, now."

"I just wanted to talk, Dan. It's me, Carson Stone."

A longer pause this time. "McGraw send you?"

"Now why would he do that?"

"I'm trying to figure that out," Hannigan shouted. "What are you doing here?"

"I'm looking for McGraw," Carson said. "I thought you and me could chat."

"You think he'll have you back, is that it?"

"We both know better," Carson called to the Irishman.

"So, you want to put a bullet in him."

"If it comes to that. I'd rather bring him back to Texas alive."

Loud laughter came from the cabin. "I always did think you had a good sense of humor, Carson."

"I'm going to get my hat," Carson said. "Don't shoot at me."

"Go on, then. Get your hat."

Carson stood and dusted himself off and retrieved his hat. He frowned at the chunk Hannigan's shot had taken out of the brim, then put it back on his head.

"Now, how about I come up there and we can talk civilized? I'm curious what you're doing out here all by your lonesome instead of riding with McGraw."

"Come on up and I'll tell you."

Carson thought for a moment. "I brought a friend with me."

"No, no, to hell with that," Hannigan said with heat. "No strangers."

"She's not anyone to fret over. Just a friend, like I said. Come out, Kat. Show yourself." A pretty face would go a long way toward loosening Hannigan's tongue. If he'd been up here awhile, the man might have been deprived of female company for a long time.

When she didn't immediately come out, Carson called

again. "Kat!" Carson called her name only, hoping Tate would have the good sense to stay put.

Kat apparently had gone for the horses, walking out a second later, leading them by the reins, just the two of them. *Good. We need to keep up the appearance there's only two of us. The sight of Tate would only spook Dan, and we don't need him nervous.*

Carson caught sight of Hannigan's pale face at the window.

"You should have told me your friend was so easy on the eyes in the first place," Hannigan said. "Might have saved a lot of awkward hat shooting."

"We'll come up, then," Carson said. "And no shooting."

"No shooting. Bring your friend and let's have a visit."

They tied their horses to a porch post, and Carson knocked.

"Let yourself in," Hannigan called from the other side.

Carson pushed the door open and stepped inside, Kat right behind him.

It was immediately apparent why Hannigan hadn't jumped up to open the door. He sat at a square wooden table in a rickety chair, left leg out straight, propped up on another rickety chair. Hannigan's trousers had been cut off above the knee of his left leg, the knee itself wrapped in dirty bandages. The bandages had been soaked in blood at one time, the blood old and dry now. It didn't seem to Carson that Hannigan was in any danger of bleeding out right in front of him.

Carson nodded meaningfully at the Spencer rifle Hannigan held across his lap.

Hannigan set the rifle aside. "No worries."

"Dan, this is my friend, Kat."

Kat nodded to the Irishman. "Pleasure to make your acquaintance."

"Pleasure's all mine. Forgive me if I don't get up." He gestured to his leg, and then to the interior of the cabin. "In fact, forgive my lack of hospitality in general. As you can see, the accommodations are . . . let's say humble."

Carson took a look at the place. A potbelly stove off to one side. A narrow bunk against the far wall. Two more rickety chairs scooted up to the table. Carson had seen worse.

"Hold on a second," Kat said. "Be right back." She left the cabin.

"Your lady?" Hannigan asked.

"It's not like that."

A wan smile from the Irishman. "It should be, boyo. It really should be."

"Yeah, well, say that after she's pointed a shotgun at you."

"Love is grand," Hannigan said, "but often complicated."

Kat returned, holding up a half-full bottle of whisky, her grin lighting up the interior of the dank cabin. "Our way of saying thanks for not shooting us."

"He shot my hat," Carson said.

"Hush."

Hannigan's eyes lit up. "Bless you, ma'am. You're obviously an angel sent from Heaven. A cup and a glass on the shelf, Carson. Be a good lad and fetch them, won't you?"

Carson retrieved the tin coffee cup and the shot glass and set them on the table as Kat opened the bottle. She filled the shot glass and then the coffee cup halfway. "I'll drink from the bottle since there's not a third glass." She titled it back and took a large gulp.

"A woman after me own heart."

Hannigan drained the shot glass, and Kat filled it again.

Carson and Kat pulled the other two chairs up to the table, and Carson sipped from the cup.

"You really are saving my life," Hannigan said. "My leg was paining me something terrible. Just terrible."

"I guess we got here just in time, then," Kat said. "I know Parson's still a few days from making his delivery."

Carson shot Kat a sour look. They weren't supposed to mention Parson.

"Oh, Parson, is it? I was wondering how you'd found me. I should be very cross with him, but I find I'm feeling more forgiving by the second." Hannigan nudged the empty shot glass toward her.

She filled it dutifully.

"I'm curious about your leg," Carson said.

Hannigan's eyes widened with innocence. "Which one?"

Carson and Kat laughed.

"McGraw and me and the boys were riding out of Fort Smith and some marshals caught us in an ambush," Hannigan said. "I was out front when they opened up on us. Took a bullet. Hurt like the devil. First time I've ever been shot, you know. Go figure that in my line 'a work. Shot my horse right out from under me, the bastards. Beautiful white mare. You remember that horse, Carson?"

"I do."

"Shot poor Martin Jessup square in the face. His own mother wouldn't recognize him."

"I don't know him," Carson said.

"Oh, that's right. He joined after you were gone. Well, trust me, it was a terrible mess." He brought the shot glass to his lips, sipping this time. "We shot back, and Gordon got one of them, and the rest rode away. McGraw wanted to make time because he figured the marshals would stir up a posse, and of course, I couldn't ride. They dropped me off here, an out-of-the-way place McGraw knew about, said they'd come back after they threw off any pursuers. Lies, of course. That was two months ago."

"You've been with McGraw for years," Carson said. "He'd just leave you?"

"It's the knee." Hannigan gestured at it, a look of infinite sadness washing over him. "It's all broken up in there. It'll be forever to heal and never the same. McGraw's not a sentimental creature. I'm no good to him now."

Carson looked at the dried blood on the bandages and winced inwardly. A knee seemed like a bad place to get shot. "How bad is it?"

"Every morning I make a trip to the outhouse," Hannigan told them. "That's an hour's work. Highlight of my day."

"Sorry, Dan."

Hannigan emptied the shot glass again. Kat filled it.

He smiled, sad and easy. "Thank you kindly, ma'am." He sipped, then seemed to fend off the approaching melancholy. "But you fine, young specimens didn't come all this way to gawk at my leg."

"McGraw," Carson said. "I want to clear my name, and bringing him in is the only way. Unless you'd like to come back and testify I had nothing to do with shooting that marshal."

"I'd love to help you, lad," Hannigan said. "But not at the cost of putting my own head in a noose. And we know that's what would happen."

"That's what I figured, and I understand," Carson said. "That leaves McGraw. He pulled the trigger, so it should be him anyway."

"And if you help us, you could get back at him," Kat said. "For leaving you here like this."

"I hold no grudge against Big Bob," Hannigan said. "It was only business. On the other hand, I don't owe him either, and Carson's telling the truth. He was quit of McGraw's gang when that marshal was shot. Carson, you'll need the devil's own luck if you're going up against McGraw and his boys, but you're innocent and you deserve your chance."

"We should drink to that," Kat suggested.

They did. Kat refilled the tin cup and the shot glass.

"McGraw talked about his hideout in the Ozarks," Carson said. "I figure he's heading there."

"You're right," Hannigan said. "But later. He wants to lay low for the winter, but not until he pulls a few more jobs. There was some loose talk about stagecoach holdups and some other things, but I never got the details. Can't help you there. But there's a bank in Fayetteville. You can get there ahead of him maybe and wait."

Kat frowned. "He would have hit the bank by now, wouldn't he?"

"Ah, there's the catch," Hannigan said. "There's some kind of payroll coming through, and McGraw's waiting for it. I've been stuck up here awhile, so maybe it's happened and I just haven't heard. But McGraw talked like it was weeks away."

Carson tried to hide his disappointment. It wasn't much to go on. A bank in Fayetteville, but when? Hannigan had confirmed that McGraw would eventually end up at his Ozarks hideout, but Carson didn't relish sitting there all summer waiting for the outlaw to show.

"One more piece of information—not about McGraw, but it might be useful," Hannigan said.

Carson perked up. "Oh?"

"Memphis stopped by to pay me a visit about three weeks after they dumped me here," Hannigan told them. "He was on some errand for Big Bob and it was close by, so he wanted to see if I was still alive. He's a friendly lad that way. Anyway, he told me Gentleman Dick Fleetwood had quit McGraw's gang to strike out on his own."

"You're kidding. Did they have a falling-out?"

"Apparently, Dick's been squirreling away his money and has now bought some gambling tables in Jasper Springs," Hannigan said. "On the ground floor of the big hotel there. I guess Dick likes running a casino better than getting shot at all the time robbing banks."

Carson grinned. "That must have bent Big Bob out of shape every which way."

Hannigan laughed. "Sure, but Fleetwood might be the only man alive who could get away with it. Bob's fast and mean, but he can't outdraw Fleetwood. He'd have no chance in a straight-up duel. He let Dick go his own way, maybe thinking he'd backshoot him some later time."

"But there's paper on Fleetwood from here to Texas," Kat said. "How does a man like that think he can just settle down and run a roulette table?"

"Oh, he's not going by Fleetwood anymore," Hannigan said. "He took the name Lawrence Cooke. According to Memphis, anyway."

"And where's Memphis now?" Carson asked.

Hannigan shrugged. "Back to McGraw, maybe."

A silent moment stretched into two.

"I don't know if any of that helps," Hannigan said. "But I wish you luck, Carson. Really I do."

"Thanks, Dan. I reckon we've taken up enough of your time."

"Are you sure there isn't anything more you can tell us, Mr. Hannigan?" Kat asked. "Other places they might go. More jobs they mentioned."

"Sorry, ma'am. That's all I know."

She nodded. "Okay, then."

Kat's hand came up from under the table, and Carson barely had time to glimpse a hint of silver before the loud, startling *pop* of the derringer painted a neat red hole in the center of Hannigan's forehead and made Carson flinch back out of his chair.

Hannigan slid from his seat and crumpled to the floor.

Carson was still trying to back away, tripping over his own feet until he backed against the bed across the room and went down, spitting every curse he knew. He finally stood, still in shock, eyes going to Hannigan's corpse.

"What the hell'd you do that for?"

"For three hundred dollars," Kat said. "What did you think we'd come here for?"

Carson cursed another blue streak. He hated being caught by surprise.

"Go outside and fetch that mule. We'll drape him over it," she said. "And then we'll get the hell out of here."

Carson went outside just as Tate came out of hiding.

"I thought I heard a shot," Tate said.

"You did. Lady Pain strikes again."

CHAPTER 8

"Fort Smith takes us out of the way," Carson said irritably as they saddled the horses and prepared to move out.

They'd made camp early the previous night, and the mood had been sullen, the three of them saying few words to one another. Carson hadn't even wanted to look at Kat, but now there were decisions to be made.

"We need to find a marshal to collect the bounty money, and the closest place I know for sure there's a marshal is Fort Smith," Kat said. "Or we can just drag Hannigan's corpse around Arkansas until we happen to trip over one."

"She's probably right," Tate admitted. "I'd have preferred to bring him alive, but what's done is done."

They argued another few minutes, but in the end, it looked like they were going to Fort Smith. Carson had to admit the sooner they got rid of Hannigan the better. The sight of him was an unpleasant reminder.

The mule slowed them considerably, and it was on the third day when they finally rode into town and hitched their horses in front of the Fort Smith marshal's office.

"Mind Hannigan while I go in," Kat said. "Hopefully, this won't take long, but you never know."

Carson sighed. "Right."

"I'll come in with you," Tate said. "Partners, remember?"

They went in. Carson waited.

Partnering with the bounty hunters wasn't turning out the way Carson expected. He blamed himself to a certain extent. Hunting for bounties was their job, and all the men in McGraw's gang were wanted dead or alive, Hannigan included. There was no point in Carson pretending it was any other way. And hell, Hannigan wasn't no saint. Carson knew that. But to sit across from a man and talk friendly and pour him whisky and then shoot him between the eyes . . .

Carson shivered. Katherine Payne wasn't anyone to be taken lightly.

And Carson had to keep in mind that Tate might not be any better when all was said and done. He had good manners and an easy way about him, but his job was still to bring back men dead or alive. Did Carson trust either of them?

Well, that's what I need to figure out, isn't it?

Tate, Kat, and a middle-aged man emerged from the marshal's office. The man looked like a tough customer, a badge on his vest and a handbill clutched in one hand. He went directly to the mule and grabbed a fistful of Hannigan's hair, lifting his head so he could see the Irishman's face. He nodded once, let Hannigan's head drop, then went back into the office with Kat.

Tate climbed on his horse and sat there next to Carson, not quite frowning but definitely not smiling.

"That go how you wanted it to?" Carson asked.

"You mean in there?"

"I mean with her and Hannigan. The man had a bad leg, and his rifle was out of reach. He'd have come along as gentle as a lamb."

Tate sighed. "No. That's not how I would normally want it to go." He sat there and didn't say anything else.

Five minutes later, Kat came out again alone, two pieces of paper in her hand. She folded one and shoved it in her pocket. She handed the other to Tate. "That's finished, then.

There's the receipt for your half. They'll wire it to your bank. Tomorrow we can get back on track after the others."

Two deputies came out of the office and moved to take charge of Hannigan's corpse.

Kat mounted her horse. "I threw in the mule. I figure we don't have any use for it, and it'll probably drop dead within the hour anyway."

"Kat." Carson made sure he said her name in a way she'd understand something serious was coming. "This ain't working out."

Tate shook his head like he knew what was coming and wished it wasn't.

Kat's eyes narrowed. "What is it that isn't exactly working out to your complete satisfaction, Carson Stone?"

"I just think we have different ways of going about things."

He thought about it a moment, chewing his bottom lip. "I made a promise to that man. I may not have said it, maybe I didn't hold up my right hand and swear, but he told me to come up to that cabin and he wouldn't shoot. In return, I didn't shoot. And we sat to talk like normal men. We both thought we'd be leaving that conversation alive."

"I see." Kat took off her hat, wiped sweat from her forehead with the back of her hand. "You've made some mistakes in your life, Carson, but Tate here thinks you're an honest man at your core, so let's say you are. I think what happened with Hannigan offended that sense of honesty. And for that, I apologize. And it was a bad surprise to be sitting there all friendly, then suddenly there I am, shooting a man dead. So I apologize for that, too."

She stuck her hat back on, and a long sigh leaked out of her. "Two months after you left McGraw's gang, they hit a bank in Bent Willow, had to shoot their way out. Hannigan shot at two men trying to stop him. Hannigan was shooting wild, all over the place, and a bullet crossed the street and shot a Methodist preacher right out of a barber chair in the middle of a shave. His wife and three daughters buried him. This world is better without Irish Dan Hannigan in it, and for shooting him stone-dead, I am not sorry."

Carson sat on his horse, not looking at her.

"I can see you've got some words trying to get out of your mouth," Kat said. "Let's hear 'em."

"I'm just trying to line them up right," Carson told her.

She waited. Time crawled by like normal, the blazing sun high in the sky beating hell out of the world.

Finally, Carson said, "You're right I don't like surprises. And you're right that I'd prefer to feel honest than not. Like I said before, I always thought Dan an affable sort, and I let myself forget who he really was, sitting there talking so friendly. I should have remembered that on my own without you reminding me, and for that you have my apology."

The tension seemed to go out of both of them.

"I think that was well spoken by the both of you," Tate said. "It's good to clear the air."

"Speaking of clearing the air, I could use a bath," Kat said. "And then an expensive meal and a soft bed in an expensive hotel room. I plan to enjoy myself before having to sleep on the ground again. I'll see you gentlemen later."

She turned her horse and headed up the street. They watched her go.

Tate turned to Carson. "I guess the next thing to do is invite you to a steak dinner. The marshal told us the best place in town to eat, and the best hotel."

"I'm not as well-heeled as you are," Carson said.

"You're no good to me if you starve to death," Tate said. "You got a lot of good information out of Hannigan. We'll track the others. You've earned your steak and clean sheets. It's the least I can do."

Carson grinned. "You'll run through your reward money pretty quick, spoiling me like that. Three hundred is a lot of money, even split two ways, but any amount of money can run out eventually."

"Five hundred split two ways," Tate said. "The price went up on McGraw and each member of his gang when they killed that marshal at the ambush Hannigan told you about."

"Well, then. Let's eat."

"Not so fast, my friend. You need a bath even more than our intriguing Lady Pain." He leaned down and sniffed himself. "Damn. So do I."

CHAPTER 9

Carson walked into the St. Julian Hotel and almost walked right back out again. He'd never felt so out of place in his life. Men in suits and silk waistcoats with gold watch chains sat in the lobby's posh chairs, smoking cigars and reading newspapers. Carson felt rough and dirty, and he turned to go.

But Tate filed in behind him and shoved him toward the front desk.

The clerk was a neat and efficient little man who smiled at Carson and Tate as if they were royalty. "Gentlemen." He nodded to each in turn. "Welcome to the St. Julian. How may I help you today?"

"Two rooms. And we're going to need baths," Tate told him.

"Of course, sir. Our rates are . . . well, this is the *best* hotel in town and . . ."

Tate took a leather billfold from his jacket pocket and counted out the appropriate amount.

The clerk's eyes widened, but to his credit, his professional demeanor returned immediately. "May I suggest rooms with baths attached? So much more private than the bath down the hall."

"That will do nicely," Tate told him.

Five minutes later, Carson found himself standing in a

room so opulent, he felt like he was the governor or the French ambassador, or anyone except dusty Carson Stone, who surely must have smelled like horse and campfire and his own stink on top. A desk and a plush divan and a canopied bed covered in red satin. A smaller room attached held a porcelain basin and a large tub. An army of servants had been turned into a bucket brigade, marching in with buckets of hot water until the tub was full. They asked if he needed anything else before leaving him to wash, and Carson had joked there was nothing left he needed except a pitcher of beer.

Two minutes later, a pitcher of yellow beer and a clean mug sat on a small table next to the tub. Carson was glad he hadn't jokingly asked for one of the saloon gals from the place down the street.

He stripped and considered his dirty clothes with a frown. He had extra socks and underthings and one other clean shirt, but only one pair of trousers. He slapped off the road dust the best he could with an open palm, then hung the trousers on a hook behind the door.

He put one foot into the tub and took it right back out again. Way too hot. He waited, and by the time it took him to get through a mug of beer, the tub water was just right. He eased into it. Muscles and joints he hadn't even realized were sore began to relax. The hot water did its magic, and Carson was in no hurry to get out of the tub. He soaked a good while and then made use of the bar of soap sitting on the side, dunked his head under and scrubbed every inch.

He might have soaked longer, but he noticed he was soaking in his own juices now, the road grime that had been caked to him now making a thick stew in the tub. He took the hint, got out, and dried off with a soft towel.

A white robe hung on a hook next to his trousers. It was made from the same fluffy stuff as the towel. He shrugged into it and tied it around himself. Then he went into the bedroom and flopped onto the bed.

He might as well try to sleep on a cloud. There was no way a human being could sleep on something this soft, but soon he felt his eyes drooping and . . .

A rap on the door.

Carson's eyes popped open. He *had* fallen asleep. Had it been an hour? Two?

"Carson, our repast awaits!" Tate's voice on the other side of the door.

Carson rubbed his eyes. "Let me get dressed. I'll meet you in the lobby."

"Don't tarry. I'm starving."

Carson winced as he pulled on his dirty trousers, but his shirt was clean, black with white buttons, and he ran his fingers through his hair until he was more or less presentable. He went down to the lobby but didn't see Tate. Just the usual swells, men with cigars and expensive suits. A woman in a long green dress and a wide hat with a parasol and . . .

It was Kat.

Carson's mouth fell open. As the late Irish Dan Hannigan had observed, Kat was easy on the eyes, but this was something different. She looked like she'd just arrived from Paris.

Not that Carson knew much about such things.

"From the look on your face, I'd say the dress was worth every penny."

"That green goes well with your hair," Carson said.

"I rather thought so, too."

"I didn't think you'd be joining us. I reckoned you might soak in the tub all night, glad to be rid of two thick-headed men."

Her quick, devilish grin again. "And deprive you of the pleasure of my company?"

That grin sent a jolt up Carson's spine. Lady Pain was dangerous in more ways than one, and he reminded himself to keep his guard up. A smile like that could put a man wrong in the head in no time flat.

Tate appeared looking dapper. He wore the same suit, although it had been brushed. A fresh, clean shirt. Shoes shined. He looked like he should have been sitting with the other swells, smoking a pipe and reading a paper, not hobnobbing with some ragged cowboy like Carson Stone.

"I feel like a new man," Tate said. "Shall we dine?"

Carson grinned. "I think we shall."

The three of them left the hotel and walked to the restaurant, which was next door and actually owned by the same people who ran the hotel and called Julian's Bistro. Carson didn't know what a bistro was. Tate said restaurant, but fancy.

The maître d'hôtel sat them at a table next to a window, so all the regular folks passing by outside could watch them eat with envy. Carson felt like some sort of circus animal on display.

An hour later, they'd consumed string beans, mashed potatoes, buttermilk biscuits, and, of course, steaks the size of a wagon wheel, the edges hanging off the plates. Kat had ordered a bottle of red wine, something called pinot noir, and Tate complimented her choice. Carson had his share, not quite sure if he liked it or not, but by the third glass, he decided he did.

"There's some kind of chocolate French thing for dessert I can't pronounce," Kat said. "Want one?"

"No, thanks, I'm stuffed," Carson said. "I don't see where you put it."

"I'll find a place."

Tate took out a drooping pipe and stuck it into the corner of his mouth, the bowl dangling below his chin. He began to pack it with dark tobacco. "Do either of you mind if I smoke?"

They didn't mind. Tate lit the pipe, and the air filled with the scent of cherry and vanilla.

Kat ate her dessert, and Carson drank some sort of after-dinner sipping liquor that you weren't supposed to throw back all at once like a shot of whisky. They sat feeling happy and satisfied. This was why they did it, Carson supposed, risked their necks chasing bad men for the big bounties, just for this moment right here, sitting in a fancy place after a fine meal, enjoying the finer things and knowing later you'd be laying your head on a feather pillow in a soft bed.

Carson looked out the window as he sipped his liquor. A man walked by, and it struck Carson that his face was familiar. The same thing must have struck the other man because he slowed his walk as his eyes locked with Carson's. The man's face turned angry as he did a quick about-face and came into the restaurant.

He stood ten feet from Carson's table, eyes shooting fire. "You dirty son of a bitch!"

"Seriously?" Kat said. "Right in the middle of dessert?"

Carson looked the man over again and realized who he was—big, bulky fellow, that huge beard, and the thinning hair on top. "What are you doing here, Hank Baily?"

"The ranch foreman said he'd fire me if I got arrested one more time for being drunk," Baily said. "Which happened because of *you*."

"Not me," Carson said. "Your own actions landed you in jail."

"That's not how I see it." Baily swept his coat back, revealing his six-shooter. "None of your fancy tricks this time. No bending a man's finger back. You don't have me by surprise this go-around. Now stand up and gun it out with me."

"Are you out of your mind, coming into a place like this and acting like an animal?" Carson said.

"He's right, old sport." Tate puffed his pipe. "Bad form."

Baily's gaze swept the interior of the establishment and realized suddenly every eye was on him, all the diners in their fancy suits and dresses. Carson remembered the feeling of not belonging when he walked into the lobby of the St. Julian, and he knew Baily was feeling the same way now.

"I'll gun it out with you at the proper place and at the proper time," Carson said. "Like a civilized person."

"I'm civilized," Baily said. "Civilized as *you*. Name the time and place."

"You know the stables at the south end of town?"

"Benson Brothers," Baily said. "Yeah, I know it."

"Dawn," Carson said. "And if you're not there, everyone's going to know you for the mangy yellow dog you are."

"Oh, I'll be there. You just make sure *your* sorry ass is there."

Baily straightened the lapels of his jacket and offered a curt nod to everyone else in the room. "Sorry to disturb your meals. Good evening to you all."

Then he turned sharply and stalked out.

"For crying out loud," Kat said.

"It was either that or shoot him here," Carson said.

"Well, that was *almost* a perfect dinner," Kat said.

"That was an unfortunate encounter," Tate said. "You're not concerned?"

Carson shrugged. "It'll all work out."

They retired to their separate rooms, and it seemed Carson's head had barely hit the pillow when it was time to wake up. He, Tate, and Kat found themselves in the saddle before dawn, ready to ride. Carson turned Jet north and trotted down the road, Tate right behind him.

Kat caught up with them, pulled her horse alongside Carson's. "Aren't you going to keep your appointment with Hank Baily?"

"Nope."

Kat looked at him blankly for a moment and then threw her head back and laughed so loudly, it startled the horses.

"That's a relief," Tate said. "It's too early in the morning to deal with a corpse."

CHAPTER 10

Carson had explained it like this: He had no interest in killing a dumb slob like Hank Baily. And he sure as hell didn't want to be killed *by* a dumb slob like Hank Baily. There was no outcome to such an encounter that Carson would have found satisfactory, so he told the guy a story to make him go away.

And then Carson Stone rode out of town and put the minor nuisance of Hank Baily out of his mind.

Until Kat brought it up again when they stopped to rest the horses.

"You're not worried what people will say?" she asked. "That they might call you a coward or something?"

Carson chuckled. "I suppose there's a time to worry about what other people think. I didn't say a proper goodbye to my ma, and now I wonder what she thinks of me. What she's heard. And when I finally set things straight, I'm going to tell her. But if strangers who've never met me judge me a coward because I didn't shoot some other stranger they never met, well, if there's a bigger waste of time, I don't know it."

"A sensible point of view," Tate said.

Kat looked at Carson seriously for a long moment. "Every time I turn a corner, there's a little something more to you, Carson Stone."

Carson smiled. "I'm also good at checkers and can whistle."

"Don't tell me," Kat said. "I like to be surprised as we go along."

"Fair enough."

"I take it we're heading for that bank," Kat said.

"I thought of that, but we could be waiting for days or weeks," Carson said. "Hell, for all we know, McGraw hit the bank already."

"I don't think so," Kat told him. "When we were in the marshal's office collecting the reward on Hannigan, I sniffed around for news, and a bank robbery would have been news. Not a word about anything like that."

"Nothing like that in Fayetteville," Tate corrected. "But there was a stage robbery three days' ride north of Fayetteville, and the bandits matched the description of McGraw and his men. I think he's in the area."

"Okay, then, let's say he hasn't hit the bank yet," Carson conceded. "But he's in striking distance. He could hit the bank tomorrow or five minutes from now. We don't *know*. I still don't like the idea of twiddling my thumbs for weeks, waiting for McGraw to make his move. I think we need more information."

Kat thought about that for a minute, then said, "Fleetwood?"

Carson sighed, then nodded. "I don't like it, but yeah, I was thinking that."

"Why don't you like it?" Tate asked.

"Of all the men in McGraw's gang, the only two who really frighten me are McGraw himself and Gentleman Dick Fleetwood."

Kat raised an eyebrow. "You don't seem the type to frighten."

"McGraw is pure mean, and as I believe I've already mentioned, nobody alive is faster than Fleetwood." Carson tsked. "Anyone brave enough to go up against those men just doesn't understand the situation. At some point, brave and smart part ways."

"And you think he'll just start spouting information if you ask him?" Tate said.

Carson shook his head. "I doubt it."

"So, how do you plan to get him to talk?"

"I was thinking he might be more likely to talk to you."

A slow grin spread across Tate's face. "Oh, I think I like where this is going."

Kat shot Carson a sharp look. "What makes you think I have the magic touch?"

"After getting a look at you in that dress last night, I reckon a man might say anything you'd want to hear."

A wide grin lit up her face. "Are you buttering me up, Carson Stone?"

Carson's cheeks went pink. "Jasper Springs is on the way to Fayetteville anyway. I figure it's worth a look-see."

"If Fleetwood's as fast as you claim, I think I'd better handle him," Tate said.

Carson sighed and shook his head. "With respect, Mr. Tate, I just don't think that's the play."

"Oh? You think you can take him?"

"I know for a fact I can't," Carson admitted. "I haven't seen you in action, but I've seen him, and I just don't think this is something we should put to the test. A straight-up gunfight isn't the way with Fleetwood. More like a job for Kat's little derringer, if you take my meaning."

"You've got a plan?" Kat asked.

"I've got a notion," Carson said. "I'm hoping it will grow up and make a plan out of itself as we go along."

Tate rubbed his chin, thinking. "I should go, then."

Kat's head snapped around to look at him. "What? Dissolve the partnership?"

"When I said you shouldn't go up against Fleetwood, I didn't mean you should go away," Carson said.

"Sorry. Let me explain myself," Tate said. "If you don't need my guns with Fleetwood, I can be useful elsewhere. We need to know where McGraw is or what he's doing. I can ride to the scene of the stage holdup and make a slow loop back south toward Fayetteville. I'll try to pick up his trail along the way, keeping an ear to the ground for rumors and so forth. We still have a partnership. We'll just be working the problem from two different ends."

"And what if you do catch up with McGraw?" Carson asked. "You don't plan to face down the whole gang, do you?"

"I don't have a death wish," Tate said. "If an opportunity presents itself and I like the odds, I'll see what I can accomplish. Short of that, I'm simply on a fact-finding mission. I propose that if any of us find ourselves in an untenable position, we fall back and regroup in Fayetteville."

"I'm for that," Carson said. "Kat?"

"I don't know. Didn't Custer divide his forces?" She shrugged. "What the hell. Why not? Like you said, we can cut out and meet up in Fayetteville if we find we've bitten off more than we can chew."

Carson made coffee, and they talked it over for another hour while the horses rested. They went over the details, discussed contingent plans, second-guessed, and expressed concerns. In the end, they agreed the plan was the best they could come up with under the circumstances. Tate saddled his horse and mounted.

Carson shook Tate's hand. "Good luck."

Tate's eyes flicked to Kat, who was tending her horse. He lowered his voice. "Don't turn your back on that one."

Carson grinned. "I'll sleep with one eye open."

Tate returned the grin, then pointed his horse north and galloped away. Carson watched him go, wishing a little that he wasn't.

Kat came up behind him a moment later. "How far to Jasper Springs?"

"Two nights sleeping on the ground. Maybe a third, but probably not if we keep moving."

Kat sighed. "I'm going to miss that big, soft bed at the St. Julian."

Carson laughed and shook his head. "Too fancy for me. I liked it once to say I done it, but I kept thinking I was soiling everything I touched."

Kat grinned, nodding. "I felt that way at first. But I got used to it, and more importantly, I got used to thinking I *deserved* it. I've had . . . well, some bad luck. Some bad times. And I decided if I wanted good times, I'd have to arrange them for myself instead of waiting for fate or the grace of God or sheer dumb luck. I don't enjoy killing, Carson, but I don't mind if it's men that deserve it and if it gets me the money to live a fine life."

"That's why you decided to get into the bounty hunter business?"

"I didn't pick this line of work. It picked me." Kat's grin faltered a moment, and when it came back, it seemed forced. "Anyway, you missed your chance to ask about that when I was in the right mood, full of wine and chocolate at the restaurant."

"Hank Baily spoiled my opportunity."

"That he did," Kat agreed. "But as soon as I put away enough money, I'll invest in something. I don't know, cattle or a hotel or something that will keep making money and letting me live the good life."

"Then you need to stop spending money in expensive restaurants," Carson said.

"Don't worry, I always stash away some of it," Kat told him. "But I have to remind myself once in a while what sort of life I'm working toward. Helps me keep my eye on the future."

"I got my hands full with the here and now."

"You never think of your future?"

A shrug. "I got a price on my head. Hard to think past that. I suppose if I could get things straight, I might find my mother. I'd hate to think she's heard I'm some kind of murdering outlaw. I'd like her to know the truth."

"Where is she now?" Kat asked.

"New Orleans. She's from a good family there, but she was the youngest of four daughters, and my understanding was she didn't expect much in the way of an inheritance. So she decided to head west with a Confederate captain looking to start over. They had land and worked it. But Pa died, and I was gone. She went back to play nurse to one of her sister's children. That's what I heard, anyway."

"You'll get there," Kat said. "We'll handle McGraw, set things right, and then you can go see her."

"Wish I felt as confident as you."

"The trick to confidence is not looking surprised when all the stuff you bragged you were going to do actually happens."

"I'll keep that in mind," Carson said. "I'll try not to look surprised if we actually find a way to take Fleetwood. Now, let's get ourselves to Jasper Springs."

CHAPTER 11

They didn't drag into Jasper Springs until four days later.

They'd been on schedule the third day, when the sky opened up midmorning and drenched them, thunder and lightning shaking the world. A farmer took pity and allowed them to hide from the weather in his barn until it blew past, but the storm raged most of the day, and they ended up sleeping there.

Carson reined in his horse on the edge of town.

Kat stopped her horse next to his. "What is it?"

"Fleetwood will recognize me," Carson said.

"What'll he do?"

"Can't say exactly," Carson admitted. "No reason he'd have anything against me, but we'd lose whatever element of surprise we might have in case that matters. Also, he might not like that I know him. He don't use the name Fleetwood here. He might not be comfortable with a familiar face, and I don't like the idea of being Gentleman Dick Fleetwood's source of discomfort."

"I see your point."

"Might be best if we camp outside of town until we formulate our plan," Carson said.

"Two nights on the ground and one in a hayloft," Kat told

him. "I'm sleeping in a bed tonight. Dick Fleetwood won't recognize *me*."

"I know you like your comfort and that's fine," Carson said. "But we still need to talk about how we should go about this."

"Agreed." She clicked her tongue, and her horse started forward. "Wait here. I'll scout it out and report back."

Carson sat in the saddle and watched her head into town for a few moments. He felt a little useless just waiting but couldn't think what else to do. He'd leave it to Kat.

And why not? She was smart, pretty, dangerous, and didn't need Carson to look after her. He surprised himself by how fondly he suddenly found himself thinking of her. Well, he was a man and she was quite a woman, so why shouldn't he think it might be nice if they . . .

He chuckled to himself. Lady Pain was steak dinners with French desserts and high-fashion dresses and expensive hotels. She had definite thoughts about her future, and Carson doubted those thoughts included some bumpkin who owned only one pair of trousers.

Still, when she wasn't pointing guns at him, Kat was a bit of okay in his book. Feminine without being fragile. Definitely not boring. Maybe once this McGraw business was over . . .

Stop fooling yourself. Just be glad she didn't blow your head off with that shotgun.

He found a small clearing behind a line of shrubs, which allowed him to conceal himself while still watching the road. He made a small fire and started a pot of coffee. While it brewed, he tended to Jet: removed his saddle, fed and watered him.

Carson sat on a log and sipped coffee. Nothing to do now but wait.

* * *

Kat's horse slopped along the muddy street through Jasper Springs. The scorching sun after the heavy rain had made the place hot and steamy. Maybe that was what caused the lazy feel of the place. Even the folks out and about their business seemed to move more slowly than normal. Jasper Springs had the feeling of a town in no hurry to accomplish anything in particular.

She tied her horse to a post in front of a place called Molly's Wayside Inn, a clean and well-kept-looking place, far less opulent than the St. Julian and presumably cheaper. Carson's point about running through her money too quickly had been a good one, but Kat had meant what she'd told him. She always made a point of stashing away a good bit of each bounty she collected. Kat had tasted the good life and wanted more of it.

But she wasn't a complete fool.

She paused a moment to look up and down the street. Jasper Springs wasn't much different from any other town. Smaller than Fort Smith but bigger than some other places. She spied the saloon across the street and down a block. A big sign said "Lucky Clover Casino & Hotel," a bright green image of a four-leaf clover on one side and a roulette wheel on the other. Kat guessed the hotel rooms were probably for the working girls and their customers and decided a room at Molly's would likely suit her better.

She went inside and paid a friendly, middle-aged woman the price of a room, which included putting her horse in the stable around back. The room was small but tidy and, as expected, quite affordable.

Kat flopped on the bed and considered her next move. She needed to scout the place out and get a look at Fleetwood, now calling himself Lawrence Cooke, but it was still early in the afternoon, and the place probably wouldn't be doing much business. She preferred hiding in a crowd over walking into a nearly empty casino and drawing attention to herself.

On the other hand, Carson was sitting on the edge of town all by his lonesome, waiting for her to scout the place out so they could form some kind of plan.

Screw it. She hopped out of bed and shrugged into a light buckskin jacket in spite of the heat. The jacket hid the .32 Rimfire in the shoulder holster. She left Molly's and crossed the street, walking a block down to the Lucky Clover.

She entered and paused to look the place over, bracing herself for that brief moment of annoyance when all eyes turned to see a woman entering the saloon.

But it didn't happen this time; nobody paid any attention to her. As predicted, there were few customers this time of day. The bar made a big circle of itself in the center of the room, and a gaunt barkeep stood behind it, wiping out shot glasses with a rag and stacking them in a neat pyramid. A customer slumped at the bar a few feet from him, a half-empty whisky bottle at his elbow.

All the tables on this side of the bar looked like the ones you'd find in any saloon. On the other side of the bar, the space was taken up with blackjack tables and a big roulette wheel. At the moment, they were all completely deserted.

The only other people in the establishment were four men at a table in the corner, quietly playing cards.

Kat crossed the room to the bar.

The barkeep looked up, taking her in with indifference. "Help you?"

"I'm not sure I'm in the right place," Kat said. "Is this place owned by Lawrence Cooke?"

"He owns downstairs," the barkeep told her. "Madam Rose owns upstairs. She runs the girls. Do you know Mr. Cooke?"

"I've never met him. A friend of a friend said this was a good place if I was thirsty. Just wanted to make sure I'd walked into the right establishment."

"Well, that's him playing cards if you ever want to introduce yourself. The man with his back against the wall." The barkeep nodded toward the corner table. "But you'll want to wait until the game's over. They've been at it since three in the morning."

"I won't interrupt."

"As for being thirsty, that's my department. What can I get you?"

"Whisky. Thank you."

He filled a clean shot glass and set it in front of her. She paid him.

Kat sipped, keeping her head down but looking at the man with his back against the wall.

He might not have been going by the nickname "Gentleman" anymore, but Kat had to admit Fleetwood was a dapper fellow. According to the barkeep, they'd been playing cards more or less all night, and the other three men at the table looked ragged, sleeves rolled up, ties pulled loose.

Gentleman Dick Fleetwood looked fresh as a daisy. A red- and blue-striped waistcoat, a jacket that looked as if it had just been pressed, a tie with a gold stickpin and a pearl. Glittering gold cufflinks. Even his shoes had a fresh shine. Square jaw. No mustache or beard, but sideburns coming a long way down. Black hair slicked back, not a strand out of place.

There was always the temptation in these situations to simply shoot the man when he was looking the other way. Fleetwood was wanted dead or alive, and there was nothing in the rules that said Kat had to give the man a sporting chance.

But the other men in the room might be his friends. The barkeep probably had a scattergun underneath the counter. Any one of them could gun her down before she could announce she'd shot Fleetwood in her legal pursuit of a bounty. Kat had stayed alive so far by being smart. She wasn't going to start getting impatient now and do something stupid.

Also, shooting the wrong man would land her in a world of trouble. She'd never seen Fleetwood before except on the wanted poster, which showed him with a beard and a mustache, and the information that Fleetwood now called himself Cooke was hardly firsthand.

No, she needed Carson to confirm it was definitely Fleetwood before she started shooting. And then, getting Fleetwood alone would be preferable to shooting him in front of people who could shoot back. But Carson needed to identify Fleetwood without being *seen* by him. Maybe it was better to leave Carson outside of town while she confirmed Fleetwood's identity another way. She'd done it before.

But that could take days, and I want to get after McGraw and the rest of his gang sooner rather than that. Tate might be trustworthy, but then again, he might not be. Maybe he was hatching some scheme to keep the McGraw bounty for himself. Hell, when did this get so complicated?

Kat sipped whisky, her thoughts going around in circles. Maybe she should find Carson and talk it over before—

"You cheating son of a bitch!"

Kat turned her head, looking at the table in the corner.

One of the men at Fleetwood's table threw down his cards, then pointed an angry finger at Fleetwood. "I show four tens and you show four jacks? That some kinda joke? All your hands been just a little bit better'n mine all damn night. Nobody has that kind of luck."

Fleetwood made a calming gesture, then said something too low for Kat to hear. Fleetwood showed no sign that he was rattled by the other man's outburst.

"I don't have to prove a damn thing because you're gonna confess. I'll *make* you confess!" The other man stood, hand dropping to his six-shooter.

There were two quick pops, and the man staggered back

over his chair and went down hard. A little silver revolver had appeared in Fleetwood's hand as if by magic.

Carson was right. I've never seen anyone so fast. Where did that gun come from? His sleeve? Under the table? The man's hand had been empty one moment, then holding a revolver the next, a .32 Marlin by the look of it.

The man on the floor untangled himself from his chair. One hand came away from his shoulder red and sticky from his bleeding wounds. His face had gone ashen, but he was still game to try for his gun with the other hand, fumbling it out of his holster. "Not dead . . . yet . . . you. . . bastard."

Fleetwood stood and fired again, a flower blooming in the center of the man's forehead. He went down hard, rattling the floorboards.

Fleetwood sighed. "I gave you a chance, Clyde. We're all tired, and you'd been drinking all night. I thought shooting you in the shoulder would take the fight out of you. I guess not. I suppose we'll need the sheriff now. Could you fetch him, Abner?"

"Sure thing, Lawrence." Abner paused to look down at the corpse and shook his head. "Clyde always was too hotheaded for his own good."

Abner left, and Fleetwood walked toward the bar, then did a double-take upon seeing Kat standing there. He'd obviously been focused on his card game and hadn't realized someone else had come in.

"I'm sorry you had to see that, ma'am," Fleetwood said. "I try not to run that sort of establishment, but occasionally these things can't be helped." He gestured to the barkeep. "A drink for the lady. On the house. My feeble attempt at an apology."

The barkeep refilled Kat's glass.

"No apology needed, Mr. Cooke," Kat said. "He went for his gun. I don't see you had any other choice."

A nod. "Quite."

His eyes went up and down her, nothing overtly lascivious, but he was clearly getting a good look, and Kat knew what he was thinking. Men's clothes and dusty from riding, but there was clearly an attractive woman underneath.

"Have we met perhaps?" he asked. "You seem to know my name."

"We've not. Your man behind the bar pointed you out as the owner."

He smiled, charm oozing out of him. "That explains it, then. I'm sure I'd have remembered you. You have me at a disadvantage."

She was now expected to introduce herself but balked at the thought of giving her real name. But if she gave a fake name and Fleetwood found out, that could be bad. She'd given her real name when checking in to Molly's. All Fleetwood had to do was ask around.

"My friends just call me Kat," she said.

"A pleasure to make your acquaintance, Kat. Why don't we get a quiet table and have another drink? I always take an interest when someone new comes into the Lucky Clover, especially one so beautiful."

She almost batted her eyes at him but stopped herself. The man worked around saloon girls every day and would have seen such a cheap maneuver a thousand times. The beginnings of a plan were beginning to form in the back of her brain.

Kat gestured down at her own appearance. "You're not exactly catching me at my best. I've been on the road for days."

"It is a lady's prerogative to put her best foot forward," Fleetwood said. "Come back tonight and I can show you the Lucky Clover's hospitality properly. Without unfortunate bloodshed."

Kat smiled warmly and hoped it came off as sincere. "I

look forward to. it." She tossed back the whisky and gave Fleetwood a nod. "Until tonight."

Fleetwood returned both smile and nod. "Until tonight."

Kat walked out of the casino without looking back. She had two stops to make before finding Carson and telling him the plan she'd formed.

CHAPTER 12

"You know he's only got one thing on his mind," Carson said.

Kat grinned. "I'm counting on it."

A dissatisfied grunt came from the bottom of Carson's throat.

Kat rolled her eyes. "It was *your* idea. Put on my pretty green dress and how could he resist. Remember?"

"I guess I didn't think it through, but yeah. It was my idea."

But that doesn't mean I have to like it.

Fleetwood was slick and dangerous. Getting him alone was a two-edged blade. Kat could take him out without fear his pals would take action, but once alone, Fleetwood might try anything. Kat could handle herself. She'd proven that. Still . . .

"You going in alone doesn't sit well, if you want to know the truth," Carson said.

Kat circled the campfire and put a hand on Carson's shoulder. "I won't be alone. I'll have big, strong Carson Stone backing me up."

"I thought we didn't want to risk Fleetwood spotting me."

"We don't." Kat crossed back to her horse, fetched something from a saddlebag, then returned and handed it to him.

He looked at the wad of clean, white gauze. "What's this for?"

"The terrible burns you got on your face and head, of course."

"But I don't have any—oh. Don't you think I'll get funny looks walking into the Lucky Clover with my face all wrapped up?"

"You surely will," Kat said. "But they'll all see a man who got himself hurt. They won't see Carson Stone."

"I don't know about this."

"Then wait here," Kat told him. "I'll let you know how it turns out."

Carson sighed, took off his hat, and handed the gauze back to her. "Just leave mouth and eyeholes, okay?"

She stood behind him and began carefully wrapping his head.

"Remember, you need him to talk first," Carson reminded her.

"I know."

"But you can't do it in a way that seems suspicious," Carson said. "Find out about McGraw's plans, but be subtle."

"I *know*."

"And then . . . I guess you shoot him?" Carson asked.

"You're not even considering taking him alive? I thought you were the delicate one."

"First, I know you don't work that way," Carson said. "Second, if it were anyone else, maybe, but this is Fleetwood, and I don't want you taking any chances."

"On this issue we're in agreement."

"But once we've got a corpse on our hands, I'd feel better knowing we have a plan. As far as the folks around here know, you'll just have shot Lawrence Cooke, and he might have friends that take offense."

"I went two places after I left the Lucky Clover," Kat said. "To the general store to buy the gauze, and then to the sheriff's office. I need a marshal to collect the bounty, but the sheriff is enough law for our purposes. I've explained what's about to happen. He'll make sure we get out of town safely. We'll find ourselves a marshal later."

"You didn't mention me, did you?"

"I didn't suddenly get stupid," Kat said. "You're a wanted man. I told him I had some help but left names out of it."

She tied off the gauze at the base of his skull, then stood back to take a look.

Carson looked up at her. "Well?"

"You're an eyeful, all right."

They worked out a few more details, and then Carson reluctantly agreed they'd planned as much as could be expected. Time to give it a go.

"Give me an hour head start," Kat said. "I need to wash up and change."

"See you at the Lucky Clover then. And be careful." Carson tugged at the gauze. It was already hot and uncomfortable.

An hour crawled by, and then Carson saddled Jet and headed into Jasper Springs. It was well after sundown by the time he arrived, and the sound of a tinny piano spilled out of the Lucky Clover and into the street.

Carson climbed off Jet and tied him to the hitching post out front. He lingered a moment, not eager to go inside.

Kat's in there. Man up and do your part, jackass.

Carson sighed and entered.

Every head in the place turned to look at him. Even the piano stopped playing.

I hate this.

He walked toward the bar, forcing himself not to hurry. Soon enough, everyone went back to what they were doing. Even the piano player picked up where he'd left off. He might be hiding the fact he was Carson Stone, but *inconspicuous* had gone straight out the window.

He sidled up to the bar, and the barkeep gawked. "Good God, mister, what happened to you?"

"Kerosene lamp shattered right in front of my face," Carson explained. "Burned all over pretty bad."

The barkeep whistled. "Must have hurt like the dickens."

"It stung a bit, yes."

"Tell you what I'm gonna do, brother. First one on the house. I hate to see a man in pain."

"That's generous. A beer, please."

The beer was warm and brown and bitter, but it was beer, and Carson drank it. He leaned against the bar and took a good look around, hoping he seemed casual about it. The place was two-thirds full, a lively crowd but well behaved. So far, anyway.

He cast about for a glimpse of Kat. Had she not arrived yet, or had things progressed already and Carson had missed it? They'd discussed a short list of scenarios, and what Carson should do for each. He didn't like the idea that she might be in trouble, and he wasn't able to—

Then he saw her at a corner table beyond the roulette wheel and blackjack dealers. She seemed to be laughing and having a good time, although Carson supposed that was part of the act. She sat with two people. One was a woman, a big pile of yellow hair on her head and way too much makeup for Carson's liking. She was dressed reminiscent of a saloon girl but carried herself with more importance.

The other person at the table was Gentleman Dick Fleetwood.

He'd shaved his face clean except for the sideburns, but Carson would know that smirk and those laughing eyes anywhere. Carson felt a pang of anxiety and turned away, sipping his beer.

Never mind. He doesn't know it's me. I just need to keep a cool head.

Carson paid for his second beer and reminded himself to take it slow. He might be standing there all night waiting for Kat to make her move. He watched the table from the corner of his eye. The three of them shared a bottle of something. Looked like it might have been champagne, but Carson couldn't be sure. He'd never had champagne.

Nothing to do now but wait.

CHAPTER 13

Kat laughed as Fleetwood refilled her champagne glass. She hadn't actually heard the joke. She'd been too preoccupied, watching for Carson to come in, but the others had laughed, so she thought she'd better laugh, too. She was relieved to see Carson finally walk into the place, slightly nervous at the moment of silence that followed, then relaxed as Carson headed to the bar for a beer, and normal conversation resumed.

"That's a sad sight." Fleetwood refilled his own glass. "Do you suppose something happened, or is he just homely, do you think?"

"An accident, I expect," Kat said lightly, as if not giving the subject much thought. "Wrong place at the wrong time."

"Poor fellow," said the woman who sat across from Kat. "I should send one of the girls around to assure him we're not prejudiced here. His money will make him handsome enough whatever's under the bandages."

The woman had been introduced to Kat as Madam Rose. Some called her the Yellow Rose because of all the blond hair. According to Fleetwood, she'd been a working girl in the Clover for nine years, had saved her money and bought out the previous madam, and had run the place another six. Creeping into middle age, she was still a fine-looking woman, now curvier with extra padding.

Some men like that, Kat thought. *I bet she still gets plenty of offers.* Kat glanced down at her own assets. Ample, if short of abundant.

Pay attention, stupid. That's not what's important right now.

She sipped champagne. "This is simply marvelous. And expensive, I imagine."

"Terribly," Fleetwood said. "It comes from France. On a ship as far as Boston. Then a train until it's off-loaded and brought by freight wagon. Each leg of the journey it gets a little more expensive, but if you can't enjoy the finer things, then what's the point, am I right?"

Rose sighed. "To think, *I* used to be one of the finer things men came in here to enjoy."

Fleetwood lifted his glass to her. "You still are, Rose. You still are. Like all good wine, you're better with age."

They all laughed.

"He's always saying such lovely things," Rose said. "It makes sharing a building with him quite palatable, I suppose."

"It's a good partnership, then?" Kat asked.

"Hmmm. Not sure 'partnership' is the word I'd use," Rose said. "I'd been saving up to buy the casino from Lucky Gavin when our darling Lawrence here came along and outbid me. You sneaky little devil, you."

"I bought it fair and square," Fleetwood insisted. "Now, don't hold a grudge, Rose. You're better than that."

"Of course not, darling. Of course not." Rose turned to Kat. "It's all just business, after all."

Fleetwood raised his glass again. "To business."

The ladies raised their glasses also. "To business!"

Fleetwood drained his glass, set it on the table in front of him, and stood. "And speaking of business, I should see to mine. Employees have a way of staying on their toes if the boss looks in on them now and again. If you'll excuse me, I'll make the rounds and return in a few minutes." He nodded to each of the ladies in turn then set off for the blackjack tables.

"May I ask how you and Lawrence know each other?" Rose reached for the champagne bottle and refilled her glass.

"We only met this afternoon," Kat said. "There was some . . . unpleasantness . . . in the casino, and Lawrence invited me back for a drink. To put the Lucky Clover in a better light, I suppose."

"A word of advice, darling." The frivolity had drained from her voice, something serious now in Madam Rose's eyes. "Don't turn your back on that one."

Kat maintained her friendly smile. "I've always been a careful woman, but are you sure you're not still a bit raw that he beat you in a business deal?"

Rose sipped champagne, head tilting, eyes going thoughtful. "I'll tell you this much. I went looking for Lucky Gavin after Lawrence made his offer for the casino. I figured turnabout was fair play and planned to up my bid. I don't give up so easily. I was told Gavin had left town. In a hurry. There were also rumors that Gavin had been strongly *encouraged* to leave town. Well . . . rumors. Who can say what's true and what's not? You wouldn't believe some of the ghastly things people have said about me over the years. All I can say is that fate seemed to have arranged that I couldn't put in a competing bid for the casino, and now Lawrence Cooke owns the Lucky Clover."

Kat sipped her own champagne and considered. Apparently, there was still animosity there. On the surface, Rose wasn't making an issue of it, got along with Cooke—Fleetwood—on a daily basis, or at least that was how it seemed to everyone.

But Kat sized her up and sensed a smart woman biding her time.

Fleetwood chose that moment to return. "Sorry to keep you waiting, ladies."

He sat at the table and grabbed the champagne bottle, saw it was empty and snapped his fingers. A man in an apron appeared, and Fleetwood sent him away to fetch another bottle.

"Are the employees all on their toes?" Kat asked.

Fleetwood gestured at the casino around him. "A well-oiled machine. Thank you for asking."

"Then I suppose it's my turn to do my part." Rose pushed away from the table and stood. "The girls know they don't get paid if they don't hustle, but it never hurts to check on them. Nice meeting you, Kat."

Kat nodded. "And you."

Rose left just as the waiter arrived, opened the new bottle, and filled each glass.

"We've talked too much about me," Fleetwood said. "What brings a lovely young thing like yourself to Jasper Springs?"

"Interesting you should ask," Kat said. "One of the reasons I wanted to accept your hospitality tonight—other than to enjoy your charming company, of course—is that you might be in a position to offer me some advice."

"Ah, now this seems interesting. Tell me more."

"I have a considerable amount of money to invest," Kat said. "And I'm exploring this area. I think it might be on the rise, and I'd like to get in on the ground floor, investing in various businesses and so on. I've worked hard for my money. Now I want it working for me."

"That's understandable. I might be able to advise you there," Fleetwood told her. "I know several sharp-minded businessmen. I'd be happy to make introductions."

"And I'll take you up on that offer when the time is right," she said. "But I prefer to move slowly. I'd like to get to know the area first. In the meantime, I need somewhere safe to keep my money, and I notice Jasper Springs doesn't have a bank."

"I see. As it happens, the casino safe is the most secure place in Jasper Springs," Fleetwood said. "I offer the same service to a number of prominent people in town. As secure as any bank."

"A generous offer, but if I'm to start making investments, I'll need to establish a relationship with a reputable bank sooner or later."

"So you'd like me to suggest a good bank in the area?"

"Yes," Kat replied. "And also help me sort through some things I've heard about various establishments. For example, I heard there's some large payroll coming to a bank in Fayetteville. I'm afraid I haven't been able to find out any details, but I'd surely feel safe with my money in a place like that."

Fleetwood scratched his chin, considering. "As it happens, I might have some inside information on that exact situation."

Kat raised an eyebrow, her expression filled with innocence. "Oh?"

"But it's not something to be talked about openly," Fleetwood said. "Too many curious ears lurk around the Lucky Clover. I have a suite of rooms upstairs, including a comfortable parlor. We can take our champagne with us and discuss banking in earnest. I do have information you might find interesting. And if we were to take the opportunity to get to know each other better, that would be nice, too."

The idea of getting to know Dick Fleetwood better made the bile rise in Kat's throat, but she smiled as if delighted by the prospect. "That sounds like a lovely idea."

Fleetwood stood and offered his arm. "Shall we?"

Carson ordered a third beer to keep up appearances but didn't drink it.

He watched Kat's table from his place at the bar. Fleetwood had gotten up to do something, and Kat remained, talking to the other woman. Then Fleetwood returned, and the woman with too much makeup went away. Kat and Fleetwood

talked, all smiles and friendly. Carson could only assume
Kat's ruse was working.

He sure as hell hoped so.

He looked around just in time to see a sturdy, middle-aged
man enter, a gleaming star on his vest. It could only be the
sheriff, Carson thought. Square jaw, neatly trimmed mustache, a Colt hanging on his hip. He had a no-nonsense air
about him.

The sheriff's eyes roamed the casino for a moment. Apparently satisfied nothing was amiss, he crossed the room at an
easy pace and claimed a spot three feet from Carson. "Whisky,
Pete."

The barkeep brought the sheriff a shot glass of whisky.
The sheriff sipped it. He stood looking straight ahead, not
even glancing at Carson.

*He knows. No way somebody can just ignore me looking
the way I do. He's working way too hard not to notice the
most-noticeable person at the bar.*

Kat might not have told the sheriff Carson's name, but
she must have made it known she had backup. Carson put
some hope into that. He figured the sheriff would just stand
aside and let the lady bounty hunter do her job, but maybe
there was some help there if needed.

Carson glanced back at the table and saw Kat and Fleetwood getting up. She took Fleetwood's arm and headed for
the stairs in the back of the room. He knew the point was to
get Fleetwood alone, but he still didn't like it.

Now it was Carson's job to go up after them, be there in
case Kat needed backup. He wasn't exactly sure how this was
going to work. He had a vague notion of listening at each
door until he recognized Kat's voice. Carson was beginning
to realize this was a pretty loose plan and was feeling more
uneasy about it by the second.

Kat and Fleetwood had now disappeared from view upstairs. Carson stepped away from the bar and made to follow.

"Stay put," the sheriff said in a low voice. He didn't turn his head to look at Carson.

"Sorry?"

"Don't look at me," the sheriff said. "Pay attention to your beer."

Carson leaned against the bar, head down.

"Don't go up there," the sheriff told him, voice still low. "It's being handled. You'll know if we need you."

"How will I know?"

"You'll know."

Carson didn't know what to do, so he sipped his warm beer.

A few moments later, the sheriff finished his whisky and headed toward the same stairway Kat and Fleetwood had used. He headed upstairs slowly, as if he didn't have a care in the world. Carson watched from his spot at the bar.

Nope. Carson didn't like it. Not one bit.

CHAPTER 14

Fleetwood ushered Kat into his private parlor and closed the door behind him.

Kat took in the well-appointed room. A plush divan. Over-stuffed chairs covered in leather. A writing desk, and a sideboard with decanters of various liquors. A window overlooking Jasper Springs's main street. A painting hung over the desk, a sailing ship plying a stormy sea.

"This is very pleasant," Kat said. "It suits you, I think."

"Thank you, Kat. Or should I call you . . . Lady Pain?"

Kat's hand dove into her handbag and closed around the derringer.

Fleetwood was on her in an instant. His huge, hairy hand clamped over the small handbag, squeezing her slender fingers against the derringer's cold metal. Kat hissed pain. With his other hand, he grabbed the back of her neck and held her still.

"This is outrageous," Kat said. "What do you think you're—"

"Shut your mouth," Fleetwood told her. "I'll break the hand. I mean it."

Kat shut her mouth and stopped squirming.

"I'm going to ease my grip and then you take your hand out. *Without* the gun." He squeezed her neck. "Or I twist your damn head off. You understand?"

She nodded.

"Nice and slow." He eased his grip.

She pulled her hand out and flexed the fingers, scowling at Fleetwood. "That hurt."

"You'll get worse than that if you don't behave." He snatched the handbag from her and took out the derringer, cocking back the little hammer with a thumb. "Hold still if you don't want to get shot with your own gun."

He groped her all over, patting her down. He reached up under her dress. Kat was revolted by the feel of his rough hand on her inner thigh but refused to flinch, refused to give him the satisfaction. He found the thigh holster and took the .32 Rimfire.

Fleetwood stepped back, one of Kat's guns in each hand, and let her dress fall back into place. "I have your claws, Kat, so now I suppose we can have a civilized discussion. It will stay civilized if you tell me what I want to know." He shifted the derringer to hold both guns in one hand, then turned to open a drawer in the writing desk. "Let's put these out of harm's way for now, shall we?"

When he was partially turned away from her, Kat rushed forward, shoving him hard with both hands. He stumbled against the desk, losing his balance.

Fleetwood would only be distracted for a second and Kat didn't hesitate. She dashed for the door and threw it open.

And ran straight into the sheriff.

"Thank God," she said. "Sheriff, it's Fleetwood. He's—"

The sheriff grabbed her arm roughly, shoved her back into the room, and shut the door.

She blinked, stunned. "What?"

"Just in time, Bart," Fleetwood said. "Any sign of her help?"

Sheriff Bart Harmon hooked his thumbs into his gun belt and stood blocking the door. "Fella downstairs at the bar, but he's not going anywhere."

"You're supposed to be a lawman. You're nothing but trash," Kat told him, barely controlled rage edging her voice.

"Bart does a good job keeping the peace in Jasper Springs," Fleetwood told her. "But he also works for me. Now be a good girl, Lady Pain, and answer my questions."

"If you know anything about me, you know I'm not really keen on that nickname," Kat said.

"I don't give a tinker's damn what you're 'keen' on," Fleetwood said. "You might be no lady, but you're sure as hell a pain. Word's gotten around about the female bounty hunter with the red hair. Now, who are you working with? That man at the bar your only partner or are there others? How do you know about McGraw's plan for the First Bank of Fayetteville and the railroad payroll? The clumsy way you asked about it would have given you away even if Bart hadn't already told me all about you."

"I have a half-dozen men with me," Kat said. "Some out front. The rest out back. You're crazy if you think you're taking me out of here as your prisoner. Your only chance is to let me go. Then we both back away and call this off."

Fleetwood's eyes shifted to the sheriff.

Bart shook his head. "Nope. Only strangers in town are her and the bandaged man."

"Nice try," Fleetwood told her. "Where did you hear about McGraw's plan for the bank?"

"A little bird told me."

"You're trying my patience."

"Then you'll love this." Kat leaned forward and spit straight into Fleetwood's left eye.

Hot pain exploded across her face, stinging needles, tears welling in her eyes. Again, Fleetwood's speed had astounded her. She barely saw the backhand that spun her head around. She worked her jaw, a sharp ache creeping up the bone.

"It's fine," Fleetwood said. "We can do it the hard way."

He took a handkerchief from his coat pocket and tied it into a gag around Kat's mouth. "Bart, can you do something about her hands?"

"Yessir, Mr. Cooke. I took the liberty of bringing the manacles." The sheriff fixed them to her wrists.

"Good man. Is there anyone in the jail?"

"Nope. Empty."

"Take her out the back way, then put her in a cell," Fleetwood said. "Don't let anyone in. Keep her out of sight. Don't tell anyone. You still have that bullwhip hanging in the stable?"

"Yessir."

Kat's eyes widened at the word "bullwhip."

"Get it," Fleetwood said. "Our lovely Lady Pain *will* be answering my questions. One way or another."

The sheriff grabbed Kat by the arm, dragged her stumbling after him out of the parlor. He took her down a different stairway to a back door and into a darkened alley behind the Lucky Clover. They followed the alley a way, and then the sheriff took her through another door.

Two cells. A desk. A rack of rifles and shotguns on the wall. Big front windows with the shades drawn.

The jailhouse, Kat realized. Sheriff's office.

The sheriff pushed her into a cell without removing her gag or manacles, then pulled the cell door closed with a heavy clunk.

He went to the front door and rattled the knob, making sure it was locked.

Kat's hands had been manacled in front of her. Easy

enough to reach the gag and pull it out of her mouth. "Sheriff, you've got to listen to me."

He wheeled on her, pointing a finger at her. "Now you just keep quiet. I'm sorry about what's happening, ma'am, but this is just the way it has to be."

"Sheriff—"

"I'll put that gag back on you. I will. Truss you up good and leave you on the floor of that cell. You get me?"

Kat took a deep breath and nodded.

"Okay, then."

He took his hat off and wiped his forehead with his sleeve, let out a big sigh. Kat got the feeling the man wasn't happy about what was happening but couldn't do anything about it. Her mind raced to think how she might appeal to him. She'd need to pick her words carefully. She wouldn't get to say much before he'd gag her again.

The sheriff put his hat back on, fixed her with a hard stare. "You just stay quiet. I'll be back in two shakes of a lamb's tail." And then he was out the back door again.

Kat wondered about Carson. Had they done something to him, or was he still out there, unaware of what had happened to her? She wanted to have hope, to think Carson was even now planning some daring rescue.

And since when have I ever needed to be rescued? I botched this one good and proper.

The back door swung open again. The sheriff entered, tossed something on the desk. Kat's eyes widened when she saw it was the bullwhip. She also saw the sheriff hadn't closed the door. Someone else was coming in.

Oh, God. This is about to get bad. Real bad.

The person who entered wasn't Fleetwood.

Kat went to the front of her cell, grasped the bars. "Madam Rose?"

The Yellow Rose of the Lucky Clover looked at the sheriff. "How long?"

"A minute or two. Any more ain't safe."

Rose stood on tiptoe, and the sheriff leaned down to kiss her hard on the lips. The kiss lingered an extra moment.

Rose broke away, patted the big lawman on the shoulder, and then took a step toward Kat's cell. "We need to talk."

CHAPTER 15

Colby Tate spent three miserable nights sleeping on the ground. He considered his skills at making camp to be adequate. He could build a fire and bed down and tend his horse, but not as well as Carson could. Carson had a knack for picking a camping spot that always somehow seemed dryer or out of the wind or closer to clean water. Tate had learned to ride at a young age, but there'd always been grooms to take care of the horses afterward. Carson had an easy way with the animals.

Well, you didn't come West to be comfortable, did you, old sport? You're here to make your fortune all on your own. You could have stayed back East and had it easy and eventually inherited the family fortune, but that comes with a price, doesn't it?

A price Colby Tate wasn't willing to pay.

The site of the stagecoach holdup was about five miles south of a place called Jones Crossroads, not more than a trading post and a water stop for the stagecoach horses. The old couple who ran the trading post related the story of the holdup. The bandits had waited for the stage to leave the crossroads and had struck at a spot where the road narrowed. They'd taken a strongbox with some money and emptied the pockets of the passengers. Everyone cooperated, and nobody was hurt.

The bandits wore kerchiefs over their faces, but everyone's guess was that it was McGraw and his boys. Tate spent about a half hour questioning the old couple about towns and places in the area, but when it came to the stage holdup and McGraw, no more useful information was to be had.

Tate suspected it had been a mistake to leave Carson and Kat, but then chastised himself. It was too soon to give up.

There are at least three small towns between here and Fayetteville. I'll ride south and west with my ears and eyes open. One never knows when or where luck will strike.

He hit a town called Liberty Grove with three hours of daylight left. Tate wasn't sure what to do with himself. He wasn't hungry or thirsty and wasn't sure if this was a good place to spend the night. There was a shabby-looking boardinghouse, and while it was probably better than sleeping on the ground, Tate couldn't quite summon up enthusiasm for it.

A bench in front of the dry goods store caught his attention. He tied his horse to the hitching post, sat on the bench, and took out his pipe. He packed it with tobacco, lit a match, and puffed. He watched the people of Liberty Grove come and go. A few nodded politely as they passed. He took out his pocket watch and checked the time. Tate wasn't completely sure how to proceed.

Asking random townsfolk *Excuse me, but have you seen a gang of vicious outlaws?* seemed a ploy more likely to alarm people and draw attention to himself than to produce useful information. Going to the local sheriff might be a way to glean the latest news, but once Tate identified himself as a bounty hunter, it wasn't something he could undo. For now, he wanted to maintain a low profile. A modicum of anonymity suited his plans better. Word of a bounty hunter in town might frighten the very game he was hunting.

He puffed the pipe and sat there and had no good ideas.

Two men came out of the dry goods store, grumbling and grousing at each other. One had a canvas sack thrown over one shoulder. The other had parcels under each arm wrapped up in paper and twine. They passed Tate, taking no notice of him, and stopped in the street ten feet away.

"I'm only talking ten minutes, Gordon," said the man with the sack over his shoulder. "Loosen up a bit, why don't you?" He wore a huge tan hat, the wide brim pushed up in the front. Red bib shirt with half the buttons undone. Sturdy denims and scuffed boots. A pair of .44 caliber Remingtons hung on his hips. An outlandishly bushy mustache hung down over his top lip and almost hid the front tooth he was missing. "I ain't had a proper drink in a saloon in a week."

"Don't talk bunk to me, Ben," Gordon shot back. "You ain't never spent only ten minutes in a saloon in your life. One quick drink will end up being a whole bottle, and we'll be there all night." The one called Gordon was wide and brawny, with a full beard and dark, hard little eyes like river stones. Black shirt and tan trousers. A single Colt Peacemaker rigged for a left-handed draw. "Bob wants them potatoes and the cabbage to go with that turkey he shot. If he has to eat hardtack another night, you can be the one tells him you're to blame."

Tate had been eavesdropping, and his ears perked up double when he heard the name Bob. *This must be Gordon McGraw, Bob's brother.*

One never knows when or where luck will strike. Indeed.

"Have a heart, Gordon," Ben pleaded. "Nobody's going to miss a meal if we stop off for one quick drink. You can hold me to that."

"Okay, fine. Quit your bellyaching," Gordon said. "A quick one and that's it."

Ben grinned, showing off the gap in his smile, and followed Gordon across the street to the saloon.

Tate watched them go, sitting quietly and puffing his pipe.

Five minutes later, they hadn't emerged, so Tate got to his feet and crossed the street. He glanced into the saloon's open door without entering. At a table against the far wall, both men sat, an open whisky bottle between them.

Either this Ben fellow is more persuasive than he looks or Gordon McGraw was more in need of whisky than he anticipated. Looks like they might be there awhile.

Tate crossed the street back to the dry goods store and took his leather-bound book from a saddlebag. He reclaimed his perch out front and filled his pipe again, smoking casually as he paged through his careful notes.

Ah. Here we are. Benjamin Mooney. Wanted for cattle rustling. Reward: fifty dollars. Not exactly a windfall.

Tate considered what useful information could be gleaned from this new circumstance. Benjamin Mooney wasn't a known associate of McGraw and his gang, at least not until now. That meant Big Bob was recruiting new members to his gang, to fill the holes left by the departures of Hannigan and Fleetwood and whoever else.

He tsked. *I doubt we'll catch the old boy understaffed.*

Tate mulled it over, and the pieces of a plan began to come together.

An hour later, the two outlaws emerged from the saloon. They didn't quite stumble. But there was an easy sloppiness to their stride, as if walking properly just wasn't worth the bother. They still bickered, but it seemed joking now. Tate couldn't hear the words from the bench in front of the dry goods store. He watched them walk to the end of the street and circle around behind the livery stables.

Tate tapped out the ashes against the side of the bench, put his pipe away, and followed.

The two men stood next to their horses, the animals watering at a trough. Gordon's was saddled, and he was loading his packages into the saddlebags. Ben's horse wasn't saddled yet.

The man occupied himself rolling a cigarette. Both sets of eyes came up to stab Tate when he came round the corner.

"Good evening, gentlemen," Tate said amiably.

"Help you with something, mister?" Gordon cinched the horse's saddle strap and made a point of paying Tate little mind.

"I thought I might help you," Tate said. "I infer your brother Bob has been recruiting men to fill the vacancies in your gang left by Irish Dan Hannigan and Gentleman Dick Fleetwood and perhaps others. Benjamin Mooney here is evidence of that."

Ben froze with the cigarette halfway to his mouth. Gordon turned slowly, his face carefully blank.

"You got the wrong fellas, mister," Gordon said. "Best be on your way."

"I know for a fact I don't have the wrong fellows, Gordon McGraw," Tate insisted. "So let's drop the charade and talk business."

Gordon and Ben traded glances.

"Not saying who I am or who I ain't," Gordon said, "but what's your business?"

Tate's smile stretched wide. "I intend to join your gang, of course."

CHAPTER 16

The sheriff had told Carson to stay put. That meant the situation was well in hand.

Right?

Carson wasn't buying it. Too much time had gone by, and nobody had come back down the stairs. On the other hand, he hadn't heard gunshots or screams or anything else to indicate trouble.

I could kick myself. I've been standing here like an idiot. Kat could be in danger.

Just as Carson pushed away from the bar, a saloon gal sidled up next to him, put her hand on his back. "Why, hello, stranger. You look like you could use some company, standing here all by your lonesome."

She had dark, glossy hair and light brown skin and eyes like coffee with a hint of cream. High cheekbones. There was a tooth missing at the far-left edge of her smile, but she had an open, sincere face that could draw a man in. On the tall side, with broad shoulders.

"Sorry, ma'am," Carson said. "But I need to be on my way."

She latched onto his arm. "Now, you don't want to hurt my feelings, do you? I came over here just to talk to little old *you*. My name is Bess."

Carson forced down a surge of impatience. "It's not like that, ma'am. I really have to—"

Bess stroked his bandaged cheek with her other hand and leaned in like she was going to whisper something lewd into his ear. "You need to listen to me, Carson Stone. This is important."

Carson heard his name and went rigid.

"Stop that," Bess whispered. "You look like somebody just poured ice water down your back. People could be watching. Act like you're interested in me."

He reached out and took her by the shoulder. He felt stiff and awkward.

"Dang, you are the *worst* actor I've ever seen," Bess whispered. "Say something, and I'll act like it's funny."

"Say what exactly?"

She tossed her head back and laughed, playfully slapping him on the arm. "Oh, now you are just a bad boy." Then she leaned in and whispered, "Now I'm pretending to tell you what I aim to do to you upstairs. You nod along like you're hearing things you like."

Carson nodded, feeling foolish.

Bess took him by the hand, turned, and led him away, looking back over her shoulder to bat her eyes at him occasionally. His hands were hard and callused. Hers were soft. Carson drew looks as he passed through the casino on the way to the stairs, the stranger with the bandaged face.

But the looks didn't linger. Everyone knew where he was going. His business with the saloon gal was his own. Bess took him up the stairs.

She led Carson to a door at the end of the hall, opened it, and gestured he should enter. He did. He looked back at her, saw her closing the door from the outside.

Carson frowned. "Where are you going?"

"She needs to talk to you." Bess closed the door.

She?

"Hello, Mr. Stone," came a voice from the corner of the room.

Carson turned abruptly, hand falling to the hilt of his Peacemaker.

"You don't need that," she said. "At least not for me."

She sat in a highbacked chair, and Carson hadn't seen her at first in the poor light. The room was lit by a single candle on the vanity. Carson could see now it was the woman with too much makeup Kat had been talking to earlier. She sat with her legs crossed, hands folded over one knee, proper as any schoolmarm.

"Who are you?"

"Rose. I run the girls here."

"You know my name?" Carson asked.

"Kat told me."

Carson wondered if that was good or bad. "Where is she?"

"In trouble."

I knew it. The sheriff told me to stay put and I should have gone with my gut instead of listening to him.

"What kind of trouble?"

"The Dick Fleetwood kind of trouble."

Damn.

Carson's mind raced. "What's all this to you?"

"We can help each other," Rose said. "We were afraid of Fleetwood when we thought he was Lawrence Cooke, somebody quick and sly. Now that we know he's Fleetwood, it's different."

"Different how?"

"Cooke was a bastard, but he was legal," Rose explained. "Fleetwood's an outlaw. An outlaw we can get rid of. But I can't do it alone. I need somebody like you."

"I'm not who you think I am," Carson said. "I don't want to tangle with Fleetwood any more than you."

"We don't have time to debate this," Rose insisted. "If you want to help Kat, we've got to get this thing started right now."

"Why don't you cut to it and just tell me straight out what you want me to do?"

"Isn't it obvious?" she asked. "We want you to kill him."

The sheriff sat at his desk, pulled out a handkerchief, and wiped his face. Kat watched him from her cell. The man was more than just a little nervous.

He was scared.

Kat lifted her hands, let the chains rattle. "Take these off and let me fix this."

The sheriff shook his head. "And then what if you don't? I'm supposed to go up against Fleetwood? Fat chance. He'll know it was me that let you out. We just have to sit tight. Rose always was the smart one. She'll have this figured."

He took a bottle from the bottom desk drawer and filled a shot glass with whisky. He sat looking at it for a moment, then shoved it across the desk without drinking. He wiped his sweaty face again with the handkerchief.

No help there. He's about to piss himself at the thought of crossing Fleetwood.

Not that she could blame him. Kat had thought she was so smart. Yeah, right, the world's smartest fly walking straight into the spider's web. She had to figure a way out of this cell, but the sheriff was too afraid to help her.

Was Carson out there somewhere planning her rescue? He might not even know where she was, might not even know she was in trouble. Or maybe he did know but had hightailed it out of town rather than risk his neck for her.

No, that thought hit her as wrong all the way through. She realized she trusted Carson completely. He was a good man, and good men could be useful if handled right. She wasn't sure about Tate and was still trying to figure him out, but she might as well have had Carson in her pocket.

The back door swung open, and Fleetwood strode in like he owned the place, closing the door behind him.

The sheriff stood, almost like he was coming to attention. Fleetwood jerked a thumb at Kat. "Get her out of there."

The sheriff opened the cell, pulled her out by one arm, and shut it again.

Fleetwood picked up the bullwhip. "Turn her around. Loop that chain through the bars up there."

Kat went stiff and felt her stomach twist. "Wait. We can talk about—"

The sheriff jerked her toward him, a warning to keep quiet. This would have to play out. He took one shackle off the left wrist, then turned her to face the cold bars of the cell. He pulled her hands up, stretching them over her head, and looped the chain around a crossbar, then shackled her again.

Kat's heart pounded so hard and so fast she thought it might climb up her throat and out of her mouth. She should say something, anything, to make this stop, but somehow couldn't think of a word. Her mouth felt so dry.

She felt Fleetwood's hands suddenly on her collar. With a great wrench, he tore the dress down the center seam. Kat gasped both at the sudden ripping sound and at the wash of air on her exposed skin.

"Look at that." Fleetwood ran rough fingertips down the flesh of her back. "Clean and white. Not a mark. We can fix that."

Kat fought down a wave of revulsion. "Don't. You . . . you don't need to do this."

"Except that I'm going to ask you questions, and I expect answers," Fleetwood said.

"I'll answer your questions."

"But that's not good enough," Fleetwood insisted. "I don't just need answers, I need answers I can *believe*. We need to get you to the point where you wouldn't dare lie, that you'd do or say whatever needed to make the pain stop because you just can't take it anymore. Once we get you to that point, *then* I'll believe whatever you tell me. You'll sing your heart out, Lady Pain, and I'll *know* every word is true."

Kat trembled, all the strength leaving her. She wanted to plead but couldn't find the words.

The sheriff cleared his throat. "Maybe . . . maybe this ain't the way, Mr. Cooke."

"You look a little green, Bart," Fleetwood said. "Why don't you get some air?"

"Mr. Cooke . . ."

"Go on, Bart."

A hesitation, and then the sheriff slipped out the back door, pulling it closed with a tiny click.

Kat took in a deep breath, then let it out slowly, trying to calm herself. Her hands stretched uncomfortably over her head, and she had to stand on tiptoe to keep the shackles from digging into her wrists. She heard the whip crack behind her, and another little gasp popped out of her mouth.

"Been a while since I used one of these," Fleetwood admitted. "But it comes back to you."

Tears of frustration formed in the corners of her eyes.

Stop it. Don't give the bastard the satisfaction.

Fleetwood flicked the bullwhip experimentally, getting the feel of it. "I put a lot of time into Lawrence Cooke, making him into a citizen to replace Dick Fleetwood. I'm something in this town. I have a new life away from McGraw and his hooligans. That's why I need to know who you've told. Marshals? Other bounty hunters? I have a secret to protect, Lady Pain, and that's what I aim to do."

Fleetwood cocked his arm back, twirling the whip, getting ready to lay one across her bare back.

Kat shut her eyes tight and braced herself.

A sudden pounding on the front door spun Fleetwood's head around. "The sheriff's not here."

"Mr. Cooke, you've got to come quick." A woman's voice. "It's urgent!"

Fleetwood opened the door, scowled down at the woman standing there. "What is it, Bess?"

"Miss Rose says—" Bess's eyes widened upon seeing Kat.

"Never mind her," Fleetwood said.

"Rose says you got to come right now," Bess insisted.

"I'm in the middle of something."

"Right *now*," Bess said. "Rose says it's life-and-death important and can't wait. I don't know what it is, but I never seen her so frantic."

Fleetwood sighed. "Tell her I'm coming."

He shut the door, tossed the bullwhip on the desk, and then stood next to Kat. He ran the back of his hand down one of her cheeks. "I don't suppose you're going anywhere. I'll be back soon, and then we'll pick up where we left off."

And then he left.

Kat blew out a ragged breath she hadn't known she'd been holding.

CHAPTER 17

Tate felt everything go quiet and still in the way that always seemed to happen when gunplay was imminent. The single lantern hanging from a post cast the rear stable yard in jagged shadows that suddenly seemed ominous. Gordon's hard eyes glistened with lantern light, the rest of his face soaking in the darkness.

Ben took a few steps away from him, right hand hovering over one of his guns.

Colby Tate remained cool, posture casual. He made no move toward his Peacemakers. He felt confident he knew how this was going to end, but it never hurt to try talking first. Anyway, he didn't need both of them dead for his plan to work.

"What's your name, mister?" Gordon asked. "I like to know who I'm about to kill."

"Colby Tate." He'd thought about lying but had discarded the idea. He didn't want to forget to reply when somebody called him John or Jack. That would be awkward. And anyway, the name didn't mean anything around here. *I don't know who they'd ask, but let them. I've never worked this area. They won't learn a thing about me.*

"But I'd appreciate not being killed just yet," Tate said. "I'm looking to get into the bank-robbing business, and I think I could be an asset to your gang."

Ben's eyes went to Gordon. "He serious?"

"Serious as a heart attack," Tate assured him.

"An asset how?" Gordon asked.

"I know that Gentleman Dick Fleetwood has left Big Bob's employ," Tate said. "So you're short a fast gun. I could take his place."

"You're fast?"

"Very."

Ben snorted. "Bob don't need you when he's got me. I'm the fast gun now."

"It's true," Gordon said. "He's pretty fast."

"I doubt he could outdraw me," Tate said.

Another snort from Ben, this time with a pinch of derision. "Go on and try me, then."

"You've been drinking," Tate said. "I wouldn't want to take unfair advantage."

Ben laughed. "See? He's trying to get out of it now."

"Not at all," Tate said. "If you'd like to reconvene in the morning after a few cups of black coffee, I'd be happy to show you—"

Ben went for his gun, and it cleared the holster. Fast.

Not fast enough.

Tate's revolvers filled his hands like a magician's trick.

The gunshot cracked thunder, and blood exploded from Ben's right shoulder. He staggered sideways, and Tate shot again, a wet, red rose blooming in the center of Ben's chest. He staggered, started to go down, but found some store of strength and tried to straighten himself.

Tate shot again. Ben spun, an arc of blood following him to the ground where he landed with a thud and never moved again.

It had all happened in a second. Gordon's hand had made it as far as his pistol hilt, but he hadn't cleared leather.

Tate turned his guns on the man. "I wouldn't if I were you."

Gordon froze.

Shoot him, Tate's instincts screamed. Gordon McGraw was Big Bob's brother and right-hand man. Tate could deal a devastating blow to the outlaw gang right now and collect a handsome reward to boot. It was the smart play. The safe play. Bird in the hand and all that.

But no. That wasn't the plan. Tate wanted all of them, but for that he had to *find* them first.

"Slowly take your hand away from that revolver, please."

Gordon obeyed.

Tate cleared his throat. "Now, about joining the gang."

Gordon's eyes narrowed. "Are you out of your damn mind? You just shot one of my guys."

"Yes, the one who claimed he was the new quick-draw artist of your outfit," Tate said. "Not quick enough, it would seem, although he was faster than I expected. Had a sort of sideways move when he drew. That's why my first shot caught him in the shoulder. Still, he's dead, and you need to replace him. Also, I wanted to talk, remember? He went for his gun first. His being dead is his own fault, not mine."

"So what now?"

"Somebody heard those shots. I'd ride out of here if I were you," Tate advised. "Tell McGraw who I am and what I've done. You can vote me into the gang or not. I'll take care of Ben. He's a wanted man, and I have a clean record. They'll believe I defended myself. But you'd better go."

Gordon moved toward Ben.

"Hold on." Tate lifted his pistol. "What are you doing?"

"Bob will be mighty put out when I come back without Ben," Gordon said. "But he'll get downright mean if I come back without them potatoes and cabbages."

"Understandable. Go ahead."

Gordon fetched the bag of vegetables, then hopped on his horse. "Jericho's. It's a full day's ride west. Not much more than a stagecoach stop. Stay on the road and you can't miss it. We'll be there or not, depending on what Bob decides."

Gordon didn't wait for a reply. He spurred his horse and took off.

Tate looked at Benjamin Mooney's rapidly cooling corpse and sighed. He lifted him with a grunt and heaved him across his unsaddled horse. Fifty dollars was fifty dollars, after all.

CHAPTER 18

The knock at the door startled Carson. He was nervous, jumping at every little thing.

"It's just Bess," Rose said. "I hope."

Carson stood behind the door, one hand on the hilt of his Peacemaker.

"He's coming." Bess's voice.

"Okay," Rose said. "Now go hide yourself somewhere until this is all over." Rose shut the door again. "You know what to do."

Carson nodded. He knew what Madam Rose *wanted* him to do, but if he'd actually do it was something he was still struggling with. It made sense in its own way. Fleetwood was too fast for a straight-up fight. Carson might as well put the barrel of his own gun in his mouth and pull the trigger. Shooting him when he wasn't looking, before the man even knew what was happening, was all perfectly legal. Gentleman Dick Fleetwood was wanted dead or alive. Probably it was how Kat would have done it.

None of that made Carson feel any better about shooting a man in the back.

Even if Fleetwood did deserve it.

"I hear somebody coming up the stairs." Rose moved all

the way to the other side of the room, opposite the door. "Wait until he's all the way in. Get a clean shot."

Carson's heart hammered in his chest.

A second later, the door creaked open slowly. "Rose. Bess said it was urgent."

"It is," she said. "An emergency. But we need to keep this quiet. Close the door."

Fleetwood stepped into his parlor and shut the door behind him.

Carson lifted his Peacemaker.

Now. Do it now and it's all over.

Carson put the barrel of his Colt against the back of Fleetwood's head. "Don't move. Don't even twitch."

Fleetwood's left hand dropped, the .32 Marlin revolver sliding from his sleeve and into his palm.

"I said don't." There was a calm to Carson's voice that was somehow more formidable than if he'd shouted. He pressed the Peacemaker's revolver against the back of Fleetwood's head with force. "I know exactly how fast you are, Mr. Fleetwood, and I know for a fact I'm outmatched. That means if you make any move I don't like, I'll put a bullet straight through your brain. I figure that's the only chance I'd have. So no more warnings. Drop it."

The .32 clattered against the floor. Carson gave it a kick, and it skittered across the room and under the desk.

"You must be our bandage-faced man," Fleetwood said. "My friends and I couldn't decide if you'd been injured or if you were just plain ugly."

"You just wonder about that all you want," Carson said. "As long as you don't move. Now, here is your one and only chance. You're wanted dead or alive. I can pull this trigger right now if I want, and it's all good and legal."

Carson spared a glance for Rose. She looked ready to chew nails. This wasn't how she'd wanted it to go. She'd wanted Fleetwood shot dead the second he'd stepped into the parlor.

"Wait. I recognize your voice."

"Never mind that," Carson said. "Like I said, you have one chance. I tie your hands, and you take your chances with a judge. The way I see it, that's a better deal than me blowing a hole through your skull."

A long moment passed, and then Fleetwood chuckled.

"Let me in on the joke, why don't you?" Carson said.

"Carson Stone. It's been awhile," Fleetwood said. "Last I saw you, you were hightailing it out of a saloon in El Paso."

"The lead was flying hard and fast, and I didn't want any of it. Besides, it was a good excuse to skip out on my tab," Carson told him. "That doesn't change anything at the moment. I'm gonna take that Colt Thunderer on your hip now, Dick, and you're going to let me or you're dead before you hit the floor."

Fleetwood spread his arms out away from his body. "Go on, then."

Carson hesitated. Fleetwood was the fastest with a gun. Everyone knew that. But Carson realized he really didn't know much else about the man or how he might be dangerous in different ways. Carson's father had fought for the Confederacy, but he hadn't been a regular soldier. He'd been a spy, often trapped behind enemy lines. He'd known a lot of tricks for fighting unarmed and had passed many of those tricks along to Carson.

One of the most valuable lessons Carson's father had taught him was never to assume you were the only one who knew those tricks.

He backed away from Fleetwood, keeping the Peacemaker trained on the back of the man's head. "Get his gun, would you, Miss Rose? I'd be obliged."

She looked back and forth between Carson and Fleetwood, moving slowly, as if approaching a wild animal. She stopped a couple of feet from him and reached for the hilt of the Colt, bending slightly at the waist.

Fleetwood's hand shot out like lightning, grabbed her wrist, and pulled her into him as he ducked. Rose screamed.

Carson followed his movement with the Peacemaker and barely stopped himself in time from pulling the trigger. Fleetwood used Rose as a shield, and the only way to shoot him was to blow a big hole through Rose first.

Carson didn't even have time to figure out his next move. Fleetwood shoved Rose hard right into Carson. She shrieked as she slammed into him. He tried to shove her aside, not gently. He'd apologize later. Right now, he needed a clear shot at—

But Fleetwood was on him, one hand closing over Carson's revolver, shoving it away, both men stumbling back into the wall. Carson tried to bring his gun around, but Fleetwood shifted his other hand to hold Carson's gun hand with both, pushing his arm back against the wall.

Carson acted on reflex, another trick from his father. He jabbed out with his other hand, the knuckle of his middle finger extended. Carson struck the center of Fleetwood's chest, a spot his father called the solar plexus. Carson was going for speed, so it was a light hit, but the effect was instantaneous.

Fleetwood made a croaking sound, suddenly unable to draw breath. His legs went out, and he went down, but not alone. He held on to Carson as he fell, both men getting tangled up as they hit the floorboards hard. Carson's Peacemaker flew from his hand. They wrestled, grabbing and pulling and rolling across the floor. Carson was vaguely aware of Rose scrambling out of the way.

Fleetwood recovered faster than Carson would have predicted. Fleetwood ended up on top of him and threw a punch that landed across Carson's jaw. The bandages absorbed some of the blow, but it still rung Carson's bell. Fleetwood produced a knife. Carson blinked at it.

Where did that come from?

Fleetwood's hand went up, knife held over his head, and Carson's hands came up to fend off the thrust.

Pop.

Everything froze.

Fleetwood sat on top of Carson, the knife poised above him but not moving. Slowly, Fleetwood's expression twisted. A trickle of blood came from behind his left ear and ran down his neck. He twitched violently just once, then toppled sideways off Carson.

Carson sat up and pushed himself back against the wall, breathing heavily. He felt suddenly hot and light-headed and tore the bandages off. He sat there for a long moment looking at Fleetwood's corpse, afraid the man would suddenly rise up again.

Carson glanced at Rose. She was on her knees, a familiar-looking derringer still clutched in one hand, a final wisp of smoke drifting from the barrel.

She tore her eyes from Fleetwood's corpse and looked at Carson. "Is that it?"

"Well . . . that's it for him," Carson said.

She looked back at the corpse again as if it were some sort of sideshow curiosity. "I never killed nobody before."

"You picked a good one to start with."

They stayed like that a few more moments, not exactly sure what they were waiting for. The muffled din from the casino below seeped into the parlor. Carson felt his breathing ease, his heart slowing.

Now what?

"The derringer doesn't make much of a noise," he said. "I don't think anyone heard."

Rose stood, dusted herself off, and Carson followed her example.

The door swung open suddenly, startling both of them. Carson's hand went to his empty holster.

The sheriff walked in, bringing Kat with him, and shut the

door again. Kat had an oversize men's coat draped around her shoulders. Both of them seemed nervous.

The sheriff's eyes went to Fleetwood's body. "Damn. I didn't think he'd do it."

"I didn't," Carson said.

"It got done. That's the important thing." Rose went to the sheriff and kissed him on the cheek. "You're okay? The both of you?"

"Your girl arrived just in time," Kat said. "It was about to get rough."

"I feel like I'm missing part of the story," Carson said.

Rose, Kat, and the sheriff all started talking at once. It took some sorting, but Carson soon had the story and shuddered at how far Fleetwood had been willing to go to protect his secret.

"So, after all this, it was you that killed him," Kat said to Rose.

Rose shook her head. "No, it was you that killed him, Miss Payne. Just like a bounty hunter is supposed to do." She handed over the derringer.

Kat took it with a raised eyebrow. "This is mine."

"Exactly," Rose said. "And when you take Fleetwood's body to the marshal in Fayetteville, the reward will be yours, too."

Carson and Kat exchanged confused looks.

"I guess you're wondering why I wouldn't take the reward for myself," Rose said.

"I was wondering exactly that," Kat admitted.

"Because you can do something for me." Rose reached into her low-cut blouse and came out with a wad of papers. She went to the desk, unfolding them and smoothing them with one hand. "This is a deed of sale. It documents that Lawrence Cooke sold me the casino downstairs. I need the signature of two witnesses. Bart's a lawman, and you work for the court, Miss Payne. That's about as legal as we can arrange it on short notice."

"You think that'll hold up?" Carson asked. "Won't there be questions?"

"Who would anyone ask?" Rose said. "Lawrence Cooke doesn't exist. If his friends ask, he got itchy feet and went to California. There's nobody to show anything untoward happened to him." She gestured to the corpse on the floor. "That ain't Lawrence Cooke. That's Dick Fleetwood. And the marshal in Fayetteville will say so. I'm a law-abiding woman. When Lawrence Cooke bought the Lucky Clover Casino out from under me, I was pretty raw about it. But there was nothing illegal in what he did, and I don't shoot men in the head just for outbidding me. But again, *that* ain't Cooke. It's a murdering bastard named Dick Fleetwood, and he got what was coming to him."

A long, quiet pause as everyone waited for everyone else to say something.

"We can't let anyone see the body," Carson said. "Not anyone that thinks he's Cooke."

"Your horses are in the alley," the sheriff said. "I checked Miss Payne out of Molly's and packed her things. You can go down the back way. Don't worry. You'll get out of town clean."

Carson looked at Kat. Another pregnant pause.

Then Kat crossed the room to the desk, stepping over the dead man on the floor. She picked up a fountain pen and signed the paper. "Congratulations, Madam Rose. You just bought yourself a casino."

CHAPTER 19

"I really wanted to sleep in that bed." Kat stood and stretched and moaned and rubbed her back.

They'd ridden all night and made camp in a copse of trees within a stone's throw of the road. They'd collapsed into their bedrolls without lighting a fire and slept until midmorning.

Carson had returned with firewood just in time to hear Kat's complaints.

"I paid in advance for that room at Molly's," she said. "Damn, I hate sleeping on the ground."

"Really?" Carson grinned. "I hadn't heard."

"Funny man."

"I wonder where Tate is. Probably somewhere sleeping on the ground, too. I feel right sorry for the both of you." Carson knelt and began stacking the wood in the space he'd cleared. "What's the reward on Fleetwood up to now?"

"Eight hundred dollars."

Carson whistled. "I don't think you'll miss whatever you paid Molly with eight hundred dollars in your pocket."

"Four hundred," Kat corrected him. "Tate's not here, but we're still partners. You can be damn sure I'll want my half if he's off somewhere shooting McGraw. Don't it rub you the wrong way you're not getting any of this money?"

"A deal's a deal," Carson said. "Clearing my name's worth more than all the rewards put together."

"I guess you're right. A deal's a deal. Still, you're pulling your weight. I'll give you that."

"I didn't shoot Fleetwood," Carson reminded her. "The madam did that."

Kat laughed, shaking her head. "Never seen a man work so hard to avoid a compliment. Anyway, you did more than I did. I don't know if you've ever been chained up to a jail cell, waiting for a man to lay into you with a bullwhip, but it was an eye opener, I can tell you."

"It don't sound pleasant."

"It wasn't, and it could have been a lot worse. It was the first time it really hit me that I can't always do this by myself. I don't like having to rely on anybody, but I like being dead even less. When it comes to somebody watching my back, I guess I could do worse than you."

"*I could do worse*, of course, being the highest compliment a man can hear."

"You're a strange man, Carson. You don't want money nor compliments neither."

Carson chuckled. "I like money as much as the next man. I just got a higher priority at the moment. As for compliments, I prefer ones about how handsome I am."

Kat smirked. "Sorry, but that shot-off earlobe spoils your looks. As for money, well, maybe Tate and I can discuss an amendment to our arrangement when we catch up with him. I'm not known for my generosity, but there's a first time for everything. Sound okay?" She stuck out her hand.

Carson stood, wiped his hand on his pants before taking Kat's. "Sounds fine." He held on to her hand, looked her in the eye. "But just until we get McGraw. I doubt I'm cut out to be a bounty hunter on a permanent basis."

"Agreed," she said. "Now, when do we get on with it?'

"I'm thinking we should put off heading to Fayetteville

until tomorrow. We already slept the morning away and wouldn't arrive until late if we started now. Let's rest here today and then get a proper start bright and early. The sheriff was kind enough to wrap Fleetwood in canvas, so that'll keep the flies off him until we deliver him to the marshal."

"Fine with me, but how shall we pass the time?"

"I have an idea about that," Carson told her. "But let me fix up some grub first."

Carson finished building the fire, brewed coffee, and fixed bacon and biscuits. They wolfed it down and finished the entire pot of coffee.

"Okay," Kat said. "You promised me something to pass the time. You're not going to pull a checkerboard out of your saddlebag, are you?"

"I should have thought of that," Carson said. "But I have something a little more useful in mind. You don't have anything to shoot with besides that .32 and the derringer, do you?"

"I like my guns just fine, thank you."

"You shoot Big Bob McGraw with either of those, you better hit him right between the eyes," Carson said. "Otherwise, he'll shrug off those beestings and break your neck."

"I thought you wanted to bring in McGraw alive."

"I do," Carson said. "But I'm not going to be religious about it if my own neck is on the line."

"I've got the twelve gauge if I need to go big."

"I guess you do at that," Carson conceded. "But I have something else in mind, to be honest."

"Go on and get to the point, then."

Carson went to the baggage and pulled out a wrapped bundle. He unwrapped it, revealing a Spencer repeating rifle.

Kat squinted at it. "That was Hannigan's?"

"I figured he was finished with it," Carson said. "He had a good supply of cartridges, too."

"You figure I shoot McGraw with that he'll die better than if I shoot him with the derringer?"

"Yup. Not only that but you can shoot at him from a lot farther away. Farther than with the shotgun."

Kat chewed her bottom lip, thinking about it. "Is a Spencer rifle any good?"

"I reckon so," Carson said. "Although you can't crank 'em out as fast as I do with my Winchester. This kind of rifle's called a carbine. Good size for you, probably."

"Okay, then. Show me."

He showed her. First, how to load the cartridges into the stock, how to cock the hammer, and how to crank a new round into the chamber. She held it to her shoulder and sighted down the barrel. Carson inspected her stance, nodded approval.

"You've fired a rifle before."

"Dad's Henry," she said. "A long time ago."

"Let's find a good spot and shoot a bit."

They found a meadow a stone's throw from camp, and Carson set up a line of rocks and wide chunks of bark on a fallen pine trunk. She shot first from twenty yards away, missing with the first five shots but knocking rocks off the trunk with the last two. Kat reloaded, and when she hit with all seven shots, they backed it up to forty yards and she tried again. They went through three boxes of cartridges like that.

"I think I have the feel of it now," Kat said.

Carson nodded. "I think so. Best to save the last box of ammunition in case we need it. We should probably find a tanner in Fayetteville and get you some kind of saddle sheath."

"Good idea."

Back at camp, Carson blew on the fire coals and added some sticks. "I can get some coffee going."

"I got a better idea." Kat went to one of her saddlebags and came back with an unopened bottle of whisky. "When I stopped to buy your face bandages, I stocked up on essentials, too."

Carson grinned. "I reckon a sip or two can't hurt."

They sat around the campfire, passing the bottle between

them. For every one of Carson's sips, Kat took three. They paused to cook dinner—more of the same but hot and filling—then returned to the bottle.

"You're not bad with the Spencer," Carson told her. "You say you've some experience with a rifle? Your dad's Henry?"

A pause. "Yeah."

Kat stared into the fire unblinking, and Carson knew she'd drifted away into a memory.

A moment later, she took a long pull from the bottle and said, "Mother died two summers before bandits murdered my father. They killed him on the road between our farm and town, took his horse and gun and three dollars."

This was the story, Carson realized. The one she'd been holding in only to tell when the time was right. Evidently she'd decided now was the time. He wanted to tell her he was sorry about her father, or that she didn't have to tell the story if it was too painful. But Carson knew when to keep shut, so he sat on the other side of the fire and waited.

"A neighbor had seen who'd done it," she continued a minute later. "I took the Henry from over the fireplace and went into town. We didn't have a sheriff at the time. A man named Cal Ambler was sheriff, but he'd recently gotten married and gone off with his bride. So there was no law. I went into town and saw my dad's horse in front of the saloon. I went inside and there they were, the four of them drinking at the bar, brazen as you please, as if they hadn't just murdered a man in cold blood. Spending my father's three dollars on the whisky, I guess."

Kat went quiet again and drank from the bottle.

Carson put more wood on the fire.

"I raised the rifle and took dead aim on the biggest, ugliest one of them and squeezed the trigger," Kat said. "I caught him on the side of the head, and brains and blood exploded out the other side. Let me tell you, that's a good way to scatter folks. Everyone went running and ducking all around, including those other three bandits. I kept firing the Henry at them, but my hands were shaking by then and all I did was shoot up the saloon. Lucky I didn't hit an innocent bystander."

Carson watched her. Kat's eyes glistened in the flickering light of the campfire. It seemed the whole forest had gone stone quiet.

"And then I looked up, and all of a sudden the place was empty," Kat said. "Just me standing over the corpse of the man I killed. I figured a sheriff would come along and take me into custody, but then I remembered we had no sheriff. The town council sent a rider to Beaumont to fetch a marshal. I didn't even care. Put me in jail. Fine. All that mattered was that I'd killed one of the bastards who'd murdered my father. I even thought about going after the other two. Anyway, the marshal showed up and said the man I'd shot was wanted dead or alive for murdering and cattle rustling, and you already know how that works. Shooting a man in the head without warning had earned me two hundred and fifty dollars. And that's how I became a bounty hunter with my dad's Henry rifle, not even knowing I was doing it."

Kat wiped her eyes with the back of her hand and took a long, loud gulp of whisky, smacking her lips.

"I'd have done the same," Carson said. "Somebody killed my kin? Anyone would have done the same."

A long, extravagant sigh leaked out of Kat. The tears had passed. She'd gathered herself. "You're probably right. Anyway, I had two hundred and fifty dollars, which was more money than I'd ever seen in my life. I sort of went a bit crazy, I guess. I had no family. Not anymore. So I drank, and bought pretty clothes and all sorts of things, and you'd be surprised how fast somebody can make that much money disappear."

Carson smiled. "I notice both you and Tate like your comforts."

Kat laughed. "You know me too well. I like good meals and clean sheets. I was almost broke, but I knew how to get money. I registered myself with the judge, all nice and legal, and set off after the bad men and never looked back. I still have a farm in East Texas, I guess. Nothing to harvest but weeds. Maybe I'll get back there someday."

"It's hard to picture you on a farm." Carson stood and stretched. "But it's probably a good, quiet way to live, if it's not too dull for you. I could use a little dull, quiet living myself. Anyway, sun's going down. I best check the horses."

Night had descended completely over the forest by the time Carson returned from tending the horses. Kat had kicked off her boots and sprawled out atop her bedroll with her head on her saddle. The fire had burned low.

Carson eased into his own bedroll and pulled a thin blanket over him. It had been an easy day, and yet for some reason he felt bone-tired. Maybe it was just his whole life finally catching up to him, the predicament of having a price on his head, the constant uncertainty of not knowing what the next day would bring.

Don't be so dramatic. Shut your eyes and go to sleep.

"Carson?" Kat's voice on the other side of the fire, soft and tentative.

"Yeah?"

"You know how I warned you that I sleep with that derringer?"

Carson grinned at the memory of their first night camping together. Kat had wanted to make it abundantly clear she wasn't some helpless flower to be plucked at the whim of strangers. "You warned me."

"I seem to have misplaced that derringer for the moment," she said softly.

Carson's eyes popped open. What was Kat trying to say? That she'd let her defenses down. Carson thought this must be some kind of invitation. On the other hand, if he were misreading the situation, it would be damn embarrassing.

He heard movement and froze.

A second later, his blanket was thrown back, and she moved in beside him, replacing the blanket and scooting in close. Kat was warm and solid next to him. Carson's heart was suddenly going like a jackrabbit's, like he was some wet-behind-the-ears schoolboy.

Kat ran a hand over his chest, snuggled in close to him, her breath hot on his neck as she spoke. "A woman could get old and gray waiting for you to make up your mind, Carson Stone."

She'd had plenty to drink, and the last thing he needed was Kat accusing him of taking advantage. Not that he hadn't thought about it. He'd thought about it plenty. But there was a way to do things. "Kat, are you sure you're okay with . . . well, what I mean to say is . . . Kat?"

No reply.

"Kat?"

Kat snored softly.

Carson chuckled quietly to himself. *The Lord giveth and the Lord taketh away.* He figured it was probably for the best.

He settled back and closed his eyes, drifting into easy slumber, Kat solid against him, her chest rising and falling with steady breaths.

CHAPTER 20

The road rose gently, and from the top of a low hill, Colby Tate could see Jericho's below, the lantern light twinkling in the windows. Gordon had been right. There wasn't much to it. A log building with a shingled roof. A barn. A corral with horses. Like any other trading post and stagecoach stop.

Tate had taken Benjamin Mooney's corpse to the local sheriff, who said he'd have to send word to the nearest US Marshal before any reward could be given out. The best he could do was give Tate a receipt for the body, the upshot being Tate wouldn't see his fifty dollars any time soon.

Never mind. He'd get back around to it eventually.

He rode toward Jericho's, wondering if there would be anyone to meet him. The landscape was implacable darkness in every direction, Jericho's an oasis of windows lit flickering orange. He watched for a moment, but other than the horses in the corral, there was no sign of movement. Would the proprietor expect anyone this time of night or not? Only one way to find out.

He dismounted in front of the log building and tied his horse to the hitching post. Tate paused and listened but didn't hear voices coming from inside, which could mean almost anything. Whoever was within might be asleep or simply not talking. Or possibly they'd heard his horse coming and were waiting quietly to see what happened next.

Tate knocked.

The sound of shuffling. A chair being pushed away from a table. "It's open."

Tate entered.

As expected, the place was a combination trading post and cantina, not uncommon for a stagecoach stop. Shelves with dry goods. Tack and harness hanging from hooks on the walls. A stone fireplace with a blaze going. Three tables and a scattering of chairs. A wooden counter to the left, with a man standing behind it. He was clean-shaven and lean, eyes bright and wary.

"I take it you're Jericho and this is your place," Tate said.

Upon hearing the sound of a cocking revolver and feeling the cold metal of a gun barrel pressed against the flesh under his right ear, Tate went stone still.

"Jericho stepped out for a moment." Gordon's voice.

The lean man behind the counter produced a shotgun and leveled it at Tate. A third man stepped out of the shadows, revolver in hand. He was stocky, with a flat nose. Tate didn't immediately recognize him from any of the wanted posters.

"Well, I'm not dead yet," Tate said. "I presume this means you're still mulling my offer."

"Presume all you want as long as you hand over those guns," Gordon told him. "Nice and slow."

Tate unbuckled his gun belt and set it on the nearest table. "Okay? We're friends now?"

"We'll see about that," Gordon said. "Get those guns, Cal."

Cal was the one with the flat nose. He took Tate's guns, moving with caution. Gordon must have warned them Tate was fast.

"We got a camp a few miles from here," Gordon said. "Bob will decide if you're any use to us or not. Either way, it's out of your hands now, so don't bother trying anything tricky."

"I understand."

Once on his horse, Gordon handed him a blindfold. "Put it on."

"I don't see why I should bother," Tate said. "If I'm to be part of the gang, it doesn't matter if I know where your camp is, and if Bob decides I'm not to join you, I doubt I'll leave the camp alive."

"You make a good case," Gordon said. "Put it on anyway or I'll blow your damn head off."

Tate put the blindfold on.

"Don't even think about peeking," Gordon warned. "Or I'll—"

"Yes, yes, you'll blow my damn head off," Tate said impatiently. "It's not a subtle point you're making."

Gordon took the reins of Tate's horse and led him. He heard at least one of the outlaws riding behind him. He sensed when they left the road, Gordon leading them into the hills. A pine bow slapped his face.

"A warning would be nice," Tate said.

"You just hang on to your saddle horn," Gordon shot back.

Tate smelled the cookfire long before Gordon announced they were approaching the camp. They'd only been riding a little over an hour, so the camp wasn't too far from Jericho's. Tate wondered if a good tracker could find where they'd left the road and follow the trail to McGraw's camp. Coming back with some help might be a good way to catch all the outlaws by surprise.

Not a bad plan, old boy, but the trick is living long enough to slip away and find a tracker.

There was no point in making plans at the moment. The situation could change a dozen times in the next hour. The only thing to do was wait and see how things went with Big Bob.

The next moment, Tate was surrounded by chatter, at least

a half-dozen men by his estimation. He was ordered to dismount and did as he was told. His hands went automatically to the blindfold, but he stopped himself. Tate hadn't been told to remove it yet. *See how cooperative I am? Just one of the gang.*

In the next moment, rough hands removed the blindfold.

Tate glanced around, taking in the camp. A few of the outlaws sat around the campfire, others tended horses, and a few more lurked in the shadows just on the edge of camp, probably on guard duty. At least a dozen of them, Tate estimated. Even if he'd had his guns, Tate wouldn't have had a chance. He'd had the vague notion that if McGraw was shorthanded, he might be down to two or three men in his gang. Then, if Tate could win Big Bob's trust and get his guns back, he might contrive a way to take them.

That plan was out the window now. Whatever Big Bob was planning with the bank in Fayetteville, it must be something big, because it looked like he was gathering a small army.

And the payoff must be something unprecedented, Tate thought. *The take would have to be big to split it among so many men and still be worth the trouble.*

A shadow fell across Tate as a huge man placed himself between Tate and the campfire. Big Bob McGraw was every bit the intimidating figure his reputation made him out to be. A tall, broad-chested bear of a man with a strangely menacing air, almost like the man was on the verge of rage just standing there. For the first time, Tate felt a hint of fear. He'd been concerned, naturally, when Gordon blindfolded him and led him into the wilderness. Putting yourself into the hands of outlaws was no laughing matter.

But coming face to face with Big Bob was something else altogether.

"So you're the fast shooter, huh?" Bob's voice was calm and utterly without menace.

Which Tate somehow found worse than if the man were shouting at him.

Tate cleared his throat and tried to keep his nerves out of his voice. "Faster than Benjamin Mooney, anyway. I hope your brother related an honest account of the altercation."

"He said Ben drew first, but you were faster," Bob said. "Still, he was one of my men. Hard not to take that personally."

"I don't apologize for defending myself," Tate said. "But I do apologize for inconveniencing you. I respect you have an organization to manage, and obviously the sudden demise of your man could cause you a problem. Fortunately, the solution is obvious since I'm ready, willing, and available to take his place."

"You talk too fancy for my liking, but you have good manners, I'll give you that," Bob said. "What is it exactly you think you'd be in for if you threw in with us?"

"As I mentioned to your brother, I'm rather keen to get into the bank-robbing business."

"So who's stopping you?" Bob asked. "No shortage of banks."

"A fair question," Tate conceded. "My understanding is that you're on to something special with a bank in Fayetteville. If I'm going to be a bank robber, I want to do it right, and I want to do it *big*."

Bob shot Gordon a hard look.

Gordon held up his hands. "Now hold on, Bob. I already asked the boys. Nobody's been talking. No loose lips in this gang. I put it to 'em hard. They know better than to lie to me."

Bob turned his gaze back to Tate. "What do you know and how do you know it?"

"Something big that isn't there yet," Tate said. "Otherwise, you would have hit the bank already. Whatever this something is must be worth the wait."

"Says who?"

"Dan Hannigan."

Tate had expected these questions and had his story ready to go, had even rehearsed it a few times in his head.

"Hell." Bob turned his head and spat. "That dumb Mick always did have a big mouth. How do you know Dan?"

"We sort of fell in together," Tate said. "Drinking buddies, so to speak."

"Yeah, that sounds like Dan."

"Dan didn't say what might be in the bank," Tate explained. "Just that he expected it to be your final big score before holding up for the winter."

"True enough," Bob said. "And what did you expect to get out of joining up with us?"

"Whatever was coming to Ben Mooney, I suppose. I expect it'll be more than I could earn robbing banks on my own."

"Maybe there's men here was friends with Mooney and wouldn't take it well if you just joined up out of the blue."

"Surely men like this understand the risks of the business."

"They do," Bob said. "Still."

"Yeah."

Bob twisted around to face the campfire and raised his voice. "Anyone here pals enough with Mooney to be upset he got himself shot?"

"He owed me five dollars," came a voice from one of the men in the shadows. "How am I supposed to collect that now?"

Low chuckles rippled through the camp.

"I'm afraid I couldn't make good on any such transaction unless I saw a receipt," Tate said to the gathered outlaws in jovial fashion. "But I'll stand a whisky at the next opportunity for any man who feels unjustly deprived of Mooney's camaraderie."

"That'll work," said the same voice.

"Now that I come to think of it," another voice rose from the campfire, "I was pretty good pals with Ben myself."

More laughter.

"Seems nobody has a strenuous objection," Bob said.

"Delightful." Tate grinned. "Does this mean I can have my guns back? I feel a bit naked without them."

Bob returned the grin. "I imagine you do. But let's say you're on probation right now. I sent somebody on ahead to check you out. I've lasted a good long time in the outlaw business. Being mean is part of it. Another part of it is being careful."

"I'm new to the region," Tate said. "Who could you possibly ask about me?"

"Never you mind, Mr. Tate." Bob's grin faded, his expression going hard again. "Just never you mind."

CHAPTER 21

"What the hell?"

Carson started awake to find Kat pulling away from him. The dusty first light of dawn had crept through the forest to surround them.

Kat stood, glaring down at him. "Just what do you think you're doing, you snake?"

Carson held his hands palms up, out in front of him. "Easy. I didn't do a thing. Your bedroll's over there."

She looked back, memory obviously flooding her eyes. "Oh, hell. I'm sorry, Carson." Her hands went to her head. "I feel like my brain's about to pound out of my skull."

"Too much whisky," he said. "I'll make coffee. That'll help."

"I'm . . . embarrassed."

"Don't be."

"No, I am," Kat said. "That was unprofessional. I'm not like that."

Carson didn't say anything, fetched the coffee and the pot.

Kat cleared her throat. "If we could just forget it ever happened . . ."

Carson paused what he was doing, then shrugged. "If that's what you want."

"It's just that . . . well, we should keep our minds on business."

"Right." Carson stoked the fire. "This coffee will be ready soon and we can be on our way."

In less than an hour, they were packed, saddled up, and on their way to Fayetteville. About midday, the rain started. Not the raging storm from before, but a miserable, all-day drizzle, soaking them to the bone. The discussion to stop and find shelter was a mere formality. Neither of them wanted to stop before reaching Fayetteville. They were eager to be shed of Fleetwood's corpse, and even Carson balked at the idea of another night sleeping on the ground. He wasn't as attached to creature comforts as Kat, but he was in no mood to chase sleep through a long, wet night with roots and rocks in his back.

They were both in a foul mood when they finally reined in their horses on the outskirts of Fayetteville about an hour before sundown.

"How do you want to handle this?" Carson asked.

"Dump Fleetwood on the marshal's doorstep and get my money," Kat said. "What else is there to handle?"

"I mean the bank," Carson said. "The marshal's going to have information we need. When the payroll arrives and all that."

"The last time I trusted a lawman, I got chained up to a jail cell ready to be whipped," Kat said.

"A fair point, but it worked out okay in the end," Carson reminded her. "I have other concerns."

Kat groaned. "Well, Carson, I can't think of anything I'd like better than to sit in the cold rain listening to your concerns. Can't it wait until I've got some dry clothes and a hot meal?"

"If you're going to talk to the marshal, it can't wait."

"Go on, then."

"If you ask when the payroll's coming into town, he'll

want to know why," Carson explained. "And if you tell him about McGraw, what're the chances he's going to want him and his boys to handle it and you and me out of the way? I haven't been associated with bounty hunters long enough to know how all this works."

"Hell, I hadn't thought of that," Kat admitted. "This is a new situation for me. Some lawmen aren't partial to bounty hunters. When we deliver Fleetwood, I'll size up the marshal. If he seems like a reasonable man, I'll let him in on McGraw. I'll also try to find out if Tate's in town."

"And if the marshal doesn't seem reasonable?"

"Then we'll figure something out," she said. "Still, best you stay out of sight. We got lucky back in Fort Smith that the marshal didn't have your wanted poster on the wall. I didn't even think of it at the time. We need to be more careful. We need to be more careful about a lot of things."

Since Fleetwood's corpse was draped across Jet, Carson let Kat lead the animal away while he went off to get them a couple of rooms for the night. Nothing fancy this time. No expensive hotel rooms with private baths or steak dinners in the window of a fancy restaurant. No Kat in an alluring green dress.

Carson was a bit sorry about that, but mostly he was tired and wet. The nearest hotel took the last of his money for two rooms. He told himself not to worry about it. Kat was good for her share. She had to be, or else Carson wouldn't eat that night.

He left Kat's key with the front desk clerk and told him she'd be along for it directly.

He went upstairs to his own room. It was simple and comfortable. He stripped off his wet shirt and hung it up to dry. Carson vowed to get himself another pair of trousers. He hung his wet socks over the bed's headboard and set his boots aside. He wanted to hang his pants up to dry, too, but Kat would probably be along any minute. The pants weren't bad, really, a bit damp but not sopping.

He flopped on the bed and lay there, looking at the ceiling.

Carson waited for Kat to show.

And waited.

He stood and went to the window, looking down at the muddy street. There wasn't much to see. A few people went about their business, shoulders hunched against the cold rain.

Carson's life had become a strange thing to him, flitting from town to town, traveling with bounty hunters and bringing the dead bodies of outlaws to marshals. He tried to remember his quiet life with his folks on the farm but couldn't quite feel it, as if it was a time described to him instead of something he'd lived himself. He told himself he wanted that quiet life again but suspected he only thought that because it was the sensible thing to think. He wondered if he could really go back to it.

And he wondered what the alternative would be.

A knock at the door.

He hastily slipped on his dry shirt and was still buttoning it when he opened the door and let Kat in. "How'd it go?"

She pushed in past him, and he shut the door again.

"Not bad," Kat said. "I think."

"You think?"

"The marshal says safety is more a concern to him than our reward," Kat explained. "He'll pay up on whoever's caught or killed. He said that's the least he could do for tipping him off, but he made it clear I'm to stay out of the way."

"What about me?"

"You don't exist," Kat said. "I didn't see your wanted poster on the wall of his office, but I still think it's best you steer clear of him. I did see posters for Big Bob McGraw and his brother Gordon. Dan Hannigan, too, but I told him to take that one down since we got Hannigan already."

"You learn anything about the payroll?"

"Day after tomorrow," Kat said. "That's when it arrives. I'm going back to the marshal's office in the morning to discuss the best way to set up the trap."

"I thought the marshal wanted you out of the way."

"Sort of a courtesy," Kat said. "The marshal seems like a reasonable sort, and I think he's grateful I brought him this information about McGraw. Probably some kind of feather in his cap to bring in a famous outlaw like that."

"I wish Tate was here," Carson said. "I feel like things are picking up speed and we don't know where he is."

"All we can do is check things out and be ready."

Carson tugged an earlobe, face scrunched in thought. "Then I guess tomorrow I might check out that bank myself. You never know. I might see something useful. I wonder how McGraw will go about it."

Kat held up a yellow sheet of thin paper. "We can go to the bank together if you want."

"What's that?"

"Bank voucher," Kat said. "For the reward on Fleetwood. I figure that'll give us an excuse to look the bank over, like you were saying. I wouldn't mind finding a good spot to set up with that Spencer rifle."

Carson grinned, shaking his head. "Again, I think you and the marshal have different ideas about what 'stay out of the way' means."

"If the marshal and his deputies want to do the heavy lifting on this, I'm happy to let them," Kat said. "But there's a lot of money at stake, and I'm not keen on leaving anything to chance if I don't have to."

Carson nodded. "Makes sense. Do you need me to put up the horses?"

"The hotel has a stable and a stable boy," she said. "Don't worry, he'll give Jet a proper rubdown. They only thing left for us to do is grab a hot meal. There's a place the next street over."

"I think I'll just sack out." He felt dog tired all of a sudden, and anyway, he didn't have any money.

"Okay. If you do go out, pull your hat down low. No point risking anyone getting a good look at you."

"Right."

"Sleep tight, Carson."

Carson didn't even remember his head hitting the pillow.

CHAPTER 22

Carson realized he didn't really know much about banks as he stood in the lobby and waited for Kat, who'd approached one of the four teller windows. They'd arrived early, and the bank had only been open for five minutes. The other three teller windows were closed.

A door to Carson's left had a sign with the words "Alfred Garrison, President." An important man in the community, Carson figured. There were leather-covered benches on either side of the door. There was another door behind the tellers, leading back to . . . a safe? More offices?

Carson could only guess. He'd been in the alley, minding the horses, for his one and only bank robbery. He tried to imagine how it would go if he tried it right now. What would he do? Stick a gun in the teller's face and demand money, probably. Was that all McGraw and his gang had done? It didn't take much to be an infamous outlaw, Carson supposed; guts and meanness and a casual disregard for the law and the welfare of others.

A man entered the bank, bald head glistening with sweat, black beard neatly trimmed and going white at the corners of his mouth and at his temples. His worried eyes darted furtively around the lobby. He wore a fine brown suit, neatly pressed, a tidy and efficient-looking man, but something in his demeanor suggested an acute apprehension.

The man wiped his bald head with a handkerchief and entered the president's office, shutting the door behind him with a quiet click.

So that's Alfred Garrison. Poor man looks like he's working on an ulcer. Running a bank must be a load of stress.

Kat crossed the lobby toward him, a smile on her face. Apparently, her transaction with the teller had gone as hoped.

"The marshal plays cards with the head teller and put in a word for me so there wouldn't be any trouble." Kat handed Carson a folded bill. "For you."

He unfolded the bill and looked at it. Fifty dollars. Carson hadn't even known bills came as high as fifty. It was only paper but somehow felt heavy in his hand. "What's this?"

"I told you that when we spoke to Tate next, we'd talk about renegotiating the terms of our three-way partnership," Kat said. "In the meantime, I no longer want to be seen in the company of a beggar. When I see you next, you'll be in better trousers, agreed?"

"Agreed."

"I'll leave it to your own good judgment to decide whatever else you need. Now, come on and let's get out of this bank."

The sun was up and already warming Fayetteville, the people out and about their business.

"Just remember, try to keep a low profile. We'll meet later for a bite to eat," Kat said. "Nothing too fancy. I don't have my green dress anymore."

"Low profile. No green dress. Want I should write this down?"

"The funny man again," Kat said. "What are you going to do while I'm talking to the marshal?"

Carson shrugged. "Take a look around town. I've never been to Fayetteville before. Buy some pants, I reckon, so I don't embarrass you. I'll keep my eyes open for Tate, too. It would be nice to find out if he actually accomplished anything."

"Okay, then. Stay out of trouble. I'll see you later at the hotel."

Kat turned and headed toward the marshal's office.

Carson turned the other way and headed up the street in no particular hurry.

A few minutes later, he paused at a red, white, and blue barber's pole. A sign in the window boasted "Haircuts, Shaves, Tonics, Toiletries, Hot Towel Treatments, and Cigars." Carson entered.

A jowly man in a white coat looked up from a newspaper. "Help you today, sir?"

Carson took off his hat and plopped himself down in the barber's chair. "Give me the works."

The marshal took the coffee pot from the iron stove, filled a cup, and handed it to Kat.

"Obliged." She sipped. A little too hot but good.

Marshal Jedediah Pike considered himself a fair man and took his job seriously. Kat could see that right away. Square shoulders, square jaw, and a fair and square attitude. Middle-aged, with a lot of years left in him, Pike had told Kat he'd been a lawman for two decades and liked it, was good at it, and planned to keep doing it until the good Lord took him. He had nothing in particular against bounty hunters.

But Pike was the man with the badge. His town. His people. His responsibility.

"So, don't take offense if I ask you to find a nice spot out of the way to watch and let me and my boys take care of business," Pike said. "Like I told you last night, I already get two paychecks. The good people of Fayetteville made me their town marshal long before I was picked to be a US Marshal, too. And the county sheriff is my brother-in-law. Your bounties are safe. Nobody's looking to cheat you out of anything. We just want to see bad men go behind bars . . . or into the grave-yard, if they force us to go that way."

"You've been fair, Marshal, and I can't ask any more than that," Kat said. "How many men have you got?"

"Plenty for the job," Pike assured her. "There's my boys and the sheriff's and some other fellas we take on temporarily whenever we need a hand. All told, I can have twenty armed men ready to go when the time comes."

"Twenty men standing on the steps of the bank waiting for McGraw and his gang to show up might draw some attention, Marshal."

Pike chuckled and refilled his own coffee mug. "They would at that, but I hope you'll give me a little more credit. There's only two ways in and out of that bank, and only one way that counts: the front door. I'll have men across the street both on the roof and along the sidewalk. Men up and down the street, too, all of them pretending to be window-shopping or about some other business. We'll be as inconspicuous as possible, let McGraw and his boys come in like everything's okay, and then suddenly they'll have twenty guns in their faces."

"Only one that counts why?"

"Beg pardon?"

"You said only one way in and out of the bank that counted," Kat reminded him. "What's the other way?"

"The back door," Pike said. "It wasn't there originally. When the bank upgraded from a small safe to a big vault, it was easier to make a door in the back and put the vault in that way. People pointed out it was probably good to have another door, anyway, in case of a fire or something. Nobody uses it. Looks like a normal wooden door on the outside, but it's backed with iron, and locked *and* barred on the inside. I guess you could have a go at it with a million sticks of dynamite, but my bet is McGraw goes through the front door like anyone else."

"You might still want a man back there," Kat suggested. "You never know."

"Two men," Pike said. "But I want most of my boys where the action's going to be. I want to make damn sure McGraw is outgunned. Either he'll see it's hopeless and give up, or my boys'll put him down like a rabid dog."

"Sounds like you've got it figured out," Kat said.

"I hope so, but I'm not telling you all this *just* as a courtesy," Pike admitted. "I know McGraw has a hideout somewhere in the Ozarks, and I make it a point to learn all I can about the bad men in the area. If you've been tracking McGraw's gang, you might have heard something I haven't. I'd be obliged for any information you can share."

Kat nodded and sipped her coffee. She'd had a conversation with Carson over an early breakfast in anticipation of this exact request from the marshal.

"He's not going to come in shorthanded," Kat said. "I brought you Fleetwood, and I told you about Hannigan. He's lost other men, too, I think. That means new faces, maybe faces that aren't on any of your wanted posters. McGraw has certainly sent one or more of these new faces to scout the bank, keep tabs on it. There's probably one of them out there right now keeping watch. If you're not sneaky about setting up your men, he'll see everything you're doing, and McGraw will know in an hour."

"That's not a bad point," Pike said. "I'll need to ask Brady if he's seen any strangers in town."

"Brady?"

"My right-hand man," Pike explained. "He should be along any minute."

"So, if you were Big Bob McGraw, how would you go about hitting the bank and stealing the payroll?" Kat asked.

"Frankly, I wouldn't," Pike told her. "Thirty thousand in gold coming by armored wagon, escorted by twenty Pinkertons. They bring it to the bank which only has four guards. They take shifts, but for something like this, all four will be there. Either the president or vice president of the bank signs for the gold, and that completes the Pinkertons' responsibility. I suppose there's a slight opening when the Pinkertons have gone and there's just the four bank guards loading the gold into the vault. I reckon that might be a possible time for McGraw to strike. Unless his gang's so big now he's cocky enough to take on Pinkertons."

"Why only four guards at the bank?"

"That's all the bank's ever needed," Pike said. "It's the first time for a shipment of gold this big. It's all new. The railroad company building all the branch lines have had some financial trouble, and they've been paying their workers in scrip. Mostly Chinese fellas. They're not treated so well, I hear, but that's none of my business until a law is broken. Anyway, these workers have been paid in scrip going on three months while the financial magicians do whatever the hell they do, and I guess it worked since the gold's on the way and the workers can finally trade it for proper money. Anyway . . . *dang*, I forgot your question."

"Four guards."

"Oh, right. Guards. This is the first time for so much gold at once. Four guards have always been plenty before."

Kat stifled an impatient sigh. "Considering the circumstances, wouldn't the bank want to hire on some additional guards?"

"That's *exactly* what the bank wanted to do." Pike grinned. "I asked them not to."

Kat thought about it for a moment. "You want McGraw to take that opening after the Pinkertons leave."

Pike nodded. "I can't have twenty men standing around forever, waiting for McGraw to decide he's ready. I need to serve him up a juicy opportunity on a silver platter. If Big Bob really does have a spy in town, he's going to hear it's just the usual four guards. I'm betting he'll wait for the Pinkertons to leave and then storm in the front door, guns drawn, catching the guards flat-footed. I'm going to tell those guards to cooperate fully. McGraw won't shoot if he doesn't have to. That'll just draw attention. When he comes out of the bank, he'll find twenty rifles pointing at him. And gold's heavy. He won't be running anywhere, leastways not fast."

"Sounds like you've put thought into this," Kat said. "Just one question."

"Let's hear it."

"What if it doesn't work?"

"Then I guess I owe twenty men a day's pay for doing nothing," Pike said. "But it's worth a chance. If McGraw doesn't show . . . well, we'll cross that bridge when we come to it."

The door opened, and a lanky man entered the marshal's office, tin star on his vest.

"Here's Brady now," Pike told Kat. "Brady, this is the bounty hunter I was telling you about. Katherine Payne."

Brady gave Kat the once-over. He was a lean type, black hair in a sharp widow's peak, cheeks scarred from acne in his youth. A splotchy, scarlet birthmark below his left eye. "Never heard tell of no woman bounty hunter before."

Kat raised an eyebrow. "That a problem?"

Brady shook his head. "No problem here."

"You round up the boys?" Pike asked his deputy.

"Yep. And I told them to keep their mouths shut, just like you wanted," Brady said.

"And then what?"

"Went to the saloon as instructed," Brady said. "Had a shot of whisky and a nice conversation at the bar with Ike Johansen about how those bank guards better be on their toes since there's only four of 'em."

"A nice, loud conversation?"

"Don't worry. Everybody heard," Brady said. "And I wasn't obvious about it."

"Good." Pike turned back to Kat. "I guess we're done here, unless you have any more questions?"

Kat handed her empty coffee cup back to the marshal. "What time's the show start?"

"Gold wagon's scheduled to arrive right as the bank closes. Five o'clock," Pike said. "Sharp."

CHAPTER 23

Carson had come out of the barbershop smelling good, looking smooth and tidy, and feeling refreshed. Hair neatly trimmed and the excess hair on his neck taken off with a straight razor. Something sweet-smelling rubbed into his hair afterward. A close shave and hot towels on his face, and then some sort of aftershave that was warm at first and then cool.

The barber had given Carson's fifty-dollar bill the stink eye. It had nearly cleaned him out making change.

He walked down the sidewalk with a fat, unlit cigar in the corner of his mouth, feeling like a big shot. A sign on the next block caught his eye. "Swinson's Haberdashery."

Carson was tempted to splurge on one of the fine suits to see if he could get a reaction from Kat, but he couldn't quite picture himself dressed like that. He'd worry all the time he'd get it dirty or spill gravy down the front.

An efficient, twig-thin man helped him pick out three shirts, all alike in cut with simple buttons down the front, one brown, one a dark green, and another white with thin blue stripes. A selection of underthings and socks.

"And trousers," Carson told the man.

"The occasion?" the haberdasher asked.

"The what?"

"Where shall we be wearing our trousers, sir?"

"Where?" Carson blinked at the man. "Everywhere. You want I should go out without trousers?"

They finally worked it out to purchase two pairs of trousers, one plain and sturdy for riding and everyday use, and another for church-going and such. Carson tried on the sturdy pair, looked at himself in the mirror. A good fit. A deep tan color that went well with his black shirt. Probably might look okay with the green, too.

"May I suggest you wear those out of the shop, sir?" He looked down at Carson's old pants, folded neatly in his hands like they were a pile of something that had found its way out of the back end of a draft horse. "In my opinion, sir, these trousers have served their purpose. It might be time to retire them."

Carson laughed. There were a lot of miles on those trousers. "I guess they do look pretty rough. I'll wear the new ones, but if you don't mind, please wrap up the old trousers. I'm sure I'll end up mucking out a barn sooner or later, and I'd hate to soil my new duds."

"As you wish, sir."

Carson stood looking out the front window while he waited for the haberdasher to wrap up his purchases. The nervous gentleman across the street caught his attention. He kept pacing back and forth in front of a saloon, almost going inside but then stopping himself. The man looked familiar.

Alfred Garrison, Carson realized a moment later. The bank president.

Garrison wiped his bald head with a handkerchief, some kind of nervous habit apparently, and then entered the saloon with reluctance.

"Your purchases are wrapped and good to go," the haberdasher said. "And we look forward to having more of your business in the future."

"Can I stop by and pick up the clothes later?" Carson asked.

"Yes, or if you're staying nearby, we can have them delivered. It's a courtesy we extend to all of our customers."

"Thanks. That would be helpful." Carson told him the name of the hotel. "Under the name Henry Adams." The fake name had been Kat's idea. Until he cleared up this business with McGraw, Carson was still a wanted man. No sense advertising his whereabouts. It rubbed him the wrong way not to use his own name, but it made sense under the circumstances.

Carson thanked the haberdasher again, exited the store, crossed the street, and entered the saloon.

He walked in and paused, letting his eyes adjust to the dim interior. The place wasn't what anyone would call crowded, but it was surprisingly busy for so early in the day. A dozen or so patrons occupied various tables, enjoying friendly conversations or equally friendly card games. An old man sat hunched over his beer mug at the bar. Carson glanced right, then left, and saw the man he was looking for. Garrison sat at a corner table. He was with someone, but the other man's back was to Carson, so he couldn't get a good look.

He ambled across the room, taking his time and doing nothing to draw attention to himself. There was a big mirror behind the bar, so he positioned himself in a spot that allowed him to keep watch on Garrison's table in the reflection.

"What can I do you for?" the barkeep asked him.

"Coffee?"

"I'd have to make it."

"Never mind, then. How about a beer?"

"Coming right up." The barkeep grabbed a fresh mug and stuck it under the tap, filled it, and set the mug in front of Carson.

Carson leaned against the bar, head down. He brought the mug up to his lips, more to block his face than to drink, and slowly lifted his eyes to look in the mirror. Garrison sat at his table, still nervous and twitchy. Carson had a better angle on the other man now, but not enough to look him full in the face. Thick brown beard. Hat pulled low, maybe trying to obscure his features, just like Carson was doing.

What am I doing here? The banker's nervous demeanor had caught Carson's attention. But that might not mean anything. *The man could just be naturally skittish. He's responsible for a lot of money. That would probably make me nervous, too. I should just finish my beer and vamoose.*

But he didn't. He stayed right there, watching Garrison in the mirror and nursing his beer.

The two men kept talking, the banker twitching and dabbing sweat, his eyes darting left and right, as if expecting something bad could come at him from any direction. The other man leaned back in his chair, relaxed by comparison.

Carson got through half the beer and didn't want the rest. He was wasting time. He should leave, go find Kat and—

The man at the table with the banker turned his head, and Carson finally got a clear look at his face.

Memphis!

The beard was new, but Carson would recognize those mischievous eyes and that sharp nose anywhere. Jimmy Bachman might be one of the few left riding with McGraw from the old days, when Carson was briefly part of the gang. Carson had always liked him well enough. Memphis had a friendly way about him, but he was a killer, no mistake.

And there he was, talking to the president of the very bank he would soon help rob.

No, sir, I definitely do not believe in coincidences.

Carson watched another two minutes, and then both men got up to leave. He needed to follow one of them. That much was obvious.

His first notion was to follow Memphis. If he could find where Big Bob McGraw and his men were hiding, Kat might be able to gather some deputies and end all this pretty quick. But Carson immediately saw a couple of problems with that idea. If Memphis recognized him and tipped off Bob, that would blow any surprise they had. Also, Carson didn't have his horse handy. By the time he fetched Jet, Memphis would be long gone.

Better to follow the banker. The man didn't know Carson, but he obviously knew something.

Carson watched Memphis and Garrison leave the saloon, waited a few moments, and then followed after them. Garrison had turned left. Memphis rode his horse in the opposite direction. Carson had been right. He wouldn't have been able to follow Memphis. He turned and followed the banker.

A block down, the banker took another right. Two streets over, Carson found himself walking along a well-to-do avenue, with nice houses on both sides. Garrison walked to the biggest house all the way down, two stories, fresh white paint and blue shutters. A neatly trimmed yard behind a picket fence. Carson had never seen a banker's house before, but this was what he might have imagined one to look like.

Garrison went inside. Carson kept walking so as not to be seen lingering, slow and casual. When he figured he was out of sight of the front windows, he stopped under the low branches of a tree near the street. He scanned the neighborhood from the shady spot. It was broad daylight, but nobody was about.

He headed back toward the banker's house, coming at it from an angle, stepping fast, and the next moment, he stood with his back up against the side of the house. He scooted along, pausing at the first window he came to, and took a look inside, ready to duck back in case somebody was there looking out. He wasn't exactly sure what he was trying to accomplish; he only knew he needed to get some notion of what the banker was up to.

Carson looked into a kitchen. Garrison sat at a small table

talking to a handsome, middle-aged woman, probably his wife. Hair pinned up, brown with only a few hints of gray, clear face, lips tight, giving her a severe look. A blue-and-pink-flowered apron tied around her.

First, she talked, and then he did. He couldn't hear anything, but the conversation seemed to get more heated as they went. He seemed agitated and she was getting the same way, apparently asking questions he couldn't answer. Then he threw up his hands, defeated, hunched over the table, a stricken expression giving him a desperate edge. He hung his head, put his hands in his face.

The woman reached for him, hesitated, then put her hand on his back, rubbing slow circles. She didn't look any happier than he did.

Carson didn't feel good about spying on the couple, but he had to know what was happening. It was too much like trying to put together one of those jigsaw puzzles, but with half the pieces missing. Whatever Garrison had discussed with Memphis, it apparently wasn't sitting well. There could be any number of reasons for that, and there was only so much Carson could learn peeping through windows.

I'll have to get more direct about this, I reckon.

Carson circled to the front of the house and knocked on the door.

A few moments passed, and Carson wondered if they hadn't heard. Or maybe they were just ignoring him, not in the mood for visitors.

But then the door opened, and the woman stood there frowning. "Yes? Can I help you?"

Carson took off his hat. He felt glad suddenly he wasn't wearing his old trousers. "Hope I'm not disturbing you, ma'am, but I'd like to speak to Mr. Garrison."

Her frown deepened. "It's not really the best time. If I might give him a message . . ."

"It's a little more urgent than that, ma'am."

She hesitated, then asked, "May I tell him who's calling?"

"The name wouldn't mean anything to him, ma'am." Carson tried to sound apologetic. "We've never met."

A mix of emotions played across her face. She was displeased, but there was worry there, too.

"If you'd wait here a moment."

"Of course, ma'am."

She closed the door and left Carson standing on the front porch, hat in hand.

Five seconds later, the door jerked open again. This wasn't the defeated banker from the kitchen table. Garrison had put on his banker's face, all business.

"I don't appreciate you not giving my wife your name," he said. "I'll ask you to please come straight to the point."

"I understand, sir," Carson said. "My name don't matter, but there's a name that might get your attention. Jimmy Bachman. Most call him Memphis."

Garrison's businesslike demeanor wavered—not for long, but enough for Carson to notice.

"I don't know what you mean," Garrison said. "I don't know anyone by that name."

Carson sighed. "Begging your pardon, sir, but I think you do."

"I'm sorry, but I can't talk right now." Garrison made to shut the door.

"Mr. Garrison, you've got to listen to me," Carson said quickly. "I can't guarantee I can help you, but then again, maybe I can. It's for sure somebody has to. Because if you're mixed up with Jimmy Bachman, that means you're mixed up with Big Bob McGraw, too, who's just about the worst outlaw there is. My guess is you're in over your head, sir, and you need a friend."

Garrison eyes went worried, and he looked past Carson, glancing up and down the avenue. "Not . . . not here. Not out in the open. Come in quickly, before anyone sees you."

The banker stood aside, and Carson entered, the door closing quickly behind him.

"Talk fast," Garrison said.

The banker was openly nervous now, no hint of the calm and collected businessman remaining. His wife stood behind him, worrying her apron with anxious fingers.

"I know there's a payroll coming," Carson said. "McGraw plans to hit the bank. Your bank."

"Are you one of Pike's men?" Garrison asked. "He said he'd kill her if I talked to the law."

"Her? Her who?"

"My daughter. She's only seventeen," Garrison said. "McGraw took her."

CHAPTER 24

"Your daughter," Carson said, letting it sink in.

And just like that, it made sense, the key piece to the puzzle.

"You're helping him rob the bank," Carson said. "You have to, or he'll kill your daughter."

"Yes." Garrison produced his handkerchief and began dabbing sweat from his bald head again. The man's nerves were frayed. "He wouldn't really do it, would he? She's innocent. Emily's never done anything to anyone."

Carson wanted to tell the man it would all be okay, but he'd spent time with Big Bob McGraw and knew it wasn't true. Even if Garrison cooperated and helped McGraw rob the payroll, he doubted this would all come out the way the banker wanted. McGraw wasn't a man to leave a witness alive. He'd want a clean slate, and Carson doubted the girl would ever be seen again.

"You've got to listen to me," Carson said. "If you want to see Emily alive again, you've got to go to the marshal and tell him what you know."

"I told you, I can't. He'll kill her."

"Send word to the marshal to meet you in secret. McGraw doesn't need to know."

"He thought of that," Garrison said. "He said he'd know. He said he's got ears and eyes everywhere."

Maybe that was true or maybe it wasn't. Carson had no way of knowing. "What were you and Memphis talking about?"

"I've said too much already. You should leave."

"You need help with this, Mr. Garrison," Carson insisted. "You can't go it alone."

His wife came forward, put a hand on her husband's arm. "Alfred, listen to the man. We can't just . . . I mean, we have to do *something*."

"Milly, stay out of this. It's too dangerous to—"

"No!" The force in Milly's voice surprised both men. "She's my daughter, too, Alfred. Just tell him."

Garrison looked at his wife with fury in his eyes, but a second later it was gone. His shoulders slumped, face bleak with despair, and Carson knew he was looking at a man at the end of his rope.

"Tell me what you and Memphis discussed," Carson said calmly. "I'm not one of Pike's men. I'm not one of McGraw's either. It's a long story, but I'm just somebody that happened along, and I want to help. I'm no friend of McGraw's, if that puts you at ease."

Garrison rubbed his eyes. He suddenly seemed so tired, like he might fall over any minute.

"Just tell him," Milly said more gently.

"Jimmy Bachman was here to make sure everything's on track," Garrison said. "I assured him I was doing my part and keeping my mouth shut. I'm supposed to open the back door from the inside and make sure there are no bank employees in the way. What happens after that, I don't know. You don't think it occurred to me to go to the marshal? Of course it did. He could have men waiting at the back door for McGraw. Set a trap for them. But then McGraw would know, wouldn't he? He shows up to the back door of the bank and finds a pack of deputies pointing guns at him, he's going to know I opened my mouth, and then where does that leave my Emily?"

Carson rubbed the back of his neck, thinking hard. He tried to view the situation like a father. There were no guarantees, not for the girl. If Garrison blabbed to the marshal, they could set the best trap possible, but there was still always the chance McGraw could squirm out of it, and then that would be all she wrote for the banker's daughter.

"I put the word around that Emily was visiting her aunt in Springfield," Garrison said. "Since then, I've been cooperating with McGraw, passing messages through this Memphis fellow, and keeping my mouth shut around everyone else. The last thing he told me was that McGraw and his outlaws were holed up in a secret spot just outside of town, ready to strike on a moment's notice. Don't ask me where because I wasn't told. All I know is I can't say or do anything that will risk harming Emily. I won't."

Carson could see the man was at his breaking point, and the last thing he wanted to do was push the banker over the edge, but if ever there was a time for the blunt truth, it was now.

"If you do nothing, Mr. Garrison, you're trusting Big Bob McGraw to keep his word he'll let Emily go when all of this is over," Carson explained. "And Big Bob is the meanest, sneakiest, least trustworthy man I've ever known. The only thing you can trust Bob McGraw to do is what's good for Bob McGraw. If you tell the marshal, gin up some kind of plan, then at least you've got a chance."

Garrison turned away, shaking his head and dabbing sweat behind his ears with the handkerchief. "I don't know. I just don't know. Every choice seems bad."

"What would *you* do?" Milly asked.

"That's a hard question, ma'am," Carson admitted. "I never had a daughter and wouldn't presume to know what you're feeling right now. Let's try this. You both stay here. Stay out of sight. Just wait. Let me poke around and try to figure something out. Don't worry, I won't go to Marshal Pike. I think it's the right thing to do, but it's your daughter we're talking about, so it's your call. I'll find out what I can and get back here fast."

Milly thought about it for a moment, then nodded. "All right."

Carson turned to leave, putting his hat on again and then opening the door. "I'll try to get back here as fast as I can."

"Wait!" Garrison rushed forward, grabbing Carson's arm to stop him. "Who are you? How are you involved in all this? I don't even know your name."

"Telling you my name wouldn't do either of us any good, Mr. Garrison." Carson was a wanted man, so as far as he was concerned, the fewer who knew his name the better. "All you need to know is that I'm mixed up with McGraw in a bad way, just like you are. Maybe helping you will help me, too. I don't know. But if it hurts McGraw and saves an innocent girl, I'm for it. Now stay here with your wife. Give each other your strength and try to have hope. And if you're the praying kind, that wouldn't hurt either."

Kat didn't find Carson in his room but didn't think much of it. The man had a decent amount of money in his pocket for the first time since . . . well, Kat didn't exactly know. Maybe for the first time ever. He was probably still shopping.

She hoped to God he was buying pants.

She walked down Fayetteville's main street, keeping an eye out for him with no luck. She ate a late lunch, then went into a general store to pick up a few items, including another box of cartridges for the Spencer rifle and a bottle of whisky. As she paid for the items, something caught her attention on the shelf behind the clerk.

"What are those?" Kat asked.

The clerk turned to look where she was pointing. "Ah, the field glasses. Yes, those came in with a shipment last week. The same kind used by our brave cavalry officers." He explained the working of them.

Kat held out a hand. "Let me try."

The clerk handed her the field glasses, and she left her other items on the counter and headed out of the front of the store, where she stood looking through them up and down the street. She was surprised at how well they worked, bringing in clear images of men and women three or four blocks away.

She went back inside. "How much?"

The clerk told her.

Kat laughed.

They dickered for a few minutes, and then Kat left with the field glasses and her other items.

Back at her hotel, she took the stairs up to the roof and found a good spot behind the "H" in the sign that said "HOTEL." She was three stories up and had a good view of the bank's front doors down and to the left. She checked the Spencer's load and leaned it within easy reach. She opened the whisky, took a healthy slug, then set it on the other side, also within easy reach. She looked at Fayetteville through the field glasses, the streets beyond the bank and the other rooftops.

Okay, bank robbers, show me what you've got.

CHAPTER 25

When it came to waking up before the sun, the outlaws were apparently just as obsessed about it as Carson. Gordon McGraw shook Colby Tate awake at an ungodly hour and announced they were leaving. Wake up, saddle up, and hurry up, no coffee, not even time to stumble to the nearby creek to splash water on his face.

They'd given him beans and cabbage and potatoes the night before. Nothing gourmet, but it had filled his belly.

What they hadn't given him were his guns. And he wouldn't get them until Big Bob decided Tate wasn't a threat.

And when will that happen? I've been without my Peacemakers for one night and I've never felt so helpless in my life.

A function of coming West, he supposed. Tate had never felt the need to carry a gun crossing Harvard Yard. It was different out here; it had to be different, because a man had to look after himself to a certain extent. Yes, there were sheriffs and marshals and the US Cavalry, but the West wouldn't need bounty hunters like Colby Tate if those things were enough to keep men and women safe on the frontier. Mountain lions, rattlesnakes, red Indians, a hundred different things that could snuff out a life that men and women might not give a moment's thought to sipping tea or a gin and tonic at the club back East.

Plenty of good reasons a man—or a woman, for that matter—got used to the feel of a Colt on his hip.

And outlaws, of course. Don't forget the outlaws. As he'd moved among them, striking up casual conversations, he'd made a careful count. Fourteen. Fifteen if you counted the man who was off running errands, one of which was to get the dirt on Tate. Fifteen armed killers. Quite a little army for Big Bob McGraw.

They rode past dawn and into the afternoon, stopping briefly to rest the horses and choke down some salted jerky for lunch. They were getting close to Fayetteville, and Big Bob called a halt on a hill just a few miles outside of town. They were looking down into farm country, small houses within shouting distance of one another, men and women out working the fields.

"Freddy, get down there and make sure it's clear," Bob said. "Wave your hat if we should come on down."

Tate watched the man called Freddy ride away toward the farmhouses. In a minute, it became clear he was veering off toward one place in particular, a little white cottage a bit off to the side from the rest of the houses. A small barn, and a corral with some of the fence missing. It was the only place that looked like nobody was working the fields.

Tate nudged his horse alongside Gordon's. "What is this place?"

"Good place close to Fayetteville," Gordon said. "Close to the bank. Old couple died of influenza a few years back, so it's abandoned. We got a couple of guys down there, but Bob's making sure. He's careful. That's how he's stayed out of the clink so long."

Tate watched Freddy dismount in front of the cottage and go inside. Tate counted to twenty waiting for Freddy to come out again. He did come out a second later and waved his hat.

"Okay, then." Bob raised his voice for all to hear. "The long way around behind that tree line to the north. Might hide us from a few curious eyes, although we won't be here that long. Let's go."

They came up on the cottage from the other side, Bob barking orders to the men. "Gordon, you're with me. You too, Tate. The rest of you get your horses out of sight into the barn. Make sure they're fed and watered."

Tate handed his horse off to one of the others and followed the McGraw brothers into the cottage. The outside looked like it could use a new coat of paint, and weeds had grown up high all along the edges. Gordon had said the place was abandoned, and it looked it.

The interior was a different story. The place had been swept clean, and the aroma of coffee brewing somewhere struck Tate immediately.

"The place is too small for all of us," Gordon said. "Front room, kitchen, bedroom. That's it. Most of the boys will have to get comfortable in the barn."

"To what do I owe the honor of being among the select few?" Tate asked.

"We're about to find out what to do with you," Bob said. "You can decide after if it's an honor or not. Memphis? Where you at?"

Tate was barely able to contain his surprise at the word "Memphis." As far as the McGraws were concerned, Tate didn't know any of these men. If any recognition showed on his face, it could give the whole game away, but there was no doubt McGraw had just called out to Jimmy Bachman. Carson had been clear that the man's nickname was Memphis.

A bearded man holding a coffeepot in one hand entered the room. Tate tried to match what he was seeing with the face on Bachman's wanted poster. The beard was new. Something in the eyes was familiar, but all in all, Tate didn't find the man standing in front of him recognizable. Tate wondered how often the wrong man was shot because of a poor likeness on a wanted poster.

"Anyone want coffee? I put it on after Freddy got here. Figured the rest of you would be along." Memphis's eyes slid to Tate. "That him?"

"That's him," Bob said. "What did you find out?"

"Our guy says he's not a lawman," Memphis said. "Leastways not one he knows."

A grunt from Gordon, halfway between surprise and relief. "I guess he's clean, then."

"I didn't say that," Memphis said. "Our man on the inside told me he never heard of the guy. That could mean anything. But he did say the marshal wasn't trying to sneak anyone in on us."

Tate raised an eyebrow. "Sneak someone in?"

"The marshal's tried it before," Bob said. "Wanted to get one of his men into our gang, find out what we were up to. When you came along, we thought he might be trying it again. Go ahead and bring us coffee, Memphis. Gordon, go get his shooting irons out of my saddlebags."

Gordon grunted and left the cottage. Memphis went back to the kitchen.

"I take it I've passed the test," Tate said.

"You're not a deputy marshal sent to spy on us," Bob said. "That's good enough for now, but let's say you should probably keep earning our trust as you go."

"And what's the best way to accomplish that?"

"To do just exactly whatever I tell you to do at the exact moment I tell you to do it."

"Sounds simple enough."

Gordon and Memphis both returned at the same time. Memphis set clean coffee mugs on the table and filled them from the pot. Gordon gave back Tate's gun belt.

Tate checked the load of each pistol, then strapped on the belt. It saddened him in an odd way how much of a relief it was to have the guns back. In a short time, they'd become a part of who he was. Mostly he just felt glad he no longer had some itch he couldn't scratch. He sipped coffee and waited for the McGraw brothers to tell him what happened next.

Gordon and Memphis pulled chairs up to the table. The four of them sat for a minute, not talking, sipping the coffee.

Finally, Bob asked, "What are the rest of the boys doing?"

"They won't bother us," Gordon said.

"He as fast as you were saying?" Bob asked.

"I reckon so," Gordon said. "He took care of Mooney with no trouble. Mooney reached for his gun and those Peacemakers were in Tate's hands almost too fast to see. Wasn't even a contest."

"Okay, then." Bob turned to Tate. "We're going in two groups. You'll be in my group. Your job is protection. Anyone tries to stop us or shoot us, it's your job to draw first. My group is me and you and him and him." He pointed at Gordon and then Memphis to emphasize his meaning. "Protection. That's your whole job."

"What about the other group?" Tate asked.

"Never mind the other group."

"What's our group supposed to do?"

"That will become clear as we go along," Bob said. "You know everything you need to know to do your job."

Tate shrugged. "I was simply curious."

"Well, keep that curiosity to yourself."

Tate held up a placating hand. "All questions cheerfully withdrawn."

"Okay, then, this is how we do it." Bob's demeanor was businesslike. "Tell the boys to give us a head start so we can get into place. Tell Jones to hook up the wagon."

"He's already doing it," Gordon said.

"Good. Tate, you're on the wagon with Memphis. Gordon and I will ride escort."

Tate didn't know what the wagon was for, but he didn't like the idea of not being on his own horse. There was always the possibility he might need a quick getaway. "I could probably cover you better if I were mounted."

"What did I tell you about how this was going to go?"

"Do exactly as you say," Tate said.

"Keep saying that to yourself until it sticks."

Tate nodded. "I'm on the wagon with Memphis."

Bob grinned. "The man can be taught."

"And our inside guy will clear the way for us?" Gordon asked.

"He knows what side his bread is buttered on," Memphis said. "We went over it a dozen times."

Bob scratched behind one ear. "And our guest?"

"Behaving," Memphis said. "Finally stopped her snivelin'."

Guest? Tate wanted to ask, but he'd been specifically ordered to curtail his curiosity.

"Best make sure," Bob said. "I don't want her trying to sneak off. Last thing I need is a problem from some brat. Get her out here."

"Okay." Memphis stood and left the room.

When he returned, he had a young woman in tow, no more than a girl, really. She was freckled and pretty, with long, brown hair in a ponytail down her back. Her eyes were blue but also red from crying. She had a hollow look, as if she'd been very frightened but was now too fatigued to feel fear anymore. Her wrists were tied together with thin rope that Memphis used as a handle to drag her along.

"How are you doing, girl?" Bob asked. "You're okay? Unhurt?"

Her eyes went to each man at the table.

Bob frowned. "I'm talking to you, girl. Answer my question."

"I'm okay, sir," she said.

Bob nodded, pleased with the answer. "See, we told you, didn't we? Mind your manners and no harm will come to you. Try to escape or get up to some other mischief and that can all change. I told your old man that he'd get you back in one piece if he cooperated. But there are many unpleasant things that can happen to you between now and then. All kinds of nastiness that can go on and on and on until death would be a welcome relief."

The girl blanched.

"But if you act right and have good manners and do as you're told, there's no reason anything bad has to happen at all," Bob assured her. "Do we understand each other?"

"Yes, sir."

"Good girl." Bob looked at Memphis and winked. "This is a well-bred young lady. She won't cause you any headaches."

Memphis took her away.

"Who was that?" The question was out of Tate's mouth before he remembered he wasn't supposed to be asking.

Bob McGraw didn't seem to mind. "Leverage. Just a little something to make sure the back door of that bank opens like it's supposed to."

CHAPTER 26

Carson couldn't find Kat anywhere. The only place he hadn't looked was the marshal's office, and he wasn't about to show his face somewhere they might grab him and toss him in a cell.

The afternoon was growing late. Whatever was going to happen, he'd need to do it himself. Kat had probably found a safe spot to watch the show, and he hadn't seen Colby Tate in days. He hoped the other bounty hunter was safe. It occurred to Carson—not for the first time—that it might have been a mistake to split up. There'd been a lot of ground to cover, so at the time it had seemed like a good idea.

But now Carson was alone. Bank robbers on the way, a young girl's life at stake, and nobody to back him up.

There's no point crying about it. Time to figure out how I'm going to handle this and get to work.

He went to his room to gather his things, shoving items into his saddlebags, trying not to wrinkle his new shirts. He glanced out the window, wondering if he'd be able to spot the marshal's men getting into position. A dozen different thoughts spun in his mind at once. He couldn't warn the marshal without putting himself at risk. Carson wouldn't be able to help anyone from the inside of a jail cell. Unless the marshal's men were the sort to shoot first and ask questions later, in which case Carson wouldn't even make it as far as a cell. He couldn't see any of the marshal's men—not that he'd necessarily recognize them anyway—getting into position, but he did see a man walking into the bank, dabbing at his bald head with a handkerchief.

Garrison!

Damn it, I told him to stay put.

But of course, why should the banker listen to Carson? The man's daughter was in peril and Carson was a stranger. Naturally, the man would feel compelled to do something, and going through with McGraw's plan was his most likely course of action. Garrison was a civilized man and would think cooperation the key to saving his daughter. The problem was that Garrison didn't know McGraw. Civilization meant nothing to a man who earned his living by flouting law and order.

He's going to open the bank's back door and let McGraw waltz right in, but not if I get there first.

Carson tossed his saddlebags over his shoulder and left in a hurry. At the stable, he saddled Jet and then rode the long way around to the back of the bank. There was a cooper and a leatherworker across from the bank's back door. Both looked closed, suiting Carson's purpose. He tied Jet behind a big stack of barrels. There was a gap between two barrels where he could spy on the back door without being seen.

All Carson had were guesses. This wasn't going to be a normal bank robbery, where McGraw and his boys stormed through the front door and stuck guns into the faces of the tellers, demanding they fill sacks with money. McGraw was crafty, and he knew somehow the marshal wasn't going to make it easy. So he'd grabbed the banker's daughter and planned to use the back door.

But there had to be more to it.

The front door. He's going to send men through the front, make it look like a normal holdup. All that shooting will cause one hell of a distraction, while McGraw slinks away with the payroll.

More guesses, but Carson couldn't figure it any other way.

He kept watch, not sure what exactly he planned to do. Would Carson step out of his hiding place when McGraw showed up and challenge Big Bob to a gunfight? That seemed like a pretty stupid idea.

But he had to do something. There was a girl's life at stake, and Carson's innocence to prove.

A moment later, two men came around the corner of the bank, each carrying a rifle. Carson watched them take positions on either side of the back door. A tin star hung from each man's vest.

Good, the marshal's not an idiot. Obviously, he'd send men to guard the back door.

Just two? It didn't seem right. Something was definitely wrong here.

But all Carson could do was watch and wait.

Kat took a slug of whisky and blew out a long sigh. Every minute that ticked closer to the payroll's arrival put her nerves on edge just a bit more. From her place on the roof, she'd probably be safe, but the anticipation made her jittery.

She took another hit of whisky, but a small one. It helped her nerves, but if she went overboard, she wouldn't be able to shoot straight. This wasn't the sort of thing Kat was used to, sitting and waiting for all hell to break loose.

The marshal had told her the payroll wagon with its Pinkerton escort would be coming from the east. She put her field glasses to her eyes and turned in that direction. Nothing yet.

She scanned the street below her, especially the area directly across from the bank. The marshal's men were being discreet, but they weren't too difficult to spot. Men casually strolling up and down the sidewalk across the street but constantly glancing toward the bank. Others loading a wagon with furniture, but rifles hidden close by under a tarp. Kat had watched them set up the ruse earlier. Obviously, none of them wore badges, but they were all either the marshal's men or the sheriff's. Some of the volunteers had been tasked with clearing civilians out of harm's way in the most discreet way possible.

Kat scanned other streets two and three blocks away, but nothing struck her as significant. She put the field glasses down and sipped whisky.

A few minutes passed. She sensed it, feeling the vibration in her bones before she actually heard anything, but a moment later it was clear, a low rumble that grew steadily. She swung the field glasses east again and saw the dust cloud first. Figures took shape in the cloud, men riding fast horses, the big, boxy silhouette of the armored wagon beyond.

Kat sighed and took one last swig of whisky. *And here come the Pinkertons, right on time.*

Since McGraw had put the fear of God into the banker's daughter, he figured leaving one man to guard her would suffice. He'd sent for a man called Old Tom to watch the girl while the rest of them handled the bank job.

Tate sized the man up the moment he entered the little cottage. Old Tom had gray hair and a gray beard and a half-dozen teeth missing from a sly grin. In his early sixties, Tate guessed. For a man to last that long as an outlaw, Tom must have been mean or clever or probably both.

And never underestimate the benefit of pure dumb luck, Tate mused.

Tate took an immediate dislike to the man. Not that he'd especially warmed up to any of the other outlaws, but there was something just a little uglier and a little seedier about Old Tom.

"Don't you worry about that pretty little thing." Tom's leer was oilier than a card sharp's hair. "I'll take mighty good care of her."

Two minutes later, Tate found himself sitting next to Gordon on the bench of a buckboard wagon, heading into town. Memphis rode a splotchy mare out front, and Big Bob brought up the rear on an enormous black stallion with a single white streak down its nose. They circled Fayetteville to come in on the north side, trotting long side streets. Memphis seemed to know where he was leading them. Nobody talked.

Memphis abruptly called a halt between two buildings and came back toward the buckboard. Bob came from behind to join them.

"That it?" Bob lifted his chin to indicated something down the street.

Memphis nodded. "Across from the cooper."

"Them two by the door are deputies?"

"Yep."

Tate looked. Two men with rifles. He wasn't close enough to see badges, but if Memphis said they were deputies, Tate had no reason to doubt it.

Bob took out his pocket watch, squinted at it, and blew out a tired sigh through his nose. "Should start getting loud pretty soon."

Tate realized the robbery was about to get underway. His eyes darted to each of the three men with him.

Tate cleared his throat. "What do we do in the meantime?"

Bob clapped the watch closed and returned it to his vest pocket, frowning. "Just can't help asking questions, can you? We wait is what we do. Now do it quiet."

When the armored wagon got close enough, she put down the field glasses and pulled the Spencer rifle into her lap. It was finally happening. This was the start of it. Kat was nervous and excited and wished it wasn't happening but also wished it would hurry up and happen all at the same time. She wiped her sweaty palms on her pants.

People cleared the streets as wagon and riders thundered along Fayetteville's main avenue, coming to an abrupt halt in a cloud of dust right in front of the bank. Men yelled instructions and others obeyed. Twenty Pinkertons in smart but dusty striped suits dismounted, rifles ready, and formed an outward-facing perimeter. Dour men who meant business.

The front doors of the bank opened, and a chubby man in a clerk's outfit emerged, followed by the four bank guards with shotguns. They formed a line behind him. People all along the street had stopped to watch.

Somebody from the wagon handed a piece of paper to the chubby clerk, who read it and signed it. That was the signal to unload the wagon at lighting speed. Men carried heavy canvas bags from the wagon into the bank double time. The contents of the bags must have been heavy because the men walked with a stoop, red-faced.

Kat picked up the field glasses and swept the area again, but there was no sign of McGraw's gang, or at least not anyone who looked like an outlaw. She didn't know what they all looked like obviously, but nobody stood out as looking especially like a bank robber.

Ugh, what the hell am I doing up here? They might not even show at all. There's a ton of Pinkertons out there, enough to give a man pause. Bob might have gotten cold feet.

No, she realized, a man like McGraw wouldn't scare that easy. If he suspected something wasn't right, he might postpone it until later. McGraw wouldn't get scared, but he was shrewd and probably knew a bad bet when he saw one. This was no ordinary bank job, and Bob might possibly have decided it wasn't worth the risk.

The thought was a relief and a disappointment all at once.

And in the next moment it was done. The payroll had been

transferred from wagon to bank. The Pinkertons mounted up and rode out, like a storm that had blustered through, leaving everything still and quiet afterward.

The chubby clerk nodded to the guards, then went into the bank. They filed in after him one at a time.

A man approached, coat thrown over his arm. He looked like he was in a hurry to make it into the bank. The final guard saw him coming and held up a hand to forestall him. Kat couldn't hear their conversation at this distance, but she could imagine what the guard was saying. *Sorry, sir, the bank is closed. Try again in the morning.*

The other man stepped in close, standing right up against the guard. The guard went rigid, alarm briefly crossing his face, but the man with the coat said something, and the guard's cool demeanor resumed.

This is it, Kat realized. *McGraw picked his man well.*

The fellow with the coat over his arm wore a brown suit with a string tie. A bland, inoffensive face. He was short. He looked like nothing more than a harmless merchant trying to do his banking before the place closed.

Kat knew better. The coat over the man's arm hid the revolver in his fist. He'd follow the guard in, looking like an ordinary customer, and then he'd prevent them from locking the door on the inside.

That's when McGraw sends in his men.

She scanned the street with the field glasses again, looking for a target. There were men, walking in both directions, and any or all of them might be in McGraw's gang. She didn't recognize any faces from wanted posters.

Come on, show me Big Bob or Gordon, or even Jimmy Bachman. Give me something to shoot at.

Kat wasn't going to wait. The money on the McGraws was too good to risk letting them get away. She'd take her shot with the Spencer if she spotted one of them.

But a second later, other men began to file into the bank,

walking in one or two at a time, casting furtive glances behind them, obviously tense and anxious. The marshal and his men had surely seen them enter. They'd be getting into position. The bank guards were supposed to be in on the whole thing and had been ordered not to resist. Right now, tellers would be doing what they were told.

Right on cue, men drove three wagons into the street. Deputies took up positions behind the wagons, a dozen rifles pointed at the bank's front door. The last of the civilians were ushered out of harm's way.

When the robbers emerged from the bank, they'd be given one chance to throw down their guns. If they didn't, there was going to be a lot of shooting.

Kat's money was on a lot of shooting.

She waited. Then waited some more. Maybe she'd been wrong about how this was going to go. She scanned the area with the field glasses again but didn't see anything that might mean—

The bank door flew open and the outlaws poured out, stopping short when they saw the line of deputies crouched behind the wagons.

Marshal Pike's voice rose above the entire scene. "You got twenty rifles pointed at you, boys. You got one chance. Throw down them guns. This can happen quiet and peaceful, or this can happen bloody."

The most pregnant of pauses.

Kat didn't see who drew first, but in the next instant, the outlaws blazed away at the deputies behind the wagons. Wood splintered and flew. Most of the deputies were behind cover, but one spun away, blood trailing, a bright red hole in his forehead.

The deputies returned fire, a storm of lead slamming into the bank robbers. Some ran to the left or tried to flee right. Others tried to back up into the bank again. Hot slugs tore into them. Men twitched and died, screaming and clutching bloody wounds.

The earsplitting racket of gunfire seemed to go on forever. The steps in front of the bank became slick with outlaw blood.

Kat reached for the whisky bottle. *Well, that's one hell of a show.*

CHAPTER 27

Carson watched the deputies guarding the bank's back door for a few minutes when another deputy rounded the corner to join them.

Good, Carson thought. *Three guards still seems kind of light to me, but every little bit helps. I should warn them. No telling how many men Big Bob will have with him when he shows up.*

But he didn't warn them. Carson stayed in hiding, watching and second-guessing himself. If he went out to warn them, they'd want to know who he was and where he got his information. He wasn't ready to reveal himself. Not yet.

The new deputy was a lean type with a splotchy scarlet birthmark below his left eye. He pulled tobacco and papers from his pocket and rolled a cigarette. He said something, and one of the other deputies set aside his rifle. Then he lit a match for the other man's cigarette.

The sudden, sharp crack of gunfire erupting on the next street made Carson flinch, dozens of shots like all Hell was breaking loose.

The deputy with the birthmark didn't hesitate. He drew his six-shooter and shot the man who'd lit his cigarette. The deputy fell back against the wall and slid into a sitting position, a bloody wound in his chest.

The other deputy tried to bring his rifle around, but it was too late. The one with the birthmark turned his six-shooter on the man and shot twice. The deputy spun away and hit the ground with a thud.

Carson's eyes shot wide, his hand falling to his Peacemaker on pure reflex. The gunfire on the next street redoubled its intensity.

Before Carson could decide what to do, the thundering sound of pounding hooves rumbled through the street. A wagon rolled into view, the man driving it yanking on the reins, the horses stomping to a halt, snorting, heads tossing.

The man driving the wagon was Gordon McGraw.

Two more men rode up, abruptly dismounting from their horses. Jimmy Bachman was one of them and the other was—

Carson's eyes narrowed.

Big Bob McGraw.

Carson drew his six-shooter. He didn't care if he were outnumbered. All Carson knew was that the man he'd been looking for was now right in front of him. He thumbed back the hammer of his Colt and stepped out of his hiding place, face hard, eyes blazing hate.

He'd been so focused on McGraw, he hadn't realized until the last moment that he recognized the man in the wagon with Gordon.

Colby Tate had joined the outlaws.

They heard the rapid pops of gunfire a block away, and then the one smoking the cigarette shot the two deputies. Tate's pistols appeared in his hands too fast for the human eye to follow, head turning in every direction in case some attack was coming.

"Easy," Gordon said next to him. "He's one of ours."

Tate realized he'd meant the man with the cigarette, who was now waving them on.

Gordon snapped the whip, and the buckboard lurched forward. Hooves hammered down the street, and Gordon jerked the reins when they were even with the bank's back door. Memphis and Bob dismounted, and Bob hammered a fist on the back door and waited.

The intense gun battle continued in the front of the bank. Tate realized the rest of Bob's gang was in the process of getting themselves slaughtered.

It's what he intended all along. Bob's using his men as cannon fodder. Split the money how many ways?

Tate's gaze shifted to the dead men on either side of the door. Dead deputies.

You fool. You think you're so clever, infiltrating McGraw's gang, but you sat there and watched two lawmen get murdered.

"Keep your eyes open," Bob snapped. "You're supposed to be watching our backs."

"Right." Tate spun, guns up and ready. The street was clear, but then, out of nowhere, a man stepped out from behind a stack of barrels, a gun in his hand. Tate swung his revolvers toward—

Hellfire! It's Carson!

Carson walked straight toward Tate, raising his Peacemaker.

Don't.

Tate lowered his own pistols, leaving himself defenseless, and quickly shook his head. *This isn't what you think.* Tate glanced at the other men. They were all facing the back door of the bank, Bob pounding on it again and hollering for someone to open up, but that wouldn't last long. Any second, they'd turn and see Carson.

Tate frowned and waved him away. *Hide, you imbecile.*

Confusion for a moment, and then Carson seemed to understand. He nodded once, then ducked back behind the barrels.

Just as Bob turned around. "You see anyone?"

"All clear," Tate said.

The door opened, and a pale, terrified-looking man stood there dabbing at his sweating bald head with a handkerchief.

"About damn time," Bob barked. In the background, the gunshots were already beginning to die down. "We don't have a lot of time. Tate, you cover us. We're going to do this fast."

Memphis, Gordon, Bob, and the deputy with the scarlet birthmark went in and out of the bank, lugging the payroll in canvas bags, the nervous banker watching the whole time. The gunfire had dwindled to almost nothing by the time they finished.

"You know how this works. I don't turn her loose until we get away clean," Bob told him. "I see a posse and she's good as dead."

"Please. I'm cooperating," the banker assured him.

"Get back inside, then," Bob said. "And just remember, you don't know my face."

The banker scurried through the door and shut it behind him.

Bob turned to the man with the birthmark. "What're you going to tell them?"

"I came to check on my deputies when you came along with a dozen men. I barely escaped with my life."

Bob scratched his chin. "I don't know. Seems thin. Probably more believable if you'd gotten killed, too."

Bob drew. He was fast. Tate could see that now. The man with the birthmark didn't even have time to look surprised before Bob squeezed the trigger, and the pistol bucked in his hand. The slug caught the man square in the chest and sent him staggering three steps back before he dropped.

"Now let's get our asses out of here!" Bob shouted.

Two seconds later, they were all riding back the way they'd come, Gordon whipping the buckboard team like he was trying to outrun the devil himself.

Tate hung on for dear life but glanced once over his shoulder.

Carson followed on that black horse of his, but not too closely.

Good man, Tate thought. *Keep up, but keep your distance. Don't let them see you.*

Big Bob McGraw had let the bulk of his gang get gunned down, and Tate didn't want to be next.

Hurry along, Carson, old boy. Don't make me take on these fellows all by myself.

One of the outlaws crawled between bodies on his belly, bleeding from a half-dozen holes. He spit curses at the deputies behind the wagons and lifted his pistol.

Ten rifles belched fire, and the outlaw sprouted a bunch of new holes, blood spraying. He went facedown and stayed that way.

Kat chuckled and drank whisky. *He was game for it. I'll give him that.*

It had been one loud, bloody show, that was for sure. Some of the robbers had retreated to the interior of the bank, where they'd returned fire for a while, but the marshal told them to give it up. They'd come out, hands up, pretending to surrender, and then suddenly darted in multiple directions. Kat thought some of them might have made it, but most had gone down in a blaze of rifle fire.

Smoke hung in the air along the street. Everything was suddenly strangely quiet. The marshal called out to see if anyone was left, but the bank guards came through the door, saying there weren't any more outlaws inside, and that was the end of it.

Except where the hell was Big Bob McGraw?

Kat looked up and down the street again with the field glasses. People came out of shops now to gawk. The danger was over, and they wanted to see the corpses. Pike's men were keeping people back. They'd be talking about this in Fayetteville for a long time.

She cast her gaze farther afield, sweeping the streets beyond the main avenue, but nothing was—

Movement caught her eye, darting between buildings, a buckboard tearing through the town hell-bent for leather, and a pair of men on horses riding escort. The field glasses brought them in close. The man on the lead horse might have been Big Bob McGraw. Even with the field glasses, she couldn't be sure. She'd only ever seen the man's likeness on a wanted poster. The man driving the buckboard might have been his brother. Sitting next to him . . .

Colby Tate?

What the hell?

He, at least, was a man she'd seen in person, and there was no mistaking it was him, especially when he turned to glance over his shoulder, giving Kat a perfect view of his face. She swung the field glasses back to see what he might have been looking at.

At first, she didn't see anything, but then a streak of black caught her eye, just a glimpse between buildings. She trailed after with the field glasses, hoping for another look, and a second later, she saw him: Carson Stone, following after Tate and the outlaws on that black horse of his.

Kat grabbed the Spencer rifle and bolted from the roof, taking the stairs two at a time on the way down. She needed to get to her horse as fast as possible and get after them.

If Carson Stone and Colby Tate think they can take off with my bounties, they're stupider than I thought.

CHAPTER 28

They rode like the wind up the dirt lane to the cottage, and Gordon reined in the team, the buckboard sliding to a halt. He and Tate jumped down, just as Bob and Memphis rode up.

Tate looked back the way they'd come but didn't see any sign of Carson. *I hope he's just being careful. I hope we didn't lose him.*

Memphis and Bob tied their horses to the back of the buckboard.

"Memphis, get the wagon and the horses out of sight in the barn," Bob told him. "We're not going to be here any longer than necessary, but I don't want to risk getting seen."

Memphis took the buckboard and horses away, and Tate and Gordon followed Bob into the cottage.

Now. Do it now, Tate thought.

Bob was fairly fast with a gun. Tate had seen it. But if Tate made his move now, he'd catch them by surprise. Memphis would hear the shots and come running, but it would be over by then, and Tate could handle Memphis all by himself with no trouble. This would likely be Tate's best chance. He could end it right now. His hands moved casually to the hilts of his revolvers.

Old Tom burst in from the other room, his hand on his gun, a mean look on his face.

Tate hesitated.

"What's crawled up your rear end?" Bob asked Tom.

"I heard somebody come in." Tom moved his hand away from his six-shooter. "Just needed to be sure it was friendlies."

"It's us, if that's what you mean," Bob said. "Where's the girl?"

"In bed. Cried herself to sleep."

I can take all three, Tate thought. *I still have the surprise.*
Tate tensed, ready to draw.

Memphis rushed in through the front door.

"Didn't I tell you to get them horses hidden in the barn?" Bob said irritably.

"Riders coming," Memphis announced.

Damn. Four now, with Memphis. Four was too many, especially with Bob being so fast. Tate blew out a sigh and made his muscles go loose. *Relax. Not yet.*

Gordon went to the window. "Who is it?"

"Too far to see," Memphis said. "But they looked like they was coming straight this way."

"I see them." Gordon squinted through the window, watching them come. "They're closer now. Yeah, it's Joe Billings and a few of the boys. Looks like four in all."

Tate remembered that Joe Billings was the name of the man who'd joked about Ben Mooney owing him five dollars.

"Tom, get out there and wait for them," Bob said. "Let them know we're in here."

Tom frowned. "Hell, they can figure that out for themselves, can't they?"

"You done just said yourself you didn't know if we was friendlies or not when we came in the cottage," Bob said heatedly. "Now get your ass out there and do what I tell you."

"Fine, fine. You don't need to get nasty about it." Tom left, slamming the door behind him.

Gordon, Bob, and Memphis turned to Tate.

Tate met their gaze and waited.

"They'll be here in a minute," Bob said. "You know why I let you into this gang?"

"Because I'm a fast gun," Tate said. "So I could watch your back when we hit the bank."

"That's right. That's part of it," Bob said. "But there's more. I sized you up as a smart man, so let's see how smart you really are. Why do you think I sent the rest of the boys in the front door, when you and me and Gordon and Memphis went around back?"

Tate knew but paused anyway, like he needed a second to think it over. "Because you needed a diversion. And the best diversion was all those fellows getting themselves shot into a hundred pieces."

Bob nodded. "Exactly so. And if you can figure that out, I have to allow the chance that they've figured it out, too."

"In which case they might not be in the best of moods when they arrive," Tate said.

"Which is why I want a fast gun such as yourself standing with me when that happens," Bob said.

"Furthermore," Tate continued, "that's a lot of men who won't be taking their share of the payroll."

Bob grinned. "I like a four-way split better."

Tate let his face go blank, and he looked Bob square in the eye. "I'm concerned you might find a three-way split even more appealing."

"Now, I said you was smart," Bob reminded him. "But don't get *too* smart. There's four men coming up the lane. Four shares. Five shares, if you throw Old Tom into the bargain. It's worth paying you one share not to pay out five to them. You're a fast gun, so you're a bad risk to double-cross. I'm greedy, but I'm reasonable."

Tate thought it over, wondered how a hardened outlaw would reply to Big Bob. "That math works fine for me, but let's all go easy around one another. There's no sense pushing trust too far."

"Then we have an understanding."

"They're here," Gordon said, still standing at the window. "Tom's talking to them now."

"How do they look?" Memphis asked.

"Pissed," Gordon said. "Harry Reubens looks all shot to hell."

"Get back from that window," Bob said. "Memphis, move over there in the corner. We don't want to get in one another's line of fire, but we don't want to all stand in a line like we're waiting for them either."

"How do you want to do it?" Tate asked.

"Nothing until I move," Bob said. "Then you'll know what to do."

The next instant, they fell through the door, Joe Billings and another man carrying the shot-up Harry Reubens between them, panting and sweaty. They lurched across the room, dropping Reubens into the nearest chair at the small table. He grunted in pain, holding his bloody guts. His face was ashen, and it looked like he might pass out any second. Billings had a nasty red gash across the side of his neck where a rifle shot had scorched him.

Tom followed them in and shut the door behind him.

It was suddenly crowded in the little cottage's front room, and Tate's eyes went from man to man as he picked his targets, knowing what was about to happen.

"You want to tell me just what in the hell happened back there?" Billings shouted, face going red. "We barely got out of there with our lives. Most of the rest of the boys didn't. It was a damn slaughter."

"Keep a civil tongue in your head, Joe," Bob warned. "It was a bank robbery, not a church picnic. Risks are part of it. I guess they must have known we were coming."

"No shit, genius," Billings said. "I thought you had a deputy on the inside. Where was our warning?"

"Maybe he sold us out," Bob said.

"Somebody sure as hell sold somebody out." Billings's demeanor had suddenly gone cold. "And I can't help but notice you fellas don't have a scratch on you. Where's the payroll, Bob?"

Bob's eyes narrowed, and he matched Billings's cool demeanor. "You want to say something, say it straight out."

"You said it was a big bank robbery, biggest one you ever pulled, so you needed a lot of men to make it work," Billings said. "Needed us right up until you didn't need us no more. Pretty convenient for the few left. That's a lot of money for not too many fellas. Pretty nice for you and your brother and Memphis. And your pet gunslinger, I suppose."

"That does seem a bit suspicious," Tom said.

Billings scoffed. "You were watching the girl. You didn't get within a mile of that bank. Pretty easy money for you."

Tom scowled. "I just did what I was told."

"Enough bellyaching," Bob said. "What do you want?"

"I reckon we want our share of the payroll right now, and then we'll be on our way," Billings said.

"That's not how it works," Bob said.

Billings's face went hard. "That's how it works now."

Tate tensed some more, then saw Billings go tense. Reubens barely knew where he was and wouldn't be reaching for his six-shooter anytime soon, but the other two who'd arrived with Billings spread out a few feet from one another, hands hovering over guns. Even Old Tom looked like he was about to reach.

They'd all gone tight as wires. Tate held his breath.

Then Harry Reubens groaned. His eyes rolled back and he pitched forward, his head smacking the table with an earsplitting crack.

All eyes in the room went to Reubens.

Except for Big Bob McGraw's.

He drew and fired.

Joe Billings did his best to react, and even managed to get his gun halfway out of its holster. Too late.

McGraw's shot caught Billings in the face. Spinning his head around, one cheek exploding in blood and flesh and teeth flying out across the room. McGraw fired again, caught Billings in the chest and put him down.

The others were already going for their guns, but Tate was faster.

He drew his Colt right-handed, and with his left hand fanned the hammer, moving from right to left. He put two rounds into each of the men who'd arrived with Billings, thunder and smoke filling the small room, and the men went down twitching and clawing at their wounds.

Old Tom had drawn, too, but had simultaneously dashed for the front door, looking to get himself out of there.

Tate's first shot caught Tom in the hip, and he staggered back, screaming like a stuck pig. He slapped a hand over the wound, thick blood seeping red between his fingers. He brought his gun around, attempting to return fire.

Tate shot again, and a bloody red hole appeared in the center of Tom's forehead. His head went back, hat flying off, and then he fell with a thud.

Suddenly, the cottage was dead quiet, smoke hanging in the air, nobody moving. Memphis gawked at the scene with wide eyes. It had all happened so fast, he hadn't even drawn his six-shooter.

Gordon rushed to the window. "I don't see nobody else."

Tate returned his empty gun to its holster. The cottage smelled like gunpowder and blood and somebody's bowels that had let loose in the last moments of dying. Tate had shot men before, but this was a lot of death all at once in a very small space. He needed air. "Open that window if you don't mind."

Gordon unlatched the window and pushed it open.

Big Bob still had his revolver in his hand, and slowly, he turned it on Tate. "You know, I am sorta warming up to the idea of a three-way split after all."

CHAPTER 29

Carson held Jet's reins behind a tall, thick hedge that lined the dirt lane leading up to the cottage. He rubbed the horse's nose and whispered, "Easy, boy. Keep quiet."

Carson had hung back when he'd seen Tate and the others heading toward the farm with the small cottage. Carson wasn't sure what Tate's play was, but he might need Carson's help. The McGraw brothers were no laughing matter. On the other hand, blundering up there without getting the lay of the land first could prove lethal.

He'd been mulling it over when he'd heard the rumble of hooves coming up behind him. He'd pulled Jet behind the hedge and waited. They rode by fast. If they'd been looking for him, they probably would have spotted him, no problem, but in their hurry, they sped past, none the wiser. Carson watched them dismount and talk to another man who'd come out of the cottage. They spoke for a few seconds, then all went inside.

By my math, that's one Colby Tate against at least eight outlaws. Not good.

Like it or not, Carson was going to have to do something to help the man. The bounty hunter was fast, but going up against eight hardened outlaws was a tall order.

Carson scanned the terrain. There were enough bushes and

trees to provide cover from his spot behind the hedges to the cottage. He'd be briefly exposed as he darted from one hiding place to the next, but hopefully those inside would be too occupied to glance out a window. Anyway, it was a chance he'd have to take if he wanted to help Tate.

He tied Jet's reins to the hedge, took a last look around to make sure he wasn't missing anything, and then ran.

From behind the hedge to a tree, then to a large stump, then an overturned wheelbarrow. Carson squatted there, panting, glad nobody had shot at him. He screwed his courage up for one last sprint that would place him below one of the windows. He needed just a bit more luck and he could make it. He tensed to run and—

A sharp spatter of gunfire sent Carson to his belly behind the wheelbarrow. It only took a second to realize the shots weren't being fired at him, and in the next second he was up and running.

He reached the cottage just as the gunfire died away and threw himself on the ground, rolling up against the cottage under a window. He lay there, chest heaving as he gulped air, one hand on his gun as he listened for whatever happened next.

The window above him opened, and Carson held his breath.

"You know, I am sorta warming up to the idea of a three-way split." Unmistakably, Big Bob's voice, filled with that smug tone he always had when he was about to shoot somebody in cold blood.

Colby Tate had known all along he couldn't trust Big Bob McGraw, but he hadn't expected the betrayal to come so abruptly. His left hand twitched, yearning to go for his other six-shooter, but McGraw's gun was pointed right at Tate's face. He was fast, but he wasn't that fast.

Tate's eyes narrowed to white-hot pinpoints. "What happened to greedy but reasonable?"

"I guess greedy won out." Bob thumbed back the revolver's hammer.

A sudden, terrifying groan rose from Harry Reubens, who lifted his head from the table and drew his pistol, firing wildly every which way.

Everyone dove in a different direction, spouting curses and waving pistols.

Big Bob shifted his aim and fired, hitting Reubens between the eyes, his head going back and then the chair tipping over, crashing to the floor. Bob swung his six-shooter back toward Tate and fired twice.

But Tate had already thrown himself to the floor, the shots passing over his head.

Gordon and Memphis both drew their pistols at the same time. Gordon took aim at Tate.

And in the next instant, Carson Stone was right there, standing in the window. Carson brought the butt of his pistol down hard on Gordon's wrist. The man grunted and dropped his pistol. It clattered across the floor.

Memphis shifted his aim from Tate to Carson, but Carson shot first.

Memphis took the lead in the shoulder, squealing in pain and surprise, but he managed to hang on to his gun. He lifted it and fired.

Carson ducked out of the way, and the poorly aimed shot drilled a hole in the ceiling.

Big Bob ducked into the next room.

Memphis turned and fled through the front door, Gordon hot on his heels.

Now Tate was up again, his other Colt in his left hand, and at the same time, Bob emerged from the next room.

He held the banker's daughter in front of him like a shield, one big hand grabbing her by the neck, his six-shooter in the other.

Tate aimed his pistol at Bob's face. He could take the shot right now, put one right through Bob's left eye without hitting the girl.

Probably.

"Using an innocent young lady as a shield is far from chivalrous, Bob," Tate said.

"Then it's fortunate for me, I don't give a rat's ass about no damn chivalry." Bob pointed the pistol at the girl's head. "I'm going to walk out of here nice and easy. You're going to let me."

"I rather thought I'd shoot you instead," Tate told him. "You were going to do the same to me, after all."

"Not a chance. And risk hitting this pretty young thing?"

Tate tried to look callous. "She's nothing to me."

"Then you'd've shot already."

Tate shook his head. *Say what you want about Big Bob McGraw, he's a decent judge of a man. He knows I won't risk it.*

The girl looked terrified, eyes wide and red, tears leaking from each corner and streaming down her cheeks. Tate's mind raced for something to say that would both calm her and convince Bob not to do anything rash.

"Go easy, Bob," Tate said in a cool voice. "Surely you know that harming her doesn't solve anything. You'll only regret it if—"

Bob shoved the girl hard right into Tate as he bolted for the door.

She stumbled toward him, and his hands came out to catch her, but he hadn't been expecting it. Tate fumbled the catch as she tried to twist away, still afraid, wanting to flee but needing to be caught. She tried to go one way, even as she tumbled, and Tate went the other, and both tangled and went down in a heap, the girl screaming and Tate trying to hush her.

She pushed away from him, kicking and elbow crawling backward until she hit the wall, sniveling and bleating like a frightened lamb.

Tate got to one knee, held his hands up, palms out. "Just calm down, will you? Those men aren't going to bother you anymore. I'm here to save you."

Carson ducked out of the window when Memphis started shooting and pressed his back flat against the side of the cottage. More gunfire, then the sound of stomping feet, a door opening, and the clamor of men fleeing.

Carson held his breath for a moment. Then Big Bob's voice again, talking to Tate. Carson listened and understood the situation immediately. Bob was holding the banker's daughter in front of his body. Carson risked a quick look through the window. No good. He couldn't get an angle on Bob, and anyway, he might hit the girl if he tried a shot.

"Damn it, Memphis, hurry up!" Gordon's voice, loud and urgent, coming from the other side of the cottage.

There wasn't anything Carson could do to help Tate, not from his place outside the window, but maybe he could do something to prevent Gordon and Memphis from getting away. He ran around the other side of the cottage just in time to see Memphis struggle into the saddle. He bled freely from his wound and didn't look good, pale and weak. He saw Carson and tried to lift his pistol again, slow and awkward.

Carson shot him again, right in the chest, and Memphis tumbled out of the saddle and hit the ground.

Gordon saw Carson. "You?" He fired his six-shooter.

Carson dove to the ground and returned fire until his Colt clicked empty.

"You're out of lead, Carson." Gordon nudged his horse forward and aimed his six-shooter right at Carson's heart.

"I don't know where you been hiding yourself, but you should have stayed there."

The crack of a distant rifle shot, and the six-shooter flew out of Gordon's hand. He yowled with surprise.

Carson twisted to look behind him and saw Kat almost a hundred yards away, standing in the stirrups, holding the Spencer rifle.

Just then, Bob came running around the other side of the building. He hopped aboard the buckboard and grabbed the reins. "Let's get out of here!" He snapped the whip, and the team took off, Gordon following right behind.

Carson looked back down the lane. If he ran back to Jet and reloaded his Colt, the McGraw brothers would have too much of a head start. He could try to catch up, but then it would be two on one. He suddenly wondered how Tate had made out in the cottage. Maybe he should check on—

A sputter and a cough. "Help . . . help me." Memphis's voice.

Carson went and knelt next to the man. Blood oozed between Memphis's fingers from the chest shot. The man wasn't long for this world.

"Good God. Carson . . . Carson Stone . . . that you?" Memphis was weak and fading fast.

"It's me, Memphis," Carson said gently. "Sorry I had to gun you like that. Just the way it is, I guess."

"Get me . . . a . . . doctor." Memphis coughed again, blood staining his lower lip.

Kat rode up and dismounted. She cast her eyes on the dying man. "That's Jimmy Bachman, isn't it?"

Carson nodded. "Yeah."

"Get me a doctor . . . and . . . I'll help you." Memphis coughed again and choked on blood. He turned his head and spat. "You're after Bob, aintcha? I can . . . I can . . . tell you where his hideout is. Just . . . a doctor."

"I already know about Bob's place in the Ozarks," Carson

said. "Anyway, Gordon saw me, and he knows that I know about the hideout. I doubt they'll go there now."

"No . . . you . . . you got it all wrong," Memphis said. "He has to . . . has to go there. Big . . . stash of money. All his . . . robberies and . . . bank holdups over the years. He can't . . . can't leave it. A . . . fortune. He'll go . . . go back and . . ."

Memphis's head flopped to one side and his eyes rolled up. Jimmy "Memphis" Bachman was no more.

Carson stood and sighed, still looking down at the body. Kat waited.

Finally, Carson looked at her and said, "That was one hell of a shot. You knocked Gordon's gun right out of his hand. I guess I taught you pretty good."

Kat shrugged. "I was aiming for his face."

CHAPTER 30

They dragged the corpses outside to clear the cottage. Kat had one arm around the banker's daughter, who still cried softly, in some kind of shock from her ordeal, Carson figured. Tate gave her some water, told her it was all going to be okay and she'd be with her family again real soon.

Carson and Tate went outside to talk. Carson brought Tate up to speed with everything he and Kat had done, the close call with Gentlemen Dick Fleetwood, arriving in Fayetteville, and Carson's encounter with Albert Garrison, the bank president. Tate related how he'd contrived to join McGraw's gang.

Carson sensed Tate wasn't completely satisfied with how he'd handled things.

"I suppose I thought I was clever," Tate said. "I was hoping to get them all at once, but McGraw had a lot more men with him than expected. I kept waiting for the situation to turn to my advantage, but I just sort of found myself swept along with the flow of events. I was fortunate not to get myself killed."

"Your plan half worked," Carson said. "We got Memphis and a bunch of them other fellows. And we saved the banker's daughter."

"Ah, yes. The girl. It was the right thing to do, although

I'm sure our Lady Pain will point out that corpses pay reward money and saving banker's daughters doesn't."

"You didn't meet Albert Garrison. I did," Carson said. "I wouldn't be surprised if he offered some sort of reward. He'll be happy and relieved she's alive and unhurt. Just a bit rattled is all. But you already said it best. It was the right thing to do. Something good needed to come out of this. Shooting Jimmy Bachman might pay a fine bounty, but it just don't feel like an accomplishment, if you take my meaning. I'm glad the girl's all right."

"If you're telling me that saving somebody feels better than shooting somebody, I won't argue with you," Tate said. "The real question is what happens now."

"It's obvious to me that we take off after Bob and Gordon," Carson said. "Memphis told us where they were going and why, but you can bet they won't stay there long. Bob will grab his stash and they might rest a night, but we can't count on more than that."

"We got dead bodies and a banker's daughter to see to," Tate reminded him. "We have to take her to town first and turn over these outlaws for the bounties. There's paper on Jimmy Bachman, at least, and I wouldn't be surprised if there were rewards for some of the others, too."

"If I wait for you to take care of all that, we'll lose the McGraw brothers."

"The point is to collect bounties," Tate said. "There's money here lying dead on the ground. Wouldn't be sensible just to leave it."

"I'm not in this for reward money," Carson reminded the bounty hunter. "The man who can clear my name is getting farther away every second we stand here jawing about it."

"Perhaps Kat can take the girl home and collect the bounties," Tate suggested. "Then I can go after Bob and Gordon with you. You don't want to take them on by yourself."

"That won't work."

Both men turned to see Kat standing in the cottage's open doorway. She closed the door behind her and joined the two men.

"How's the girl?" Carson asked.

"Finally calmed down," Kat said. "But she needs to go home to her family."

"What did you mean before?" Tate asked her. "What won't work?"

"I can't go back to the marshal with this many dead bodies and no payroll," Kat explained. "They'll know I had help, and they'll have questions. You've got to come with me, Tate. Two of us is more believable. Hell, it's true, even."

"The girl has seen me," Carson said.

"She's seen a man with a six-shooter on his hip, and that's almost every man this side of the Mississippi River," Kat said. "Where there's two bounty hunters, a third doesn't seem so strange. They might send a wire to check out Tate. They'll get his bona fides. I'll tell him our third partner is a man named Grant Alford who's trailing Big Bob and his brother. If they check Alford's bona fides, they'll come back just as good, and then I'll insist we need to hurry on our way to catch up with you."

Carson frowned. "And what happens if the real Grant Alford happens along?"

A mischievous grin quirked to Kat's lips. "That's the beauty of this particular fib. When I saw Alford last month, he told me he was headed straight for Montana. He won't be wandering through by chance. The point is, we need to tell the marshal something that makes sense to him, so he doesn't hold us up with a lot of questions and suspicions. Trust me, with that payroll stolen, they'll be jumping on anything that doesn't smell right."

"That still leaves our dear friend Carson to take on the Brothers McGraw all by his lonesome," Tate pointed out. "Don't get me wrong, Carson, you're a capable fellow, right up there with Gilgamesh, but you alone against those two . . . well, I'd cheer for you, but I might not bet on you."

Carson rolled his eyes. "Thanks."

"And I'm not recommending he takes on anybody," Kat said. "But Carson's right. He needs to be on his horse and after them in the next five minutes. They won't lay low at Bob's hideout for long, but all Carson needs to do is tail them. Keep track of where they are until we can catch up. You've got a brain in your head. You'll figure some way to leave us a message."

"The general store often doubles as a post office in some of these small towns, I've noticed," Tate suggested. "A reasonable place to leave us a note."

Carson scratched behind his ear, face scrunched up in thought. "Yeah, that might work. Okay." He'd never been to McGraw's hideout in the Ozarks, but he gave Kat and Tate directions the best he could according to what he'd been told.

"Well, I can't think of anything we're leaving out, so I guess the only thing to do is mount up and ride," Carson said.

Tate offered his hand. "Once more into the breach, old boy." They shook.

Kat gave Carson a sisterly peck on the cheek. "Try not to get killed."

A sheepish grin from Carson. "No promises."

And then he hopped onto Jet and was gone.

Carson rode hard until well after sundown, not willing to give up the chase, but the first time Jet stumbled in the dark, Carson called it quits. A horse with a broken leg wouldn't help him catch up with the McGraws.

He found a likely spot, built a fire, fed and watered Jet. He cooked a simple meal and ate without really tasting it. His mind was on the road ahead, but also on those behind. He wished he could have been there when Garrison was reunited with his daughter, Emily. He wished he could get the image of Memphis's dead face out of his mind, all that blood over his bottom lip and down his chin. Carson wished a lot of things.

He wished he had one of Kat's whisky bottles, but then was glad he didn't. A mood like this was just when a man wanted whisky, and probably just the time he shouldn't have any.

Carson chastised himself for thinking such a way. *You're no philosopher, stupid. You ain't the one that went to Harvard.*

He put his head on his saddle. Sleep was a long time coming. How far ahead were the McGraw brothers? *They'll have to stop, too, and rest that team. The buckboard won't make as good time as a single rider on horseback.* Carson managed to gin up a meager morsel of optimism, and two minutes later he was asleep.

He awoke the next morning at the first hint of dawn and started riding without coffee or a hot breakfast. A hunk of jerky and a swallow from his canteen would have to suffice.

The road to Big Bob's hideout went north and east through a place called Eureka Springs. Carson had never been there but had heard some vague talk one time about healing waters and white men flocking to the place to cure their ills after the government took the area from the Indians.

Carson didn't know about any of that, but if there were people, maybe he could ask if two men had passed driving a buckboard.

It was nearing midday when Carson rode past land that had been cleared, the first sign of civilization all day. He rounded a gentle bend in the road, and a sprawling farmhouse and a barn came into view.

Carson turned Jet up the lane toward the house but reined in the horse halfway when he saw the house's front door standing open. He waited a moment and listened. Somewhere far away, a dog barked.

"Hello the farmhouse!" he called out. When he got nothing in return, he tried again, louder. Still nothing.

He rode the rest of the way at a walk, dismounted, and tied Jet to a porch post. He climbed the steps and paused in the open doorway. "Hello?"

Carson could smell it even before he stepped inside and knew what he was going to find.

Three in the front room, all head shot. Flies buzzed. The bodies lay at awkward angles where they'd fallen. The stink of blood mixed with gunpowder, not heavy but clear enough. Two of the bodies were close together, a middle-aged man and a handsome woman only a few years younger. The man across the room was older. Maybe the father. His face was twisted in fear and pain, drying blood down his face.

Carson knelt, touched the side of the man's neck with two fingers. No pulse—not a surprise—and the skin wasn't quite warm, but not stone-cold either. Carson wasn't sure how to interpret that. He didn't think these people had been dead overnight.

He stepped over the old man and went into the kitchen. The cupboards stood open. The larder had been raided. The butchers had ransacked the house and stocked up.

There was no reason to believe the McGraws had done this.

Except that Carson was certain they had.

He went out the back door and into the barn. The first thing he saw was the fourth dead body, a young man in his early twenties. Maybe the son. The second thing he saw was the buckboard. Carson recognized it as the same one Bob had driven away from the cottage near Fayetteville. There were two horses also. They'd been lathered with sweat and hadn't been rubbed down. The buckboard team, Carson realized. They stood tranquilly, munching hay. There were no other horses in the barn.

Carson deduced the situation with little effort. Bob and

Gordon had needed supplies and fresh horses. They'd found this place and had simply taken what they'd wanted. Maybe the family had tried to resist, or maybe they'd been shot to assure their silence.

Either way, they'd been murdered callously, simply because they were in the way.

Carson felt hatred boil up from within, and if McGraw had been there right at that moment, Carson wouldn't have cared anymore about bringing the man in alive. He would have pulled his Colt and started shooting until one of them was dead.

He looked down, realized he was making fists so tight his knuckles hurt. He let out a long breath, calmed himself.

Carson didn't know the family but assumed they were regular, normal folk. They didn't deserve this. Nobody did. He wanted to bury them but knew he couldn't afford the time and felt bad about it. It couldn't be helped. Their murderers were getting farther away every second.

He took oats for Jet and left.

CHAPTER 31

It wasn't a town—not yet anyway—but it was trying hard, and would get there soon.

Eureka Springs was mostly rows of mismatched tents and mud roads and men and women coming and going to and from a hot pool of bright blue water. Steam rose from the water. Buildings were being erected as well. A large, boxy wagon painted yellow and green advertised *Dr. Ambrose's Miracle Healing Water*.

One building, half erected, with canvas walls, had a sign out front that read "Whisky Springs Saloon & Eatery." The bar was a thick plank between two barrels. There wasn't much to the place, but it was still packed; too crowded, in fact, for Carson's comfort even though a beer would have hit the spot.

Not that he had time to relax, but he felt he needed to go into some establishment and try to get some information. Surely somebody had seen the McGraw brothers pass through.

Carson kept riding, passing through the tent town to a wider street where there were a few proper buildings and more under construction. *I don't know what magic is supposed to be in the spring water, but it's brought folks from all over.*

He wondered if Kat and Colby Tate had concluded their

business with the marshal in Fayetteville and were on their way after him. At first, Carson's association with the bounty hunters had merely been a necessary business arrangement, but he had to admit he'd grown accustomed to having traveling companions. Tate was affable, and Kat . . . well, Kat's appeal was a mixed bag. She was intriguing, no doubt, but she reminded Carson of a high-strung, thoroughbred horse. Beautiful to look at, but walk behind it and you might get your head kicked in.

He slowed Jet to watch a crew of men working on a two-story building. Men sweating hard, wielding hammers and saws. A beefy fellow, his red shirt sticking to him, carried an armload of scrap lumber around behind—

You've got to be kidding me.

The last thing Carson expected to see in Eureka Springs was a familiar face—unless, of course, that face belonged to one of the McGraw brothers. But this fellow wasn't Bob or Gordon. Carson shook his head. *Of all the people . . .*

Then he got an idea.

Carson tied his horse to a post in front of the feedstore across the street and followed the man carrying the scrap wood, making sure not to be seen. They rounded a ramshackle storage shed, and the man added the scrap wood to a pile. Carson double-checked to make sure the man wasn't carrying a gun.

Then Carson crossed his arms, grinned, and said, "Hank Baily, you sure do turn up in the damnedest places."

Baily spun, surprised to hear his name, then looked at Carson, slack-jawed, eyes vacant. Then his eyes shot wide with recognition, and he reached for a gun that wasn't there.

"Now that ain't friendly, Hank," Carson scolded. "I didn't come to fight."

Baily grabbed a length of wood from the pile, cocked it back as if prepared to give Carson a swat if he came any closer.

"Now, you just stay back, ya hear me, ya sumbitch? Cowardly skunk, sneaking up on a man when he don't have his gun!"

"Damn it, I told you I didn't come here to fight," Carson said. "Just calm down."

"I waited a damn hour for you to show up in Fort Smith for us to gun it out," Baily shouted. "But you didn't show, you lily-livered bastard. But you're real brave now with an unarmed man, ain'tcha?"

"Hank, if we'd both showed to that gunfight, I'd have shot you dead," Carson said. "Is that what you'd have preferred?"

"I'd have shot *you* dead, ass!"

"No." Carson shook his head. "Listen to me. When we cross paths, I make you look bad. Think about it. You don't get the better of me. I get the better of you."

"That why you're here, ya piece of dung? To get the better of me again?"

"No."

"What, then? What are you doing here?"

"I want to apologize."

"Yeah, well, you can kiss my fat—" Hank blinked. "Wait. What?"

"I'm apologizing."

Hank's face went blank. Carson could have sworn he heard the rusty clank-clunk of the wheels slowly turning in the man's head.

"This some kind of damn trick?"

Carson shook his head. "It's not a trick. I see you've got a new construction job. Good for you."

They stood like that a moment, Hank still holding the length of wood, ready to strike. Baily was trying hard to understand what was happening.

Damn, Hank, you poor dumb animal, just simmer down. I'm not going to do anything to you.

"So, if you're apologizing, you admit I lost my other job because of you," Hank said.

"Well, no. That was your fault, Hank. What I mean to say is . . ." *What do I mean to say?* Carson put together his next sentence carefully. "You had some bad luck, and I guess I was part of it—not the *cause* of it—but I was there, so I . . . uh . . . suppose I understand why you might associate me with that bad luck." *Just accept the damn apology, you thick slice of ham.*

Baily stood there, mouth hanging open, still not sure if Carson was putting one over on him.

"It takes a big man to accept an apology," Carson said. "I'd like to buy you a beer. Or a shot of whisky."

"*You* want to buy *me* a shot of whisky?"

"Yes."

"And it takes a big man to accept an apology?"

"That's right."

"Well . . . yeah, I guess." Hank lowered the club. "I mean, sure. I'm big enough for that. If a man offers an apology, I'm man enough to accept it. Right?"

"Right."

"Okay, then." Hank tossed the piece of wood back on the pile. "I mean, if you're apologizing, there's no need for a gunfight. I'm not un . . . uh . . . uncivilized."

"Of course. Let me get you that whisky."

"Not now," Hank said. "Hell, the boss is probably already wondering where I am. I only had this job two days," Hank said. "I'm done in an hour."

"In an hour, then," Carson told him. "I'm new around here. I'd like to ask some questions about this place."

"Okay, then. See you in an hour."

Carson walked around for a while, leading Jet by the reins. Eureka Springs looked to be a place at the tail end of inventing itself, proper buildings slowly taking over a village of tents. It had the feel of a gold-rush town, but cleaner and less manic. Carson never heard of nobody jumping a spring water claim. By the time he circled back to the construction site, Hank Baily was off work.

He was sweaty and wore his hat back on his head, vest unbuttoned. To Carson, it looked like Baily had put in a hot day's honest work. Carson had never worked construction but had always liked being outdoors and working with his hands. He could handle tools. He'd need to do some kind of work when all this McGraw business was finished.

Baily approached, appraising Carson with a raised eyebrow, as if suspicious he still might be the butt of some joke. He wore his gun now, but Carson didn't sense any hostility in the man.

"Wasn't sure you'd really show," Baily said.

Carson smiled. "How about that drink?" He described the saloon he'd seen on the way into Eureka Springs, the bar fashioned from a plank between two barrels.

"Naw, that place is always too crowded," Baily said. "And they charge an arm and a leg for a shot of whisky. Follow me. I know a place. Sorta like a private club."

Baily led Carson down a long row of tents. They emerged into a small clearing where there was a blacksmith's shop and a stable. "'Round back. Come on."

They circled around the building, and a long, mahogany bar ran the width of the stable's back wall. A large canvas tarp had been stretched overhead for shade. A few mismatched tables and chairs.

"Kinda early, so nobody's here yet." Baily slapped his hands on the bar a half dozen times. "Hey, Wendel, where you at? Couple thirsty fellas here."

Carson ran a hand down the smooth, rich brown wood of the bar. It was a quality piece, intricately carved scrollwork at the ends. The bar was a far cry from a plank across two barrels. "Where'd this come from?"

"Some hotel in Little Rock," Baily said. "Half the place burned down, and they pulled this bar out of it. Wendel put it here until he could sell it to one of the saloons they're building, and somebody brought a bottle one day, and it just ended up being a gathering place."

A sweaty, muscled man in a leather blacksmith's apron came around the corner. "Who's shouting?"

"Roy, you seen Wendel?" Baily asked. "Where is he?"

"How the hell do I know?" Roy said. "He don't hang out all day waiting for you to show up and ask for a drink."

"Okay, okay, simmer down. What about that kid who helps out sometimes?"

"Yeah, I'll send him 'round." Roy vanished back around to the other side of the stable.

"It'll just be a second," Baily assured Carson.

A kid showed up a minute later, curly red hair and a gap between his two front teeth. He had a slow look about him but hopped to it quick enough when Baily demanded a bottle and two glasses. Carson paid him, and the kid stashed the money in a cigar box under the bar.

Carson and Baily took one of the tables. Baily opened the bottle, licking his lips in anticipation, and filled each glass with clear liquid. Carson held up his glass and squinted at it dubiously.

"Kind of a homebrew. Moonshine. It'll strip the paint right off your insides." Baily tossed the shot back in one go and smacked his lips.

Carson shot his back, the liquid searing his throat and belly, he barely got it down, sputtering and coughing, his throat raw with fire.

Baily laughed and refilled Carson's glass. "Got a kick, don't she?"

"I'll just sip this next one," Carson said.

Baily shot back two more quick ones and then started talking. Carson didn't even have to ask the man any questions. Others filed in two or three at a time, taking up the other tables. Baily had launched into some sort of abbreviated version of his life story. Not abbreviated enough, as far as Carson was concerned.

In a few minutes, Baily's story had arrived at his and Carson's first meeting in the saloon in Clemmensville. He seemed to regret the whole incident.

"It's not like I was out to get you personally or anything like that," Carson said. "But you just can't put your hands on a woman like that. I know a lot of men think there's a different set of manners for saloon ladies, but I don't see it that way."

Carson was surprised and pleased to see Baily had the good grace to look embarrassed. "Yeah, I know. You're right. Just that I don't always know how to act when people start insulting me and making me feel stupid. Everyone's always treating me like I'm some damn fool."

Carson felt bad, not a lot but a little. He'd been one of the people who absolutely thought of Baily as a fool. *Must be tough for the man. He's just smart enough to know when he's being insulted, but not quick-witted enough to mouth back. So he resorts to bullying and violence.*

It didn't excuse bad behavior, but Carson thought maybe he understood Baily just a little better.

"Listen to me, yammering on like some jackass," Baily said. "Tell me what brings you through Eureka Springs."

Carson had been waiting for just that question. "I'm looking for some people. I know they came through this area, but I'm new around here."

"I been here about a week," Baily said. "Not too long, but I've met a good number of people. I can help you ask around, maybe. Who's these folks you're looking for?"

Carson leaned in and lowered his voice. "A man named Bob McGraw and his brother, Gordon, but they might not be using their real names." Carson went on to describe the two men.

"Wait just a damn minute. Do you mean Bob McGraw the outlaw?" Baily asked. "Big Bob McGraw? What the hell you after him for? You don't strike me as no lawman."

"Personal business," Carson said. "Let's say he done me a bad turn, and I'm looking to set things right."

"Well, you got some fair-size stones on you, I'll say that." Baily filled his glass again. "Going after a fella like McGraw."

"Don't misunderstand. It's not something I'm looking forward to," Carson said. "Just something that needs to be done."

"I'm trying to think if I seen anyone what matches that description." Baily's face scrunched up as he bent his thoughts toward remembering. "Lot of folks pass through here."

"McGraw's supposed to have a place northwest of the springs," Carson said. "A trail up into the Ozarks. I've never been, but that's how it was explained to me. A trail pretty close. But for all I know, there's a dozen trails, or a hundred. I have to narrow the search somehow."

Baily scratched the stubble on his jaw, then twisted in his chair to talk to the men at the table behind him. "Hey, Rico, you seen old Johansson today?"

A haggard, middle-aged man with a cigarette stuck in the corner of his mouth shook his head. "Not all day. What you want him for?"

"Because I'm trying to help my good buddy Carson here." Baily gestured to Carson. "Johansson used to work that copper mine, didn't he?"

"Ain't no copper mine no more," Rico said.

"That ain't the point." Baily was close to slurring his words, the moonshine starting to have its way. "I need somebody been up there."

"Yeah, that's Johansson, then," Rico said.

"Okay, then, where is he?"

Rico frowned. "I done just told you, I ain't seen him all day."

"He's probably at home," a cowboy shouted from three tables over, picking up on the conversation. "I saw him walking toward the springs, and he's got a shack near there."

"Oh, hell, I know where that is." Baily rose from the table, gesturing Carson should follow. He began to walk away from the makeshift saloon, more or less stable on his feet, then paused and went back and grabbed the bottle. "A little something for the road."

"Where are we going?" Carson asked.

"To see the Swede."

Baily drank and rambled as they walked. Carson led Jet. Every few minutes, Baily would pass the bottle over to Carson, who would sip the smallest amount humanly possible just to stay sociable. Baily went on about women he'd known and men he'd been in fisticuffs with. It sounded like a lot of lies and exaggerations to Carson, with the occasional accidental truth just to keep everyone on their toes.

They passed a huge, arched sign proclaiming "Healing Waters."

"Them's the springs," Baily said when he caught Carson looking. "The water is diverted into various tubs, and soakers can pick the temperature they like."

Carson watched a moment as various men and women in thick robes got in and out of large tubs. "Does the water really have healing properties?"

"The hell if I know. I'll stick to this." Baily took another slug from the bottle.

They passed the springs into the forest beyond, following a narrow road that hugged the base of a low hill. Carson was glad for the shade but had walked about all he wanted. "How much farther?"

"Right up here." Baily pointed ahead. "Swede built this shack way back before anyone cared about the springs. They struck copper up the mountain and opened a mine, but it turned out to be a bust. Mine was barely open a year when it closed down."

"This Swede fella was a miner, then?"

Baily shook his head. "Naw, but he made his living off the miners, going up and down the mountain delivering things— mail, dry goods, whisky. That's what made me think of him. He's been all over this place. He might have a guess where your outlaws are holed up."

The shack came into view a few seconds later, and Carson might have missed it if Baily hadn't pointed it out. The shack had certainly been there a while, and it looked like the forest was trying to reclaim it. Shrubs grew up to the windows, vines crisscrossing the gray wood. A carpet of dead leaves over the wooden roof shingles, a thin, tin chimney poking through and showing a layer of rust.

Carson spotted a small corral several yards off to the left with goats and an old swayback horse.

"Swede Johansson!" Baily called. "You in there, Swede?"

A moment passed, and then two, and then the door creaked open and an old man hobbled out. White hair, white beard, eyes set deep, almost disappearing into a wrinkled face, mouth sinking in on itself for lack of teeth. Trousers with so many patches it was difficult to discern the garment's original color. Suspenders over a red undershirt.

Even from where Carson was standing, he could tell the man hadn't bathed since the Polk administration.

"Who's that yelling my name all over creation?" The man's accent was thick, but he was easily understandable. "State yer business!"

"It's me, Swede. Hank Baily."

"Who?"

"Hank Baily. I brought you that big supply of nails you took on your route last week, and we talked for an hour."

"Oh, yah, I remember. The man with the hooch that tasted like kerosene."

Baily held up the bottle. "Want a slug?"

"No, thanks. I got six teeth left, and I don't want them melted out of my head." Swede's eyes shifted to Carson. "Who's yer friend there?"

"My good buddy Carson," Baily said. "He's looking for somebody. And I thought you could help him."

"Looking for somebody?" Swede's bushy eyebrows twitched. "Lots of somebodies in this world. What makes you think I know your particular somebody?"

"The men I'm looking for are supposed to have a place near your old stomping grounds, up around the copper mine." Carson described the men and related what he generally knew of the location of Bob's hideout.

Swede nodded, tugging at his beard. "Yah, yah. I know the trail. Goes zigging and zagging up into the mountains. Most of the cabins are run-down and abandoned. I think I seen the men you described a few hours ago, but there weren't two. There was three men."

Carson didn't like the sound of a third man. McGraw's gang had been whittled to two, and the idea he was building it back up again already didn't sit well. "Describe this third fella."

"Tall, wide, and ugly," Swede said. "One of his hands was a hook."

"A hook?" That wasn't anyone Carson knew. He would have remembered a hook.

Baily's eyes widened. "Was it his left hand that was the hook?"

Swede nodded. "That's right. Left hand. Looked wicked mighty sharp, too, I can tell ya."

Baily whistled.

"What?" Carson asked.

"He's one mean bastard," Baily said. "Don't know his name, but most folks just call him Angus. Local leg breaker for hire. Seen him put that hook through a fella's eye once. Right into his brain and killed him stone dead. I guess you got guts going after Big Bob McGraw, Carson, but I don't know nothing 'bout him firsthand. Angus I seen in action. You don't want no part of him."

"Why ain't he in jail?"

Baily shrugged. "Self-defense or something. Who can say why anyone gets away with anything? Alls I know is what I said. You do *not* want no part of him."

Carson sighed. "I don't want no part of any of this, but them's the cards that were dealt. Mr. Johansson, can you tell me which cabin they were heading for?"

"Call me Swede, and no, I can't. I make a monthly run up the mountain to the few folks still live there—dry goods and whatnot. Sometimes there's mail, but not often. I passed them on the way down as they were heading up. We all nodded politely at one another, and that was it."

"Can you take me up there?" Carson asked.

"You're welcome to come along next month when I do my route," Swede said. "Glad for the company."

"Obliged, but I've got business that won't wait that long."

Swede shuffled his feet. "Well, I suppose I could show you the trail in the morning. Point you in the right direction."

"Any chance you could show me now?"

"Now? I was just about to cook up some supper."

"I'd pay you a dollar," offered Carson. "It's important."

"A dollar, huh? Well, I can't afford to pass that up. Let me saddle Bessy, and then I'll take you." Swede ambled away to saddle the swayback.

"This is as far as I go," Baily said. "Got to get back to work tomorrow, which I can't do if Angus kills me with a hook through the face."

Carson stuck out his hand. "I'm obliged to you, Hank."

"Handshake? Naw, that ain't gonna do it." Baily swept Carson up in a tight, sweaty bear hug, slapping him on the back. "Happy to help. Glad to do it. Hell, what are best friends for?"

Carson rolled his eyes, but he found himself smiling, too.

CHAPTER 32

When Carson had mounted Jet and ridden away from the cottage, leaving Memphis and the other dead outlaws in his wake, Kat and Tate had stood a moment in silence, watching him go. When the pounding of Jet's hooves finally faded and Carson was out of sight, Tate sighed and said, "Well. Now what?"

"You know now what," Kat told him. "We load up these dead men and collect our money."

"Don't forget the girl," Tate said. "We need to return her to her parents. I imagine they're worried sick."

"I haven't forgotten," Kat assured him. "Gather whatever horses haven't run off too far, and I'll go tell her to stay inside the cottage for now. She's seen enough dead bodies."

"I suppose that's best."

Tate retrieved the horses, and an hour later, they'd thrown the corpses over two horses and were ready to depart.

"Get the girl and we'll go," Tate said. "There's an extra horse for her, so neither of us will have to ride double."

"Go in the barn first and see if there's any extra rope or leather straps," Kat told Tate. "I want to make sure these bodies are good and tied down."

"They aren't going anywhere."

"If we have to break into a gallop and a body bounces off, are you going to be the one that goes back to fetch it?"

Tate threw his hands up. "Fine. It's not worth arguing." He headed for the barn.

Kat waited a moment to give him a head start, then looked at the cottage door. The girl wouldn't come out until Kat went to fetch her, which was just how Kat had arranged it. She followed Tate into the barn.

He was on the far side, pulling a coil of rope from a peg. He glanced over his shoulder and saw Kat. "This should do it, I think. I still don't think it's necessary, but better safe than sorry, eh?"

"Other than Memphis, there's only small bounties on two of the others, I think. Not a big score," Kat said. "Especially not split two ways."

Tate turned and grinned at her. "'The world is not thy friend, nor the world's law, The world affords no law to make thee rich; Then be not poor, but break it and take this.' The Bard's way of telling us to take what we can get, I suppose. Never mind. The McGraw brothers will fetch us a tidier sum."

"Still." Kat tsked. "Splitting it two ways just doesn't have the same appeal as keeping it all for myself."

Confusion crossed Tate's face. "That's not really the plan. Anyway, safety in numbers, remember?"

"I remember." Kat kept walking toward him, casually, an easy way about her, as if she were just saying things that happened to be crossing her mind on the spur of the moment. "But that's when Bob had himself a big gang. It's just down to two of them now."

"The two most dangerous ones," Tate reminded her.

"And the two with the biggest bounties," she said.

Tate lifted his chin, eyes narrowing. "My dear Lady Pain, surely my ears deceive me, but it almost sounds as if you're dissolving our partnership."

"Dissolving. Our. Partnership." Kat said the words like

she was discovering how they tasted in her mouth. "That's one way to put it."

Kat lifted her arm suddenly, and the little derringer in her fist spat fire.

Tate's hands had been full of rope, yet she'd still known how fast he was, and so she'd shot fast, not taking the best aim, and the slug caught him high on the shoulder. He staggered back, eyes big as dinner plates, hands falling to his Colts but getting tangled in the rope.

She took a step forward and fired the second round, this time making sure to aim. The shot caught him right in the heart, and he spun around and went down, landing face-first in the dust. Kat kept one eye on him as she broke the derringer and took out the spent brass, then reloaded two fresh rounds. Then she pointed the little gun at Tate again as she inched closer, ready to shoot if he so much as twitched.

Kat kicked him, and when he didn't move, she kicked again, harder.

Dead. No doubt about it.

Her plan couldn't have gone better. Tate was too fast with a gun for a square fight, but that had never been Kat's style anyway. She'd gotten him into the back of the barn, so the banker's daughter wouldn't see, and had kept the small derringer in the palm of her hand, so he didn't see it until it had been time to shoot. That Tate's hands had been full of rope was an extra bit of luck.

Katherine Payne had never intended to share the bounties. With Carson gone, it had been the perfect time to eliminate Tate. She'd make up a story for Carson when the time came.

Kat went back to the cottage to fetch the girl.

"Where are the others?" she asked. "The two men who were with you?"

"They're chasing after those bad men. Never fear. You're safe now." Kat smiled warmly. "Now let's get you home."

CHAPTER 33

Dusk's gloom had nearly overtaken the forest by the time Swede brought Carson to the trailhead.

"This is as far as I go today," the old man said. "It'll be full dark soon and it's a narrow trail. It can get tricky. You sure you can't wait until morning?"

"I'd rather," Carson said. "But I can't."

"You'll see the first cabin about halfway up," Swede explained. "Roof's caved in. Nobody's lived there since the mine closed. Get up a little farther and the next cabin belongs to Pete Lamonte. He don't cotton to company, so I'd steer clear of him."

Carson made a note of it. He was already biting off more trouble than he needed. Getting shot for trespassing wouldn't help.

"Then the next couple of cabins are abandoned, so no point worrying about them," Swede continued. "The two cabins near the top got folks in 'em. Xavier Jones lives up there with some Indian woman, and then the next cabin over is Gil Morgan's place, but he sort of comes and goes. Ain't seen him in a while, come to think of it. But probably you won't even make it up that far."

"Won't I?"

"I just mean, you probably won't need to," Swede said.

"Once you pass Lamonte's, there's a trail that veers off to the left. Easy enough to miss in daylight. Good luck in the dark. But it wanders around to a couple more cabins. I ain't been that way in years because nobody lives down there, but I can't think where else them three fellas might've gone. Would seem the perfect place if they're looking to stay hid."

"And there's no sign I can look for?" Carson asked. "Nothing to mark the trail that branches off?"

"Nothing formal," Swede said. "Although now that I think of it, horses passing through might break some branches. Let you know if anyone's used that trail recently or not."

"Still seems like a poor bet in the dark, doesn't it?"

"Here, take this." Swede reached into one of his saddlebags and came out with a lantern. It had seen better days, dented and pitted with rust. "You can return it on the way back. That's me betting you're coming back."

"I appreciate the vote of confidence."

"I don't suppose I need to tell you that lantern will make it easier to see, but also easier to be seen," Swede said.

"The thought had occurred to me," Carson admitted. "How fidgety is this Lamonte character?"

"Stay on the path and you're fine," Swede said. "He'll leave you be if you stay off his property."

"Good to know. How far along this branch trail do I go until I come to the first cabin?"

"Maybe a quarter mile. I suppose you can use the lantern to find the trail, then put it out after that."

"Pretty much what I was thinking."

"Still a good chance you'll trip in the dark and break your fool neck," Swede told him.

"Your concern for my well-being is touching."

Swede laughed. "I just want to be sure I get my lantern back."

"I'll do my best." Carson offered his hand.

Swede shook it. "Good luck, young fella."

"Thanks."

Carson turned Jet and headed up the mountain.

He didn't get far before night descended fully. He paused to light the lantern, then nudged Jet forward at an easy walk. A half hour later, the trail narrowed and grew significantly steeper. Carson held Jet's reins in one hand and held the lantern aloft with the other, making sure both he and the horse could see the path. It seemed a long time before Carson finally came to the first cabin.

Swede had been right that nobody could live there. The dilapidated cabin perched on a steep slope to the left, roof fallen in. It looked like only thick, overgrown shrubs and weeds kept the whole mess from sliding down the mountain.

Carson kept going.

He came upon Lamont's place a few minutes later. The cabin was well kept, a candle flickering dirty-yellow light in the window. Carson braced himself as he rode past, half-thinking a rifle shot would split the night and knock him out of the saddle.

But Swede's advice had proven good. Carson stayed on the path, and nothing happened. He let out a breath he hadn't known he'd been holding as he put Lamont's cabin behind him.

He spotted the trail veering off to the left two minutes later. Swede had been right again when he'd predicted the horses passing through would leave their mark. Hedges had been shoved aside, branches snapped. Carson dismounted briefly and knelt, studying the ground. Fresh hoof marks, sharp and clear even in the dim lantern light.

It could be three other men, in which case whatever they were doing was none of Carson's business.

But he didn't think so.

I'm a quarter mile away from the McGraw brothers and some leg breaker with a hook for a hand. Now what?

Carson was making this up as he went along. That was fine yesterday, but not today, not when he was so close. He was nervous before, when he thought he was only going up against Bob and Gordon. That was more than plenty. Now there was the unknown factor of a man called Angus, and according to Hank Baily, Angus was the devil in boots. Carson wished Tate were here. He could use a fast gun at his side. Or Kat and her sneakiness.

But there was only Carson.

Then he remembered the dead family in the farmhouse and steeled himself. The men responsible had a dose of justice coming to them, and Carson determined again that he would be the man to make it happen. Maybe that justice would happen in front of a judge.

Or maybe at the end of a gun barrel.

Carson mounted Jet and rode on.

He rode about a hundred feet to make sure of the trail, and then he put out the lantern. He was surprised at the extent of the sudden darkness, but his eyes adjusted. There wasn't much moonlight, but it was enough, and he continued down the trail until he came to an opening in the undergrowth. He dismounted again, led Jet through the opening in the hedges, and tied him to a tree limb. Carson planned to go the rest of the way on foot and sneak as close to the cabin as possible. He wasn't sure how long he'd be gone, so he gave Jet a drink from the canteen and a handful of oats.

Then Carson set off down the trail, stepping quietly and carefully. He resisted the urge to hurry. He wanted to get there, find out what the McGraw brothers were up to so he could form his plan, but his intelligence told him to go easy. *You want to trip and break your fool neck? Or worse, make a bunch of blundering noise and alert them you're coming? You'll get there soon enough.*

Almost as soon as he'd completed those thoughts, he glimpsed flickering illumination through the foliage to his right. Carson left the trail, working his way toward the light, trying to step quietly. It was slow going, but he forced himself to be patient, and a few minutes later, he found himself kneeling next to the trunk of a fat pine, watching a cabin and trying to figure the best approach.

Weeds and shrubs had grown up around the place, evidence of a long absence, or maybe that the owner simply wasn't concerned about upkeep. Orange-yellow light in the windows, and gruff voices reached Carson from across the yard, although he couldn't quite make out what was being said. It was a good-sized cabin, bigger than the others he'd passed.

Off to the left, a picket line stretched between two evergreens, five horses tethered there. Carson felt a stab of concern that maybe there were more than the three men inside he'd expected, but it occurred to him a couple of the animals were likely packhorses.

Carson watched and waited a few moments. He needed to get closer to hear what they were saying. He started to rise and then immediately froze when he sensed movement among the horses. Carson held his breath, pressed himself against the trunk of the pine.

Gordon came from around the other side of the picket line. He rested a rifle lazily across one shoulder and headed back toward the cabin in no particular hurry. If Carson had moved a second sooner, he would have revealed himself. He watched Gordon climb the steps of the cabin's front porch and enter. Shadows played across the window.

Carson made a slow scan of the entire area but didn't see anyone else. As far as he could tell, all three men were inside now. He blew out a ragged breath, counted to three, and fast-walked toward the cabin, crouching low. He eased himself up under an open window and squatted there. The window was too high up for him to look inside even if he stood, so he waited and listened.

"Checked the horses and had a look around." Gordon's voice. "All quiet for now."

"Good." Bob. "Then we can do our business in the morning and get out of here before anyone finds us."

"You can't be thinking Carson's coming after us," Gordon said. "I don't figure him for having that kind of nerve."

"Yeah, well, you tell me what to think, then. You were as surprised to see him as I was."

"I reckon. What do you think he wants?"

"Been thinking 'bout that since Fayetteville," Bob said. "Been thinking about that quick-draw artist you let pull the wool over your eyes."

"You still on about that?"

"You brought Tate into the gang, so that's on you."

"Dang it, Bob, you wanted the fastest gun to cover us when we hit the bank, and that was Mooney until Mooney got himself shot," Gordon said. "So Tate took his place. You okayed him. It's on you as much as it is on me."

"Whatever. We'll finish this argument another time," Bob told him. "The point is, there's no way this Tate fella tricks his way into our gang right when Carson shows his face and it's a coincidence. And what about that woman who showed up out of nowhere taking rifle shots at us? I'm telling you, this was some kind of coordinated effort."

Gordon blew out a big sigh. "Go on and talk me through it, then."

"You say Carson don't have the spine to come after us," Bob said. "Maybe, maybe not. But if he's got help, he don't need to be so brave. He knows generally where this hideout is and what we look like. Could be he's just pointing the way for the other two."

Gordon tsked. "Tate didn't strike me as no lawman."

"Bounty hunters, I figure," Bob said. "Think about it. Prices on our heads keep going up. Couple ambitious bounty hunters grab Carson and get him to spill what he knows about us. It all adds up."

Carson swallowed hard, listening to Big Bob and his brother work it out. The outlaw was mean and tough, but he was smart, too. He had to be, Carson reckoned, to avoid jail so long. Bob had thought about it long and hard and had it just about exactly right. Never mind they didn't think Carson had the nerve to come after them himself.

I got the nerve all right, Bob. You just wait and see.

"What about the woman?" Gordon asked. "Never heard of no woman bounty hunter."

Then another voice, one Carson didn't recognize. A guttural mumble. Carson didn't catch the words.

"You got something to contribute, Angus?" Bob asked.

"Did the woman have red hair?" Angus's voice was deep and rough.

"That's right," Bob said. "How'd you know that?"

"I heard tell of some woman bounty hunter a while back. Red hair," Angus said. "They called her lady something. Lady Pain, now's I think of it. Don't rightly remember her proper name. But I can't think there's too many women bounty hunters, so it's probably her."

"You're probably right," Gordon said. "Although I don't see how knowing does us any good."

"I'd rather know than not know," Bob said. "Knowing might come in handy later on. So let's assume the worst. We got bounty hunters coming after us, and Carson Stone can lead them right here. I don't like waiting until morning to vamoose, I can tell ya, but I don't really want to stumble my way up to the mine in the dark. You know what you're supposed to do, right?"

"Yeah, I know," Angus said. "I wait here until—"

"Not here, damn it," Bob snapped. "Up to the mine."

"I meant here on the mountain," Angus shot back. "I know what to do. We'll all go up to the mine at first light so you can fetch your stash. Then you two take the other way down the mountain. I wait here for three days to see if anyone comes snooping around, and if they do, I make sure they never snoop again. Just one question."

"Ask it," Bob said.

"Why don't all three of us wait and get the jump on anyone who's following you?" Angus asked. "The more guns the better, I'm thinking."

"I told you already, we got business that can't wait," Bob said. "We can't afford to have anyone follow us, but we also can't afford to sit around with our thumbs up our asses for three days when somebody might show, or might be they don't. That's your job."

"My job don't sound so good suddenly."

"What are you bellyaching about now?" Gordon asked.

"You said somebody might be following you, and I'm supposed to handle him," Angus said. "Now you say it might be three somebodies, one being Lady Pain and another a quick-draw artist. I feel we might need to rethink what I'm being paid for this."

"Rethink, my ass."

"Easy, Bob," Gordon said. "Angus, we're paying you a hundred dollars up front to show we're serious, and then another five hundred when you come find us at the meetup place. Now that's real money, and you know it."

"Not real enough if I'm too dead to spend it," Angus said. "We never talked about no bounty killers."

"Tough man. Hard man," Bob said sarcastically. "What did you think we were paying you for? To fend off schoolmarms?"

"How about this?" Gordon proposed. "We pay you the agreed price plus a hundred extra for each additional person you have to kill. How about that?"

"I want a thousand dollars," Angus said.

"You dirty son of a bitch!" Bob raged. "It'll be a cold day in hell before I—"

Bob cut himself off, and suddenly nothing but tense silence came from the cabin. Carson was sure the heated discussion was about to come to blows. The silence stretched.

When Bob spoke next, he was eerily calm. "Fine. A thousand dollars. Have it your way. But I expect something for my thousand dollars. If the Seventh Cavalry comes up the mountain in the next three days, I expect you to handle them."

Angus laughed. "I'm just as tough and as hard as you've heard, McGraw. You'll get your money's worth."

"Pass the bottle around, then," Bob said. "One more stiff one, then we hit the sack. I'm serious about an early start. We'll leave the horses and take the short path up. Faster than taking the road all the way around the other side."

There was some general grumbling and muttering, and a few minutes later, the interior of the cabin went dark. Carson waited, listening.

All quiet.

Carson considered his options. He could bust into the cabin, take them all by surprise while they were sleeping, but there were too many unknowns. He didn't know how they were arrayed inside the cabin. Were they light sleepers? All it would take was for one to get off a shot at him. Maybe the door was barred. Carson cursed himself for not asking Swede directions to the mine. He simply hadn't figured it was a place he'd need to go, but it would have been a good plan to get there ahead of them and maybe set up some kind of ambush.

The only thing Carson could think of was to wait until morning and then follow them up the trail to the mine. Maybe he could pick them off as they came out or . . .

Hell, I don't know. I'll need to get up there and see. Maybe I'll get an idea as I go.

Again, Carson wished Tate were with him. Carson had to be smart and patient and wait for his chance.

He remembered Bob saying they'd leave the horses and

take a foot trail, so he eased quietly away from the cabin and made his way back to Jet. He unsaddled the horse and gave him additional water and oats. He stroked the horse's nose. "You wait here, boy."

He took his bedroll and his Winchester rifle and headed back to the cabin. He found a hiding spot where he could watch the front door. Carson would naturally wake up with the dawn. He always had. And anyway, he'd hear the three men as they left the cabin. One way or another, Carson would be up and after them at first light.

He checked his rifle and leaned it against a tree, where he could grab it quickly. Then he spread out his bedroll and stretched out on it. His head spun with a thousand thoughts, butterfly nerves in his belly.

Hell, I'm never going to get to sleep.

But two minutes later, he snored lightly, deep in dreamless slumber.

CHAPTER 34

It was already full light when Carson snorted awake.

He sprang to one knee and grabbed the Winchester. He'd overslept. Of all the damn times to—

He heard voices from the cabin. The smell of fresh coffee wafted across the yard. Carson hadn't missed them. For all of Bob's talk about leaving at first light, they'd ended up dilly-dallying. Carson sat and watched and pulled a strip of jerky from his pocket. He bit off a chunk. It was slightly better than chewing an old boot.

Half an hour later, the three men left the cabin. It was Carson's first look at the man called Angus.

Carson had always thought of Bob as a big man. He was called Big Bob, after all. Angus was something else alto-gether. He was thick and muscled like a bull, and at least six and a half feet tall. No beard or mustache, but long sideburns down his jaw to a chin the size of an anvil. A huge .44-40 Remington revolver hung on his right hip. As advertised, his left arm ended with a wickedly sharp iron hook instead of a hand.

Carson shook his head. *I'm thinking this is a bad idea after all.*

But he was already committed. He gave the men a head start, then slipped from his hiding place, Winchester clutched in his hands, and headed for the cabin. Once there, he eased around the corner and had a look. He barely glimpsed the men through the trees. He gave them a moment, then found the path and followed it. It quickly turned steep, angling up the side of the mountain. Wooden beams had been put into place here and there to make crude steps. He paused often, cocking his head to listen. He didn't want to lose them, but he didn't want to stumble into them either.

Carson reached the top just in time to see the three men vanish into the wide mouth of the mine. He knelt in the shade of a scrawny pine and surveyed the area. The opening to the mine shaft had been dug right into the rocky mountainside, framed by thick beams to keep it stable. The plateau had once been forest but had been cleared for the mining operation. Fat stumps still humped up from the ground here and there. Piles of rock everywhere. A pair of narrow-gauge rails led from within the tunnel to some kind of dumping area on the far side of the clearing. Obviously for mine carts. Stacks of empty crates and rusted shovels and pickaxes littered the place, all signs of an enterprise that didn't quite work out.

Carson didn't know much about mining, but it was clear that somebody had expected this to be a serious operation at one time. But from what Swede had told him, the whole thing had gone bust. Men who expected to get rich were left penniless.

Now the mine was just an out-of-the-way place for Big Bob McGraw to stash his ill-gotten gains.

There was an overturned mine cart halfway between Carson's hiding place and the entrance to the mine, wheels rusted so solid they'd never turn again. To Carson, it seemed a good spot from which to cover the mine entrance with his Winchester. He sprang up and ran for it.

Halfway there, he spotted Gordon, appearing suddenly at the cave's mouth. Gordon's eyes shot wide, and he drew his revolver and fired.

Carson dove behind the mine cart, then popped up and cut loose with the Winchester. In rapid-fire succession, Carson squeezed the trigger, levered in another round, fired again, and then again, the whipcrack of the rifle shots splitting the morning air, the spent shells tinging on the rocky ground next to him.

The shots struck the wall of the mine two inches from Gordon's face, dust, shards, and chips flying up. Gordon flinched and scurried back into the cave.

Damn it, you shot too fast. Take better aim next time. Carson hurriedly loaded fresh cartridges into the rifle and took aim at the mine entrance, waiting for one of the outlaws to show his face. He waited. And then waited some more.

Be damned if Carson was going to get any closer. This wasn't exactly how he wanted this to go, but he had the mine covered good and knew they knew it, too. He could wait longer than they could. Carson's guess was that there'd be more shooting eventually, but they'd want to talk first.

Sure enough, Big Bob's voice echoed from the darkness a few seconds later. "Now, is that any way to say hello to old friends, Carson?"

Carson didn't say anything and kept the Winchester trained on the mine.

"I can tell something's on your mind, Carson," Bob called. "Let's talk this over like reasonable people."

"I stopped at the farmhouse where you left the buck-board," Carson shouted. "I guess you must not have found that family so reasonable, huh, Bob? Did they object to lending you their horses? If that's your notion of reasonable, I'm happy to oblige you; just stick your face out for a quick look-see."

A long pause, then Bob shouted, "Three of us and one of you. We better work this out, I'm thinking."

Carson said nothing. Come on, you bastard. Stick your head out for a peek. I dare you.

"Or maybe you're not alone after all," Bob called. "You got your quick-draw pal with you? Tate?"

"Come say hello to him," Carson shouted.

"I'm not sure I believe you," Bob said. "Have Tate shout us a hello so we know you're not bluffing."

"And give away his position? Fat chance," Carson said. "You want to talk to anyone out here, you do it through me."

Another long pause. Carson wondered if they believed him. Probably not.

"You still haven't told us your gripe," Bob said. "Them folks in the farmhouse was no kin of yours."

"Maybe I'm tired of getting blamed for things you done," Carson said.

"The marshal? I can't help what people think, Carson. The law draws its own conclusions."

"Well, they can draw 'em up fresh after I bring you in," Carson said.

"Is that the plan?" A faint chuckle from Bob. "I surrender to you and then come quietly and confess to a judge how I'm the bad man who does all the murdering, and Carson Stone was just in the wrong place at the wrong time?"

Carson grinned in spite of himself. It did sound pretty ridiculous. Big Bob McGraw wasn't going to come quietly any more than Carson was going to sprout wings and fly to California.

Still . . . he had to make the offer. "I reckon surrendering to me would sting a little less than this Winchester if you try to make a run for it. At this range, I don't like your chances. Throw your guns out, for starters."

"We'll mull that over," Bob said. "In the meantime, a counteroffer. You might be biting off more than you can chew here, son. How about you go on your way, and then we'll forget you inconvenienced us. The longer this goes on, the more I'm likely to take it personal and get upset."

"Then I hope you have a good store of food and water and a deck of cards to pass the time because I guess we're going to be here all day," Carson said.

"See, now I'm getting upset!"

Carson sighed. This wasn't working. He switched tactics. "Angus!" he called. "You hear me, Angus?"

No reply.

"None of this is to do with you, Angus!" Carson said. "My beef's with the McGraws. You walk out. Go your way, and I'll go mine. No sense for you to get tangled up in something that might get you killed."

"You go to hell," Angus shouted from the depths of the mine.

"What did they pay you to stay behind?" Carson called. "Must have been a pretty penny to stay behind and do the dirty work while Bob and Gordon left you. I'm guessing they had some business that just wouldn't wait, right?"

Everything went quiet now. Even the birds in the trees seemed to be thinking over Carson's words.

"That's one of Bob's old tricks, isn't it, Bob?" Carson shouted. "He leaves because he's got some business, and there's always somebody else holding the bag. It's some sucker that gets shot up while Bob and his brother slink away."

"You don't know what the hell you're talking about," Bob barked.

"What'd he say he was going to pay you, Angus?" Carson asked. "Five hundred dollars? Hell, I bet it was a thousand. Maybe more than that. Might as well have been a million, because you were never going to see it. I bet he gave you a few measly bucks now, and said he'd pay you the rest when you met later . . . except there was not going to be no later because he was planning for me and Tate and the rest of my boys to fill you full of lead. And even if you did survive, he was never going to show at that meetup. If I'd have showed an hour later, it would have been you all on your own against me and mine."

Now the silence had an eerie tension to it, or maybe that was just Carson's imagination. His hands were sweaty on the Winchester.

"Face it, Angus. You've been had."

The silence stretched.

Then, a few seconds later, harsh voices echoed from the mine. An argument. Yelling and cursing, the three men shouting over one another. Carson's ploy had had the desired effect. Angus was turning on the McGraw brothers, at least enough to be suspicious of their motivations. Their argument kicked up another notch in volume.

And then the sharp report of a pistol shot reverberated from the mine.

Everything went still.

One shot. That probably wasn't working in Carson's favor. If Angus had gotten the drop on the McGraws, there would have been two shots, one for each brother. As it stood, Carson had to figure it was Angus who'd caught the lead. A shame. It had been a good ploy. Carson held out hope that maybe Angus had gotten a piece of one of the brothers before going down. He grinned at the thought of that hook sinking into Bob's flesh.

Carson waited.

He wondered if they'd call out to him, try to strike a deal. When they didn't, Carson wondered if he should be the one to start talking. Maybe they'd listen to sense.

Although Bob McGraw's notion of sense didn't exactly match up with everyone else's. Maybe if Carson talked to Gordon instead. Bob's brother always seemed a tad less volatile.

A noise echoed from the mine, the rough scrape of metal

on metal. Distant at first, it came from deep in the mine but then steadily grew louder. Carson held the Winchester in a white-knuckled grip, trying to understand what he was hearing.

An odd, rhythmic sound came from the mine, strangely familiar . . . klink-klak . . . klink-klak . . . klink-klak . . .

Something was happening, and Carson didn't like it. He spotted a stack of crates twenty yards to the right. It was slightly closer to the mine entrance but at a different angle. On the off chance the McGraws had estimated his position from the sound of his voice, he decided to move, leaping to his feet and dashing to the crates.

The rhythmic, metallic sound from the mine picked up speed. Klink-klak klink-klak klink-klak klink-klak—

A line of mine cars erupted from the mouth of the tunnel, one, two, three, four of them all bursting forth into daylight one after another, creaking and jostling on rusted wheels. At the end, Gordon pushed them, running full speed, puffing air, face read and gleaming sweat from the exertion.

Carson swung the Winchester to the tail end of the mine cars and took a bead on Gordon's head.

Big Bob rose from the lead mine car, a six-gun in each hand. He cut loose on Carson, the lead flying. The crates splintered and shook all around Carson from the storm of pistol fire. Carson flinched away and threw himself to the ground, dirt and rock kicked up on both sides of him as Bob poured it on.

Carson cursed and scooted around to the other side of the crates. Gordon had been just enough of a distraction to allow Bob to pop up from his hiding spot in the front mine car. Carson had fallen for it like a fool.

He had to hand it to Bob. The guy was a reckless lunatic sometimes, but he had guts.

The barrage of gunfire let off, and Carson carefully peeked around the corner of the crates. Bob and Gordon were hightailing it toward the edge of the plateau and the path back down to their cabin. Each man had a stuffed saddlebag over each shoulder.

That just figured. Bob wasn't about to skedaddle without his stash.

Carson leaped from his hiding place and stepped into the open, raising the Winchester. He had time for one good shot before Bob and Gordon disappeared down the side of the mountain.

And then a steam locomotive slammed into Carson's back.

At least, that was what it felt like. Carson flew forward, the Winchester tumbling away. The ground and the sky traded places, and a second later, Carson landed hard, skidding across the rocky ground. He rose to his feet, still half-dazed, legs weak, his hand dropping to his gun.

He drew the Colt, but he was too slow.

Angus swatted, a big, sweeping backhand, and the iron hook hit Carson's six-shooter with a sharp ting. The Colt flew out of Carson's grip.

Angus bled freely from a wound high on the left side of his chest. One of the McGraws—probably Bob—had gotten the drop on the huge leg breaker but hadn't killed him. Maybe Angus had fled deeper into the mine or had played possum, waiting for the brothers to leave.

Not that it mattered at the moment.

Angus swung his hook directly at Carson's face, and both of Carson's hands came up to grab the big man's forearm. Angus had the strength of a mad bull, and it was all Carson could do to stop the point of the hook two inches from his eye.

With his good hand, Angus snatched Carson by the throat. And squeezed.

Carson felt his air cut off immediately. He worked his mouth but couldn't get breath. A moment later, darkness crept in at the edge of his vision, spots dancing before his eyes. Another thirty seconds of this and he'd be finished.

Carson let one hand go of Angus's forearm. He was now fending off the hook with only the other hand, and it wasn't enough. He turned his head, and took a nasty cut down his right cheek. He would have screamed if he'd had the air.

With his free hand, he jammed a thumb directly into Angus's gunshot wound, felt it sink deep into the soft, bloody flesh.

Angus hollered agony and eased his grip on Carson, allowing him to move in a step.

And kicked Angus square in the crotch with every ounce of strength he could muster.

Angus opened his mouth to scream, but it came out more as a plaintive keening before devolving into a hoarse grunt, the man's face going purple as he took three wobbly steps back, then tilted to one side, hitting the ground with a hard thud. He lay there, using all his strength to breathe in and out, tears leaking from the corners of his eyes.

Carson had gone to his knees when Angus let him go. He knelt there, sucking in air, his throat raw. He gathered himself, stood, and shook Angus's blood off his thumb. He'd stopped himself just in time from wiping the thumb on his new pants.

"Help . . . h–help me," Angus croaked. "Oh, hell, man . . . you've got to . . . got to get me a doctor."

Carson ignored him and fetched his Colt from the dust and holstered it. Then he went and picked up his Winchester.

He returned to Angus, who was still moaning agony on the ground and pointed the Winchester at his face, holding it casually with one hand. "Why fight me, idiot? It was a McGraw that shot you. Which one was it?"

"Bob."

"Yeah, I could have guessed that."

"Sorry," Angus said. "Instinct, I guess. I just wanted to get away."

"Well, you didn't."

"Come on, man. Get me to a doctor."

"Stay here." Carson went to the edge of the mountain and looked down, but he didn't catch a glimpse of either brother. They were long gone. By the time he got back to Jet, it would be pointless to follow. He didn't even know in what direction they were going.

He went back to Angus and asked, "Where were you supposed to meet them?"

"Y–you've . . . got to help me." Angus coughed. "Give me some water."

"I asked you a question."

"What's it matter? You said they weren't going to meet me anyway."

"I don't have nothing else to go on," Carson said. "You tell me anything you think might be useful, and I'll think about that doctor."

"Coffeyville," Angus said. "Just over the Okie line into Kansas."

"Stay here," Carson said. "I'm going for my horse, but that means I got to bring him up some other way, and I don't know what that is."

"I'm . . . I'm getting dizzy."

"How do I get back up here, dammit? You'd better tell me before you fade."

"Back out to the main trail from McGraw's cabin and then all the way up. Then circle around south and back down another trail. You'll see it."

"Okay, then. Don't wander off."

Carson went back down the mountain as quickly as he could without losing his footing. He paused briefly at the cabin, but it was empty. The McGraws had taken Angus's horse, and

Carson cursed. That meant he'd have to drape the huge leg breaker over Jet for the trip down.

Jet waited patiently where Carson had left him. He mounted the horse and headed up the mountain, following the trail as Angus had described. Carson found the mine again soon enough, and Angus was right where he'd left him. The big man lay unmoving. Carson checked for signs of life. He was unconscious but still breathing.

It took every ounce of muscle Carson could muster to get Angus onto Jet. Carson stood there panting and wiped sweat from his brow. "Okay, Jet, I'm going to let you take it from here."

The horse snorted as if to say, Thanks a lot, pal.

Carson took Angus down the mountain, and when he reached Eureka Springs, he asked the first person he saw where he might find a doctor.

CHAPTER 35

The doctor told Carson that Angus would live.

Carson hadn't asked. Still, he had gone to all the trouble of hauling the man's carcass down the mountain, so he supposed he was glad it hadn't been for nothing. The doctor cleaned the shallow wound the hook had made down Carson's cheek.

He'd lost too much of the day to set out for Coffeyville, and he wasn't sure that was where he wanted to go anyway. He believed what he'd told Angus, that the McGraws had never intended to meet him or pay him a nickel, let alone a thousand dollars, and it was a long way just to prove he'd been right. On the other hand, he didn't have any better ideas.

He found Hank Baily at the makeshift saloon. Hank was happy to see him and seemed impressed that Carson had bested the mighty Angus in hand-to-hand combat, and let out a high-pitched whistle when he heard the red line down Carson's face was the direct result of Angus's hook. Carson told him the fight might have come out a lot different if Angus hadn't already been shot. A bullet will take a good bit of fight out of a man.

Carson had a couple of beers too many while he watched Baily make half a bottle of whisky vanish. He didn't quite get drunk, but he came close. Baily told him where he could find an inexpensive flophouse. It wasn't fancy, but it was clean, and for the first time in memory, Carson slept though breakfast.

He splashed water on his face, the wound stinging, dressed, and headed back up the mountain to McGraw's cabin. The trip was much faster—and safer—in daylight. He searched the cabin carefully, hoping for some clue as to Big Bob's plans.

Nothing.

On his way back to Eureka Springs, he stopped by Swede's shack and returned his lantern. They passed a half hour in idle chitchat.

I'm stalling, he told himself. I need to figure out what the hell I'm going to do.

Feeling defeated, he slunk back to Eureka Springs.

Coffeyville was a lie. The more he thought about it, the more he trusted his original instinct that Big Bob had fed Angus a line of bull about the meetup. Obviously, Bob and Gordon were headed anywhere but Coffeyville, Kansas. The only reasonable thing Carson could figure to do was head back toward Fayetteville. Maybe he'd meet Kat and Tate on the way. Possibly, the bounty hunters had gotten some new information from the marshal.

He hoped so, because Carson had blown his chance. The McGraws were a hundred miles away by now.

Before leaving town, he'd need to leave a message some-where for Kat and Tate. He went by Hank Baily's construction site, hoping to ask him if there was a post office or some such where he could leave a letter. A sweaty carpenter told Carson that Baily had run off on some errand. Carson thanked the man and led Jet away at a slow walk.

A minute later, somebody yelled his name from behind.

"Carson!"

Carson turned to see Hank Baily running after him, hat-less, shirtsleeves rolled up. Baily huffed and puffed, face red.

"Easy, Hank," Carson said. "You'll give yourself a heart attack."

He stopped in front of Carson, bent double, panting. After he caught his breath, he said, "Thought I'd missed you, buddy."

"You shouldn't have put yourself out," Carson said. "But as long as you did, can you point me to a post office or someplace I can leave a message? There might be some folks trying to find me."

"Never mind no post office," Baily told him. "Follow me."

Baily turned and headed away. Carson called after him, but Baily kept going. Carson shook his head and followed. In a minute, it became apparent that Baily was leading him yet again to the makeshift saloon behind the stables.

"I don't have time for a drink, Hank!"

But the man just kept going, beckoning for Carson to follow.

They rounded the corner, and Carson immediately spotted a familiar redhead leaning back in her chair, boots propped on the table, a whisky bottle and a glass in front of her.

"Kat!"

"Mr. Baily said you'd probably be along sooner or later," Kat said. "Figured I might as well get comfortable."

"I'll get two more glasses." Baily went to the bar.

Kat's eyes slid to Baily, then back to Carson. "Your new best friend?"

"Seemed a better arrangement than him trying to gunfight me all the time," Carson said.

Baily returned, pulled up a chair, and filled two shot glasses without asking permission. He slid one of the glasses across to Carson. "She was asking around for you earlier and lucky I just happened to hear. I recognized her from Fort Smith and said, hey that's my pal Carson's lady friend. I figured I'd best run after you. Otherwise, you'd miss each other. Good thing I caught you just in time."

Kat offered Baily a sweet smile. "We're obliged to you, Mr. Baily."

"Happy to help." Baily tossed back his whisky.

"Aren't they going to miss you at the construction site, Hank?" Carson asked.

"I got a fella covering for me just this once." Baily refilled his glass.

Carson looked at Kat. "Lucky us."

"Mr. Baily says you've been busy." Kat filled her own glass and tossed it back.

Carson sighed and related his endeavors since they'd split. Baily hadn't heard the full, detailed account before and listened, wide-eyed and rapt. Carson finished his story and shrugged.

"Sounds like we're going to Coffeyville," Kat said. "I know you don't like it, but what else do we have to go on?"

"The more I think about it, the more I just can't believe they'd actually tell Angus where they were going. Has to be some kind of diversion." Carson looked around to see men had begun to fill the tables around them, workers from Baily's construction crew. Maybe they were starting the weekend early. "Anyway, I told my story. I think I should hear yours."

"What's to tell?"

"You can start by telling me where Colby Tate is," Carson said. "I thought I'd find you both together."

"That the fancy-talking bounty hunter?" Baily asked.

"That's him," Kat said. "Carson, I just don't think he has the stomach for it."

Carson's eyes narrowed. "That doesn't sound like the Colby Tate I know."

"I know. I was surprised, too," Kat admitted. "But think about it. We haven't known him that long. None of us know one another really, not through and through. I think it was the time he spent with those outlaws. I think it unnerved him, knowing they could discover who he was any second. He thought maybe he'd bitten off more than he could chew with Big Bob. He took his share of the money for the others and said he was heading back East."

Carson sighed again and felt deflated. It was a blow to hear it, no doubt. He'd come to consider the Harvard man a friend, and it just didn't seem right, him up and leaving with the job half-done. "Damn."

"It is what it is," Kat said. "Now, we need to decide about Coffeyville."

Carson snatched up his shot glass and threw back the whisky, setting the glass down again hard. "Hell, I don't want to go to Coffeyville."

"Coffeyville, Kansas?" said a man at the next table.

Carson twisted in his chair to look at him, one of the construction workers, cut from the same cloth as Baily, brawny and hairy. "That's right. You from there?"

"Nope," the construction worker said. "I helped build the depot there a couple of years back for the Leavenworth, Lawrence and Galveston Railroad. Good work and fair pay, but I don't blame you for not wanting to go. Not exactly a hotbed of social activity, and the ugliest women I've seen this side of the Mississippi."

Carson froze and stared at the man. Something had tickled a memory.

The construction worker frowned. "You okay, mister?

"Can't you see the man's thinking, Lester?" Baily interjected.

"Sorry," Carson said. "You did what there?"

"Helped build the depot."

"But the railroad company. Which one?"

"Leavenworth, Lawrence and Galveston," Lester said.

"Mister, you might not know it, but you just did me a favor." Carson pushed away from the table and stood.

Kat stood, too. "Are we going?"

"Yes."

"Where are we going?"

"Coffeyville, Kansas."

Confusion crossed Kat's face. "I thought Coffeyville was a bad bet."

"It just got a lot better," Carson said. "Now hustle up. We're losing daylight."

CHAPTER 36

Upon hearing Carson was leaving, Hank Baily swept him into another sweaty bearhug. For a moment, Carson thought tears might actually well up in the man's eyes. They exchanged goodbyes and solemn vows of eternal friendship, Carson the whole time pretending not to see Kat's smirk.

An hour west of Eureka Springs, Kat finally asked, "Okay, out with it. What changed your mind?"

"Gordon ain't Big Bob's only brother."

"I know that," Kat said. "He's in Huntsville. So what?"

"No, I mean another brother," Carson told her. "Elvin McGraw. He's the oldest of all four."

"News to me. Where's this information coming from?"

"Colby told me. Didn't mean much to me at the time, but when Hank Baily's friend mentioned the Leavenworth, Lawrence and Galveston Railroad Company, it brought it all back."

"I don't follow."

"Elvin works for the Leavenworth, Lawrence and Galveston, and we just learned the railroad has a depot in Coffeyville," Carson said. "Just maybe Bob didn't pull the town out of a hat when he told Angus a place for their meetup. Maybe he's going to see his brother."

"It could still be a goose chase," Kat said. "And Bob's got

a head start on us. Even if that's where he was going, he might be long gone by the time we arrive."

"If we wait for guarantees in life, we'll be waiting until we're old and gray," Carson said. "They might be there. Or Elvin might know something. Or who knows? It's still a risk, but a better one."

"Then I guess we'd better get along to Coffeyville." Kat spurred her horse, and it trotted ahead down the road.

Carson followed.

Full dark descended, and they were still short of the Oklahoma line.

Kat tsked. "Sleeping on the ground again. You do know how to show a girl a good time, Carson."

"I don't think we'll see many hotels cutting across Indian territory."

"As long as we don't see any Indians," Kat said.

They made camp and ate. Small talk was minimal. They were both bone-tired, falling asleep immediately, heads upon saddles.

They rose before dawn, coffee and hardtack. They didn't waste time and crossed into Oklahoma by full light. There was no sign of Indians, but both Carson and Kat kept a sharp watch just the same. Most of the current Indian troubles were farther west, so they were cautious but not fearful. They rode all day, setting a steady pace and stopping only long enough to rest the horses. At nightfall, they stopped short of the Kansas line and camped along the Verdigris River. Kat didn't even try to attempt polite small talk, citing three nights in a row sleeping on the ground as her absolute limit. The next morning, they headed north along the river, looking for a place to ford and happened upon a trading post for fur trappers. A man there ran a ferry made of rough-hewn logs and took both Carson and Kat across the river for a nickel.

By lunchtime, they were plodding into Coffeyville.

Hank Baily's construction crew pal had warned it was a

nothing sort of place, and to Carson's observation, there certainly wasn't much to suggest excitement. On the other hand, Carson had seen shabbier towns, or towns with more unpleasant folk. Dull wasn't the worst thing a town could be. People watched Carson and Kat as they passed, but with curiosity, not hostility.

Carson politely touched the brim of his hat at the next pedestrian, an older man who looked like a shopkeeper. "Beg pardon, sir, but how would I find the train depot?"

"All the way through town to the other side," the shopkeeper said. "Small building right next to the tracks. Can't miss it."

"Obliged to you."

"No trouble at all. Have yourself a good day, young man."

They traveled the dirt street past shops and dwellings to the other side of town. The depot was little more than a shack and a small, covered platform next to the tracks. They tied their horses to the hitching post and dismounted.

"Maybe I should go in on my own," Carson suggested.

Kat raised an eyebrow. "Why's that?"

"A man with a chunk of ear shot off traveling with a gun-toting, red-haired woman might ring a bell with some folks," Carson explained. "On my own, he might notice the ear, or maybe not. In any case, I'll be less of a spectacle without you."

Kat grinned. "I guess I can take that as a compliment."

Carson returned the grin. She was indeed a good-looking woman. "Take it as you like."

"It might not even be Elvin in there," she said. "Might not even be anyone at all."

"I'm about to find out."

He climbed the two steps up to the platform, crossed it, and tried the depot door. Locked. He noticed the "Closed" sign. There was a small ticket window next to the door. It was closed, too, but he could see inside. A man in the back was moving some crates around, a gray vest over a white shirt with the sleeves rolled up and a clerk's visor. His back was to Carson.

Carson knocked on the glass.

The man started and turned around, and in that instant, Carson knew.

In his younger days, the man was probably as brawny as Big Bob, but Elvin was stooped and older now, black hair shot through with gray. The wicked gleam in Big Bob's eyes at the thought of any petty cruelty was absent in Elvin's, which were simply a tired brown, observant but unenergetic.

"Ticket window ain't open until in the morning," Elvin said. "They ain't sent me the final schedule yet."

"Elvin?"

Elvin's eyes narrowed. "Who are you?"

"Sorry to bother you. I'm looking for Elvin McGraw."

"I'm Elvin Webber."

Carson frowned. "You're not Bob McGraw's brother?"

Elvin sighed. "I wondered when somebody would be along. You a marshal or something?"

"I'm no kind of lawman," Carson said. "I used to ride with Bob."

Elvin took a step closer, getting a better look at Carson. His eyes went to Carson's mangled ear, and he nodded. "Where's the woman?"

"The woman?"

"The redhead."

Carson thought to lie, but then immediately decided it was the wrong play. "She's outside. We didn't want to crowd you."

Elvin looked back at the crates, then at Carson again. "People drop stuff off here to be put on the weekly train. Gets a might cluttered if I don't keep up with it. Let me finish getting things in order, then I'll meet you. Maybe twenty minutes. There's a place called the Bluebird Café. Good coffee."

"Obliged," Carson said. "The Bluebird. Twenty minutes."

The café was located halfway back down the street they'd come to find the train depot. Carson told Kat about his exchange with Elvin on the way.

The Bluebird Café was simple and small, a half-dozen tables with three or four chairs at each, all empty. A haggard woman in her fifties wiped her hands on an apron and said to pick whatever table they liked. Kat insisted on the one in the corner and sat in a chair with her back to the wall.

"I don't suppose it occurred to you he'll round up his brothers to come gun us while we sit quietly sipping coffee." Kat drew her .32 revolver and held it on her lap under the table.

"I thought of it, but I don't figure it that way," Carson said. "He don't seem the type."

"You'll forgive me if I'm not keen to risk my life on whether or not you're a good judge of character."

Carson ignored her and waved over the woman with the apron. "Two cups of coffee."

"I'm hungry," Kat said. "What's to eat?"

"Beef stew and corn bread," the woman told her.

"Okay, bring that," Kat said. "Thanks."

Elvin walked through the door exactly twenty minutes later and sat down at their table. The woman brought him a cup of coffee without him having to ask.

"I saw them," Elvin said, anticipating the question. "But they're long gone now."

Carson spared Kat a glance before returning to Elvin. "You could have told me that back at the depot."

"I'm sure you have some follow-up questions," Elvin said. "Questions go better with coffee." He spooned sugar into his cup.

"When did you see them last?" Carson asked. "And where did they go?"

"Yesterday morning," Elvin said. "I got 'em on the train heading out, and by now they've switched trains heading west."

"West, huh?" Carson scratched the stubble along his jaw. "That doesn't narrow it down much. There's a lot of west out there."

"I suppose that was the idea," Elvin explained. "They got tickets all the way to California but might get off sooner. I told them not to tell me where. I don't want to know, because if I don't know, I can't tell anyone. The point is, they're long gone. Bob told me somebody would be along. Maybe the law. Maybe you two."

"And this is supposed to discourage us, I reckon," mused Carson. "Make us give up and go home?"

"I reckon," Elvin said.

"Then why tell us at all?" Kat asked. "You could've just said you hadn't seen them."

"Maybe you'd believe that, and maybe you wouldn't," Elvin said. "But if I'm honest and tell what I know, I reckon I've washed my hands of it. I'm not like Bob and Gordon. I'm a law-abiding citizen. You're a bounty hunter, ma'am, and that ain't exactly the law, but it's close enough I don't want to be on the wrong side of it. I'm in a strange, in-between sort of place. I don't want anything to do with my brothers and their crooked ways, but kin is kin, and I'll help avoid bloodshed if I can."

"Is that why you changed your name to Webber?" Carson asked. "So you wouldn't be associated with your brothers?"

"I didn't change it. Webber was my father's name. He died, and my mother remarried," Elvin explained. "The new husband was McGraw, and the next three boys were his." He stared into his coffee, and a change seemed to come over him, a sad memory approaching from a long way off. "He didn't much see me as his responsibility, so I went my own way at age fourteen. Got a job with the railroad and stuck with it. I figured they could be a happy family without me . . . except that didn't quite work out either." He paused to sip coffee, seeming reluctant to continue.

But Carson was too curious to let it go. "What do you mean by that?"

"I guess he wasn't of a mind to look after his own boys any more than he was to be a father to me," Elvin said. "He took off to parts unknown when Bob was only six. There was no man around to raise 'em up right, show 'em how a proper man acts. They got into trouble a lot, and, well, you know how that went. I always thought maybe I could have done something then, been some kind of big brother. Maybe it would have mattered." He shrugged and finished his coffee. "What's done is done."

"Well, it sounds like we missed them." Carson looked at Kat. "I can't think of any more questions. You?"

She shook her head. "I guess not."

"I appreciate you're in a difficult position, Mr. Webber," Carson said. "You didn't have to talk to us, but you did. We're obliged."

"You sticking around or hitting the trail?" Elvin asked.

Carson rubbed his eyes with a thumb and blew out a heavy sigh. "Hell, I don't know. I don't know anything."

"I guess we need to figure that out," Kat said.

"If you decide to go, see Lucille about getting some grub to take with you," Elvin suggested. "She'll wrap it up for you. I'm an old bachelor and do that sometimes, when I don't feel like cooking."

"We'll consider it."

Elvin stood. "Well, that's it, then. Sorry it didn't work out for you." He nodded to each of them and left.

They sat for a moment, not talking.

Then Kat said, "You believe him?"

Carson nodded. "Yeah."

"I was afraid you'd say that. We're done, aren't we?"

"We could follow them to California," Carson said. "Which

won't do us much good if they get off in Utah. Hell, they could be anywhere."

"That's it, then. Well, it was nice working with you, Carson." Kat stood and holstered her .32.

"Where are you going?"

"To see if there's anything like a hotel in this two-bit town," Kat said. "It's too late in the day to make it very far, and I'll be damned if I'm sleeping on the ground tonight. You?"

"I don't know. I hadn't thought that far. Maybe I'll see if there's a saloon. I could use something stronger than coffee."

"Then maybe I'll find you there after I get a room. If not, well, it's been fun."

She winked at him and walked out of the Bluebird Café and didn't look back.

CHAPTER 37

Coffeyville's only saloon, as it turned out, sat directly across the street from the Bluebird Café and was called the Prairie Mermaid. An enormous oil painting behind the bar drove the point home: a mermaid perched on a rock before a foamy green sea, her bottom half all fish and her topless upper half definitely all woman. The proprietor had served fourteen years as a bosun's mate aboard a whaler, squirreling away his money to open a dockside pub someday, but when the time had arrived, he'd decided he was sick of ships and the sight of the ocean. So he'd headed west and then dropped anchor in Coffeyville, Kansas.

Carson had learned all this while talking to the man and slowly working on a bottle of whisky. The old sailor might have claimed to be sick of the sea, but a big, wooden ship's wheel hung on the wall over a battered, upright piano, and a brass bell sat at one end of the bar to be rung whenever anyone bought the house a round, or for any similarly significant event. All reminders of a past life.

Late afternoon crept into early evening, and the barstools filled up around him. Carson had gone around and around in circles, trying to think what he should do next until finally he decided to stop thinking altogether, letting himself go numb and blocking the idle chatter all around him.

A hazy, uncertain amount of time passed, and then Carson felt a tap on his shoulder. He turned to see Kat standing there, a package under one arm, her other thumb hooked into her belt.

She looked at him with bright eyes, head cocked to one side, and lit up the room with a quirky grin. "You drinking that all by yourself?"

Carson grabbed the bottle and another glass and gestured to an unoccupied table by the window. They sat. Carson noticed not so much time had passed after all. There was still a good hour of daylight.

"Thought you went looking for a hotel." Carson filled both shot glasses.

She set her package on the table, took her glass, and sipped. "Old widow rents out her spare rooms. Nothing fancy, but it's a bed."

Carson eyed the package. It was wrapped with brown paper and tied with white string, a neat bow on top. "What's that?"

"I got it at the Bluebird," Kat said. "One of those meals Lucille packs up that you can take with you, like Elvin told us. My plan is to head back to my room, kick off my boots, eat fried chicken, and forget the McGraw brothers exist."

"There's worse ways to pass an evening." She didn't invite him to share the chicken, and she sure as hell hadn't invited him to share her room at the widow's house. Carson had been drinking just enough to feel sad about it, but not enough to make a fool of himself.

"What are you going to do now?" Kat asked.

Carson emptied his shot glass and set it on the table in front of him. "I've been thinking about that a lot."

"And?"

"And I'll try thinking about it again tomorrow."

"You must have some notion."

Carson shrugged. "Head west, maybe."

"After McGraw?"

Carson shook his head. "No. Just seems like a good direction. I'd thought about going back to find my mom, but I don't want to face her, not with a bounty still on my head. But I'm all done chasing Big Bob McGraw. Did my best. Didn't work out. I mean, if we cross paths, then, yeah, I'll start shooting and explain later, but I'm not holding my breath."

Kat finished her drink, stood, and gathered her package. She bent and gave Carson a kiss on the cheek. "Take care of yourself, Carson. We probably won't see each other again . . . but you never know."

She gave his shoulder a squeeze and left.

Yeah. You never know.

Carson sat there, feeling glum, and stared out the window. Even the whisky had lost its appeal. Chopping wood and mending fences on the Taylor Ranch seemed a lifetime ago. He wished he were back there.

Across the street, Elvin Webber emerged from the Bluebird Café, juggling three of the brown paper–wrapped packages like the one Kat had earlier. Carson watched the man turn toward the depot, and a few minutes later he came back the other way, driving a beat-up surrey, pulled by a tired, gray mare, the packaged meals on the seat next to him.

Carson watched Elvin go. Either the Bluebird was the only place to eat in town, or Elvin really liked the food there. Something about those packages pricked Carson's curiosity, but he was too lazy to chase after it.

A minute later, the realization drifted in all on its own. Three meals? The other two weren't for his family. He'd said he was a bachelor. No wife or kids.

Carson stood, felt the whisky in his legs. He rubbed his eyes, took a couple of deep breaths, and left the saloon, crossing the street to the Bluebird Café. He was well aware that he was grasping at straws. Three meals didn't necessarily mean three men. Elvin might have been a glutton. Or maybe he was thinking ahead to the next day's breakfast and lunch. There could have been a dozen explanations.

And yet Carson knew none of those explanations mattered because they weren't true. Call it instinct, or—and Carson had to admit this to himself—he may simply have fallen in love with a notion that meant he hadn't failed, that he could still accomplish what he'd set out to do, that the slate could still be cleaned.

He entered the café, and Lucille looked up at him, her tired eyes bland and unwelcoming. "Well, I'm closing up, but I suppose I could rustle you up something simple and quick."

"No, ma'am, I don't mean to trouble you," Carson said. "I was in here earlier."

"I remember. With Elvin and that red-haired woman."

"Yes, ma'am, exactly. I was actually looking for Elvin. Had something pretty important to tell him."

"Oh, you just missed him. I'm sorry. He picked up some meals to take with him."

Carson worked hard to look dejected. "Damn. Pardon the language, ma'am. It was sort of important. You know where I can find him?"

"It's no secret, I guess," Lucille said. "He has a place down in Copperhead Gorge, along the creek."

"The creek?"

"Copperhead Creek," Lucille explained. "Although it's way bigger than a creek, really. Just not big enough to be a proper river. It feeds into the Verdigris. Elvin has a place there. Leastways, that's what I heard. Never been myself."

"Would you be able to give me directions?"

"Like I said, I never been there, but my understanding is it ain't hard to find. Happy to share what I've heard."

"That would be most helpful, ma'am," Carson said. "Thank you kindly."

CHAPTER 38

Kat woke up in her room at the widow's house, yawned and stretched and swung her feet over the bed. She stood, went to the vanity where a pitcher of water and a basin waited. She splashed cool water on her face, blinking the sleep from her eyes. Morning light crept in through the window.

Coffee. I need coffee.

She rubbed water behind the back of her ears, splashed some on her neck, dried and dressed, then packed up and left the room, thanking the widow on the way out. She headed toward the Bluebird, walking slowly, in no particular hurry.

Kat hadn't done too badly for herself. She lamented the loss of the big prizes, Big Bob and Gordon, but she'd collected on Memphis, and it had turned out there'd been smaller rewards on all of the other men. Not having to split with Tate had made the smaller bounties more worth the trouble.

She braced herself for a tinge of guilt, but it never came. Colby Tate was someone who'd been in the way of what she wanted to accomplish. He was the competition. Katherine Payne was fully aware, in some abstract way, that she'd done something wrong, at least as defined by the laws of the land. All her life she'd had to fight tooth and nail to get what was hers, to make a place for herself in the world, and the laws were made by men like Tate to benefit men like Tate, the rich and the powerful from back East who didn't give a damn about a woman like Kat, who was just trying to get ahead.

By the time anyone found Tate's body in the abandoned barn, Kat would be long gone, and the murder would be blamed on the McGraw brothers anyway.

She walked into the Bluebird Café and asked Lucille for coffee and a couple of biscuits to take with her.

"I thought you'd left town and headed north with your man," Lucille said. "Or did you decide to stay a while?"

Kat looked confused. "My man?"

"From yesterday," Lucille said. "You were in here with Elvin and that good-looking fella. Shame about that chewed-up ear. If I was fifteen years younger . . ." Lucille winked.

Ah, she meant Carson. "He doesn't belong to me. Did you say north?" Carson had told her he was considering a trek west, or he might have changed his mind and headed south to see his mother. Even east was a possibility if he was looking to take the same ferry back across the Verdigris.

North didn't figure.

"He came back in, looking for Elvin," Lucille said. "Had something to tell him or ask him or . . . heck, I don't know. I mind my own business. That's how I keep out of trouble. I gave him directions to Elvin's place. Like I told him, it ain't no secret. Anyone in town can find the man if they want."

"Would you mind giving me those directions, too?" Kat asked. "I'm thinking I might need to catch up with Carson after all."

Lucille grinned. "Not your man, huh?"

Kat returned the grin. "Am I that obvious?"

Elvin Webber's place hadn't been hard to find. It wasn't some outlaw hideout in the Ozarks, after all. It was just a place where a man lived. It was a nice house, with a barn and a pigsty right next to it with a half-dozen good-sized hogs.

It sat well up the bank from Copperhead Creek, which must have been named during a drought, because it was fast and deep enough to be a small river, a fact Carson had discovered when he'd taken Jet down for water.

He'd waited all night, and now watched the house from a shadowy clump of bushes that gave him a good angle on both the house and the barn. If Carson had guessed right, there were three men inside, and he wasn't keen to try three on one again, although Elvin was hardly cut from the same cloth as Angus. Carson figured all he had to do was wait and the odds would get better.

Five minutes later, he was proved right. Elvin emerged from the house. It looked like he was dressed for work down at the train depot. Just as Carson had thought, Elvin was a dutiful employee of the railroad. He watched Elvin go to the barn and enter. Carson saw he was hitching the surrey. He'd be on his way soon. Carson headed back down around a bend in the road, a spot he'd picked earlier. He waited.

A few minutes later, Elvin came around the bend, the horse pulling the surrey at a slow, easy trot. Carson stepped out of his hiding place, one hand held high, commanding Elvin to stop. He wielded the Winchester with the other hand, leveling the barrel at Elvin's chest. The surrey slowed and stopped, Elvin reining in the horse. Carson took hold of the horse's bridle to keep the animal still.

Elvin saw the rifle pointing at him and tensed, but a second later, all the tension leaked out of him in a sigh. "I thought I had you buffaloed."

"You did."

"Then what tipped you off?"

"I saw you later coming out of the Bluebird," Carson said. "One man. Three dinners."

"Maybe I'm just a big eater."

"Maybe." Carson saw Elvin wasn't wearing a gun, so he

leaned the Winchester on his shoulder. "I was just playing a hunch."

"Now what?"

"Now you ride on," Carson told him.

"Why stop me at all?" Elvin asked. "You just could have stayed hidden."

"I believed what you told me yesterday," Carson said. "About you being in a sort of in-between place, doing what's right on one side and your brothers on the other. Must be hard to know what to do. I think you're a good man who got stuck with bad choices, and you're just trying to do your best. I'd hate for you to get a half mile down the road and then hear something worrisome and come back and get caught up in something that might not go your way."

Elvin sighed again, looked over his shoulder, then back at Carson. "I guess I'd better get that depot sorted. The morning train likes to get the freight loaded quick as possible so they can stay on schedule."

Carson let go of the bridle and stepped back. "I'd never stand between a man and his job."

"You have a good day." Elvin touched the brim of his hat, then flicked the reins, and the surrey lurched forward.

Carson watched him go. Elvin Webber didn't look back.

In his hiding spot back in the bushes, Carson watched and waited.

An hour slipped by, and he began to wonder if he'd need to force the issue. He'd had no breakfast and no coffee, and he hadn't slept. His mood wasn't the best, nervous and irritable. This time, Carson intended to seize the first opportunity that was offered. Shoot first and ask questions later. It might not have been sporting, but Big Bob McGraw didn't deserve a sporting chance. He deserved to be shot stone-cold dead. Carson no longer entertained the luxury of bringing the man in alive.

As soon as Carson had finished thinking such thoughts,

the front door of the house swung open, and out came Bob, yawning and scratching his rear end. No jacket, shirt untucked, sleeves rolled up. He rubbed his eyes and started walking at a casual pace.

Carson lifted the Winchester and took aim, lining up his sight on the big man's broad chest. He began to squeeze the trigger.

Then stopped.

Bob wasn't wearing a gun.

Carson's thoughts raced. I can still take him alive. He's unarmed, and a shot might bring Gordon anyway, or leastways put him on alert. If I can take Bob quietly, I can turn my attention to Gordon. One at a time's a lot safer than two at once. He eased off the Winchester's trigger.

Part of Carson was relieved. Bushwhacking a man from hiding—even a man like Bob, who surely deserved it—didn't sit well. Bob being unarmed made taking him alive an acceptable risk.

Carson watched Bob walk to the outhouse and shut himself inside. He glanced back at the house. No sign of Gordon. Carson figured his best chance was to catch Bob on his way back from the outhouse. Clocking him a good one in the back of the head with his rifle butt should put him out of commission.

And if that didn't work out, Carson could still shoot him.

He sprang from his place in the bushes and sprinted for a thick-trunked bur oak. Carson put his back to it and waited, clutching the rifle to his chest. Bob's return trip would bring him right past the tree, and that was when Carson would strike. He glanced occasionally back toward the house, but there was still no sign of Gordon.

The outhouse door creaked open, then slammed shut again. Bob's heavy footfalls trudged toward him. Carson tensed. This was it. The footfalls came closer, dry grass crunching.

Then, abruptly, the steps turned, grass crunching away from him.

Carson frowned. Where the hell's he going?

He chanced a peek around the tree trunk and saw Bob heading toward the pigsty, the big man reaching into his shirt pocket. He pulled out a small pouch, rolling paper, and matches. Bob rolled a smoke, shoved it into the corner of his mouth, and struck a match, puffing the cigarette to life and blowing gray smoke into the air. He leaned against the rough-hewn, split-log fence of the pigsty and smoked, watching the hogs snort and root around.

Carson headed for him, a tight grip on the Winchester. He was betting that the snorting of the hogs would cover his footsteps in the dry grass. He approached closer, his heart-beat quickening. Bob puffed his cigarette and blew smoke, oblivious.

Now Carson was almost right on top of him. He cranked the Winchester back to hit Bob at the base of his skull with everything he had. One good strike with the rifle butt and the big man would go down. Not even five steps away and—

Bob turned and saw Carson, the outlaw's eyes shooting wide.

Carson picked up speed to close the final few feet but stumbled as he brought the rifle down. The Winchester's butt slammed across Bob's jaw, spinning his head around with a loud crack even as Carson's momentum carried him forward. He slammed into Bob, and both of them crashed through the split-log fence into the slop of the pigsty. They went down, sinking into the mud and the filth, hogs squealing like mad and scattering.

They both staggered to their feet at the same time. Bob's eyes were covered in mud. He took a wild swing and missed Carson by a mile. Carson slammed the Winchester into his gut, and Bob grunted, bending double. Carson swung the rifle like a club, connecting with the back of Bob's head.

Everything inside Bob went limp all at once, and he collapsed face-first into the mud. Carson succumbed to poor footing and also flopped back into the mud. He sat up, spitting filth from his mouth. He wiped his eyes clear—Just in time to see Gordon walking toward him, lifting his pistol.

Carson tried to get to his feet, slipped in the mud again.

Gordon's pistol spit fire. The mud three inches to Carson's left erupted with the stray shot. Carson fumbled for his Colt, his fingers thick with pig filth. The slippery six-shooter flew from his hand and sank into the mud.

Gordon fired again, and Carson felt and heard hot lead speed by, less than an inch from his ear.

Gordon kept coming, thumbed back the hammer of his revolver. This close, there was not one chance in hell the outlaw would miss again.

Carson swallowed hard, stumbling back in the mud. I'm going to die.

A rifle shot split the air, and Gordon's hat flew off. His head spun, eyes going wide. The next shot made him flinch, and he turned and ran into the barn.

Carson righted himself and saw Kat approaching at a gallop. Thirty feet away, she reined in her horse and dismounted, the Spencer rifle trained on the open barn door. Gordon flew out, his horse running full speed. Kat fired, but Gordon leaned low in the saddle as he raced past. Kat went to one knee and fired as the outlaw fled. She levered in another cartridge and fired again, but by then Gordon was around the bend and out of sight.

Kat lowered the Spencer. "Damn it."

Carson trudged out of the pigsty, big glops of mud plopping off him. "That's the second time you've saved me from getting shot by Gordon. I owe you."

"Yeah, well, it's the second time I let the bastard get away, too," she said bitterly.

"How'd you even know to come look for me?"

"Lucille." Kat related her conversation with the café owner. "I thought you might have been on to something, not that it did us any good."

"Oh, I think it did us some good." Carson gestured to the unconscious man in the pigsty. "We might have lost the little fish, but I landed the big one."

Kat came to the edge of the broken pigpen and looked. "Hot damn, is that Big Bob?"

"Yep."

"Is he dead?"

"No," Carson said. "I gave him a good knock on the head. He'll have a good, long snooze, but he'll be okay."

"I'll find something to tie him up with." Kat looked Carson up and down, wrinkling her nose. "In the meantime, you might want to clean up."

Carson looked down at himself. "I reckon I am pretty muddy."

"I got some bad news for you, slick." Kat pinched her nose closed with thumb and forefinger. "That's more than just mud."

Carson laughed. "I've smelled better."

"Head down to the river."

Carson looked down at Copperhead Creek, then back at Kat.

"A quick dunk under the water isn't going to do it. Take your time," she said. "I'll give you your privacy. Come back up when you're finished."

"Right." Carson's eyes went to Bob. "Tie him up first thing. I don't think he'll come to anytime soon, but better to be safe."

Kat waved him away. "I'm on it. Now go clean up, stinko."

Carson fetched his guns from the pigsty. He needed a change of clothes from his saddlebags, so he took Jet by the reins and led him down to the edge of Copperhead Creek. He looked back once to make sure he was alone before stripping off his clothes. He washed them the best he could in the cold water, beating them against a rock and wringing them out. He hung them on a low tree limb to dry.

Carson let Jet roam loose to feed on some grass as he ventured knee-deep into the river. It was cold, the current a lot swifter than it looked. When he was waist-deep, he dunked under, then came up sputtering and shivering.

Damn, that is cold. What must it be like in winter?

But he realized he was grinning. It didn't matter if he was covered in pig crap. He'd done it. He'd tracked down Big Bob McGraw and had taken him alive. Carson Stone was going to clear his name. He dunked under the water again, wishing he had a bar of soap.

CHAPTER 39

Kat wished she'd asked Carson to pull Bob out of the pigsty before going to bathe. She went in, her boots sinking into the muck, and took Bob by the ankles. She grunted and heaved and dragged him clear, then tied his wrists and ankles with rawhide strips she'd found in the barn. The big outlaw wasn't going anywhere even if he woke up.

She glanced down at the river, but Carson was out of sight behind some trees. She'd told him to take his time, but she still needed to hurry.

Kat went into the house and began to search, under the beds, in every cabinet and closet.

Nothing.

She stood in a tidy living room, hands on hips, and made a slow turn, eyes raking every corner. It had to be here, didn't it? She supposed not. The outlaws could have stashed it somewhere else, obviously, but if it had been her, she'd want to keep it close.

Kat looked down, her eyes narrowing on the rag throw rug she was standing on. One corner had been folded over. Had she done that, kicked it maybe as she walked past? She didn't think so. She booted the rug to the side and examined the floor underneath. The room's floorboards were each six to eight feet long except for the ones that had been hidden by the rug, cut roughly three feet by three feet.

She knelt and pried the first board up with her knife. It lifted away easily. It had been just sitting on the crossbeams below. The next three boards weren't nailed down either, and she removed them quickly, then looked into the hidey-hole below.

Kat reached in, grabbed the top of the canvas sack, and heaved.

And was almost pulled down into the hole. Damn thing's heavy.

She widened her stance, took hold with both hands, pulled the bag out, and set it on the floor next to her with a metallic clink. She hurriedly opened the sack and peered within. Gold coins. Just as she'd hoped, it was the take from the bank robbery in Fayetteville. She pulled out the rest of the sacks to discover well-worn saddlebags underneath. She opened them and riffled through the mix of coins and greenbacks. This must have been Big Bob's stash that Carson had told her about. There must be over twenty thousand dollars here.

Kat took it all in. The payroll gold and Bob's stash all together represented more money than she'd earn in the next ten years of chasing down bounties. Ten years of haunting dank saloons and skulking after scum. At any moment, one of them could get the drop on her. Kat could take a bullet. She'd been lucky so far, but luck always ran out.

Really, the decision was easy.

There was only one loose end to take care of. Kat reloaded the Spencer and headed for the river. She stepped lightly, reached the bank, and followed the sound of splashing. She came through a stand of trees and saw him.

Carson stood in the fast-moving water up to his chest, splashing his face and working his fingers through his wet hair. Kat moved to the very edge of the river, raised the Spencer, sighting down the barrel.

When Carson saw her, a second of confusion crossed his face, followed by alarm. He twisted underneath the water just as she fired. Kat followed the white blur of his body along the bank, cocked the rifle, and fired again. Carson disappeared into the deep center of the river.

Kat cocked the gun again, cursing, still following the edge of the river. She couldn't have missed, not from that close. It was impossible. She leaped atop a large, flat boulder that afforded her a long, clear view of the river for at least a quarter mile. She brought the rifle to her shoulder and waited. If she'd missed, he'd have to come up for air. She rested her finger on the trigger, ready to squeeze at the first sign of him.

She waited.

A full minute went by, and Kat's eyes darted between banks and scanned up and down the length of it. Two minutes, then three.

She lowered the rifle, nodding to herself. She must have hit him. It was the only explanation. He was hit and the current had taken him down and deep. She felt relief. It was done, the hard part at least. Now, for the rest of it. There was still plenty to do.

Kat found where Carson had left his soiled clothing and his guns. She picked up his rifle and heaved it as far as she could into the river. The Colt Peacemaker followed next. She tossed the clothes in last, and the current took them rapidly downstream.

She climbed the bank back up to the house, found Bob where she'd left him. Kat considered putting a bullet in his head. Corpses were much less trouble than live men.

Kat laughed to herself. No, just this one time I'll take my man in alive. I suppose I owe Carson that much at least. And anyway, she was beginning to suspect the marshals were thinking of her in a bad way because she always brought in her bounties dead. Yes, it was all good and legal, but she was getting a bad reputation.

Big Bob would be the biggest bounty of her career and she'd bring him in alive. The more Kat thought about it, the more she liked it. A fitting end to her career. She could head into retirement in style.

Joplin was a full day's ride, but half the day was gone. So, she'd set out immediately. When she'd been in the barn earlier, she'd seen a wagon and a team of horses. Plenty big enough to tote a trussed-up Bob McGraw, along with all the gold. She'd need to make sure Bob was tied with extra rope. Kat didn't plan to turn him loose until she turned him over to the marshal in Joplin. Then, by stage or train, he'd make his way back to El Paso for trial where—Kat presumed—he would be found guilty and hanged.

That was probably why they occasionally wanted these outlaws alive, she mused. It would be a shame to cheat honest citizens out of a good hanging. Her eyes went back to Bob. Big man. Heavy. It would be a chore getting him up and into the wagon.

Well, nothing worthwhile ever came easy.

Carson's arms, legs, fingers, and toes were all nearly frozen to the bone, but he didn't dare come out of hiding.

Eventually, she'll think I drowned. Or that her shot hit its mark. But how long will she wait? Kat's a tenacious one, make no mistake.

When Carson saw Kat looking down the Spencer's barrel right at him, he twisted away and went deep, the rifle's report muffled by the water. Something hot scorched his lower back, and even now he wondered if he was bleeding to death. He kicked sideways, making for the far bank even as the current took him downstream. He held his breath until his lungs burned, and then held it a little longer.

When he finally come up for air, he hit his head on a rock. The current took him to an overhanging chunk of riverbank among the reeds. There was barely a two-inch space where he could stick his nose and mouth out of the water for air.

And so he stayed like that and waited.

And waited.

Had an eternity passed or half an hour? Sore and frozen, he finally came out and paddled weakly back to shore. He crawled up on the bank, looking and listening. No sign of Kat. He made his way back along the edge of the river, pausing occasionally to listen.

His clothes and guns were gone.

Carson swore every vulgarity he could think of.

He looked behind a rock, where he'd stashed his boots. They were still there. He pulled them on and stood looking down at himself. He was a sight and that was for sure, standing there dripping in nothing but boots.

A stinging throb at his lower back reminded him he had bigger problems. He reached back and winced when his fingers grazed the wound. He gritted his teeth and felt around. A shallow gash across his back. It didn't feel so good, but it wasn't much of a wound, maybe not even worth bandaging. If he'd been a second slower ducking under the water and twisting away . . .

I just had to teach her to use that Spencer, didn't I?

So much for good intentions.

A rustle in the bushes startled him, and his hand went for a gun that wasn't there.

Jet poked his nose out of the shrubbery and snorted.

Carson sighed relief. "Thank God. At least I've got one friend left."

He went into the saddlebags for clothes and got dressed.

"Follow me," he said to the horse. "I need to check something."

Kat was gone, and so was Big Bob. No horses or wagon in the barn. Carson checked the house, and immediately saw the hole in the floor. It didn't even take him a full minute to put two and two together. The money, the girl, and the outlaw. All gone.

Carson supposed the money was too much of a temptation. The question was, what would Kat do now? If she thought Carson shot or drowned, there weren't any witnesses. With all that money, would she even bother with the bounty on McGraw? He wouldn't put it past Kat to put a bullet in the back of the man's head and dump the body in the woods.

But then, why take him in the first place? Would there ever be a pile of money big enough for a person like Kat? Bob McGraw was worth four thousand dollars, and if Kat got used to thinking of that money as hers, she probably wouldn't let it go easily. So she'd need to take him somewhere and hand him over to a marshal. Coffeyville was too small. Joplin? Topeka? Wichita?

Carson could only guess, and if he guessed wrong, he could waste a lot of time riding the wrong way.

But he didn't need to guess. He knew where this would all end up. If Kat turned in Big Bob for the reward, Bob would end up in El Paso for his trial.

Carson left the house and mounted Jet. "Come on, boy. We got a long ride ahead of us."

He headed for the Verdigris and took the same ferry back across the river. Oklahoma stretched ahead, wide open and empty.

CHAPTER 40

Carson didn't see another living soul for the next three days, as he angled across Oklahoma toward Fayetteville. He'd be able to get supplies there, and maybe news. He had enough money for a new Colt Peacemaker, but it would take everything he had left, and he still needed to feed himself all the way to Texas.

As for news, the capture of an outlaw as notorious as Big Bob McGraw would cause talk. Carson needed to know. Was McGraw on his way to El Paso in shackles?

He hit Fayetteville just as the sun was setting. Carson decided supplies could wait until morning, and he pointed himself at the nearest saloon to catch whatever gossip he could. A single beer wouldn't hurt his budget too bad. He pushed through the swinging doors into smoke and piano music.

The place was full, and it took Carson a minute to squeeze in at the bar. He ordered a beer, nursed it, and listened to the chatter around him. A couple of farmers lamenting the lack of rain. Others saying there'd been far too much rain. A couple of merchants working out a business arrangement.

And, of course, the bank robbery was still fresh in everyone's minds. Carson had been watching the back door at the time, but stories of the incident painted a gruesome picture. The scene in front of the bank had been a bloodbath. There was still no sign of the payroll, or the surviving outlaws, which told Carson that either Kat hadn't turned Bob McGraw over to the marshals, or, if she had, word hadn't reached Fayetteville yet. After listening to the talk all around him for an hour and making two beers disappear down his throat, Carson decided he hadn't really learned anything useful. He needed to get out of here and find a place to bed down for the night, and then, in the morning, he could—

Carson felt something cold and hard press into his ribs. Somebody big crowded him from behind.

"Just take it easy, Carson. Let's not nobody do nothing sudden."

Carson recognized the voice immediately. "You do show up in the damnedest places, Gordon."

"Well, I reckon I'm passing through, same as you," Gordon said in a low voice. "I'm wondering if you happen to be on your way to El Paso."

Carson turned slightly so he could face the man.

Gordon increased the pressure in Carson's side. "Easy."

Carson glanced down. Gordon had a stubby pepperbox pressed into his ribs. It wasn't Gordon's usual weapon, but Carson supposed it was easier to conceal than the big Colt on his hip. Gordon himself had gone out of his way to change his appearance. He wore a hat with a wider brim, hair cut close to his head, face clean-shaven. He didn't resemble his wanted poster so much anymore.

Men and noise pushed at them from all sides. In the crowd, it just looked like two men having a chin-wag.

"So, what happens now?" Carson asked.

"We go outside and have a private chat."

"About what?"

"Your red-haired, bounty hunter friend, for a start."

"She's no friend of mine," Carson said.

"You can explain it outside."

"I'm not going to help you shoot me, Gordon. We can talk here."

"I'll shoot you in here just as dead. Try me."

"Then what's the difference?" Carson asked.

"Getting shot now or getting shot later."

A fair point, Carson thought. Maybe he could think of something, make some move. It was better than just standing there taking a bullet without trying. Gordon prodded him with the pepperbox, and Carson began to sluggishly maneuver through the crowd.

"Don't get ahead of me," Gordon told him. "I'll let you have it right in the back."

Carson did as he was told, moving slowly, just a man looking for the exit. His eyes darted back and forth, looking for an opportunity. Should he make his move in here, where it was crowded, or outside? Once outside, Gordon would ask his questions, and Carson would only be able to stall for so long. He had maybe two minutes to figure a way out of this.

Unless some miracle falls out of the sky.

"Carson!"

Carson froze and looked for the man shouting his name.

"Carson, over here!"

"Just keep going," Gordon whispered.

"Carson! Buddy!"

Hank Baily pushed his way through the crowd and planted his bulk squarely in front of Carson and Gordon. He had a sloppy grin on his face and grabbed Carson by the shoulder. "Holy hot damn, buddy, what are you doing here?"

Baily wasn't drunk, but Carson could see the man was headed in that direction.

He felt the pepperbox press into his back.

"Good to see you, Hank," Carson said. "But I'm sort of busy at the moment."

"Aw, hell, come on and have a drink with me," Baily insisted. "I finished that construction job and got paid, so drinks are on me. Heck, they like me so much, they're keeping me on. We're building a Methodist church on the edge of town here starting Monday. So I got until then to spend my pay."

Gordon frowned. "You heard the man, friend. We're busy. Step aside."

Baily's eyes narrowed, focusing on Gordon. "Who in the hell are you?"

"I'm the man telling you to step aside," growled Gordon.

"Well, I'm talking to my good pal, Carson, so why don't you shut the hell up and piss off?"

Carson braced himself. He was pretty sure what was about to happen.

"I'm not saying it again, you slack-jawed moron," Gordon shouted. "Get your fat ass out of our way right now or—"

Baily's fist came up with surprising speed and smacked hard into Gordon's jaw. Gordon's head spun around and he was knocked back, stumbling into the men behind him. Spilled beer. Angry shouts. Shoves from all directions.

Gordon lifted the pepperbox, and a woman somewhere screamed. Men closest to the scene tried to scatter but ran into others in the crowded room. Carson grabbed Gordon's wrist and aimed the pepperbox at the ceiling just as it went off. Dozens of people threw themselves to the floor.

Baily rushed forward and slugged Gordon in the gut. Gordon bent in half, and Baily brought a vicious uppercut to his chin. Gordon's eyes rolled up, and he dropped the pepperbox. It clattered across the floor of the saloon. Gordon listed to the side, then went down hard, rattling the floorboards, and lay there unconscious.

Others in the saloon began to stand up and come closer for a look.

"You're the one who's slack-jawed, ya sumbitch." Baily snapped his fingers at the unconscious man.

"Somebody go for the sheriff!" called the barkeep.

The murmur in the room began to rise again.

"I sure the hell am glad to see you, Hank." Carson went to one knee, unbuckled Gordon's gun belt, then stood and buckled it around his own waist. It felt good to have an iron on his hip again. "Hank, I've got to get out of here. You need to listen to me."

"Go?" Hank blinked in confusion. "Go where?"

"There's no time, man, so listen. You just punched Gordon McGraw into dreamland."

"The outlaw?" Baily looked down at the unconscious man, suddenly worried. "Oh, hell, he ain't going to wake up, is he?"

"There's a big reward on Gordon, and you just earned it," Carson explained. "You hear me? That's your money."

Baily brightened. "A reward?"

"That's right," Carson said. "Just don't mention to the sheriff I was here. It's a long story. I'll explain some other time. I've got to git gone."

"Okay, buddy," Baily said. "Sorry you have to rush off before you can see your friend."

Carson paused. "What?"

"I thought that's why you was in town."

Could Baily be talking about Kat? If she was in town, Carson needed to know. Katherine Payne had a lot to answer for, not least of which was that she'd tried to murder him. "Hank, if you've seen Kat, you've got to tell me where. I need to find her."

"What? The red-haired lady?" Baily waved away the notion. "Not her. Your other friend. The fancy-talking fella."

"Colby Tate?"

"He got himself shot, if I heard tell right," Baily said. "Laid up in the hospital."

Carson let Baily's words soak in. "Tell me where this hospital is."

* * *

The two-story, white-washed clapboard building about a half mile away was tidy and clean. A doctor happened to be working late. He was a stooped old man with a battered black bag, and he was making the rounds when Carson wandered in, holding his hat to his chest. He'd missed visiting hours, but the doctor didn't make an issue out of it.

The upstairs ward was one large room with a line of ten beds going down each side. There were only three patients: a farmer who'd been kicked by a mule, a young woman with a disturbingly wet cough in her chest, and Colby Tate, who slept in the bed all the way at the end of the left-hand row.

"He'd lost a lot of blood by the time I got to him," the doctor told Carson. "He took two bullets, fortunately from a relatively small caliber pistol. The one in his shoulder thankfully didn't hit anything vital. The other shot would have hit his heart except for this."

The doctor took something from his coat pocket and handed it to Carson.

Carson looked at the Harvard pocket watch, the one Tate seemed to cherish. A small slug of lead had lodged into the works just left of center. Carson wondered if Tate would lament the loss of one of his prized possessions or be glad it had been there to stop the bullet. Maybe both.

"The wounds are no longer the problem," the doctor explained. "He got a bad infection, and the fever's had him unconscious most of the time. The good news is the fever finally broke this morning."

"Can I talk to him?" Carson asked.

"The man needs his rest," the doctor said. "You're welcome to wait, but don't wake him. If he comes around on his own, you can speak with him."

"I appreciate it, Doc."

Carson pulled up a chair and sat next to the narrow bed, crossed his arms, and waited. Colby Tate looked pale but seemed to be resting comfortably. It was eerily quiet in the hospital ward, and Carson's mind wandered. Kat had told him Tate was through, that he'd had enough of chasing outlaws and was headed back East. What could have happened to him after he'd parted ways with the lady bounty hunter? Carson considered what to do next, where to go. He supposed he'd still make for El Paso.

He snorted awake, realizing he'd drifted off, his chin down against his chest. He lifted his head when he heard his name, wiped the sleep from his eyes.

"Carson," came the voice again. "Good . . . to see you . . . old sport."

"Colby." Carson focused on the man in the hospital bed. "How are you doing?"

"Been . . . better, I guess." Tate's voice was weak. He was still drowsy. "What . . . what's . . . happened?"

"Looks like you got in the way of a couple of bullets," Carson said. "But don't you worry. You'll be fine. All you need is some more rest, according to the doc."

"Kat . . ."

"She's not here at the moment." Carson didn't see any point in going into the details, at least not yet.

"It was . . . Kat." Tate's voice began to fade.

"What do you mean?" Carson asked. "Kat what?"

"It was . . . Kat . . . who shot me."

Carson suddenly felt leaden but let out a long sigh. On some level he'd known, and it had all gelled when Tate actually said the words. Of course it had been Kat. She'd tried to gun Carson in the river, so why not Tate, too. It should have been obvious a lot sooner. He vowed not to let a pretty face pull the wool so completely over his eyes in the future.

Tate chuckled weakly, and it came out half wheeze. "She . . . doesn't like . . . to share bounties, I guess. Sly little . . . minx. Should have . . . guessed."

"I'm on my way to El Paso after this," Carson said. "You just rest, Colby. If I see her, I'll take care of her for both of us.

You can count on that. We'll get the last laugh yet." Carson didn't really believe it, but it sounded good. Anyway, it might bolster Tate's spirits to hear it.

But the Harvard bounty hunter had already fallen asleep again.

CHAPTER 41

Carson stopped only long enough to rest Jet and sleep just enough to keep from collapsing. He ate in the saddle and was sore, dusty, and exhausted by the time he rode into El Paso midmorning of the eleventh day since he'd set out from Fayetteville. Jet was a strong horse with a big heart, and he'd given Carson everything he could.

He tied Jet to the hitching post outside a saloon he never thought he'd step foot into again. He paused before entering, stroking his horse's nose. "I haven't seen her in a long while, boy. Sort of nervous."

Jet tossed his head and snorted.

Carson frowned. "Easy for you to say."

He sighed, hooked his thumbs into his gun belt, and walked into the saloon.

There were only two people inside. A stick-thin man in a white apron swept the floor, a barkeep preparing for the day. Hunched at one end of the bar was a saloon gal with hair so orange, it had to be fake. She looked a bit long in the tooth for a saloon gal, but that was how she was dressed, her corset pushing her milk-white assets up for the world to see. There was a bottle and a shot glass in front of her. For some, it was never too early to get started.

The barkeep looked up from his sweeping and eyed

Carson. "Not quite ready to open just yet. Maybe give us a few minutes. You in town for the hanging?"

Carson raised an eyebrow. "Hanging?"

"That outlaw called Big Bob McGraw," the barkeep said. "Trial ended yesterday, and they found him guilty. They're building the gallows now in front of the courthouse. Have a seat. I'll get you a drink in a minute."

"Don't trouble yourself," Carson said. "Just looking for one of your girls."

"Not open for that yet either."

"Not looking to do business," Carson clarified. "Just need to ask one of your ladies a question or two. Her name's Annie, on the short side, dark hair in tight curls."

The barkeep shook his head. "Lot of girls through here. Don't remember no Annie."

"Gone almost a year," said the woman at the end of the bar. "We can find you another gal. Plenty here with dark hair."

"Gone where, ma'am?" Carson asked. "If you don't mind me asking."

"Rancher up and married her away from us," she said.

Hearing that made Carson feel odd. Not bad exactly although definitely not good. Just odd.

"I just saw her the other day," the woman said. "She was in town to testify at the trial. She looked well."

The barkeep's head snapped around to look at the woman. "Testify? Wait, you mean she's that Annie? I had no idea she used to work here."

"You'd be surprised the women that's passed through here, Jack," she told the barkeep. "Not all the girls are lifers like me."

Jack shrugged and kept sweeping.

"Ma'am, if you could tell me where to find her, I'd be grateful," Carson said. "Some nearby ranch, I take it."

"Annie's married now, son," the woman said. "Best leave it be."

"I understand, but I promise it's not like that," Carson

assured her. "If she's happy, I'm glad for her. But I left sort of sudden last time I saw her, and I just need to tell her a couple of things and ask a question or two. Sort of turning the last page in a book before closing it shut, if you understand my meaning."

She looked at him for a long moment, then said, "I guess I can understand that. Okay, I'll tell you."

The land west of El Paso was wide and flat, and Carson saw the ranch house, barn, and corral long before he reached it. He didn't see people. There were a half-dozen horses in the corral. When he reached the place, he dismounted and waited a few seconds.

When nobody showed themselves, he called, "Hello the ranch house!"

"Around back!" A woman's voice.

Only two words, but Carson immediately recognized the voice as belonging to Annie.

He left Jet and rounded the house. She stood amid four long clotheslines, each stretched between two poles, white sheets gently billowing in the easy breeze. She was still as pretty as ever and yet looked like a completely different woman. No makeup. A plain blue dress that any rancher's wife might wear. Her hair pulled back hastily, a few loose strands hanging past her face.

She spoke without looking away from her chore. "If it's about that horse, you've come at a bad time, I'm afraid. My husband and the boys are riding the property line, rounding up strays and such, but you can look at the animal and make up your mind, I guess, and then I can let him know what you decide."

"Annie."

Her eyes jerked to him, and there was suddenly recognition

there. "Carson?" She nervously tucked the loose strands of hair behind an ear.

"Hello. Sorry to . . . well, sorry if I'm catching you by surprise."

"Like I said, my husband is off . . . I have a husband."

"I know," Carson said. "Congratulations. Good man?"

"Paul is normal," she said. "I guess that don't sound like a high compliment, but in the saloon you meet all kinds, brutes and outlaws and drunks, and even nice ones once in a while, like you. Paul is just . . ."

"Normal."

"Yeah."

"No kids yet?"

Her slim hand went to her flat belly on reflex. "Trying."

"I'm glad. You'd be good with some kids. A good mom."

And that coaxed a smile out of her.

"I was hoping you could tell me about McGraw's trial."

"Oh." She nodded. "I suppose you would want to hear about that, wouldn't you?"

"If you don't mind."

"I told them, Carson," Annie said. "That it was Big Bob and not you that shot the marshal. I'll be honest, I'm a little ashamed. I should have told the law a long time ago you weren't involved, that it was Bob. It must have been hard for you."

"Hard for you, too," Carson said. "It's not easy to speak against a man like McGraw, knowing what he could do to you."

She laughed nervously. "You should have seen him in that courtroom. When I testified against him, he started yelling that he'd kill me. Kill me and plenty worse. He tried to get at me, but a bunch of deputies held him back. I used to work in a saloon, and I thought I'd heard every mean thing a man could say to a woman, but Bob was able to surprise me. In that second, I regretted it, wished I'd never come forward. It's a frightening thing to have a red-faced man shout he'll kill you if it's the last thing he ever does. I almost felt he could kill me right there with his words. But he didn't, and I'm glad, glad that I spoke up for you, Carson. Better late than never."

"I'm grateful," Carson said. "And I mean that."

"I'll still be glad when he's hanged," Annie admitted. "To know he's gone for good."

"I guess I can appreciate that."

"You should go to the law," Annie suggested. "You're clear now. Tell them to take down all those damn wanted posters."

Carson laughed. He hadn't actually seen a poster with his face on it recently, but he said, "That's a good idea. The likeness never did me justice anyway. Okay, then. Thank you, Annie."

He turned to go.

"Carson."

He turned back.

"Carson, if things had been different . . ."

Carson looked around, at the house and the barn and the billowing laundry, at Annie in a blue dress. He smiled. "Oh, I don't know. I think you did just right for yourself."

Annie returned the smile.

"You take care." He touched the brim of his hat, then left.

He mounted Jet and rode back the way he'd come. He felt strange and tired and good. Carson thought about staying to watch McGraw hang, but he knew the sight wouldn't give him any satisfaction.

And exactly what will give me satisfaction?

Carson didn't know. His life was his own again, and that, too, was a strange feeling.

Still, Annie's advice suddenly seemed prudent. Carson had been a wanted man for a long time. What did it mean for his name to be cleared? He'd hate to get shot next week, or next month, by some bounty hunter who hadn't gotten the word.

When Carson got back to El Paso, he headed for the marshal's office.

Where he found chaos.

A man lay dead in the street, and a woman sobbed over him. People crowded around, men yelling. The door to the jailhouse stood open.

A tall man with a drooping red mustache appeared in the doorway. A tin star was pinned to his vest.

"One of you get down to Clem's," he shouted. "Tell them to round up everyone they can find, and to hurry the hell up!"

He vanished back into the jailhouse, and Carson followed.

"What's happened, Marshal?" Carson asked.

The marshal unlocked a gun cabinet and began pulling out rifles. "Jailbreak."

"McGraw?"

"Hell, yes, McGraw; who do you think? Caught two deputies off guard, killed them and took their guns. I told them not to turn their backs on the bastard. Look, mister, I don't really have time to talk. I'm trying to get a posse together and get after him."

Carson's mind raced. Big Bob had vowed to kill Annie if it was the last thing he ever did, and Annie was out on her ranch all on her own, her husband and the other ranch hands miles away.

"Marshal, there's a girl named Annie who's in danger," Carson said. "McGraw's going to kill her."

"Who?"

"Annie. She testified at the trial against McGraw, and he's going to kill her!"

"Annie Chambers?" the marshal asked. "Paul's wife?"

"If that's her married name, then I guess so." Carson realized he'd never bothered to find out.

"Doesn't make no sense," the marshal said. "Revenge can wait. His first goal will be to escape."

"You don't know the man like I do, Marshal."

The marshal paused, as if seeing Carson for the first time. "Just exactly who are you, mister?"

"Name's Carson Stone."

"Why does that sound familiar?"

Carson explained. "And McGraw is just about the meanest man to ever draw breath. If he's got rage in his heart, he won't be able to do anything else or even think straight until the fires of vengeance are quenched."

"It's going to take me a few more minutes to get this posse together," the marshal told him. "I understand your urge to help her, but fastest thing might be for you to get out there and warn her yourself."

But Carson didn't hear. He was already out the door and in the saddle, riding at a full gallop.

CHAPTER 42

The Golden Spur was the biggest, most luxurious, and therefore most expensive hotel in El Paso. Katherine Payne had been very comfortable since arriving on the same train that had brought Big Bob McGraw back to town in chains.

The marshal in Joplin had suggested the whopping five-thousand-dollar reward on McGraw's head might find its way into Kat's possession more quickly in El Paso, where the trial would be held. This turned out not to be the case, and Kat now figured the Joplin marshal had pulled a fast one on her, trying to wriggle out of a bit of tedious paperwork.

Apparently, five-thousand-dollar rewards took longer to process than lesser amounts, which was how Kat found herself still stuck in El Paso.

Not that it had been all bad. The suite was the biggest in the hotel, and she'd eaten well and drunk well and done a good bit of shopping for her upcoming journey, including six large steamer trunks. She purchased a lot of new clothing, but what mostly filled the trunks was the payroll in gold and Bob's stash of ill-gotten gains. Sturdy padlocks kept the curious from looking inside the trunks.

Kat had considered not waiting. She had more than enough money. But she'd earned that reward for McGraw, and five thousand dollars was nothing to sneeze at.

So she'd wait, and there was more than enough champagne to make the waiting bearable.

She refilled her glass and sipped, thinking about her upcoming voyage.

Kat had decided to quit the States altogether. She had a comfortable cabin booked on a ship leaving New Orleans that would take her to New York, and eventually to France and Paris. It would be a long trip, but she wasn't in a hurry. Feather beds all the way.

I'll never sleep on the ground again. I'll do exactly what I please from here on out.

She reclined on a plush chaise, wearing only a thin shift and flimsy bloomers, and sipped more champagne. Perhaps a late lunch. Or a nap. She closed her eyes, and imagined herself in some trendy Paris café, a handsome count or baron desperate to woo her.

Gunshots jerked her abruptly from her fantasy.

Kat fell off the chaise, spilling the remainder of her champagne. She gathered herself, rushing out onto the second-floor balcony, and looked down into the street. There was a commotion less than half a block away, a crowd gathering. Kat leaned out over the balcony and determined the scene was unfolding in front of the jailhouse.

McGraw. It had to be something to do with the outlaw. Curiosity got the better of her, and she scrambled to get dressed. She had a score of new, stunning frocks and the accessories to go with them, but those weren't the clothes she needed now. She found her pants and the man's shirt, and put them on. She rolled up the sleeves and shrugged into the shoulder holster with the .32.

Excitement pulsed through her veins, and in that moment, she learned something about herself.

Katherine Payne liked this. She enjoyed the excitement, the potential danger of running toward gunshots instead of away from them. Could she really run off to Paris? How much luxury could one woman stand before it became boring? She'd need to give these new thoughts serious consideration.

But not now.

She looked for her boots, tried to remember the last time she'd worn them. She found them near the huge porcelain tub where she'd kicked them off for a bath after checking in. Kat headed downstairs, through the lobby, and out into the street.

The crowd had been pushed back, and a dozen men stood in the street with their horses, the marshal with the big red mustache and a deputy handing out rifles.

"Marshal, what's happened?" Kat asked.

"Getting this posse ready to go, Miss Payne," the marshal explained. "McGraw's on the loose, and somebody said they saw him on the south side of town. Probably making for the Mexican border is my guess. He might steal a horse. We have to move fast."

"What about that Stone fella?" One of the posse volunteers spoke up. "He said McGraw was heading to Paul Chambers's place."

Kat tensed. "Stone?"

"Fella named Carson Stone," the marshal told her. "I ain't got time to explain how he's all mixed up in this."

"Did he say—" Kat almost asked, *Did he say anything about me*? but stopped herself. "Did he say anything important?"

"Just that he thought McGraw might be headed out to Chambers's ranch because of some grudge against his wife, but that don't make no sense to me. We already know he's headed south." The marshal climbed atop his horse and raised his voice. "Okay, boys, let's ride!"

A shout went up from the posse, and they thundered down the street.

Kat ran for the stables to saddle her horse. Carson hadn't said anything to the marshal, not about her. The situation could still be salvaged. Carson could still be silenced. She cursed herself. Kat had been certain she'd hit Carson with a good shot while he was bathing in the river. His body hadn't surfaced. She wouldn't be so careless again. Kat would see the bullet enter Carson's body, watch the life leave his eyes.

Taking off after Carson was a risk, but what other choice did she have? If she ran, it would be without the gold. By the time she arranged a wagon to take the steamer trunks away, Carson could have talked. The marshal might believe Carson, or maybe he wouldn't, but all he had to do was search her hotel suite and he'd find the gold. No, the only thing to do was shut Carson's mouth. Permanently.

She lost several minutes asking around for directions to Paul Chambers's ranch, but soon enough she was on her way, the Spencer loaded, the .32 revolver and the derringer ready for action.

Kat eventually found the ranch, and she knew it was the right place because she recognized Carson's black horse tied outside. She dismounted and cocked the rifle, searching for faces in the windows of the house. She spared a glance for the barn but didn't see anyone there either. The marshal had said Carson had ridden out here to warn some woman. Kat would probably have to kill her, too. She couldn't risk what Carson might've told her.

She went to the front door and put her ear against it. No voices or anything moving. She chanced a glance into one of the windows and saw an empty front room, a cold stone fireplace, a long, wooden table with four simple chairs on each side. Kat twisted the lever, and the front door creaked inward. She eased inside, stepping lightly, the Spencer up and ready. Floorboards groaned beneath her boots.

Kat paused at a hallway and glanced down it. Bedrooms, maybe. She still hadn't seen or heard anyone. Her palms were sweaty on the Spencer. A steady wind moaned through the house. She went back to the kitchen. A smaller table, a water pump next to a sink, a large iron stove. The back door stood open.

Outside, she saw rows of bright white sheets hanging on lines, blowing and billowing in the hot Texas wind. She watched a moment, and then some of the sheets blew one way, the next line of sheets blowing the other, and in the second gap, she saw him standing at the far end of the row, Carson Stone, his back to her.

I'm not missing this time.

Kat stepped outside as she lifted the rifle, setting the site on a spot between his shoulder blades. Slowly she squeezed the trigger—

Pain exploded in the back of her head with a metallic clang. The world tilted, and she went down. She pushed herself to her hands and knees, but it took all she had, arms and legs watery. Kat managed to lift her head, squinted at a woman in a blue dress standing over her and clutching a shovel to her chest.

"I didn't knock her out." The woman's voice sounded like it echoed from the bottom of a deep well. "You want me to hit her again?"

"Don't," Carson told Annie. "You got her good enough."

He picked up the Spencer and leaned it against the house. Then he went back to Kat, knelt in front of her. She groaned and tried not to move. He reached in and took the .32 from her shoulder holster, emptied the ammunition onto the ground, and tossed the revolver next to the Spencer.

"I'll take that derringer now, Kat. I guess I don't have to tell you to move real slow, or a shovel up against your skull will be the least of your troubles."

Kat muttered something but handed over the derringer without trying anything. Carson stuck it in his back pocket.

To Annie, he said, "Get a cord or some thin rope or something to tie her hands."

Annie scurried into the house.

Carson took Kat under one arm and heaved her to her feet. She groaned and looked shaky, but she stood on her own.

"Ambushed me pretty good, didn't you?" Kat said.

"Didn't know it was you," Carson admitted. "We heard the horse and thought it was Bob."

"I don't think he's coming," Kat said. "Marshal says he's headed to Mexico."

"Mexico can have him."

Annie returned with a length of thin cord and handed it to Carson. He began to tie Kat's wrists.

"Can we talk about this?" Kat asked.

"Talk all you want," Carson said. "If I listen or not is another story."

"There's plenty of gold, Carson."

"You think I care about that?"

Kat took a step closer, pressed against him, her eyes searching for his. She seemed not to care that Annie stood three feet away, watching with open curiosity.

"Listen to me, Carson," Kat said. "When I say plenty of gold, I mean plenty enough for two. Think about it. We could have a life together, traveling far and living high. You and me."

But he wasn't listening, wasn't even looking at her. He was looking past her across the wide prairie. "You were wrong about Bob."

Kat frowned. "What do you mean?"

"Bob didn't go to Mexico."

Both women turned to follow Carson's gaze. A figure sat on a horse a few hundred yards away, too far to see who it was, but they all knew already.

Annie gasped.

"I guess everything just got complicated," Kat said.

Carson sighed. "He's coming this way."

"Oh, no." Annie began to shake. "Oh, no, no, no."

Carson took her by the shoulders. "Easy. Breathe. Can you listen to me?"

Annie nodded.

"Untie me," Kat said. "Two of us against him."

"Stay shut," Carson said. "I'm talking to Annie. Annie, is there a room in the house with a door that locks?"

"The bedroom."

"Take Kat into the bedroom and keep watch on her." Carson took the derringer from his back pocket and handed it to Annie. "Just keep her quiet and out of the way. She can be tricky. Don't let her talk you into anything. Close the shutters and lock the door."

"What about you?"

Carson turned back to watch Bob approach, and his face went hard. "I'm going to finish it."

Annie took Kat by the arm and dragged her back into the house. "Come on!"

Kat paused in the doorway, looked back at Carson. "If you're a little bit fast, you're faster than most. Somebody said that once."

A wan smile flickered across Carson's lips. "I guess we'll see."

CHAPTER 43

Annie pushed Kat into the bedroom ahead of her, then slammed the door and locked it.

"Listen to me," Kat said. "You've got to untie me, and then we'll have a chance. I know how to use that derringer better than—"

"Quiet!" Annie pointed the gun at her with a shaking hand. "Just . . . sit on the bed and be quiet." She went to the window and closed the shutters.

Kat did as she was told and sat on the bed. The last thing she wanted to do was provoke the other woman, who was nervous and jittery. This was the sort of circumstance where pistols went off by accident, and Kat didn't want to be on the wrong end of it.

She looked around the room, her gaze coming to rest on a vanity. There was a pincushion full of pins and needles, next to it a pair of sewing scissors. Kat edged across the bed.

Annie's face pressed against the shutters. She was trying to see through a crack.

"What's happening out there?" Kat leaned toward the vanity and grabbed the scissors.

"I . . . I don't know," Annie said. "I can't see anything."

"Keep looking." Kat held the scissors between her knees and began to saw on the rope around her wrists.

Annie kept watch, then suddenly took in a sharp breath. "He's here."

Carson stood and watched him come. He was strangely calm. He should have been afraid, he supposed. Just a little bit fast, Carson thought. Carson was no Colby Tate with a gun, no Gentleman Dick Fleetwood. Just a little bit fast perfectly described Carson.

And Big Bob McGraw, maybe.

Bob's defining characteristic was his pure meanness, his ruthless way, but he was no slouch with a six-shooter, and he'd killed enough men that he wouldn't shy away from killing one more. It would be nothing to him, and Carson wondered if his sheer eagerness for blood would give Bob the edge.

McGraw was close enough now that Carson could see his face, lips curled into a derisive smirk. He reined in his horse about forty yards away and dismounted.

Carson faded back into the linen forest of bedsheets.

He waited, moving quietly among the sheets, shifting his head back and forth in an attempt to catch a glimpse of McGraw. The sheets fluttered one way and then another, and every time Carson thought he caught sight of movement, the sheets would shift again, obscuring his view.

"Carson!" McGraw sounded much closer now. "Hiding behind laundry ain't going to save you. Maybe I just start shooting and see what I can hit. How about that?"

"Sounds like a waste of lead." Carson immediately moved to one side, then stepped back to the next row of sheets in case McGraw tried to follow his voice and pin down his location. "How about a straight-up fight like men?" Carson moved again, going back a row.

"You're the one hiding, Carson, not me."

The voice surprised Carson, coming more from his left than he'd predicted. McGraw was on the move, too.

"I should thank you," McGraw called. "For gathering everyone I'm going to kill in one lonely place. When I finish you, I'll see to the women. I'll shoot that red-haired bitch first."

Carson moved away from the voice, circled around.

"That saloon whore I plan to strangle with my own two hands," McGraw called. "And I'll take my time, too. You can count on that. I made her plenty of promises that day in court for speaking against me. Yeah, we'll have us a high old time. You'll be dead by then, so I have to tell you about it now."

McGraw moved as he talked, and Carson kept track of him. He was getting close.

"Come to think of it, I guess there's no hurry," McGraw shouted. "We could have us a lot of fun before I snap her neck. Annie always was good at pleasing a man."

Carson wanted to tell McGraw to shut his filthy mouth but realized that was exactly what the outlaw wanted, for Carson to speak up and give away his position.

"You won't be able to save them, Carson! You'll be dead, and then I'll do whatever I'll do, and that will be the world, and I'll be God of it, and it'll end when I'm finished."

Carson turned slowly, hearing the voice but seeing only bleached white sheets.

He's right in front of me. I know he is. I could shoot right now.

But if he was wrong . . .

"Carson!"

And then a hot Texas gust blew through like God's own breath, lifting the sheets like angel wings, like the Red Sea parting. McGraw stood directly in front of him at the other end of the row. The two men faced each other, legs apart, hands hovering over six-shooters.

A little bit fast . . .

Carson's eyes narrowed and met McGraw's. The world seemed to freeze in place, an eternity filling the gap between heartbeats.

The wind died, the angel's wings closing again.

McGraw drew.

And so did Carson.

Both pistols cracked thunder as the sheets fell back into place, closing around them. Carson stepped back, hand patting his chest, looking for the blood. He was sure he'd been hit, certain the life was leaking out of him even as he searched for the wound.

But there was no wound. McGraw had missed. Carson's head went light with relief.

And then the relief vanished, dissolving and floating away like dust on the breeze. Heavy footfalls came toward him, McGraw breathing hard and snorting like an old bull. The next instant he came through the sheets, and Carson flinched back at the sight of him. McGraw's face was red and sweating, rage and hate filling his eyes. He looked like he was about to rip into Carson with his bare hands.

And now Carson was afraid, this mad animal version of McGraw like some force of nature.

McGraw grabbed at one of the sheets as he stumbled forward, leaving a bright red streak on the clean white linen. He fell, pulling sheets off the line, tangled in them as he hit the earth, rolling on his back. He lay there, not moving, eyes open to nothing. The sheet across his chest began to soak through with blood.

Carson stood, looking down at the outlaw, not sure what to feel or if he felt anything at all. He couldn't bring himself to think of Big Bob McGraw as a man he'd defeated. More like some natural calamity—a storm or an avalanche—that had come and gone, leaving Carson shaken but standing.

He gathered himself for a few moments, then headed back through the rows of sheets toward the house.

And then stopped short when he looked up and saw Kat and Annie standing in the doorway. Kat stood behind the other women, holding the derringer to the back of her head. Annie's eyes were wide and frightened. The ugly purple bruise at the corner of her mouth told Carson what had happened inside.

Carson rubbed the back of his neck and sighed. "Right now you're thinking about who to shoot first, but what you don't understand is that it won't matter."

"Sounds like you got it all figured," Kat said. "Tell me what you're thinking, and I'll tell you if you're close or not."

"You can't let me and Annie live," Carson said. "Because we'll talk, and then you'll never get away with that payroll gold. You've got two shots in the derringer. If you shoot Annie first, that gives me time to draw, and if I can outdraw Bob McGraw, I'm pretty sure I can take you."

"So maybe I shoot you first," Kat said. "Then I've got your old girlfriend here as a shield."

"That's the better play, but I'm a little out of range for that peashooter. You'd be taking a chance. I'd be sad if you shot Annie, that's for sure, but I'd still get a shot at you, and I doubt I'd miss." Carson tsked and shook his head. "But like I said, none of that matters."

"And just why the hell not?"

"Because you didn't finish the job with Colby Tate," Carson said. "He's recovering nicely in a Fayetteville hospital."

Kat's eyes widened slowly, her face going pale.

"Word's on its way that you shot him," Carson said. "Could be that the marshal in El Paso knows already. They'll know you shot him, and that whatever tale you spun about not finding the payroll was a lie. You can shoot me and Annie, but it won't help you. They know everything. Your secret's out."

Carson searched Kat's face and could see she was groping for a way out.

So Carson obliged her.

"I just shot Big Bob McGraw, so frankly, I've had my share of shooting for today," Carson said. "And as I've already said, shooting us won't do you any good. So how about you get on your horse and go? I won't stop you. Ride in any direction you like. You don't shoot, and I don't shoot."

Kat licked her lips, thinking. Then, very slowly, she backed into the house, pulling Annie along with her, still using her as a shield until both women were out of sight. Carson waited a few seconds and then a few more, and then wondered if he'd misjudged.

He headed for the back door as he heard a horse whinny and gallop away fast. The next second, Annie came running out the back door again. She threw herself into Carson's arms and cried against his chest, fear and relief and every emotion mixed together all coming out at once. He hugged her back and wondered if he was holding her up or if it was the other way around.

"You're not going to have to worry about Big Bob McGraw ever again," Carson said.

"Oh, thank God." Annie wiped away tears, smudging her face. "Thank God."

"But you're going to have to wash some of those sheets over again," he told her. "Sorry about that."

EPILOGUE

Well, that's just my luck, Carson thought.

The reward for Big Bob McGraw had already been issued to Katherine Payne, never mind that she wasn't there to collect it. The law was the law. And there hadn't been time to issue a new reward in the short gap between McGraw's jailbreak and Carson Stone shooting the man cold dead. Carson had gotten a number of free drinks and slaps on the back for gunning the notorious outlaw but not one thin dime.

Paul Chambers had shaken Carson's hand and thanked him for being there to save his wife.

Carson's luck wasn't all bad. The railroad company had been glad to get their payroll back and gave Carson a five-hundred-dollar reward. It took a few days for the money to arrive, but a fancy hotel was happy to give Carson credit until the money arrived. The manager said it was the least he could do for the man who'd rid Texas of such a no-good, murdering skunk.

So Carson spent a few days eating steak and drinking whisky and basking in the strange warmth of freedom. He wasn't just free to come and go physically. He was free of the weight of being a wanted man that had burdened his soul. It would take some getting used to.

The money finally arrived, and it was time to go. He saddled

Jet and tied him to the hitching post in front of the hotel, then went into the lobby. Even after settling his bill, he had plenty of money for whatever came next.

Carson just didn't have any idea what that might be.

He went back outside to find a man waiting for him.

"Hello, old sport." Colby Tate grinned. "You're looking good. Where are we off to now?"

Tate looked lean. He'd lost a few pounds in the hospital but otherwise seemed healthy. The walking stick he leaned on was the only indication that he was still on the mend. He wore a new tan suit and a silk waistcoat with a burgundy-and-gold-paisley pattern. New shoes polished to a bright gleam.

"You look expensive," Carson said.

Tate laughed. "An interesting compliment. But my question was not rhetorical. What's next for you?"

"A fair question," Carson said. "I'd thought I might head to New Orleans to see my mother, let her know her son's not an outlaw." A shrug. "I might just write her a letter. I want to see her again, but I want to accomplish something first. Be somebody. Hell, I don't know. I'm figuring this out as I go. I'm this far west already. Might as well keep going."

"I thought you might be at loose ends." Tate handed Carson a rolled-up piece of paper. "I have a new enterprise in mind and could use a capable partner."

Carson unrolled the paper and felt his stomach flutter at the sight of her. It was a good likeness. The words underneath the illustration read Katherine Payne, AKA "Lady Pain." Wanted Dead or Alive. 1000 Dollars Reward.

Carson rolled the wanted poster back up and gave it back, shaking his head. "No, thanks."

Tate looked surprised. "She tried to kill you, too. You don't want another chance at her?"

"More like I don't want to give her another chance at me."

"Understandable," Tate said. "But I think we might be

heading in the same direction. I propose we ride together at the very least. For the sake of safety as well as good company."

"And to give you a chance to talk me into going after Kat, I reckon."

Mock innocence crossed Tate's face. "Perish the thought."

The two men climbed into their saddles.

"How far do you think we can get today?" Tate asked.

"Depends on how many hours of daylight are left."

Tate reached into the pocket of his waistcoat and pulled out the Harvard watch. The .32 caliber slug was still stuck in the face. "It seems my watch has stopped."

"Never mind," Carson said. "The world is its own clock. The sun rises and the sun sets. The trick is getting as much done in between as you can."

Carson Stone spurred his horse forward and Colby Tate followed, the distant horizon inviting them onward.

PROLOGUE

They were all killers, and they filled the small office with their menace.

Not that Bill Cartwright was intimidated. He'd just turned fifty and had accomplished more in his years than ten ordinary men in ten lifetimes. He was formidable in a bigger and more lasting way than a simple assassin, a wealthy man by any measurement. If he wanted women, he had only to snap his fingers. If he wanted champagne from Paris, he could bathe in it. He made men and broke them every day as a matter of routine. If he wanted expensive things or exotic pleasures, he simply had to pay for them.

But what he wanted now was power, and that couldn't be bought; no, not quite. His money would help, of course. As with any such undertaking, money could solve a myriad of problems.

Thus the killers. The problem solvers.

And then Cartwright would be on the path to the power he craved. Idaho would be a state soon. It was coming. Even a blind man could see it. And when such things happened, certain men would rise—smart, crafty men who'd had the foresight to position themselves, who'd made themselves ready to seize such an opportunity.

Cartwright took a cigar from the humidor, clipped the end,

then lit it with a gold desk lighter big enough to choke a mule. He sat back, puffing, giving each of the killers the once-over, taking their measure.

The Mexican looked so obviously a killer, it was difficult to take him seriously. But he'd come highly recommended, a man both ruthless and cunning. He wore a black sombrero, crisscrossed bandoliers over a red shirt, and a black vest. He cradled a garish, gold-plated Winchester, intricately engraved with a thorny, twisting vine. His mustache looked as if a ferret had taken ownership of his face. Carlos Ruiz stood stoically, waiting for whatever Cartwright was about to say.

The Englishman was something different. Slender, shorter than average, mousy hair thinning and so blond as to be nearly white. Bland, watery eyes. He stood, timidly clutching a bowler hat to his chest. He didn't look like a killer. He looked like a man there to balance Cartwright's books. *Don't turn your back on the quiet ones,* Cartwright's mother had been fond of saying. The man's name was Nigel Evers.

The two brothers worked as a team. Larry and Barry Hanson were both cut from the same cloth, as one might imagine with brothers. Lean and hard and tall. They looked like any other cowboys in off the trail. The older one—Barry—wore his Peacemaker for a left-handed draw, and when he grinned, he showed off a gold front tooth. Larry had one cheek perpetually bulging with chewing tobacco. They'd do just about any dastardly thing for money, and their résumé included arson, armed robbery—of both train and stagecoach—cattle rustling, extortion, and murder of every variety.

Cartwright wasn't sure what to make of the fifth killer. The jury was still out on that one.

Well, time to get this meeting started. Cartwright puffed his cigar and said, "You don't know me."

The killers said nothing to this peculiar statement. They knew more was coming.

"I want to look you in the eye, let you know that this is

serious business," Cartwright said. "And I expect results. I get the results I want, and you'll all be well-rewarded. If I don't get the results I want, then I'll be unhappy. They say misery loves company, so if I'm unhappy, I can promise you'll be unhappy with me. You take my meaning?"

The killers offered a sort of vague, group shrug in return. They were hard types and wouldn't intimidate easily. He wouldn't want them if they did.

Cartwright blew out a fresh stream of blue-gray cigar smoke. "Yeah, I think we understand one another. But I reiterate: You don't know me. You fail or get caught, I'm not to be mentioned. You get drunk and my name falls out of your mouth, I'll bury you so deep, them laborers will be digging you up in their flower gardens. You keep your mouths shut or I'll see they get shut permanently."

Not even the shrug this time. These individuals weren't accustomed to being spoken to in such a way. Cartwright didn't give a damn. It had to be said.

"The man who initially contacted each of you is named Doyle," Cartwright reminded them. "You need something or you have a question, see Doyle. When it's time to be paid, see Doyle. As soon as you walk out the door, forget my face."

"Why bother to meet with us at all, then?" The question had come from Larry. He was either stupider or braver than the others. Not that it mattered.

Cartwright took a long draw on the cigar, letting Larry's question hang in the air. Larry shifted from one foot to the other, glancing at his brother, then back at Cartwright.

Cartwright exhaled smoke, then said, "Because I'm the boss, and what I say goes. And if you've never seen me, I'm just an abstract concept, some ghost issuing commands from the ether. But I'm not a ghost. I'm reality. And reality sinks in."

Another pregnant pause. None of the killers had anything to say to that.

Cartwright stood and yanked a cord dangling over his head. From somewhere, the sound of a muffled bell reached them, and a moment later, an efficient little man in a striped suit and slicked-back hair entered the room with five sheets of paper. He handed one sheet to each of the killers.

"Mr. Doyle has presented each of you with an identical list," Cartwright said. "There are forty-three names on the list, the location where they can be found, and a dollar amount to be paid for their corpses. Your mission is simple. Kill. Any questions?"

They shook their heads, mumbling there were none.

"I suggest you check in with our Mr. Doyle every few days," Cartwright said. "There's always a chance I'll be adding names to the list. Now go. Do your jobs."

The killers began to file out of the room.

"Not you." Cartwright pointed a finger at the fifth killer. "I want to talk to you."

She paused, one eyebrow arching into a question. "Oh?"

Cartwright smiled in a way he knew to be charming. "Just for a moment. Indulge me."

The woman considered a moment and then nodded her consent.

The other killers left, Doyle following and shutting the door behind him.

The woman had a good shape and a pretty face and sly eyes. Her skin was clear and very white. Lips a glistening red. Glossy, black hair pulled into a tight bun at the nape of her neck. A flat-crowned, black bolero hat perched at a jaunty angle atop her head. She wore a red jacket, cropped just above her waist with black lapels, a white blouse underneath. Tan pants tucked into high, black boots. Altogether, a tidy, eye-catching package.

"And what can I do for you, Mr. Cartwright?" she asked.

"I just wanted a chance to exchange pleasantries," he said. "Perhaps get to know each other a little better."

"I thought the point of your speech earlier is that I *don't* know you."

Cartwright chuckled. "Fair enough. But you're not like those other hired killers. That's obvious."

"You mean you're not sure if a woman is up to the job?" She reached into her jacket and came out with a long, thin cigarillo. She stuck it into her mouth and leaned forward. "Do you mind?"

Cartwright lit her cigarillo with the desk lighter. She puffed. The smoke hung in the air between them, cloying and sweet. "What do they call you?"

"Kate."

"Just Kate?"

"Like you, I often find it useful to be forgettable. Last names have a way of sticking to people."

"May I offer you a drink?" Cartwright moved toward a sideboard with a collection of bottles and decanters. "There's a rather good sherry."

"When I've crossed forty-three names off this list, I'll have my fill of champagne," Kate said. "For now, some of that coffin varnish will do me just fine."

"As you like." Cartwright filled a shot glass with whisky and handed it to her.

She tossed it back in one go, then wiped her lips with the back of a slender hand. She handed the glass back, nodding at the bottle. "I'll sip this one."

Cartwright refilled her glass and poured himself a sherry. They sipped, reconsidering each other.

"I've known enough women to know that murder can certainly be in a woman's heart, so I don't doubt you've the will for it," Cartwright said. "As for being up to the job . . . well, that's what I'm hoping to determine. Frankly, I notice you don't even carry a gun."

"Well, they're so awfully heavy." She batted her eyes comically. "And I'm just a frail little girl."

"You're having some fun with me."

"A little. Have faith, Mr. Cartwright. Pistols aren't the only way to kill. Now, I must take my leave, if you don't mind. There's work to do." Kate offered her hand, palm down, expecting a gentlemanly kiss on her knuckles.

Cartwright grinned. He was all too happy to oblige. He reached for her hand.

Kate flipped it over quickly and, as if by magic, a gleaming derringer appeared in her tight fist, the double barrels pointed at his chest. Cartwright felt a stab of panic, his heartbeat thudding rapidly. He took a moment, composed himself, and forced a smile.

"I mean, I do *have* a gun," Kate said. "More than one, in fact. But if all you wanted were guns, you could buy them by the wagonload. What I offer is far more valuable." She tapped the side of her head. "A certain kind of know-how."

"I believe you've made your point."

Kate lowered the derringer. "Sincere apologies if that startled you. I just wanted you to know you're getting your money's worth."

Cartwright was tempted to be cross with her. He let it pass and let his intrigue intensify instead. "There's more to you than meets the eye, Kate. I think I'd like to find out more. Over dinner?"

Her smile brightened the room. "I guess a gal's gotta eat."

CHAPTER 1

Carson Stone looked down the Spencer rifle's barrel at the shabby camp below. He huddled in his heavy wool coat under the low-hanging branches of an evergreen. Only September and already the nights were cold, the mornings slow to warm, a white mist creeping across the forest floor.

He fought off a shiver. *Idaho sure ain't Texas.*

He panned left to right with the rifle, looking for signs of life among the circle of tents. Last night's coals in the cook-fire still smoked. A picket line stretched between two skinny ponderosa pines, three horses tethered there. It wasn't the worst spot for a camp if a fella was looking to hide himself. Ten miles deep into the Payette Forest, up in the rocky foothills about thirty-five hundred feet. It wasn't a place anyone would have happened upon by accident, an area at the top of a hill but surrounded on all sides by rock walls, like the indention of a thumb smashed into the top of a mashed potato mound.

They'd never have found the place if not for the Indian, a rangy Bannock on the run from Howard after the surrender. He'd given them detailed directions for a dollar. How the Indian had come to have the information Carson didn't know, but he'd perfectly described the huge Bavarian, and there was no doubt it was the man they were after.

Carson glanced to his left to check Tate's progress.

Colby Tate worked his way down the narrow crevice between two boulders. He'd be out of sight for a moment when he circled below Carson, but he wasn't worried about Tate. The bounty hunter could take care of himself. Carson's job was to cover him if anyone tried to hit Tate from his blind side.

How do I let Tate talk me into these things?

But Carson knew the answer. Money. Carson had ideas and plans, and very few of them came for free. He'd wintered as a cattle hand on a ranch in Colorado. When the spring thaw had rolled around, Tate had returned and said he needed help with a job. They'd tracked four cattle rustlers, brought them in alive and, after splitting the reward with Tate, Carson had made as much in three days as he had working the ranch all winter.

So, when Tate had taken off after a notorious murderer and robber, Carson tagged along. Half of a five-hundred-dollar reward was nothing to sneeze at. They'd chased the outlaw as far as Cheyenne, and the job had gone bloody. Carson had remembered why he'd wanted no part of bounty hunting, had sworn he was finished with it, but then the next job had gone smoother, and so had the one after that, and pretty soon both men looked up and found they'd stumbled into Boise.

That was where the local sheriff had told them about the Bavarian.

Tate disappeared from view, and Carson slowly swung the Spencer back the other way, eyes peeled for movement.

As Carson had already observed, it was a good place for a camp: hidden, sheltered from the wind, the only drawback being what Carson was doing right now. Shooting down into the sunken area made the place a killing ground. He could pick off ten of them before they even knew what was happening.

Of course, he'd have to spot them first.

And he doubted there were ten of them. Reports varied,

saying the Bavarian rode with a few men or a dozen, depending
on who was telling the tale and how much whisky they'd had,
but Carson figured three horses meant three men.

On the other hand, there were four tents.

So who the hell could say?

Carson could see Tate below him now, one of his twin Colt
Peacemakers in his hand as he crouched halfway behind a
boulder, with a good view of the tents.

"I'd like to address the gentleman in the tents if I may,"
Tate shouted. "I know it's a bit early in the morning for
unpleasant surprises, so if you'd please give me your full attention, we can get through this with as little bloodshed as
possible. Your complete cooperation is absolutely crucial to
your continued good health."

Carson grinned. Colby Tate sure must love the feel of
words flying out of his mouth because he never chose to say
things fast and simple.

"I strongly suggest throwing your guns out first," Tate
continued. "Followed slowly by your person. It goes without
saying that having your hands up and not making any moves
that could be interpreted as hostile will serve to facilitate a
smooth conclusion to this whole affair."

Nothing. Somewhere in the distance, a bald eagle screeched.

"Indicating that you've heard my instructions and are has-
tening to comply would now be a good idea," Tate called.

A moment later, "Just who in the hell are you?"

Carson couldn't be sure which tent the voice came from.

"A fair question. My name is Tate and I'm a bounty hunter.
My colleagues and I mean to collect the two-hundred-and-
fifty-dollar reward currently being offered for Hans Mueller.
This actually brings me to my next point. There's no paper
that I know of on anyone else here. If Mueller gives himself
up without a fuss, we'll leave without troubling the rest of
you. I think that's a very generous offer and I'd like to hear
your opinion."

A moment passed. "Opinion?" asked the same voice.

"Yes," Tate said. "I'd like you to weigh in on my proposal. I don't detect a German accent, so I take it you're not Mueller, but rather one of his compatriots."

"I ain't Mueller," the voice confirmed.

"Just so. I imagine it would save you and your other friends a good deal of stress if Mueller would give himself up without a lot of tedious shooting."

"You go to hell, bounty hunter," shouted a different voice.

Carson swung the Spencer to aim it at a tent two over from the first voice. He had a better fix on them now.

"These men are my friends. They won't give me up without a fight." Thick accent. The words sounded like Zese men are my vrends. Zey von't giff me up vithout a fight.

"Now hold on just a minute, Hans," the first voice said. "Let's be smart about this."

"I quite agree," Tate said. "Listen to your friend, Hans."

"Just do what the man says, Hans," the first voice said. "You'll take him peaceable like and he gets a fair trial, right, mister?"

"As long as everyone cooperates," Tate said.

"You hear that, Hans? Just play along with the fella."

"You go straight to hell, Ralph McNally," Hans shouted. "This could be a trick. You want I should get shot?"

"I'll shoot you my own damn self," Meriweather shouted back. "I know what tent you're in. No sense all of us getting taken. Now get out there with your damn hands up."

Grumbling, then cursing in German, and then, "Fine, okay. I'm coming. But you don't shoot, yes?"

"I don't shoot, yes," confirmed Tate.

Movement in the corner of Carson's eye drew attention. He swung the Spencer to the far-right side of the clearing, where a man emerged from between two boulders. The man was tall and stooped and stork thin, with buckteeth and a battered hat pushed back on his head. He was pulling up his pants as he walked, and Carson figured the man had been off doing his business.

Stork Man suddenly understood what was going on and ducked back against one of the boulders, eyes going wide as he hurriedly buckled his belt. Carson assessed the situation. Tate faced the tents and couldn't see the newcomer unless he happened to turn his head. Carson could shout a warning, but that would give away his position.

The Bavarian emerged from his tent. Hans Mueller was a beefy man, with a glistening bald head, clean-shaven pink cheeks. He wore a big Colt Dragoon on his left hip. He raised his hands and looked nervous. "No shooting, remember!"

"Unbuckle that belt and let it drop," Tate told him.

The Bavarian hesitated.

Carson took aim at Stork Man. He didn't want to shoot if he didn't have to. Tate had told the truth when he said they were only interested in Mueller. *Just walk away, friend. Better for all concerned.*

Hans moved his hands slowly toward his gun belt.

Stork Man drew his six-shooter.

Don't do it. Don't do it. Don't—

Stork Man took aim.

The Spencer bucked in Carson's hands, and Stork Man spun away, blood trailing from a hole above his left temple, six-gun flying and clattering along the rocky ground.

Tate's head came around to see what was happening, and that was when the Bavarian drew.

But Tate was fast and fanned his Colt three times. The blasts made a neat triangle of wet red dots across Mueller's chest. The beefy man stumbled back into his tent and fell over, smashing it flat.

A shotgun blast shook the world, and Tate dove behind his boulder. It had come from Ralph Meriweather's tent, and another blast immediately followed, buckshot scorching Tate's boulder.

Carson emptied the Spencer into the tent, levering one cartridge in after another.

Silence. Smoke hung in the air.

"You okay?" Carson called.

"Unscathed," Tate said. "What are you doing?"

"Reloading the Spencer. Want to take a look?"

"Do you think you got him?"

"No idea."

"You alive in there, Meriweather?" Tate called. "My partner's going to open up again in ten seconds if you don't say something. We've got ammunition to spare."

Ten seconds went by and they heard nothing from Meriweather.

"You don't really want me to shoot up that tent again, do you?"

"Never mind," Tate said. "Cover me. I'll take a look."

Meriweather had a hole in his head and a very surprised look on his face.